HOUSE OF TABLES

HOUSE
OF TABLES

Ileen McDuring

Grey Warbler Press
Dallas, Texas

THIS IS A GREY WARBLER BOOK
PUBLISHED BY GREY WARBLER PRESS

Library of Congress United States Copyright Office
Catalogue: TXu 001-853-308
House of Tables / Ileen McDuring. — 1st ed.

Grey Warbler ISBN: 978-0-9895050-0-0 (trade)
978-0-9895050-5-5 (eBook)

Manufactured in the United States of America

10 9 8 7 6 5 4 3 2 1

Dedication

To my partner and husband, David—my *Love, Laughter,* and *Friendship* defined.

Dad (1942-2013)

In the hearts of adventurers and musicians,
the memory of him beats strong and strums joyfully.
His footprints echo with us on each hiking trail.
Dust and wind carry his laughter.
Prop blades on jet streams
spin tales from profound silence.
Yet we hear him still.

CHAPTER ONE

Cadie Walsh stared at the blinking command prompt on the otherwise blank screen. She'd been at the computer since three o'clock that morning. Fifteen minutes had ticked away since opening the prompt.

Why not stop for the day?

She got up to gaze through her office window overlooking a large, wooden deck. Judging the shadows in her garden, she figured it was nearly two o'clock. *Eleven hours.* She massaged the side of her neck and then shrugged her shoulders. At twenty-six years old, she was too young to fall overcome by cumulative sleep deprivation, especially for a software engineer, and there was no real reason to take advantage of her work hour flexibility. Stopping now or at five o'clock wouldn't make a difference to her social schedule. There were no friends to call or social requirements demanding her presence. No long commute. She looked back at the blinking cursor. The steadiness reminded her of an evensong mantra, but the cursor seemed more beautiful.

Remember, remember, remember . . .

That was it. She was mapping a path to . . . to what? Nothing came to mind. Cadie looked again at the garden before turning on heel and walking out of her home office to the kitchen. The regular travel between computer and coffee pot was cathartic and productive. She couldn't count how many times she solved coding problems during the ritual of making and drinking coffee.

She touched the side of the French press with the back of her hand.

Hot enough for now, she mused. On second thought, she dialed up the warming plate's temperature. She might want another cup before shutting down for the day.

She refilled her coffee cup, doing nothing to stop the coffee grounds' silt from flowing into it. She liked it that way. From a green sugar bowl on the counter, she withdrew two cubes and then turned and leaned against the sharp counter edge. She held up a cube to the light and looked at the crystals before placing the sugar between her front teeth and holding it there. Carefully, she sipped from her cup and let coffee seep through the sweet cube. Once the delicate web of crystals broke apart, she swirled the remaining crystals around in her mouth.

A corner of her lips lifted in an awkward and irregular smile. She loved how the robust coffee transformed from bitter to sweet, the warm lump moving from solid to gritty-sweet entropy then finally collapsing into solution.

Cadie held up the second cube.

First the milk and then the sugar.

The smile disappeared. The words were Sister Mary Trea's.

Not *Sister Trea* nor *Sister Mary*. Sister . . . Mary . . . Trea.

Cadie frowned.

Retribution was bad enough, but retribution for drinking hot tea through cubes of sugar was the worst. Well, not the worst, but bad enough that Cadie rarely drank coffee without remembering the nun. How many times had the nun slapped sugar from Cadie's hand?

"Milk, followed by sugar and *then* tea into the cup. Milk, sugar, tea," screeched the nun.

Cadie held tight to the cube and placed it between her teeth. She spoke around the sugar. "Not anymore."

She rarely took milk now, and on the rare occasion she did, the milk followed the coffee or tea; sugar last. In delightful revenge, she lifted the cup to her lips. Control of the ritual, now pure reward, no longer belonged to Sister Mary Trea.

Beside her at the kitchen counter, Sister Mary Trea, invisible to all but Cadie, picked up a similarly invisible wooden spoon and swung it through the air. It was nothing, so nothing hit Cadie on the hands, the arms, the upper thighs.

"Impertinence, Cadie. To bed without supper," shouted Sister Mary Trea.

Not ever again, thought Cadie, wishing that her assembly of conscience included more than the dead nun and other vague figures in dark habits. She returned to thoughts about the unique passage of coffee worming its way through a dissolving network of . . .

That's it. A network.

"You think I'm fit to do my job at all?" she asked the empty room.
No answer from Sister Mary Trea.

Cadie looked around and knew she was utterly alone. She worried about the day when information might hide so well in the crooks and crannies of her brain that further answers wouldn't be possible. Puzzles that remained puzzles no matter how many lumps of sugar or cups of coffee she consumed. Looking at the time, she topped off her cup and quickly returned to her computer. It was a quarter after two.

Why do I insist on mapping permissions for my team?

Invariably, with each new member, Cadie wondered why she didn't let the IT department handle the simple task. She avoided her team at office headquarters as much as possible. This time she told herself it had to do with mothering her code and tending the web that shielded software keys and programs. Many respectable espionage companies made hack jabs at it on a regular basis. There had never been a breach in her team's security. As long as Cadie was around, there never would be. Therefore, recruited engineer Daruska Cesta from the Czech Republic would be set to go on Monday morning.

Cadie had handpicked Daruska—if email and phone calls counted as handpicking. But Cadie would leave it up to her team to show Daruska around the office. Bobby Pullman, Cadie's boss, company owner, and a growing shadow in her conscience, would make apologies for his protégé. Daruska was the kind of person that needn't see her younger boss face to face in order to do good work. Cadie knew that. Bobby would explain to Daruska why only one team leader in his company telecommuted. Soon Daruska would see that Cadie had the mind and work output of several engineers . . . as long as everyone left her alone.

Generated by Bobby, it was a company secret or joke, you might say, that Cadie had some kind of PTSD, and all were "best advised to steer clear and let her do her thing." Cadie knew one side of the secret though: When she asked for something, she got it. It never occurred to Cadie that anything other than her practical engineering needs were behind easy access to the best computers and electronics.

With mild unpleasantness, Cadie remembered the afternoon she had asked Bobby if she could skyrocket on her company's bandwagon toward greener employment solutions.

✝ ✝ ✝

BOBBY LAUGHED WHEN Cadie walked into his office two minutes after the corporate memo hit email inboxes around the building.

"Everything okay?" he asked when she walked through the door.

"I want to telecommute," she said.

"You would?" Bobby teased with a broad grin.

"Yes."

Her poor attempt at a crooked smile made Bobby laugh, which upset her stomach.

"*If you'd only stayed, you could be teaching at the convent now,*" said Sister Mary Trea's voice.

Cadie ignored her, but a bead of sweat formed on her brow.

Bobby saw that Cadie wasn't remotely aware of the reason for his amusement and became serious. "Did you see that team leads and managers aren't eligible for telecommuting?" he asked.

"Yes."

"Cadie, I really need you . . . "

Cadie cut him off before he could say *here. I really need you here.* "How about a trial period?"

"I don't know . . . what would I get in exchange?" He was joking again.

"A better brain on the job."

Bobby laughed. He didn't imagine that was possible.

"*This isn't a job,*" came Sister Mary Trea's voice. "*This is vanity and playtime, not going to make the world better by any means.*"

Not like beating children into believing in God, thought Cadie.

"Two weeks," he said. "First, type up your plan for running the team remotely, including how you will manage on-site lab tests."

"Thank you," said Cadie, any chance of a smile hijacked by thoughts already centered on the plan.

Bobby laughed again. "Go on, darlin'. Give me the report when you can get around to it."

Cadie left his office.

BOBBY PULLMAN WASN'T SURPRISED when the report was on his desk two hours later and IT personnel had loaded Cadie's car with everything she needed to run an internationally recognized team from home. As Bobby watched Cadie get in her car and drive away, he knew the trial would take. When it came to robotics and artificial intelligence engineering, the girl didn't have failure in her bones.

+ + +

THE DOORBELL STARTLED CADIE. She hurriedly completed a mapping function before answering the interruption.

"Go away," she said under her breath before opening the door to the FedEx delivery man.

She disliked the chit-chat banalities that sprang from unexpected telephone calls or persons without invitation standing on her front porch. It gave her no time to prepare. What to say, how to stand, what were the rules of chit-chat anyway? Though elementarily robotic, she functioned a little better when it came to planned, work-related social exchanges. But impromptu communication and non-working social events that demanded immediacy and quality social interaction left her nearly speechless.

She signed for the package without saying anything more than "Thanks." The driver jogged down the sidewalk to his truck as she closed the door.

Shrugging her shoulders, she sighed loudly, walked to the kitchen with her package, and set the box down on the island. She wanted to open it, but was too nervous. Instead, she grabbed two more sugar cubes and went back to her computer. While she worked, the networking permissions nearly a mindless activity for her, Cadie thought about the small package waiting in the kitchen.

DURING THE LAST COMPANY PICNIC, she'd decided to order the kit. After all, a deep ancestry was better than no ancestry at all, at least better than her recent ancestry that began at the now-closed Catholic orphanage in Dallas, Texas.

At St. Fina's, where the Irish Sister Mary Trea had named and caged her in the dysfunctional tribe of heavy-handed abuse, no ancestry but Sister Mary Trea's was passed on to Cadie. At St. Fina's, her rotating classmates were the "daughters" she had woken to each morning. They shared breakfast, clothes, and a common hatred borne of misfortune. Each girl was a near copy of one another, empathy set asunder and filled with fear. The orphanage was one of those where deference, if given by the nuns, was cause for terror rather than reward or elevation or, most of all, affection.

Sometimes the day arrived that each girl silently had wished and dreamed for, when the newly adopted daughter left with a flush of immodest tears on her cheeks. Closing the final door that separated her from the orphans, the girl blew kisses of magnanimous affection to those left behind. On occasion, the remainders saw the lucky girl, the *ragazza fortunata*, adopted by a family from St. Fina's congregation. Then the girl, sitting on her new dais of family, ignored her old classmates, for they could point at her and say, "Orphan."

Those lucky, adopted girls were usually the same girls, too, who had received the most kindness. They were sheltered in a private dormitory away from the *Mary Janes*, girls the nuns found a little too nondescript, too sullen, or too smart for their own good.

Sister Mary Trea always said, "Cadie, you're too smart for your own good." Either that or, "You're attractive, Cadie, but beauty takes a sure hit by a sullen demeanor."

No, the other girls were those who stood out, either from beauty or a single unique feature that got them into the "supper club."

The supper club was special time. It was time with potential single fathers who came to see the pick of the litter—time spent in a series of small, private dining rooms shut off to the Mary Janes. When the girls left the orphanage grounds with their potential daddies, supper club time was time at the Texas State Fair or Six Flags. The big water park was popular in the summer. In the winter, they saw the latest movies. But they *always* dined on orphanage grounds.

When such deference became too much for the supper club girls, when they grew too sullen or the realm of nondescript somehow caught up with them, the nuns shuffled those girls to the Mary Janes' dorm. And the Mary Janes asked all sorts of questions about the supper club. The more they asked, the quieter the young witnesses became. The former supper club girls became the tightest-lipped of any girls Cadie ever knew. The most liked in the supper club, the ones who could turn on a smile at the drop of a hat never stayed long at the orphanage. Cadie once overheard Mother Fara Verena say those girls "knew how to work it." Single dads adopted those girls quickly. The girls adopted by couples were the remaining cute and youngest. Couples brought those girls back to church services. But the supper club girls disappeared in their new lives, never seen again. So, either way, and as far as Cadie had been concerned, being a Mary Jane was the kiss of death if a girl wanted a family. She always figured the supper club girls just knew better how to survive.

Now that she could make her own decisions, Cadie held a season-long box seat at the theater of *la familia*. She watched families at the company picnics and conjured ways to shun orphanage memories by acting on the cultural theater's stage of social outings and intermingling. She'd experimented with social props to make her integration easier—at least to take up space and time if talking or smiling proved too difficult or impossible. She'd tried smoking, but had stopped halfway through the first cigarette. Smoking, she figured, would cause dementia in the long run. Nursing the popular beers at the company BBQs helped her decide that she didn't particularly like the taste or the smell of beer. She didn't even have the prop of electronic social networking. There was never a phone affixed to her hand so that she could text between bites of food or faltering dialogue. Who would she call or text? Everyone she knew at the picnics came from the office. She eschewed the local gyms for her evening walks in her neighborhood and the rowing machine in front of her own television. What was the point of running on a treadmill beside someone with speaker buds jammed in their ears while reading closed captioning from television rows hanging from gym ceilings?

CADIE FINISHED THE NETWORK MAPPING and walked back to the kitchen. At the freezer, she rummaged for and selected a TV dinner *du jour*. In movements that were second nature, she dispatched the chosen chicken penne into the microwave. While her meal cooked, she moved to the pantry and stood before her makeshift wine cellar.

Opening the kit called for a special celebration. The bottle she pulled from the pantry wall was the same as every other. She blew the dust from the bottles and counted what remained. It was nearly time to order another case from Fredericksburg. Only nine bottles remained of her usable cache. The remaining, two-case stash of the Texas Malbec varietal was for testing. One bottle for each year on her birthday; the last she would open on her sixty-fifth. She wasn't a connoisseur, but love had gripped her when Bobby presented her with a bottle as part of her Christmas bonus the previous year. She wanted to see if one batch of love could last until retirement. If it did, that was acceptable. If it improved . . . well then, it would be something better than acceptable.

Cadie returned to the kitchen and opened the wine. She watched the red sluice pour into her glass. A sip, then she held her breath and let the bouquet sit on her tongue for a minute. The 2008 Malbec wasn't something she drank every day, but she thought the wine, with its spicy mint and cherry apricot body, complemented her boxed dinners. Even alongside Indian or Chinese frozen cuisines, its flavor was satisfyingly exotic.

Do it now, Cadie.

She swallowed the wine and grabbed the paring knife from the utensil drawer, mostly empty except for a three-piece knife set, wine bottle opener, and wine bottle vacuum pump that came with two stoppers. She quickly sliced through the tape on the sealed box that held the kit. The box flaps popped open just as the microwave beeped. She returned the knife to the drawer.

Cadie retrieved her hot TV dinner and inverted it onto a red and white plate embellished with an old English castle. The plate was part of a four-piece set purchased at a department store fire sale in Fort Worth. The idyllic scene on the dish seemed lonely to her. The few people, foreigners to the esquires of social nobility, walked outside the thick stone walls. Cadie picked up her food and carried it with her wine to the adjoining living room. There she deposited herself on a golden paisley wingback chair salvaged from a luxury second-hand store. Grabbing her remote, she flipped through dozens of digitally recorded shows and finally settled in to watch the first film of her favorite French trilogy.

"I'll open the kit after dinner," she said aloud to herself.

"It'll only lead to trouble," answered Sister Mary Trea.

"Probably," said Cadie. "If I believed in that kind of trouble."

Invisible hands pulled at Cadie's hair, a small rod struck her cheek.

Cadie felt nothing and picked around the chicken for the scant pieces of overly steamed broccoli.

+ + +

PROMPTLY AFTER EATING, CADIE stopped the movie and returned to the kitchen. She cleaned and dried the dinner plate and fork and returned the pieces to their places. For a few seconds she stopped to listen to the neighborhood dogs howl in harmony with emergency vehicles passing through nearby. There were infinite scenarios for their transit, she imagined—a dinner-time heart attack or a fall down a flight of stairs. Maybe a cat caught in a tree. Someone or something that had had enough of whatever it was that killed them little by little every day, every minute, every second. The sirens grew faint. The dogs' howls waned to moans and then went silent.

Without further delay, she pulled the waiting package toward her, pushed aside the opened flaps, and extracted a box a bit larger than an old VHS tape.

Cadie set the light-weight packing on the counter, leaned onto her elbows, and cupped her face in her hands to study the outside of the blue, black, and white box with a little orange rectangle centered near the bottom. A single human profile, more male than female, strode along the box's blue horizon.

"A Landmark Study of the Human Journey," she mouthed, reading the words.

She still couldn't believe she'd ordered the *Genographic Project* kit from National Geographic. Inside the box lie the path to analyzing and archiving her DNA results. Cadie broke the kit's seal with her fingernail. From the spread-out contents, she first read the directions.

It only took a moment to find her unique ID number and compare it to the kit number on the side of the box. Confirming that it was truly a double blind study and satisfied that her name could never be associated with the kit's identification, Cadie walked to the sink and poured a glass of water. She swished her mouth thoroughly and spat it out. She returned to the island and withdrew a long swab, one of two, from an individual plastic sleeve. She checked the directions again.

Swab for thirty seconds.

While she swabbed the inside of her cheeks for DNA cells, Cadie let herself imagine how her ancient ancestral map would look. What branch had her maternal ancestors followed? The path would be quite different than her short lifetime migration from Dallas to Fort Worth. The human genomic path went beyond mere generations of hundreds of years. Genomic paths were ancient, the first biological writings preserved from a time before pen and paper, before webs and nets of algorithms stored on colossal servers.

As far as Cadie could remember, the Human Genome Project was the first time she had felt the kind of excitement that other people attached to people, places, and things much earlier in life. It happened while waiting outside her biology professor's office during her college freshman year. Nestled among other old and new editions of various scientific periodicals on a rickety magazine rack, she'd found the year-and-a-half-old *Nature Magazine.* The twisted double helix on its cover beside the title "The Human Genome" was what first attracted her to open the magazine's pages and find the article heralding breakthrough research. It only took a second for Cadie to recall from her eidetic memory the words that first teased the possibility of family and heritage, all the things that mattered so much to everyone around her, but that she didn't have.

> The human genome underlies the fundamental unity of all members of the human family, as well as the recognition of their inherent dignity and diversity. In a symbolic sense, it is the heritage of humanity [. . .] in a sense we are both collectively and individually, defined within the genome.

The science writers had gone on to state that the completion of such knowledge would "strike a personal chord" with every person. For orphans like her, who had nothing tangibly heritable but their selfsame bodies, Cadie had instantly known the truth of the words. She had rooted for the scientists to succeed and had followed the project like a schoolgirl chasing a first love.

And she had only had to wait six months, until April 2003, when the dauntless scientists completed mapping the three billion base pairs found in human DNA. In those billions of base pairs was the invariant information that connected all life, all families, all lines, flora and fauna.

Now here she was, trying to see where she fell along the only line that could offer any clues about her past—even if it was only a road map tens of thousands of years old. Though she often felt that maybe she wasn't on the line at all, her results would be proof. There was no mystery in proof. Because she was alive, she *had* to be on one of those lines that migrated, with the rest of the human race, out of Africa.

The second hand on her watch marked thirty seconds, and Cadie pulled the swab from her mouth. She opened one of the small liquid vials that would preserve the cheek cells during transport and held the swab over it. She looked at the swab's saliva-laden tip, excited that a Cadie-ness she didn't know and couldn't see teemed there. With a push of her thumb, the swab head detached from the plastic stick and slowly floated to the bottom of the vial. Cadie secured the vial's lid and checked her watch. It was almost six o'clock. She placed the vial into the return package and checked the instructions again.

"Do the second swab in eight hours. Okay."

That would be at two o'clock in the morning. She shrugged, turning away from the box to locate her bottle of wine. Time was of no matter. She was often still awake then anyway, and there was no requirement to rise early the next morning, a Saturday, to work, though she knew she would. And waiting another eight hours was nothing compared to the more than five years since the launch of the *Genographic Project*. That's how long it'd taken her to get the nerve to send off for the test.

Cadie released the wine stopper and poured a second glass, again vacuuming the air from the bottle. She checked her watch one more time before walking through the kitchen door and onto her back porch.

+ + +

DR. ALECK TURINA SAT under the shelter of his garage, if he could call it shelter. Every day for the last four weeks, temperatures scalded over a hundred degrees. No end in sight. The heat index, unmitigated by the shade in which he sat, hovered near one twenty. He sat in an old slingback camp chair and sweated profusely under the leather band of his cream-colored panama hat. The brown curls of his boyish mop glistened with perspiration. He watched the shadows lengthen behind his house. Only a few more minutes, and the sun rays would sink behind the tall oaks lining the west side of his long driveway. Then he could move his chair into the open air and out of the garage that felt more like a furnace.

He checked the large copper clock his mother had hung for him on the beige wall beside his electric shrub trimmer and leaf blower.

Almost six o'clock. He watched the second hand move around the clock's face. Grinning, he stopped counting the seconds when he heard Cadie's back door open and close. He waited for the familiar rummaging sounds to echo from under her expansive covered porch.

Often he waited as long as twenty minutes during her preparations, knew her habit of walking the curved path in her backyard. He listened for her quiet footsteps, sometimes catching an ephemeral glance of her between the tall fence slats as she moved through her carefully landscaped garden. Quietly refilling his iced tea glass from the pitcher that sat on the blue cooler beside him, Aleck thought about his neighbor.

OF ALL THE CRAFTSMAN COTTAGES in the neighborhood, Cadie's house sat closest to the front sidewalk. That left her with the largest backyard in the Ashwood Division. Aleck guessed the yard was half a football field's width, maybe three quarters as long. It wasn't a yard by strict definition, but an urban, botanical forest inherited from the previous owner and kept to standard without adding or taking anything away. Among two grand oaks, pines, arborvitae, and magnolias of diverse sizes, an array of perennial shrubs and evergreens were crammed and tucked. Several varieties of Japanese maples, along with Eastern and Texan redbuds, blazed yearlong color from the understories of the larger trees, along with a few hardy roses.

She spent her time in her backyard; her front yard and sidewalk simply an access for unexpected visitors, deliveries, and late evening walks when she could move more freely under the cover of darkness. Once a week during the long grass-growing season, a small crew attended to Cadie's front yard—coming and going in a matter of minutes without ever ringing the front bell for payment.

According to next-door widow, Beatrice, who used the same crew, Cadie directly paid the yard contract by mail. Twice a year, the same crew hauled in enough compost and mulch to maintain the back garden. Beatrice said that Cadie did the other plant maintenance herself.

"Not that her pruning requires much work," Beatrice said.

Tolerated well enough by most as the neighborhood gossip, Beatrice Beauregard interested Aleck. He liked the way her stories held promises of social nuances he could incorporate in lectures at the college or for the sociology textbook he was writing. Beatrice was a chief gossiper, annoying as it was at times, but a chief gossiper was valuable when it came to deriving behavioral rules and structure from a neighborhood's small social group.

Furthermore, Beatrice was interesting in her own right. She wasn't at all reticent when she spoke of wanting her belongings burned when she died.

"I don't want to live on in the gewgaws or gimcracks they find in my house. Lord no, let me live on in my roses. They feed off the blood they draw from the thorns now. They can have my ashes, too."

Beatrice had shown everyone the scrapbook that held her last will and testament and the photos of her plants. She had labeled her roses according to who was to receive which. The yellow rose left to Aleck, the pink to her widowed sister, and the red to the Garcias who lived on the other side of Cadie's house. Beatrice's house would also go to her sister, who had one up on Beatrice when it came to fascinating behavior, for the sister ran a cotillion for dogs.

"She started it right up after seein' one of Coolidge's *Dogs Playing Poker* paintings," Beatrice had told Aleck.

At the Masterson Cotillion for Not-Just-Any Canine, dogs were either daintily or smartly dressed according to gender. The classes began with frantic owners learning to dance with their dogs. Then people arranged the dogs and themselves around tea tables set with species-appropriate biscuits and tea. Everyone on the street had heard more than one story about how the dogs had the hardest time minding their manners, still devouring the doggie tea sandwiches and cookies. One day Aleck planned to watch the cotillion in action. In the meantime, he marveled that, year after year, the classes hit capacity. He summarily assumed that Ms. Masterson tried desperately to recreate the magic of her own cotillion days—when teachers, as long as numbers permitted, forced boys to dance rather than stand nervously against a wall.

Beatrice had her own way of reliving things. But Aleck's extensive mental catalogue of social exchange theories had not shed light on why Beatrice went to the daily trouble to bake and deliver cookies, along with her stories, to the Corral Street residents. The cookies, he hoped, were more than a means to pass along and gather stories.

Yet Beatrice's tales were useful to Aleck when it came to hearing about Cadie Walsh. Everyone knew that Beatrice was the only person on the street for whom Cadie would open the door, aside from the occasional drivers who delivered the technologies that supported Cadie's job as a software engineer.

"She does her grocery shopping on weekday mornings," Beatrice told everyone.

Everyone believed her, too, because witnesses to the opening of the Walsh garage door were rare. Not one neighbor had ever seen Cadie leave the house during weekends. Only twice had Aleck been in his driveway when Cadie, sunglasses donned and slowly driving her yellow Yaris Liftback, had emerged into their alley.

He knew that there was something more to Cadie than the recluse everyone thought her to be, something in the way that she returned his wave, her fingers and wrist stuttering, foreign-like, to match his confident gesture.

THE SOUND OF A SLIDING panel coming from the teak sideboard on Cadie's porch focused Aleck's thoughts. He looked at his clock again. Exactly twenty minutes after six. When he heard the amplifier's buzz, Aleck silently picked up his chair and moved it to the driveway. He went back to fetch his cooler. After he settled into his seat, he opened the cooler and lifted out the uncorked half-bottle of white wine and a cold glass prepped on the ice.

Moments later, Beatrice rounded the tree line at the other side of his yard and walked into his driveway. By then, Aleck sat comfortably with one ankle propped on a knee, a glass of wine safely cradled in the chair's built-in cup holder.

The older woman couldn't help but notice the golden tan of the young scholar's legs, thinking that maybe, forty years ago, Aleck would have been interested in her.

Aleck grinned when he saw her. Beatrice nodded and held a wrinkled finger to her lips, her nightly reminder that he must silently choose his cookies from the basket she carried. He smiled and gave two thumbs up when he saw the contents—plain sugar cookies, hot. He took two. Beatrice handed him a third and, before turning to leave, tugged at one of Aleck's soft curls peeking below his hat band. Then she shuffled away. There was little time to finish delivering her baked goods before the nightly alley ritual commenced.

TONIGHT'S RITUAL BEGAN with an allegro drumming against the side of Cadie's acoustic guitar retrofitted for electric amplification. Its sound was an arrhythmic heart chased by looming shadows. As the drumming continued, the last garage doors on the block opened, inhabitants emerging to sit in lawn chairs especially commissioned for the occasion. A simultaneous inhalation by the residents lifted and held against the high pressure of thick, humid air. When the first lively notes escaped from Cadie's lips, they breathed again, looked at their companions or gazed into cold drinks that quickly condensed into beads on the outside of their beverage containers.

The reverberations of Cadie's guitar strings vibrated through the alley, arresting each resident to watch, unblinking, for the conjured fog to roll in, like it had the first time Cadie's voice had echoed along the street. Each remembered how the sounds had first drawn them trancelike from their homes. Each had stood and tasted salt suddenly saturating the air, and the raised hair on their bodies and the nape of their necks had made them want for jackets.

It was like that every evening, the depth and tonal purity of Cadie's singing often lasting hours at a time. Her haunting voice and strange words accompanied by guitar left her neighbors afraid that the music would disappear as suddenly as it'd arrived two years ago—when Cadie had bought the house for a song of a bargain at the beginning of the housing crash.

Aleck, who was a linguist and sociologist at the University of Texas at Arlington, had told his neighbors that it was mostly in Irish "Gaeilge" and Scottish Gaelic that Cadie sang. Stashed in his music collection were now several dozen Celtic and Irish CDs. Instrumental. Vocal. Full Orchestra. Cadie's voice matched . . . no, it surpassed the best of them. The guitar hooked to the amplifier emitted proofs that ages of strumming were bundled and reborn in the girl's fingers. From what Aleck heard, Cadie had found a fret fingering to match any instrument. For weeks at a time, she never repeated one song. Aleck sadly comprehended that many of Cadie's tunes and lyrics were one-time compositions, never replayed or remembered.

Nobody argued with Beatrice that Cadie, who could be traveling the world with her talents rather than sitting alone and playing with strings of software code in a home-office cottage, was a virtuoso in song and instrument. But such virtuosity confused and frightened Aleck. Long-exposed to many intelligent and talented types, Aleck knew that Cadie Walsh's peculiarity of synchronicity pushed him beyond his understanding and analysis of human behavior and history.

AN HOUR INTO THE PRIVATE concert, Aleck noticed the directional arc of Cadie's voice migrate. She'd moved. He filled his wine glass, stood up, and stretched before walking to the end of his driveway. He looked down the alley. Mr. and Mrs. Garcia sat in chairs positioned just outside the path of any through-passing cars, though cars had never passed through the alley when Cadie played. Aleck raised his hand and nodded to them. Mr. Garcia grinned, motioning for Aleck to move toward the back of Cadie's fence. Returning the grin, Aleck shrugged his shoulders and tiptoed into the easement behind his neighbor's yard. On any other street, they would scold or call the police for his particular brand of voyeurism, but the Garcias and Beatrice first suggested it. Now everyone in the neighborhood egged him on. It was his job to confirm, by peeking through Cadie's fence, when the nightly concert concluded. Aleck knew that his role was not one of practicality, for the retirees had more in mind—matchmaking to be specific. Everyone could hear when the music ended. But Aleck persisted with the mischief, telling himself that his curiosity was for greater evaluation of sociological study. He kept secret his personal desire to know Cadie Walsh.

In the dense shade of a large magnolia, Aleck leaned forward and peered through the one fence slat providing the best view. Cadie lay stretched atop a gigantic teak chaise lounge covered with red, orange, purple, pink, and fuchsia cushions and decorative pillows. Today, like most days, she wore a pair of broken-in jeans and a T-shirt, this time aqua-blue. One leg hung over the side of the lounge. A bare foot rested on the painted, ship deck gray of the wooden porch. Her guitar, which she strummed slowly, lay balanced across her torso, her movements the fluid maneuverings of an artist at one with her instrument. Cadie's head, turned to the side, almost rested against the guitar's head stock cradled on her left breast. Above her a slow-moving ceiling fan with fabricated palm leaf blades spun, moving her long, brown tresses in soft waves, as ripples move across calm water after a swan's passing.

Aleck took slow, shallow breathes as he watched. He withdrew from the fence to fill his lungs and then resumed his watch.

It pained him that he could not see the color of her eyes. Even now, as she sat upright and stared toward the back of her yard, he couldn't see what light spectrums, shaded by the porch's canopy, danced around her irises.

As he squinted for a better view, the sound that Aleck liked most when she played it came from her guitar. This time, though, the piercing, flute-like note startled him. Between the guitar's haunting wails and light strumming, Cadie began the most possessing of her musical laments. The repose in her voice conveyed something deeper than sorrow, maybe love in all its exclusivity. In this case, fleeting.

Aleck shook his head and leaned away from the fence to take a sip of his wine. When he looked back through the slat, Cadie had returned to her prone position. Her guitar, again resting on her slender body, rose and fell with each breath. It seemed to Aleck then that the guitar was, so far, Cadie's only love. Blushing at the intimacy of what he saw and at his own thoughts, he pulled away from the fence.

With a nod to his neighbors, he returned to his chair. In him beat a great craving to know what events had caused Cadie's sequestered self and what had blended innocence with fiery, passionate song.

IT WAS ALMOST DARK when Cadie pushed her amplifier into the sideboard's depth. In front of the speaker, she nudged in her guitar case before closing the heavy doors and going into the house. Like a curtain closing on a fairy-tale finale, the sound of a handful of simultaneously closing garage doors hummed along the alleyway.

Inside 2940 Corral Street, Cadie's rowing machine and the beginning of another movie drowned all outside noise. The second swab waited on the island counter.

CHAPTER TWO

"**W**HERE DO YOU *really* come from?"

Since reading those words on the National Geographic website a year before, edgy impatience had sparked a bit of new life in Cadie. With the kit sent off, it was now a matter of waiting. And six to eight weeks seemed a dreary long time to wait for DNA isolation and analysis from the swabs carrying her cheek cells.

When laid out, her DNA's double helix would become a large table of the four amino acids that she remembered from her college biology class: (A)denine, (C)ystosine, (G)uanine, and (T)hymine. Each acid bound itself to another acid to form sequences of three nucleotides, in this case allowing for a possible sixty-four, three-letter word combinations. The combinations were explanations that would unlock, row by row, a small secret of Cadie's larger genetic history. On paper, the beginning lines of a sample genetic table looked like this:

ATTCTAATTTAAACATTCTCTGTTCTTTCATGGGG
AAGCAGATTTGGGTACCACCCAAGTATTGACTCA
CCCATCAACAACCGCTATGTATTTCGTACATT . . .

Variations in the letters along her DNA code string would show her maternal wanderers' transitions. Cadie's anxiousness increased as she waited. Which varying letters of her DNA would plot her path? What would her sentence, finite drawn from infinite, reveal of sequel lines attaching sloughed saliva to a human ready for definition?

Several times a day she tracked her kit's online progress. She fueled her eagerness in the way she keyed her secret ten-digit, alphanumeric identification number, playing the covert DNA operator looking for something so complexly hidden until recent decades. Illuminated and now easily available knowledge was only clicks away . . . as long as she didn't lose her secret code. There wasn't a person at the *Genographic Project* who could identify her with her analyzed swabs, and the thrill of tracking her kit didn't allow Cadie to think that she could just order another.

Cadie thought of it as a one-shot, succeed or fail enterprise, like the migration paths her ancestors—her mother's mother, that mother's mother's mother, and so on . . . back to the mitochondrial Eve—had followed. And each of those mothers had left her one thing: mitochondrial DNA. Until the development of the Geno 2.0 kit, it was impossible to trace paths of her paternal line. DNA history of Y chromosomes stopped with each son. Had she a brother, his DNA could identify the paternal line of ancestry passed from father to son. There was no brother. For now, her X chromosome was all that remained to "mark" the spot on a maternal line only, and never identifying exact persons.

IT DIDN'T TAKE LONG for her kit to reach Houston. Someone as equally as anonymous as Cadie logged the kit into the system. Soon, the kit's status rendered itself on Cadie's computer monitor: *Kit received*. Not long afterward: *Batch created*.

Batches were intimately familiar to Cadie. She often developed her own to simplify repetitive software engineering tasks. It soothed Cadie to associate her common day with a new batch of initiated behavior differing wildly from her natural habits.

Once created, they shipped off her DNA batch to a separate research lab. There, the last three steps of Cadie's genomic typing would move through carefully constructed and provable steps.

Her distractibility increased. Rather than engineering side projects, as she normally did while waiting for her robotics algorithms to compile, Cadie researched the intricacies of DNA isolation. Next to come, incubation, a process that would burst the membranes of her cheek cells and allow her DNA to bind with silica-coated iron beads awaiting collection.

Cadie imagined the cells born with history, something that for the first time could tell her who she was and bind her to a place, as her cheek cells had bound themselves to the swab. Those cells, if she was lucky, might give a better view of what she'd never had: a family.

Sister Mary Trea's voice interrupted her thoughts. "You walked away from it."

"I never had it," said Cadie.

She felt the sting on her hand, a memory of punishment for impertinence.

"Never speak that way of Our Mother," hissed Sister Mary Trea.

Cadie stiffened. "She isn't my mother. Definitely wasn't yours."

It was enough to drive the voice from her head, and Cadie relaxed. From her cells, she hoped to be reborn of something iron-like—strong, useful, and protective—an element so common that Cadie Walsh might find the key to fit in anywhere, with anything, and with anyone. Once and for all. Maybe, then, Sister Mary Trea would rest away from Cadie's thoughts.

FOR THE THIRD TIME that day, Cadie closed her browser after checking for her DNA results. She walked into her bedroom to change out of her jeans and T-shirt, slid into black slacks and ballet flats before pulling on a lightweight gray sweater.

"Don't know where you got that idealism, Cadie."

Cadie ignored the voice. Sister Mary Trea persisted.

"You'll be the same Cadie after those results come through."

Cadie pulled her hair into a tidy chignon and turned to face the full-length mirror. The reflection she saw *was* the same person she'd be after the results—the person who dreaded going into the office for software design meetings with the team or influential clients. She was the reflection of a person who fluently sold abstractions of proto-robot designs. She was the person who, when asked by her boss if she had "anything new goin' on in her life," wouldn't know what to say.

Leaving her reflection, Cadie walked into the garage. From a wall shelf, she grabbed the sunglasses she'd bought her sophomore year of college. Lifting her keys from an iron hook under the shelf, she unlocked her car, bracing herself against a displaced wave of warm air that tumbled out. She sighed. Even more eternal than wanting her reflection to change and Sister Mary Trea's voice to stop, she wished for an end to the office trips, infrequent though they were.

+ + +

AT THE BUILDING DOWNTOWN, Cadie dreaded going into the brightly lit offices. Inside, several balloon bouquets floated above various cubicles. Vibrant buzzing permeated the space, often common when her fellow programmers uncannily sensed that free cake and other desserts were on the horizon. Cadie summarily dismissed the afternoon as one of the "birthday," "new baby," or other delicious "life announcement" occasions soon to infiltrate her meeting with glee and gibber jabber.

She made a mental note to get to her point early on, before cake-generated interruptions resulted in days of interminable follow-up emails. That much enthusiasm, combined with sugar, rendered programmers useless. For days, they would ask for repeated design clarification and reminders of their project responsibilities. Every such email requiring repeat instruction slowed down project deliveries. As Cadie passed the last row of blue cubicles, her boss emerged from his office and looked down the hall toward her.

Bobby Pullman, a thirty-year-old computer whiz kid who had struck it smart and made his first million by the time he was twenty-two, looked barely older than Cadie. He grinned and waved grandly toward her, cowboy boots already headed her direction.

"Howdy, Cadie," he bellowed.

He never worried about how his voice carried through the room or into the headset receivers of customer service reps ironing out client difficulties. Robotics customers didn't perform any better than toaster users when it came to reading a manual or using common sense; ego had something to do with it.

Cadie, distracted by the text printed across Bobby's black T-shirt, smiled meekly. Every day he wore the Stetson hat, cowboy boots and jeans, and a black T-shirt. Before his daughters were born, the text on the shirts displayed computer world idioms, phrases that only programmers and computer people understood and found funny. Now his shirts sported pictures of his daughters with sales pitches and sponsor logos for soccer teams and peewee baseball. Sports that he proudly announced were now co-ed at the youngest ages. Today's photo was a picture of his daughters wearing matching sombreros and sitting astride mules.

She liked her boss, which is more than some could say. He was one of a handful of people she'd met who, upon getting her name, didn't ask her where she went to church. He could tell you in one breath why anything goes in Texas, like jeans and cowboy hats at Bass Hall or beer and ketchup with lobster. As far as Bobby was concerned, there was one way to do things in Texas—the Texas way. The Texas way meant getting your job done and getting along. That's all.

When Bobby was a few steps away, Cadie tried to think of something to say that didn't have anything to do with the meeting.

She went with the obvious. "Cake today?"

"Chocolate, too," he grinned, reaching for and shaking her hand. Cadie nodded.

Talking was never your forte, said the nun.

Cadie offered a thin smile. To buy time, she glanced at a new poster on the wall and then walked into the conference room.

Bobby grinned even bigger and followed. "So, Cadie girl, what's new?"

Cadie finally thought of something as she connected her laptop to the digital projector. "Does the cake have chocolate frosting, too?"

"Thank goodness, it does," Bobby chuckled. "Last birthday, somebody asked for some sort of yellow, lemony thing."

Cadie forced another close-lipped smile. *What was new?* She dove quickly into her delayed answer. "Nothing new on my end. You know . . . "

"I wish I didn't know." Bobby rolled his eyes. "I do know that we gotta find somebody for ya."

Get out of shutdown mode, Cadie. Restart, restart, restart.

Bobby, knowing Cadie enough to realize he was about to send her into a social tailspin, moved away from the subject and toward the door. There was more to her than what others thought. He could feel that something held her back, something that no one could see.

"Just call us all in when you're ready," he called over his shoulder as he left the room.

"Okay," she said.

You handled that one well.

The nun migrated from Cadie's mind and sat down across the table from Cadie.

"No thanks to you," answered Cadie, for a moment forgetting where she was. "He's a world different than you."

And that was true. For Bobby Pullman, every stray was one he could save . . . or gently put out of its misery. Cadie at least liked that he kept trying to pull her out of her broken shell rather than place her into one.

THAT AFTERNOON, HURRICANE REMNANTS from the Texas coast hit Fort Worth. Happy to be at home again, Cadie sat at her desk and watched the rain. The smaller trees in her backyard bowed under the tempest. She hoped they were deeply rooted enough to bear the storm. The smaller maples and understory trees might have done with staking, she thought, before the hurricane arrived with wind and rain that now sluiced horizontally past her house. Big, missile-like drops sailed in under the porch eaves and pelted the sideboard that cradled her amplifier, and Cadie wished she'd brought it in with her guitar already leaning against her desk.

Between looking outside and wondering about the state of her yard, Cadie alternately attended to programming tasks and logged in to check her DNA results. Each refresh of the screen showed the same status it had for days: *DNA Isolation Complete.*

She wondered how much longer it would take before her isolated DNA underwent PCR amplification, which would heat and cool the molecular particulates. Inside little thermal cycler tubes, her swirled particulates would release answers as the hurricane released its rain. The final stage: quality control. Mere time was all that separated her from microscopic matter that would tell how she was the same as, or different, from other ancient peoples.

+ + +

FOR THE NEXT TWO WEEKS, it rained daily. Corral Street's yards, now fully saturated with the plumped water table, sloughed bits of bark and mulch over landscaping barriers and into the street. Under the hazy glow thrown off by the streetlights, Cadie took her nightly walk.

She wished the air cooler than it was, wanted a short break from the stifling heat. She twirled her umbrella. Wet, circular sheets shot out and merged with softly falling rain. She was almost tired.

Since the rains had started, there had barely been time for her evening guitar playing. Eating in front of the television and watching movies had gone by the wayside. Instead, she had eaten at her desk and programmed. For the current project, however, the intensity was over. She could relax a little, look forward to playing guitar and watching television from her long list of recorded sitcoms and movies. The programming cycle was always the same with each project—ramped-up, frantic plunges into drowning work hours, a little rest during testing, another rush to deliver, and then a smidgen of downtime during tweaking as a new project rose through the ranks of customer demand. Rinse and repeat. Cadie knew she didn't want it any other way.

She hopped down into a gutter and kicked through the black water with her rubber galoshes. The water partly splashed her jeans, soaking her knees. The cool hand of a phantom yank at her collar caused her to freeze for a second. She jumped from the gutter to the sidewalk and looked over her shoulder.

"Leave me alone," she said into the night.

"Stay out of the water," snapped Sister Mary Trea.

Cadie glared into the darkness and then stepped back into the gutter, kicking the water again.

+ + +

SOMETIMES IT'D BEEN WORSE for her than the other girls, sometimes better, but everyone had known that Cadie Walsh belonged to Sister Mary Trea. Many delighted in rumoring that Cadie really was the nun's daughter, that Sister Mary Trea had skulked away to downtown Dallas one night and come away with what she'd always wanted. They whispered it was her revenge for banishment from the Old Country, for running off with a beau her daddy didn't like. That it was the fixedness of the nun's affection toward that beau that had prompted her order to "re-distribute" her across the ocean—all the way to Texas to help raise and teach daughters of Christ whom nobody else wanted to own.

Of course, Cadie went into the orphanage as many girls did—straight from the hospital. Only Cadie's biological mother didn't get up from the table and walk away, or walk into the hospital after a secret home delivery to hand over the small infant. No questions asked. Cadie's mother was a DOA Jane Doe. Cadie got lucky and survived for Sister Mary Trea to be the first to hold her. And in the custom of that privilege, Sister Mary Trea was the one to name Cadie and the one to hold first chair in her discipline and upbringing.

It was Cadie's luck that she was the only girl Sister Mary Trea first held. Sister Mary Trea's improbable visit to the hospital the day Cadie was born made her the only nun to hold just one baby who came into the orphanage.

The other girls never understood that, what it was like to be the only one.

Cadie had Mother Fara Verena's untimely death to thank for that moira. Thanks to the rattlesnake that came out of the rock garden and bit the old woman's ankle as she sipped tea and ate lemon cookies. The old nun thought the bite nothing worse than a mosquito attack and succumbed with a half-eaten cookie in her mouth. Thus, the others sent Sister Mary Trea to find Sister Georgia attending the hospital ward that day. Only, Sister Georgia wasn't there when Sister Mary Trea arrived. Sister Georgia had had a vision about a snake, was on her way back to the orphanage when Sister Mary Trea walked into the emergency room. Two going out of the world, one coming in, and Sister Mary Trea lucky as hell.

"You aren't the replacement we were hoping for," interrupted Sister Mary Trea.

"We never are," said Cadie. "But you could have told me something, anything."

"It wasn't important."

Cadie stopped answering and kept walking.

The nuns gave Cadie no information about her Jane Doe mother. Not the color of her hair or eyes. Not the woman's reason for being at the hospital. Not if anyone searched for the dead woman. Cadie had long ago gone through all the paper archives for the days leading up to and following her birth. There was nothing. Her life and name had started with Sister Mary Trea, and Sister Mary Trea had held as tightly to the infant as any woman has ever held a child. It had left Cadie feeling that she'd been nothing more to the nun than a piece of chocolate or a hard gumdrop that wasn't for the sharing, a sweet only purposed for devourment. And the results of Sister Mary Trea's "mothering" had been . . . had been?

The thought, suddenly interrupted by something far more important, stopped Cadie's foot mid-kick.

"The results."

She turned and started running for home.

Down the street, Aleck emerged from his front door and stood on his porch. At first, he thought something was wrong when he saw Cadie running. Ready to aid in a rescue, he stepped out into the rain. But he forced himself to be still when he saw that her movement wasn't fear-driven. She glanced sideways toward him as she came even with where he stood.

"Hi, Cadie," he called into the rain.

She continued running but lifted her hand, an almost run-of-the-mill wave.

Invulnerable to the rain, Aleck watched her until she cut into the alley entrance between his and Beatrice's properties.

OUTSIDE HER GARAGE, CADIE stamped her feet and keyed in the entry code. Before the door opened halfway, she bent down and ran under it, dropping her umbrella beside the car as she ran into the house. Behind her, she left a trail of wet prints.

How could I have forgotten?

It'd been two weeks since she'd last checked her genographic DNA results.

"You wanted to forget."

"No. *You* wished I would forget," Cadie argued with the nun.

Water from her galoshes puddled on the floor as Cadie sat down at her desk and clicked on her password file. She typed in the master keycode. From the opened matrix, she copied her National Geographic *Genographic Project* identification code and then clicked the login page link. She tapped her fingers across her wrist rest as the website loaded. It only took a second to paste in her kit ID and code. Two, three, four, five taps as she waited for the results.

For half a minute, she stared at the returned Web page before shooting up from her chair. She ran toward her pantry, her wet boots slipping on the tiled kitchen floor. Without stopping, she adjusted her momentum and hopped on one foot and then the other to pull off her boots and socks. She snatched a bottle of wine and ran with it to the kitchen counter. With her free hand, she pulled the damp rain jacket over her head, and then freed herself of her wet jeans. In her haste to open the wine, she broke the cork, had to shove it into the bottle. She poured a glass without straining the bits.

Wearing nothing now but her tank top and hipsters, she took her glass and stepped over the trail of wet clothes on her way back to her office. Taking a deep breath, she slid into her computer chair to confirm what she'd seen.

On the screen wasn't the regular *Track Your Kit* list. Now there was a map with a red line diverging into a distorted chicken claw. It stretched its way from Africa and clawed its way into northern and eastern Europe. She logged out, refreshed the login screen, and re-entered her code to double-check the link. It was true. Her DNA analysis and quality control were complete.

She navigated back to the National Geographic's *Genographic Project* results page. Under the map with its red line was the title: YOUR GENETIC HISTORY.

"You can't believe it, Cadie," said Sister Mary Trea.

"That I know it is true is what scares you," answered Cadie.

The nun tried to twist at Cadie's arm and then subsided again.

Taking a sip from her glass, Cadie began to read about *her* branch, *her very first* branch, on the human family tree.

CHAPTER THREE

CADIE'S FIRST IMPRESSION of the world map showing her results engrossed her with emotions both extrinsic and remote. Her path was one among twenty-four primary haplogroups, groups with similar combinations of DNA sequences at different places on the shared ancestor chromosome. All haplogroups emerged from the point of origin labeled "Eve." So the mirage of her single line seemed illusory, for there was, instead, a great interconnectedness shown on the world map, a single blood family occupying a single house.

Shifting her focus back to the mitochondrial Eve and the haplogroups that were specific branches of the human family tree, Cadie counted six times from the ancestral point of origin that her DNA had mutated. Each mutation changed the directional course her ancestors had followed before ending at a single nucleotide polymorphism (SNP) mutation, a mutation that predicted collective ancestry along her antediluvian path.

The first six super-haplogroups were L1, then L2, L3, N, and R. Her final genetic mutation occurred at the super-haplogroup U. There, Cadie's geographical path branched into three directions and became the claw that scratched her origins on the earth and imprinted on her a new label: Haplogroup U5.

Cadie correlated U5 as a new association, like the ones she used in programming. In this case, it was a command from the simple swab that produced and displayed her modified file name extension: Cadie Walsh = the association of U5. U for uncommon, unknown, unseen, un–, un–, un–.

She carefully read through her results explaining that mitochondrial Eve appeared between 150,000 to 170,000 years ago. Then between 100,000 years ago and Eve's birth, the world's female ancestors moved in all directions throughout Africa, the continent holding, almost exclusively, the L1/L0, L2, and L3 haplogroups.

Cadie's ancestors, though, followed the 70,000-year-old L3 route out of Africa, where the L3 path ended and coalesced into the 50,000-year-old N haplogroup. It was there that the real incubation of modern humans blended at the eastern Mediterranean and western Asia regions.

Feeling lightheaded, Cadie checked the wine level in her glass. She hadn't taken more than a couple of sips.

"Wine is for communion," whispered Sister Mary Trea.

"Not now," said Cadie.

She picked up the glass and took another sip.

"You never could obey, could you?"

"Not any better than you. I knew about the flask under your mattress."

It was enough to silence the voice in her head. Cadie knew the lightheadedness had to be from the results.

She looked at the map again and imagined the women of her family at one point coexisting for several thousand years with Neanderthal hominids before moving on to spread out into haplogroup R. The results said that those belonging to the 50,000-year-old haplogroup R were explorers. Some went back into Africa, some moved into the Middle East and on to Central Asia, and some moved west into present-day Turkey. Cadie's ancestors followed the north route, across the Caucasus Mountains of Georgia and southern Russia. That is where her haplogroup began to form.

Like the R and N super-haplogroups, the ancient U5 branch of Cadie's DNA ceased to yield genetic clues more recent than 50,000 years ago.

Cadie thought it a beautiful computation that could link her backwards by 50,000 years—one mother at a time. She knew, of course, it was impossible to link her maternal ancestors by name. There was no Cadie, begat by Regina, begat by Maggie, begat by so on and so forth for 50,000 years. There was only U5 Cadie. Still, it was more than she was an hour ago. She read on.

Rather than following the U6 haplogroup south, back into North Africa, Cadie's U5 mothers turned and headed north into Scandinavia.

Cadie sat back in her chair.

Scandinavia? Fie.

The Scandinavia kind of cold was a far cry from the Texas heat. She barely endured the mildest Texas winters. That migration north was most likely painfully slow, each generation slowly adapting to the harsher and harsher conditions of the north. Cadie wondered how easily she would have adapted. Would she have been a death along her family's path?

UN-association, thought Cadie. She leaned closer to the computer screen to read more about her genograph:

> U5 is quite restricted in its variation to Scandinavia, and particularly to Finland. [. . .] likely the result of geographical, linguistic, and cultural isolation.

> At much lower frequencies and lower genetic diversity, the U5 lineage has also been found in some North African Berber populations in Morocco, Senegal, and Algeria. [. . .] likely the result of re-expansions after the last glacial maximum around 15,000 years ago.

> U5 individuals also live sporadically in the Near East [. . .] their distribution in the Near East, largely confined to surrounding populations such as Turks, Kurds, Armenians, and Egyptians [. . .] the result of back-migration of people who left northern Europe and headed south [. . .].

> They had left northern Europe and headed south [. . .] as though retracing the migratory paths of their own ancestors.

The last line particularly caught Cadie's eye, and she had what she guessed was her first conscious and familial emotion. It was an aching understanding, a conscious connection to the ancient peoples who carried the U5 DNA. She had used modern science to retrace her migratory path. Had her ancient mothers subconsciously turned away from the cold north and gone in search of their warmer origins?

She leaned back and sipped her wine, frowned bitterly when the oxidized wine hit her tongue. She looked at the time on her monitor—two hours had passed.

"Look at this tomorrow, Cadie," she said. She got up and went to start the kettle for coffee. "You have at least another few hours of project work tonight."

She sang softly as the water began to boil. How brave, or desperate, was someone to just turn around and start off in a new direction?

+ + +

CADIE SPENT THE WEEKEND comparing her genographic map with current geographic maps. Her desk was strewn with multiple National Geographic and online map printouts, all marked with frenetic scribbles and arrows. The disarray overflowed from the desk and onto the floor—one idea after another discarded. She arranged and rearranged placemarks, one placemark for each U5 location mentioned by National Geographic: Morocco, Senegal, Algeria, Turkey (which included the Kurds), Armenia, and Egypt.

One of the claw points was easily referenced and identifiable: Finland. Two of the U5 genetic points were unreferenced. At the middle point, Cadie compromised and placed a mark at the border shared between Estonia and Russia. She spent more time determining a placemark at the third point, a location that could fall easily into areas of Lithuania, Poland, and Russia. After several printouts, she finally settled the last placemark inside the Polish border at Warsaw.

For a moment, Cadie allowed herself the mental calculation that, given a minimum of three mothers every hundred years between herself and Eve, she potentially had 4,500 mothers along the great span. It was a severe and overwhelming mockery that, from so many mothers, she was a motherless daughter.

Cadie comforted herself by associating the same comical mockery on the mitochondrial Eve. *She* was a woman who never realized nor could comprehend that she'd become the mother of all present-day humans.

Looking at her new map, Cadie saw a forgotten placemark. She moved her cursor to the U.S. and marked Fort Worth, Texas. It was for herself, the opposite end of her 150,000-year-old origin. With her placemarked path complete, Cadie printed the last map.

She tapped her fingers. What she could do with her results now was a source of uncertainty. She wanted to make a connection of some kind, with either persons or places, a connection more than the double-blind association of DNA results. Traveling would have to wait until she cleared her student loan balance. That would take three years with the triple payments she made. Then she could travel . . . *if* there weren't engineering projects demanding undivided attention and direction.

She returned her attention to the online results to glean any idea that hadn't occurred to her previously.

A twelve-question form was available for test participants. Upon agreeing to load her results into the *Genographic Project* coordinated by National Geographic, clients' answers helped improve the mapping process. Cadie answered the questions, doubting that her results could help improve their maps. She hadn't, *couldn't*, answer the questions about her last known ancestors.

At the bottom of the Web page, a question printed in big, bold letters asked: "What else can I do with my results?"

She clicked on the link to "Learn More." It directed her to the *Family Tree DNA* website promoting a free transfer of her National Geographic DNA results to their database. They dangled the true genealogical carrot—a breakthrough.

Cadie frowned. That wouldn't help someone with zero genealogical references. The best she could hope for was a shared female ancestor, and that couldn't happen; it was out of the question. She imagined approaching a stranger.

"Say, I'm related to you a ways back—*50,000 years back*."

If an institution for the genealogically insane existed, that would land her in it. She quickly tossed out the idea of loading her results into the family tree database and went back to studying her map.

The rationality of molecular genetics brought Sister Mary Trea's voice to the surface again.

"There is nothing but the Church—nothing beyond these walls more faithful."

The phrase was one of the orphanage's favorites, but Cadie had heard it the most from Sister Mary Trea.

Cadie shuddered over what would have happened if the nun had convinced her to stay with the order. Her closest guess was that her role would have reversed from student child to caretaker of the dying nun. But since rationality, according to the nun, was a dogmatic sin, and abuse never moved Cadie toward affection, it was without regret that Cadie had never gone back to the orphanage or the church after starting college. When the orphanage closed shortly before her college graduation, she still hadn't driven by St. Fina's. Not even for a parting glance of Sister Mary Trea. The other nuns departed every which way throughout the States to teach other orphaned girls. Sister Mary Trea returned to Ireland to finish out the last months of a cancer-shortened life, leaving behind her mantra of dogma heavy in Cadie's memories.

The doorbell rang, followed by quick rapping on the door. Cadie started from her chair and pushed the nun from her thoughts.

UNDER A DRIPPING UMBRELLA imprinted with green, leaping frogs on the black webbing, Beatrice Beauregard stood. She wielded before her a plate of warm peanut butter cookies, testament of the aroma trapped and condensed under the porch. Using the cookies as a self-invitation to step past Cadie, Beatrice dropped her umbrella on the porch and walked directly toward the girl's kitchen.

"Cadie, dear, my goodness. It's been ages since I've seen you, worried you caught the sick bug. 'Course, there's nothing better than a few cookies to cheer a body, sick or well."

Cadie reluctantly followed her plump neighbor into the kitchen but left her front door open, so the fishwife wouldn't get the idea to linger more than necessary. It surely couldn't have been that long since the always uninvited Mrs. Beauregard last popped by. Upon a mental review of several weeks, Cadie realized it'd been almost two months. She swallowed a sigh. It seemed like yesterday.

"I'm well, Mrs. Beauregard . . . "

Beatrice interrupted. "Now how many times have I told you to call me Beatrice? I absolutely insist, my dear. No sense in standing on formality. We're a little family on this street."

"Yes, Mrs. B . . . I mean Beatrice."

The motherly woman, diverting her attention to scan the space around her, missed Cadie's awkward smile.

Cadie pulled a simple white platter from her cabinet and began transferring the cookies from Mrs. Beauregard's bright cake plate.

"Oh, no, dear," the older woman exclaimed when she saw what Cadie was doing, "You can bring my plate by anytime, or when you've eaten the cookies. We never have had a chance to sit down and really visit at my house."

Cadie transferred the cookies faster.

"I'm in the middle of a big project. Wouldn't want you to wait for your plate," Cadie said. It was best to avoid conversation discomfited by social inadequacy.

"You needn't go to the trouble, dear."

Beatrice's tone was convincing, but she enjoyed the advantage of extra minutes to see what the girl had been up to for the last few weeks. She knew that she daren't ask Cadie why the Corral Street residents hadn't heard her singing as often. The girl usually sang even when it rained, as long as her back porch offered enough protection to keep the musical equipment dry. But the Corral Street garage doors had opened expectantly each night during the rains, and then the doors had shut. Forlorn residents had drifted back inside to the silence of their private lives.

Making her rounds to gather news nonetheless, Beatrice had learned that nobody had spotted Cadie outside her house at all. It was the fresh snicker doodles delivered to Aleck that yielded the story of Cadie's strange running in the rain.

Talking as she moved around the kitchen, Beatrice looked for anything new—anything out of place.

"I'd be happy to drop by next week to collect the plate, dear. If you're too busy to get out, that is. Really, it's no trouble—no bother at all."

She moved toward Cadie's office door.

"I always go by Aleck's to collect my plates . . . 'course it never takes him more than a couple of days to finish his cookies."

Beatrice threw an irritable glance at Cadie's slender figure. What she would do to look like that—except eat fewer cookies or exercise, beyond pruning roses.

Keeping her eyes on the cookies, Cadie marveled at the verbal fluidity of people like Mrs. Beauregard. But when Cadie noticed Mrs. Beauregard poke her head around the office door frame, Cadie dumped the remaining cookies on the platter and bound toward her office.

"Oh, my," exclaimed Beatrice when she saw the papers littering the desk and floor. "You *have* been busy. My, my," she said as she swept into the office and out of Cadie's view. "Poor dear, let me help you pick these up. So sad when I see people get overwhelmed. I say people ought not burn themselves out thataway."

By the time Cadie made it to Mrs. Beauregard, the woman, with one hand balanced on the edge of the desk, was rising from a bent position. She tightly clutched dozens of pages in thick fingers made strong from decades of mixing heavy cookie and bread dough by hand.

"It must be some project, dear. Normally immaculate in this office."

Cadie jumped forward. "Let me help you, Mrs. Beauregard."

"Beatrice."

"Right . . . Beatrice."

Beatrice took a small step back from Cadie, using the moment to assess the pages she held. Her glittering eyes met Cadie's.

Cadie blushed slightly, took the pages, and hurriedly bent over to gather the other pages off the floor and into a quick pile.

"I'd be happy to help, dear. Anytime you need some company for cleaning, you can certainly call me." Beatrice glanced at the computer screen and the other pages on the desk as she talked. She didn't know a lot about computers, but it didn't look like a normal software project to her. "My dear, I've never seen so many maps. Are you taking a trip?"

Cadie collected the jumbled paper stack from her desk. With the rest of the printouts, she laid the bunch upside down on one of the sofa chairs on the other side of the room.

"No, Mrs. Beauregard, I mean Beatrice. Just a bit of research."

Beatrice, narrowing her eyes, didn't buy it. From what she'd seen, it opened as good an opportunity as any to travel down the crafty path of both successful and unsuccessful matchmakers.

"You know, Aleck's parents originally moved here from Spain. That's not too far from Morocco."

Certain now that Mrs. Beauregard had seen the maps, Cadie winced.

"Did you know he *inherited* his cottage from his parents when they moved with his younger sister back to Spain ten years ago?" It was an ages-old selling point, men with real property to their names.

Cadie shook her head.

"He did. His parents signed the deed over outright to Aleck half-way through his bachelor's degree. The rest of us on the street helped keep watch over the house while he was away at graduate school. Mowed, replaced timers and porch lights, all that."

Beatrice intently watched Cadie for signs of interest. Nothing. The girl nervously worked the paper piles into orderly stacks.

"His mother is Italian, his father Spanish—related to some famous Spanish composer, not that that matters." Beatrice artfully lowered her voice then and pretended to mutter. "Certainly explains his good looks."

No sign of agreement from Cadie. She was wondering about the composer.

Beatrice raised her voice again. "The Turinas said they missed their friends and family and something else about being able to walk for fresh breakfast *churros* with coffee."

Cadie's diverted movements slowed, and Beatrice paused.

"How nice to be close enough to walk to a little café," said Cadie, musing. She disliked driving for necessity or the smallest of conveniences. She imagined the Turina's walk to their local café, stopping often to chat with neighbors before settling in with coffee and pastries and engaging in lively discussion with long-time friends.

Beatrice frowned. That was *not* what she wanted the girl to focus on. It irritated Beatrice that someone of Cadie's beauty hadn't immediately pursued, or even talked to, the single man next door. Especially one as equally beautiful in form, face, and intelligence as Cadie was herself. In Beatrice's humble opinion, Cadie was nothing short of Bohemian.

"They visit Aleck once every two years, you know. He still gets lonely, I imagine . . . " Beatrice sighed and cast her eyes to the floor before finishing. "He doesn't have any other family here in the States, not one person."

As the successful matchmaker she considered herself to be, Beatrice moved quickly after releasing the arrow aimed at lonely heartstrings and shuffled from the office.

She gently squeezed Cadie's arm as she passed. "You let me know how this cookie batch turned out." She moved on to collect her plate before walking to the front door.

Without speaking, Cadie followed Beatrice toward the humid night air gushing into the house. Beatrice stepped through the doorway and turned back to Cadie.

"You have a good night, dear. I'm just down the street if you need anything, anything at all."

Beatrice, fiddling with her umbrella, didn't hear Cadie respond, "Good night, Mrs. Beauregard."

Instead, she pushed the leaping frogs in front of her and shuffled out into the rain. She was excited. Many conjectures could be made from the maps in the girl's office, and once she'd dried herself from the incessant rain, Beatrice had to decide who on the street would be the next to know.

IRATE OVER MRS. BEAUREGARD'S INTRUSION, Cadie stopped in the kitchen to make a pot of coffee before going back to her office. Regardless of the woman's double-edged concerns, she had a gross disregard for privacy. Cadie frowned at the platter of cookies. She couldn't know for certain but correctly inferred that untold varieties of cookies were bound for delivery along Corral Street, along with Mrs. Beauregard's neighborly speculation about Cadie's mysterious maps.

As Cadie poured a large mug of coffee and stacked four warm cookies on a napkin, her thoughts gradually returned to her genetic results. Despite the interruption and unease the woman brought, there was no need to let it thwart the enjoyment of her favorite cookies with fresh coffee and research.

CADIE MUNCHED ON THE COOKIES and read through general information for the various placemarked locations. Soon intermingled with her maps was a slew of Wikipedia pages—histories and religions of places with exotic foods and different cultures. She clicked through the numerous links and realized how minimal her knowledge was of the places—her trivia reduced to what books of prayer and theodicy placed in abundance over books of history at the orphanage. At university, her brief induction into the oversimplified Texas and American history brought to near falsity had mirrored the orphanage's lax teaching. The courses had been something to breeze through without much effort in order to get back to her focus on the technical architecture of software programming.

The pit of Cadie's stomach tightened. Would an association with any variety of these cultures be as easy as the first time she'd picked up a guitar in college—familiar and innate as the ability to understand and follow static rules in one's mother tongue? Shrugging her shoulders, Cadie doubted it. The only path to answering her questions was to make the associations. And to do so, she'd have to find groups, recent descendants of her placemarked locations, in the Dallas-Fort Worth area. There was a near-zero chance that those descendants would be U5 offspring, but that didn't matter. It was close enough to find people who brought to America the culture of her U5 places. Any connection was better than nothing.

To test the water, Cadie decided to choose no more than four cultural groups. Socially, she could barely manage one person at a time. Four new histories and meetings would be a challenge. She started a spreadsheet to track the contact links for her chosen groups and then placemarked a new map.

Her first choice was easy: Finland, the population with which she shared, in probability, the most genetic identity. She easily located a Meetup group for Dallas Finns. Placemark one. Next, she chose Morocco and Turkey. Placemarks two and three. From each of the major areas on her map, that left Poland.

Again, Cadie pulled up the information page for Poland and clicked to go directly to the religious demographics.

Devoutly religious . . . and Roman Catholic.

Cadie frowned. She was determined to make an association different from one she knew only too well.

She reluctantly returned to the Family Tree DNA link and submitted her information. Perhaps, she hoped, her submission would flesh out her DNA a little further, just enough for her to choose a final placemark. Unexpectedly, the data loaded almost instantly and returned a kit number and identification code. She logged in using the new access keys and navigated to the *ancestral origins* page. The row and column table on the computer screen showed a list of low-level U5 HVR1 matches by modern countries compared to total persons tested with those sharing her results. It didn't faze Cadie when she saw that Poland wasn't anywhere on the list.

As an alternative, she looked instead for the country with which she shared the highest percentage of matches. That was the Czech Republic. Cadie's eyes widened as she looked back to her map and stared at the outline of the land-trapped country just southwest of Poland. Her strange, unspeakable dreams crowded her thoughts. One of her few secrets was that, for as long as she could remember, she'd dreamed in Czech. She understood and spoke Czech in her dreams and woke without knowing a word of it.

Cadie queried for Czechs in the Dallas-Fort Worth area. Forty minutes south of Dallas lie her jackpot—Ennis, a town with Czech immigrants and their descendants. Satisfied, she dropped her fourth and final placemark over the Czech Republic.

On her spreadsheet, Cadie marked two objectives: Learning and Contact. She quickly navigated a list of online books and ordered one used history book for each of the countries—Finland, Turkey, Morocco, and the Czech Republic. Trepidation grew in her as she looked at the map and her list of initial contact email addresses.

"They'll go into the void or be read by someone who will think you a lunatic," said Sister Mary Trea.

Cadie, nodding, concurred on that point. Who out there had their DNA tested and then contacted groups of people so different from their childhood group—just took the past and walked into the present with it?

"Thousands have done it," Cadie finally defended.

That was true according to National Geographic. Still, with deep mistrust in herself, Cadie wondered if her DNA was a sign of regression rather than progress. She breathed in deeply and reminded herself that, as in her software world, any great progression first went through serious regression testing.

Program yourself, Cadie. Just run your sequence.

She clicked on the Finnish Meetup "Contact Us" link and watched a blank email message open. Its unpopulated white space dared her to populate the message with text. She typed, deleted, and typed again. There simply was no easy way to initiate such foreign correspondence.

Dear Finnish Group:

I am interested in contacting someone regarding your meetings. Though not Finnish, I recently participated in the National Geographic *Genographic*

Project and learned that my maternal DNA (ancient ancestry) is of the U5 branch—represented by 50% of modern Finnish (esp. Saami). I would like to meet your group and participate in some of your culture and heritage.

Thank you for your time. I look forward to hearing from you soon.

Best Regards,

Cadie Walsh
(817) 555-3645

Cadie read and re-read the message. *I am a lunatic.* For a long time, she held her fingers over the "alt" and "s" keys on her keyboard. *Just run your sequence, run your sequence, Cadie.* With her free hand, she picked up another cookie, closed her eyes, and took a bite. At the same time, she pressed down on the keys to send the message.

The message was gone from her outbox when she opened her eyes. Wanting to claim for herself some reward in the first active step on her journey toward social achievement, she turned off her computer, gathered her final maps, and shoved them into a folder. She discarded into the trash the unused preliminary maps and then took the last of her cookies and coffee into the living room. There she selected a movie. She promised herself to send the other three initial contact messages by the end of next week.

There'll be no excuses, Cadie. It's just another project deadline.

CHAPTER FOUR

CADIE WOKE TO A CLOUDLESS, blue sky and immediately went into her backyard to investigate what effects the two-week rain had deposited on her garden. She moved down the long center path toward the back fence, occasionally stepping aside and disappearing on lateral trails. Touching each plant or tree she passed, her movement released bright scents from the diversely textured evergreens.

At the youngest and smallest maple sapling, she stepped from the flagstone path. Before she could test the tree's root stability, her feet sank into a sloppy soup of richly composted soil. She hopped back onto the path just as the sludge engulfed her sandals. The tree forgotten, she trekked to the spigot at the side of her house. Mud clods fell from her heels, marking the stone path in testament of where she had been.

After rinsing her feet and discarding her wet sandals on the porch, Cadie went inside. It was time to clear her desk of her personal project and start a proper workday.

THE REMAINDER OF THE MORNING fragmented with programming and Cadie checking her inbox for a response to her first query. By noon, there was still nothing from the Finnish Meetup group.

At lunchtime, Cadie abandoned eating at her desk. She took her vegetable soup with her to the porch and set it on the wrought iron accent table beside the chaise lounge. She unlocked and opened the sideboard before reclining on the lounge to eat her meal. Looking at the guitar as she ate, she was happy that the sweeping rain had moved on to dissipate in the west Texas desert. She much preferred to play her guitar outside. She finished her soup and then strummed low notes, providing a mellow backdrop for the songs she absent-mindedly sang as she thought of other things.

Who would respond to her strange requests? If she found Moroccans in DFW, what cultural ethnicity would they be, and would they agree to meet her? Would Turkish Muslims be willing to share the content of their lives with an Irish-instructed Catholic orphan? And was polka dancing a requirement to get to know the Czechs?

The only answer Cadie had to her questions was a shameful flush of embarrassment. Her naive questions illuminated her education's narrow scope and the limited latitude of her experience. But if she didn't send her contact queries, then it would be only by a hair's breadth that she wouldn't devolve into a secular version of Sister Mary Trea. *That* Cadie would be nothing but a barely living wraith that similarly crept, suspiring her ancient songs when she thought nobody watched or listened. Cadie didn't want to die like the nun, who'd taken her lumps in the States and then returned to Ireland to expire near an absent, long-ago lover. Near a treasured village unaware and griefless over the nun's carcass hidden inside the thick walls of a countryside convent. Sister Mary Trea's last breath as an orphan of the Church was a devolution of the worst kind, a waste.

TWO HOUSES AWAY, BEATRICE paused from examining her roses and inclined her best ear toward Cadie's yard. It was odd for Cadie to play her guitar midday, but Beatrice walked to the curb and strained harder to hear. The notes, quiet though they were, confirmed that it was Cadie playing. Beatrice scanned the alley for other neighbors. Seeing no one else, she swept her rose cuttings into a garbage bag and hustled into her house. There were cookies to bake and distribute with her news of Cadie's noontime playing outside—confirmation of absolution from the rainy, songless days.

Cadie stored her guitar in the sideboard before going inside. To release herself from the nun's grasp, Cadie knew change was necessary. But was change as easy as programming functions for new actions, as systematic as building one of her robots? Could life, like the logical leaps in her programs, absorb neoteric operations, so that the result was something new—something that acted not only on the previous model of its wiring and experience, but also moved beyond its perceived environment?

"I taught you all you need to know."

"You taught me less," argued Cadie with the nun.

"What did I tell you about opening doors?"

"Not every trigger is bad," said Cadie.

That was it. Her personal queries to make contact with strangers were really triggers. Every programming action had a trigger. Her genographic search triggers were leaps to integrate a shrouded past with a static present. Combined, they would create future, undetermined events—a future that would require adaptation if she wanted to do more than simply survive. If the first queries didn't work, then she'd simply create more triggers.

She began to feel the same excited and nervous pressure that built when she compiled lines of code or watched one of her robot prototypes reach out to pick up objects or change direction when it sensed obstacles. Impatient to watch her life unfold in such a way, Cadie resolved to send out the remaining queries before going to bed.

+ + +

THE FINAL WEEK OF AUGUST passed into the first days of September. The history books sat untouched on the ottoman in Cadie's office. Instead, she read through thousands of code lines to track down a recent glitch in a new robotics system, a software bug inserted by a team member's daft inattention.

That team member escaped the dirty work by flying to Iowa, overseeing the exhumation of an aunt believed to have been poisoned by her brother, the programmer's father. In the event of foul play, the aunt had left, in her will, a small fortune to Amnesty International. Nobody thought to check the lady's stomach for poisoned dog meat prior to burial. When the dog turned up missing after the father quit his job and embarked on a three-month cruise, a few questions arose. So up came the body, too. From daily updates from Iowa, Cadie figured Amnesty International would get their money after all.

In the meantime, she programmed one test after another to find the bug corrupting their product's arm-control system. From one coffee refill to the next, she grimaced each time she saw the unopened tomes on the chair. Digesting the new worlds between the book covers would have to wait. She couldn't stop. Tonight was the engineer's do-or-die day of reckoning to find and fix the bug before overshooting the product's release date. If that happened, she'd lose hundreds of thousands of dollars for her company when the original contract price dropped with each day delivery was overdue.

Cadie pushed herself harder and harder as the evening progressed. On the horizon, another storm rolled toward Fort Worth. If she failed to deliver, the storm would coincide with a loss of cutting-edge perfectionism her company so successfully marketed. For her it would be a loss of professional meticulousness. A first. She delved on deep into the night.

DARK CLOUDS ARRIVED OVER Corral Street as Cadie submitted the repaired and tested code fix into a new build. Satisfied that everyone at the office would wake to a fully functioning product, Cadie began to close her computer programs. Just before exiting her email program, a response from the Islamic Center flashed upon her screen and faded. Outside, heavy rain pushed by strong winds began to pelt against her house. Cadie took a deep breath and opened the message.

Salutations of welcome came from Basir and Kamil Celebi. They expressed their joy to share and promote family interfaith dialogue and extended an invitation for Cadie to attend an *iftar* dinner in their home. The message congratulated her good timing.

"You have contacted us during Ramadan and will be able to share Turkish customs during our happiest month," stated the response.

Cadie looked at the details of the correspondence. Saturday night—two days away. She tried not to think about the brut rigors of socializing and commanded herself to accept the invitation. Her finger hovered over the mouse button.

Do it, Cadie. It simply triggers an action.

"Don't open the door."

The sound of the nun's voice in her head gave Cadie the courage she needed. She pressed the button and watched the reply message disappear. Invitation accepted.

A second later Cadie heard a loud crash that sounded like a nearby transformer blowing. Her computer screen went dark, along with the other lights in the house. Cadie stood.

There's nothing I can do to take it back now.

She walked in the dark to her bathroom and undressed before fishing her toothbrush and toothpaste from the chrome medicine cabinet, which rasped and snapped shut with antique consistency. As she brushed her teeth, Cadie watched the mirror for any reflection of light. *Two days.* Two days to brace herself, to defy the physics of her stagnant life and force herself to attend the dinner.

For now, though, she only wanted rest. Well familiar with her house in the dark, Cadie walked directly into her room and sank onto the bed. Following her nighttime ritual, she cocooned herself in the white cotton voile of her thick comforter. She thought for a second about her coworker's aunt. *The woman had seen it coming,* thought Cadie, *but going by way of dog stew probably hadn't been on her list of ways she might go.* Cadie shook her head and closed her eyes. It was the hardest road, understanding people. And she was just now unlatching the gate. Before she could think anything else, sleep overtook her.

A SHARP CREAKING SOUND followed by a loud explosion from her backyard startled Cadie awake. She looked at the alarm clock. Its glowing red numerals had gone with the power outage. Cadie rose from bed, moved to her bedroom window, pulled aside the heavy curtains, and peeked through the wood blinds.

The entire neighborhood was plunged into the darkness, the street lights' glow absent. Cadie held her ear close to the window but couldn't hear anything over the wind gusts.

The crash was louder than the wind. That or it was a dream.

She moved away from the window and groped for her clothes beside the bed. She put on her jeans and T-shirt and walked slowly toward her office.

There, she fumbled around her desk for her cell phone, hoping it had enough of a charge to give her the time. She found it under a piece of paper; it rewarded her with its glow when she pressed a side key. It was five o'clock—a couple of hours before sunrise. Dropping the phone, Cadie walked outside.

It was just as dark in the open air as it had been in the house. Her toes curled and uncurled over the wet porch slats. The air eddied around her, leaving her wet and cold. She counted five steps, eight steps, turned left, and then walked until she stood near the sideboard. Pacing forward a few steps, she let her toes dangle off the porch, over the first step leading down to her backyard path.

She peered toward her garden, straining to see the familiar skyline of large trees. Dark shrouded everything. Heavy rain surged sidelong under the porch's eave and soaked her head to toe. Cadie shivered and walked back inside.

This time she checked the charge level on her cell. Fully charged. *Good.*

She would call Bobby in a couple of hours to let him know that her neighborhood was without power, that she'd need to investigate the crash as soon as it was light. With any luck, Bobby wouldn't ask her to go into the office and watch their clients ooh and aah over the new product. Not that Bobby liked having her there for those meetings, anyway.

Knowing that time would be her enemy as she waited for Bobby's day to dawn, Cadie went to shower in the dark. She wished her guitar wasn't in the sideboard. She had no candles by which to read, and Sister Mary Trea's voice was always loudest when Cadie wasn't busy, busy.

On cue, Sister Mary Trea spoke. "You wouldn't have been a good nun," she said. "Never could handle austerity."

"Candles aren't calling cards for austerity." Cadie cut short her inactivity under the hot water and toweled off. "And you know why I don't like candles."

"Complain, complain. It was only a little burn."

"Burns."

"You had to be everyone's friend, didn't you? But you learned not to talk unless spoken to, did you not?"

"If that's not austerity, I don't know what is," said Cadie. She quickly donned clean jeans and a T-shirt and bound her hair in a dry towel.

SISTER MARY TREA WAS SILENT when Cadie walked to the kitchen. Cadie rummaged through a cabinet for her rarely used pot, which she filled with water and placed on the gas stove to heat. At least she could have coffee.

While the water heated, Cadie robotically prepared the coffee press. She hooked her thumb over the glass rim, as a guide to keep from overfilling the vessel. When the coffee had brewed, she retired to her office with a large mug and two sugar cubes. She settled into one of the overstuffed sofa chairs and propped her heels on the cushioned window seat. Languidly, she waited for daybreak.

At 6:30 a.m., Cadie picked up her cell phone and hit the speed dial button for Bobby Pullman. On a product release day like today, he would already be at his office desk, ready to wow his clients with another flawless and on-time project.

Bobby answered before the second ring. "Cadie girl," he said with a smile in his voice, "Looks like we've got another winner on our hands. Last-minute, too. I saw the time on the last email you sent out. Never ceases to amaze me. What's goin' on this mornin'?"

"Good morning, Bobby. The storm took out the power in my neighborhood last night. It's still out. Do you need me there today?"

Bobby leaned back in his chair and rolled his eyes. He mulled over how long it would take the girl to stop standing on formality. When would she realize she could do no wrong in his eyes? Nobody he'd ever met, except maybe himself, had her dedication and ability. It was dedication by choice or innate drive—likely both. He'd bet on it.

"You're just fine stayin' there, Cadie. We'll handle everything on this end. Already tested out the robot this mornin'—works great. Good job there."

Bobby waited a moment for a response, hoped this time Cadie would jump at the compliment. When she didn't, he continued.

"Why don't you take the day off? You have a million comp hours comin' to ya anyway."

"Okay, Bobby. Call if you need anything today—I'll keep my phone with me."

"Better yet, Cadie, why don't you turn off your phone as well?" His voice was firm.

"Goodbye, Bobby. Good luck on the presentation. I'll talk to you later."

"Later, Cadie girl."

Tossing her phone away, Cadie rose from her chair and pulled the towel away from her head. Still-damp locks tumbled over her shoulders and halfway down her back. Cold moisture sank in where her hair touched her T-shirt. Cadie leaned over the window seat to look outside. She held her breath so as not to fog the glass.

The rain had tapered to a drizzle, the wind to a soft breeze.

Cadie turned and walked to her dark bathroom. She threw the towel toward its hook. When she didn't hear anything hit the floor, she went to her closet to grab some socks and her galoshes. The ground was certain to be soft again.

A minute later, she left the house without a rain jacket or umbrella, preferring to feel light rain against her face. She stood in the drizzle and surveyed her backyard. Something was different.

She jumped from the back porch and started down the path, slowing as she neared an adjacent trail lined by parallel rows of thirty-foot-tall arborvitaes. The path curved toward Aleck's driveway and then swung in a wide arc to the back of her yard before connecting again to the main path. Through the tight, evergreen-formed hedges, Cadie sensed more light than usual filtering in. She turned right and headed through the trees, touching the soft emerald foliage as she walked. Hundreds of droplets fell from the branches and splattered across the toes of her rain boots, the path, or held onto branches immediately below. She moved on. Nearing the trail's turn where it came nearest the fence she shared with Aleck's property, Cadie stopped short. A pair of fallen evergreens rested, dying, across the path and stretched out past the broken fence. The entirety of Aleck's driveway was blocked. The tip of one evergreen rested gently against the trunk of one of the large oaks in Aleck's west yard.

So that's what caused the noise.

The base of the trees had the majority of their root systems ripped from the ground, the roots fanning out in woody, vertical blossoms. The tree farthest from the fence had fallen first, taking with it the one in the way of its downward fall. On their descent, the force had buckled and then broken the fence. Two, eight-foot-wide panels and three fence posts were down. Scattered wood splinters lay about Aleck's driveway. Transfixed by the damage, Cadie crossed over to her neighbor's property to survey the destruction.

When she was satisfied that the fence was the greatest casualty, that and her now discontinuous tree rows, she turned her focus to the problem of removing the downed trees. Ideally, before Aleck returned from work and found his garage entry blocked. Cadie began to worry. There was no Internet in the house, certainly no paper phone book, and still no data plan on her phone since she was always in front of her desktop. She would have to find a café with wireless connectivity to arrange for tree removal services—all before nature strong-armed her to face Aleck on his own turf.

With a plan devised, Cadie spun around to return to her yard and found herself face to face with Dr. Aleck Turina.

She jumped back.

Aleck was leaning against the fence a few feet to the side of the chasm that opened between their yards.

Belying her initial response, Cadie's face was expressionless, a survival throwback mechanism learned at the orphanage.

Aleck's bemused look, on the other hand, hadn't changed. First, when Cadie had walked by him unawares with her jeans tucked into the French galoshes covered with little multi-colored flowers. Now, by how much his presence had startled her. He calmly sipped from a steaming coffee mug, wanting her to talk first.

"Oh, I . . . I didn't see . . . ," she stammered. She swung a hand and her gaze along the broken boughs. "The trees . . . ," she faltered.

Aleck extended his hand and walked carefully toward her. "Aleck Turina," he said, "Nice to finally meet you. Cadie Walsh, isn't it?"

His voice was warm and confident, but his British accent startled Cadie again—not what she'd expected from a Spanish-Italian descendant. Knowing that she had to satisfy the social cadre of handshaking, Cadie turned squarely toward him.

Her long hair, previously hiding the full contours of her profile, fell away and unveiled her face.

Aleck stopped walking. Before Cadie could take his hand, his outstretched hand dropped back to his side. He didn't blink.

Cadie's eyes, an impossible color highlighted more so by her light olive skin, were nothing like he'd imagined. Trace hints of green flecked with light brown created an overall golden glow, an eerie color-blending luminescence that simultaneously coalesced and fragmented as her eyes moved. Cadie blinked, blinked, and blinked again.

On the fourth blink, Aleck became aware of Cadie's hand still extended to him. He regained his composure and shook her hand.

"Nice to meet you," he said again.

Cadie quickly dropped his hand and stepped back woodenly before she spoke.

"Mrs. Beauregard said your parents were Spanish and Italian. I didn't expect a British accent."

If Cadie noticed his quizzical look, she didn't show it. Aleck kept silent for a few seconds, waiting to see if she'd jump in and talk more—the nervous talk of people thrown out of their element.

She held silent.

Aleck assumed she hadn't registered his initial reticence to answer her question. Few people were so cold, so unfeeling, that they didn't at least exhibit nervousness when bumping up against or defying social norms. Even fewer weren't able to see that social norms existed. However unjust a society's focus was on this, that, or the other norm, people couldn't help but feel shame when a norm got the better of them. But here Cadie stood, expressionless, and unashamed. He found it intriguing and refreshing.

"My parents moved to Britain when I was six months old," he answered before he lost her attention. "When they finished their research there, we briefly returned to Spain when I was six, then from Spain to the U.S. My British nanny stayed with us until they returned to Spain with my sister. I guess it rubbed off."

Still she said nothing.

Aleck smiled. "Want some coffee? Have a full pot inside."

Cadie declined with a shake of her head. "I need to find someone to clear the trees . . . sorry they fell into your drive. I have to go out to hunt down wireless Internet . . . only way I can get a phone number for a tree service. Power's down."

Her literality amused Aleck. Nobody in the neighborhood had power. He guessed it wasn't often she let others infer things on their own. Given her initial response, it was probably rare, indeed, when she offered anything personal about herself.

"Doubt you'll get anyone out here today. Power is out for blocks, trees down everywhere. They'll be plenty busy for the next several days."

Cadie motioned at the trees. "But the driveway . . . the fence." Her agitated movement was the barest hint of her distress.

"Tell you what," started Aleck slowly, trying not to seem eager. "I could cut them. Have a chainsaw in the garage—wouldn't take two tics. Not going to work today, at any rate."

Cadie looked at him questioningly.

He pointed at the ground in front of them.

"The trees . . . can't get out . . . ," he said.

It couldn't hurt to appeal to her rationality.

Suddenly grasping the obvious, Cadie nodded.

Aleck pressed his sale further. "Could even fix the fence and repair the damage in your yard if you supply the materials," he said.

He would have offered almost anything to walk into Cadie Walsh's yard, the forbidden garden palace that shielded its mysterious and acutely awkward inhabitant. The lack of deception in Cadie's verbal and bodily language conferred upon Aleck layered exhilarations—exhilaration and the frightened sense that Cadie Walsh was a paradox, requiring a bit of restraint from his normally gregarious personality.

Cadie shoved her hands into her back pockets.

Aleck took the move as her unconscious signal of intent to decline his offer. He quickly thought ahead.

"My gate on the other side of the yard is always locked," she said.

"I could make another gate on this side if you like . . . might be able to salvage some of the fence slats that way. It'd be a quick way to secure your yard while I work at removing the root systems."

Cadie frowned.

Aleck forced himself to take a sip of coffee before hurrying forward with his argument. "That way, I wouldn't have to go back and forth across your yard. You wouldn't see me, could just unlock the gate in the afternoon before I get home from classes."

For a moment, Cadie stared at the trees. She didn't like the idea of someone going back and forth across her yard, seeing her playing guitar, or interrupting her work. But a gate where the trees had broken through would keep him away from the middle of her garden. It was reasonable.

"I'll pay you what the tree service would have charged."

"No need. Seems like a nice adventure for the day. Better than staying inside a dark house."

Cadie nodded.

Taking the nod as agreement to his proposal, Aleck turned and walked toward his garage. He stopped after a few steps and looked at Cadie. She was now staring at the damaged fence.

"Maybe we'll have power by the time I clear the trees from my driveway," he said. "If I can get 'em out, then I might be able to have the gate up and locked before it's too dark tomorrow evening."

Cadie looked at him. "I need a keyed lock."

Aleck grinned as Cadie walked toward her yard. Of *course* she wanted a lock with a key, he thought. For Cadie's straightforward approach, a key was the ideal way, the only way, to open or close something. Combinations could be tricky.

Cadie agilely scaled the fallen trees and broken fence, only pausing when her feet landed firmly inside her own yard. She raised her head slightly toward Aleck.

"Thank you."

The utterance was clear and firm, but her eyes wavered on Aleck's face only as long as it took to say the words.

Before Aleck could respond, she disappeared into her urban forest.

CHAPTER FIVE

THE SOUND OF THE GATE closing on its new hinges would mean that Aleck had finished hanging the adjoining portal between their two yards. Cadie watched her clock. When she couldn't wait any longer, she commanded herself to go ahead and drive to the Celebis' home. She'd just have to lock the gate when she returned. She left without going into the yard to tell Aleck goodbye.

"You'll regret this," said Sister Mary Trea as Cadie pulled onto the interstate and headed toward North Dallas.

Cadie escaped from the voice by woolgathering as she drove. She observed herself as a stranger might, examining the course she had followed in making her contacts. She let herself daydream about where it would lead.

This triggered action she commanded upon herself wouldn't mirror the romance of the movies she watched at night when she was too tired to program or too exhausted to sleep. She wasn't one of those traumatized heroines who prayed for the providence of true love so that they could finally see a god—so that they could control love. She was a Cadie propelled beyond Sister Mary Trea's teaching that there would be nothing but fear and hate in this new place. Fear, hate, and sadness existed everywhere people castigated dialogue. Punishment for attempting dialogue was lack of intervention. Cadie knew about that, too. No one had intervened when Sister Grace had twisted and broken her arm for questioning theological contradictions.

No, this Cadie raced away from one stigma toward the epicenter of another, and she was glad to disregard hateful totalitarianism. What would happen would happen.

IN THE EYE OF HER manufactured tempest, Cadie stood on the Celebis' doorstep and tentatively rang the doorbell. She rocked from heel to toe on the red-tinted grass "Welcome" mat thick under her shoes and waited for Basir to answer the door.

Cast sharply under the porch light, she was conscious of eyes on her. Neighbors previously moving along the sidewalks radiating warmth from the relentless sun had stopped walking. They stared at the woman on the Celebis' porch. She was the only female in sight not wearing the *hijab*. The doors of neighboring houses opened, revealing gray shapes that curiously examined the strange girl.

Using her utmost discipline to stand rooted, Cadie felt that the culturally selective neighborhood saw her as a foolish marionette cast in the wrong play. She inspected the flowers and packages of fig-date *burfi* in her hands, hoping the sweets suitably replaced wine as a hostess gift. The burfi was a favorite snack of hers, and the man in the aisle at the Indian supermarket had assured her that the sweets were *halal*.

When the door knob began to turn, Cadie lifted her head but adjusted her gaze downward when a small face below the knob's height peeked out from behind the opening door. A small girl with big brown eyes grinned at Cadie. The girl fully swung open the door when she saw the treats in Cadie's hands. Three older girls ran up to help the little one.

From growing up with a hundred different girls, Cadie guessed the children's ages ranged from four to eight years old. Cadie stared over their heads. Beyond the large foyer was a broad great room, at least 50 square feet. Floor to ceiling windows, shielded by heavy embroidered red draperies maybe 15 feet long, lined the cavernous room. No adults were visible. Cadie smiled slightly. Little girls weren't so strange to her.

"Ummm, hello, I'm . . . "

"We know," interrupted the oldest girl. "You're Cadie."

The girl jumped forward to relieve Cadie of the flowers. She ran into the great room and then disappeared through a side entry Cadie couldn't see.

Caught in a limbo of sorts, Cadie glanced back at the street, hoping the girl was on her way to retrieve an adult. It didn't look like the neighbors planned to move on until Cadie went inside or left. And leaving was exactly what Cadie had in mind when a small hand slid around her wrist and pulled her forward. At the same moment, a woman entered the great room and turned toward the door. Cadie stepped inside without looking back at the street.

THE WOMAN GLIDED INTO the foyer. Two delicately charcoal-lined eyes smiled nervously below a two-toned pink hijab the woman wore with a flowing long shirt and pants. Her voice preceded her.

"Beril. Close the door. How many times have I told you?"

The smallest girl left Cadie to close the door. She raced back to Cadie's side and fingered the hem of the silk blouse that fell just below Cadie's hips. By then, the woman was in the foyer. She extended her hand and slightly bowed her head.

"Cadie, I'm Kamil Celebi. Welcome to our simple home."

"I wasn't sure . . . this is . . . this is burfi," said Cadie, placing the sweets into her hostess's open palm. The moment was more awkward than she'd imagined it would be. She hastily added, "Thank you for having me to dinner."

Kamil nodded and handed the burfi to the tallest girl. She re-extended her hand to Cadie.

This time Cadie shook the offered hand.

"These are my granddaughters," said Kamil, motioning toward the girls. "Beril, Derya, Nazan, and Sam, the oldest. They visit from Turkey, but are U.S. citizens."

Sam jumped away from the group. "Dede! Cadie is here. She brought flowers."

Cadie followed Sam's gaze. Two adult males approached. Cadie reminded herself to place her hands behind her back liked she'd read, to keep from accidentally shaking her host's hand.

The oldest male hurriedly approached Cadie and stretched forth his hand. His smile was warm, almost jolly.

What am I to do now?

Kamil nodded in approval when Cadie looked at her for instruction. Cadie obeyed and shook the hand.

"Cadie, I am Basir," the man said. "Welcome to our humble home. Please forgive our tardiness—we just finished prayers." Basir turned to introduce the man behind him. "This is my son, Zahid. He visits from Turkey with my granddaughters. They, I see, you have had the pleasure to meet."

Bowing his head toward Cadie, Zahid also reached to shake her hand. "A pleasure."

"Thank you," said Cadie, nodding in return.

Basir motioned toward the great room. "Shall we?"

The girls ran forward and disappeared through the entrance from earlier. After taking several steps, Cadie saw that they'd rushed past a kitchen dining area and now clamored around a kitchen counter by the sink. Sam stood on a stool and reached for scissors organized among other cooking tools in an orange pottery vessel.

"No, Sam. I will get them," said Kamil, hurrying toward the girl.

Sam hopped down to make way for her grandmother.

Basir motioned Cadie to one of three leather couches.

"Please . . . sit."

Cadie sat down where she could keep Kamil in sight. The woman busied herself with the flowers. The two men sat on another of the couches.

Not sure how to begin, Cadie sat with her hands on her lap and looked around the room. Covering the other walls were several various-sized carpets. The engineer in her deconstructed the pieces as handwoven art.

Basir turned to Zahid. "Cadie independently contacted us, the first to do so regarding an *iftar* dinner." He then looked at Cadie to explain. "Everyone else interested in our program of friendship are from churches or synagogues. We do iftar dinners for them at their worship places."

"Is this true, Cadie—that you called directly?" Zahid's look was one of amused disbelief.

"I emailed."

Basir and Zahid exchanged smiles.

Unable to guess what was so funny, Cadie changed the subject.

"So, you are visiting from Turkey, Zahid?"

"Yes, I study medicine there—almost finished. Then I return home to U.S."

"He is already a doctor," said Basir proudly. "He works in Turkey for two years to visit my family there . . . his first time. I never traveled out of U.S. since I was born here, but Zahid—he wanted to know his other family."

Zahid nodded benignly.

"You understand this, of course," continued Basir. "Like your U5 family."

Cadie nodded and looked toward the kitchen. Kamil busily cut the flower heads from the stems, leaving only inch-long stems below each blossom. The hands commanding the scissors didn't look old enough to belong to a grandmother. Cadie turned back to the conversation.

"Is your wife visiting with you, Zahid?"

Frowning, Zahid looked away.

Basir interjected, "Molly died . . . giving birth to Beril."

"Oh, I'm sorry," said Cadie. *Stop asking the unthinkable.*

Couldn't have said it better myself, came Sister Mary Trea's retort.

Again, Cadie looked at Kamil, who was distributing the flowers among the four girls. The children, waving the perennials in the air, ran from the kitchen toward another wing of the house. Cadie liked the idea that the blossoms had become toys rather than ornaments placed in cold crystal. The nuance made the Celebi home feel less austere and foreboding. Cadie told herself to relax.

Kamil wiped her hands on a dishtowel and then walked to the entrance of the great room.

"The food is ready," she said, gesturing toward a simple oak breakfast table set with off-white and gold dishes.

"Very good," said Basir. He indicated for Cadie to precede the men into the next room. "We will eat now."

Kamil gathered the soup bowls from the four place settings.

Cadie looked around for a "kids' table," but there wasn't one. She wondered if the children had already eaten.

Basir pointed Cadie to one of the side seats. "We sit in the kitchen nook—more cozy for talking during family dinner."

Cadie looked around her. There were no implements or symbols of material religion on the dining table, counters, or walls—very different than her experiences in the orphanage where iconography and religious objects pervaded even the commonest of places. Instead, images of oranges decorated most of Kamil's pottery. On a large wall of the kitchen dining nook hung two six-foot-tall paintings depicting two different orange trees—one in bloom and one fully laden with the fruit at different stages of ripening. Cadie liked the brush strokes of the Asian-style paintings. Cadie moved to her seat.

"Normally," continued Basir, "We say something like this before eating: *Bismi-llāhi r-rachmāni r-rachīm*—'In the name of God, Most Gracious, Most Merciful.' But we also give a prayer at the end: *Al humdu lil Allahil lazi at'amanaa wasaqaana waja'alana minal muslimeen*—'Thank you, oh Allah, for feeding us and making us amongst the believers.'"

Cadie nodded and sat down. She liked that Basir's words were informational rather than forced upon her.

Across from her, Zahid glanced occasionally between his father and Cadie. He never stopped smiling.

Kamil returned to the table with two bowls filled with soup that looked little different from canned tomato soup. She set a bowl in front of Cadie and Basir before returning for the last two bowls.

"This is *tarhana*. It takes a very long time to make," said Basir.

Cadie waited for Kamil to sit down before picking up her spoon.

"Tarhana does take a long time—mine, three weeks," said Kamil, motioning for Cadie to eat.

What took so long to make soup?

Cadie let the thick, tomatoey liquid roll slowly over her tongue. The soup had a fermented flavor. She couldn't discern the ingredient that made it so.

"The yeast makes the special flavor," said Kamil, intuiting Cadie's next question.

"A very common Turkish dish," said Basir.

"It is good—I've never tasted anything like it."

Everyone nodded in agreement.

Cadie concentrated on moving her spoon through the soup, hoped that someone else would speak next. She took a few more bites and wondered what she was doing there.

Zahid finally spoke, "So, what is it you do, Cadie?"

"I'm a software systems engineer—robotics."

More enthusiastic nods.

"This is a good job, then?" said Kamil.

"Very good," said Basir, adding, "I am a doctor, like Zahid. Being a doctor is how I met Kamil."

Blushing deeply, Kamil nodded but remained silent.

Cadie changed the subject, asked Kamil what she did.

"She is an artist," said Basir before Kamil could answer. He waved his arm toward the walls in the great room. "The carpets."

"I could tell they were handwoven," said Cadie. "Beautifully engineered."

Kamil barely smiled at the compliment. "My family's custom. Perhaps later I will show you my loom."

"I would like that," said Cadie, blushing. Not only had she been invited to a personal home after a very unusual self-introduction, she was now invited to view one of those deep recesses always shielded from precursory guests.

She scooped the last of the soup from her bowl, hoping there was a place she could buy the special food pre-made.

KAMIL EXCHANGED THE SOUP bowls for a simple romaine lettuce salad dressed with a creamy egg and lemon sauce. It reminded Cadie of Caesar dressing, without the anchovies. Next, Kamil served a beef-vegetable stew ladled over rice along with a dish she called *boerekas*. Cadie liked the flavor balance of the cut beef cubes sautéed with creamy eggplant, zucchini, green beans, and tomatoes seasoned only with salt and pepper. But the boerekas, crispy phyllo dough pastries rolled into cigar shapes and filled with either ground beef or a cheese mixture, were Cadie's favorite thus far.

"The cheese boereka is white and cheddar mixed," said Kamil. "You call the white 'feta,' I believe."

Cadie nodded. It was the same kind of cheese in her Greek chicken bake, only her pre-cooked, frozen, and reheated foods couldn't compare to what she ate now. After sampling her first cheese boereka, Cadie took a bite of a beef boereka and looked inside the roll to determine what she was eating.

"With black currants, pine nuts, chopped onion, and tomato," explained Kamil. Her eyes conveyed pleasure over Cadie's interest.

"They . . . they are the best things I've ever eaten," praised Cadie.

"Nothing more than commonplace, Turkish home cooking," said Basir. The loving look he gave his wife overshadowed his humility.

THE DINNER CONVERSATION continued slowly. Cadie was happy for the frequent interruptions from Zahid's daughters who, together or individually, stopped by the table to nibble from small plates as they each expressed hunger.

"It is not fun for them to sit long at the table with guests," explained Basir. "We let them play and eat when they are ready."

Kamil began removing the dinner plates. Cadie sensed it was now quite late but kept from checking her watch. It had been well after eight o'clock when dinner started.

"Will you take tea, Cadie?" asked Kamil.

"Yes, please."

Kamil walked into the kitchen and returned with the burfi pieces stacked on a plate.

"What are in the squares?" asked Basir.

"They are of figs and dates," said Kamil. She then looked at Cadie. "Basir loves figs."

"It's true," said Basir looking at his wife before turning to Cadie. "Kamil also made a dessert that we hope you will enjoy." He took a piece of burfi and bit into it while waiting for tea, giving no indication of whether or not he liked the sweet.

Zahid took a piece and ate as well. Cadie sat in silence as the men chewed. Several minutes later, the smell of black tea floated from the stove. Glancing over her shoulder, Cadie realized that Kamil had been making the tea all the while. Disappointed now that her back was to the kitchen, Cadie turned in her chair to watch the tea-making process, observing the smaller vessel atop a larger vessel that Kamil had placed directly over the flame.

"It's a *samovar*," said Kamil, tapping the pot's side with a long, metal spoon heat-proofed with a wooden handle.

Finally, Kamil poured the hot water from the larger container into the smaller one. She refilled the emptied vessel with cold water, joined the unit over the heat again, and waited for the cold water to boil. While they waited, Kamil placed a bowl of sugar cubes and a new platter of boerekas on the table.

"These are filled with walnut mixture," explained Kamil. "Sweet." She returned to the stove and poured amber-hued tea into clear glass cups similar in size and shape to tulip flowers.

The dinner outdid itself with each new food. Though she didn't cook, Cadie was a great purveyor of ready-to-eat foods that included all kinds of fruits and nuts, especially walnuts.

As Kamil placed the cups on the table, Basir took another piece of burfi.

The smell of the tea in front of Cadie returned memories of the orphanage. The orphanage had most times been harsh, but Cadie liked hot tea. She'd had plenty of it over the years. Tea was dependable warmth, even when bitter.

Cadie was pleasantly surprised when she took her first sip. It was nothing like others she'd tasted. Its base flavor was similar to the black tea Sister Mary Trea had strained from leaves in porcelain pots, but this had a fuller, deeper taste. Cadie suddenly looked forward to having another cup from the pot steeping on the stove, even if it meant longer-endured, awkward silences.

Without thinking, she reached out for a sugar cube, placed it between her teeth, and took her next sip of tea. The startled looks around the table were hard to miss. Cadie, realizing what she'd just done, put down her cup.

Geez, Cadie. Self-control.

Sister Mary Trea flashed before her eyes. The old voice intoned displeasure. *What have I told you?*

"I'm . . . ," she started, reproving herself. "I'm sorry. It's a habit."

Laughing, Basir dismissed the apology. "It is nothing. You looked like a regular Turk."

Zahid and Kamil nodded. Zahid was grinning.

"It is better to drink it through the sugar cube, is it not? We also do this," said Basir.

The nun frowned, disapproving.

Justified by her hosts, Cadie reached for one of the new boerekas.

The phyllo pastry, though crunchy, melted in her mouth around the walnut mixture. The taste and textures reminded Cadie of baklava, but she preferred the Turkish sweet and its more substantial nut filling compared to the thin spread of nut meats between baklava's numerous doughy layers.

"Where do your parents live, Cadie?" asked Zahid.

Cadie stopped in mid-chew and looked down at her half-eaten pastry. *Haven't we covered the basics?* They knew what she did for a job, where she worked, where she lived. They even knew that she'd grown up in Dallas. She hated when people asked where her parents lived, what they did.

She hesitantly looked at Zahid. "I was raised in a Catholic orphanage in Dallas. My mother, a Jane Doe, died giving birth to me.

Nobody knew her—she had no identification on her, and no one came looking for her," answered Cadie, rattling verbatim the words she'd memorized from her file.

It was Zahid's turn to be uncomfortable. "My deepest apologies," he mumbled softly.

But the cadre of implications in Cadie's disclosure about being raised a Catholic and being an orphan provoked more questions from the Celebis. Did she still go to Catholic church? No. Was the orphanage still functioning so that she could meet with the people who raised her? No. Was she still a Catholic? No—just an engineer. To stop the torrent of questions, Cadie asked one of her own.

"How do your beliefs impact your daily lives?" She directed the question to Basir.

Both Basir and Zahid described their adherence to being Muslim as compassionate devotees to common proscriptions for peaceful living. They spoke of the *Quran* with reverence and of Ramadan, the month of fasting and becoming closer to God, as the most special month of Islam.

"During this month, we do many things . . . ," said Basir, pausing to search within himself for the aspect that reverberated most with him, a succinct idea for what could be Cadie's first and last meeting with Muslims. "During this month," he continued, "we refrain from more than just food during the day—we refrain from gossip or backbiting."

Cadie thought of Mrs. Beauregard.

"Avoiding gossip is a noble thing . . . maybe the noblest," she said, keeping to herself the annoyance brought on by memories of Mrs. Beauregard's visits. "I think some justify gossip with prayer lists."

Zahid laughed. "This is good humor."

"It is very possible," said Basir, seriously considering the veracity of Cadie's statement.

Cadie looked at her empty tea glass. It was certain, she thought. She couldn't count the times at the office when a coworker was sick and another said they would tell their prayer group. Over the course of the day, one person after another would drop by the cubicle and say, "You're on my prayer list." Those same coworkers never came around to discuss the other person's real thoughts on things, or good news. Bad news, tragedy, and sickness: the lifeblood of gossipers. Prayer lists were vehicles of self-exultation and congratulation, a means to avoid really listening to other people. Domino, domino, domino—they all fall down, thought Cadie.

Kamil rose from the table. "Coffee?" she asked without waiting for an answer before walking to the stove.

Cadie nodded. *Of course, coffee. Wonderful coffee.* The anticipation of hot coffee pushed memories of Mrs. Beauregard from her mind. This time she turned around and paid close attention to the brewing process.

Directly onto the flame, Kamil placed another strange vessel, a long-handled brass container that looked like an upside-down funnel. She added sugar, then water and coffee. She spent more time watching the pot than doing anything else. Only a few times did she stir the coffee.

"It's an *ibrik*," said Kamil, noticing Cadie's gaze. She let the froth on the top of the coffee twice rise to the container's rim. Then she poured the dark liquid into porcelain, espresso-sized cups.

For warmth against her cold tension, Cadie took her small cup and wrapped her hand around it. She relaxed as she breathed in the rich scent. Her first taste of Turkish coffee released in her an alluvium of unidentified emotion.

Before she finished her first cup, the conversation at the table began to move more smoothly and rapidly. During the second cup, Cadie suddenly began telling the Celebis things about herself that she'd never told anyone—the life at the orphanage, how she'd spent her days, how she'd accidentally fallen into the engineering profession.

After several minutes, Basir laughed and raised his cup of coffee into the air. "It's the same for us. We say, 'Conversation doesn't flow until coffee is served.' In coffee there is kinship—the beginning of friends."

Cadie couldn't help but think it might be true.

IT WAS MIDNIGHT BEFORE CADIE and Kamil began to yawn at the dinner table. The conversation wound down, the children long before having shuffled away to fall asleep in other rooms in the large home. The plate of burfi was empty, the sweets mostly eaten by Basir.

"I should probably go," said Cadie apologetically.

"One more cup," urged Basir.

"An early day," said Cadie.

Kamil nodded and rose first from the table. Basir and Zahid followed and helped walk Cadie to the entrance.

In the foyer, Cadie again shook hands with Zahid and Basir. Before she had a chance to extend her hand to Kamil, the woman moved in for a hug. Cadie turned sideways and nervously returned the embrace.

"Please return soon, Cadie. I will show you where I make my carpets."

"I would like that," said Cadie. And then her next thought popped out of her mouth before she could stop it. "Could you teach me how to make the Turkish coffee and walnut boerekas?" She chalked up it to the resulting warmth from the unexpected hug.

"I will," said Kamil. Nothing but her eyes smiled and she gave Cadie another hug. "I will teach you all the Turkish cooking you want to learn. We will make many walnut boerekas if you like."

TAKEN ABACK ON THE DRIVE home, Cadie was amazed by how well the evening had gone, was more than relieved she'd behaved halfway . . . normally. At least she thought she had. She felt as she often did after working on ill-advised and dictated "hack jobs" to devise last-minute solutions to impossible problems.

After submitting hacked code into its final build, too late in a project to change anything else, it never failed that she thought of all the ways her "solution" might break, and irreparably harm, the system. Then it would work, and she went about improving the code afterward.

By going to the Celebis, she'd run a similar program on herself. Her compilation to make contact with total strangers had not broken the cadre of human social interaction. It had made her feel good despite her nervousness.

Maybe I can go through with meeting the Finns, Moroccans, and Czechs.

In the revelry of heightened emotions from a successful social evening, she suddenly wanted to thank someone or something for the satisfaction she felt. At the very least, she had to thank her genome. It had driven her social need. But then as Cadie drove around the alley toward her house and her headlights briefly illuminated the new gate separating her backyard from Aleck's driveway, she realized more than just her genome needed a thank you.

+ + +

THE THINGS YOU COVET, you give.

Sister Mary Trea's words formed, in part, Cadie's foundation of logical reciprocity. People usually wanted something in return for the gifts they gave. Cadie guessed that the nuns had wanted affection and attention, but what they gave the girls at the orphanage didn't mirror what the old women had missed out on. For them, gifts were never for the sake of gift-giving, even gifts to feed the hungry somehow benefited the future reproduction of the human genome, even if the people who worked at soup kitchens or flew immunizations to Africa weren't around to see it.

So the only way that Cadie could figure how to thank Aleck was to ask what she would want to receive as a gift of thanks.

IT DIDN'T TAKE HER LONG to decide. She stopped working mid-afternoon on the day following her dinner with the Celebis and drove to her favorite Dallas bakery.

When Cadie arrived, a line snaked from the pastry counter, around the bistro tables painted a variety of pastel colors, and ended a half-dozen people deep outside the door. Everyone but Cadie was with someone. Strangers in line smiled and mentioned to others why they had come—weekly tradition, word of mouth, the only place to get such and such baked *just* right. The line moved quickly. Within the hour, Cadie turned away from the counter and headed to her car without having spoken to anyone but the clerk. She carefully carried the coveted pink pastel box with the oval gold label affixed to the top.

Not until she made it home did Cadie open the lid and lower her face to sniff the contents. The sweetness wafting from the box had an ownership over her. The perfume of buttery sugar, milk, eggs, vanilla, and flour activated her taste buds as well as memories of watching girl after girl leave the orphanage as she stayed behind.

Everyone wanted a family of their own. *That* was different. Cadie had never coveted anything more than the pastries—when parents of their newly adopted girl presented her with various pastel boxes of gourmet cupcakes and petit fours from exclusive Dallas bakeries. *Just to see a smile.* The adoptees had carried their boxes of sugary redemption away from the orphanage and left the other girls with the thin, stale air of nothingness. Cadie, however, knew the boxes were more than that—a final contract, signing on the dotted line. The couple wanted a rounded-out family, a child to adore them, to learn from them, to mirror them. The girl wanted safety, allowance to think, taught to evaluate evidence, not to have indoctrination beaten into her. In the end, the girl would toe the line to have her own room and the honor of saying, "My mama this, my daddy that."

But Cadie knew something more than Sister Mary Trea's voice compelled the vehicle of thanks to Aleck. The pastries formed a linear feeling of gratification, thankfulness that a kind deed could remind her of something she'd wanted so much, yet forgotten. Giving them away might displace the old nothingness with a sweeter memory. She wasn't racking up a smile in exchange for the box. It was clear exchange for the repair of her fence and cutting away the fallen trees.

THE DILEMMA SHE HAD now was how to deliver the pastries. She second-guessed the appropriateness of the thank-you gift. Thinking it might seem forward to just drop by with something as delicate and intimate as cake, Cadie decided she couldn't deliver them directly to Aleck's door.

She walked onto her back porch and watched the trees in her garden, hoping to see some clue for how to present the gift. The trees whispered nothing to her. The roses greeted her with little but a grand flourish of late-season blooms. Cadie sighed and stepped back to sit down on the yellow Adirondack chair nearest her chaise lounge. As soon as her hamstrings hit the planks, she jumped back to her feet.

That would work.

She pulled the chair off the porch and carried it down the path. At the trail between the arborvitae rows, she turned and went until she was a couple steps shy of the new gate. There she set down the chair, turning it so that it faced the gate. The chair nearly blocked the width of the small trail. Cadie sensed that Aleck would understand that he wasn't to pass beyond her makeshift gift delivery device. She squeezed past the chair, her foot raking through and leaving a rut in the thick conifer needles under the edge of the trees. She ran back to collect the pastel box in her kitchen and the medium-pointed permanent marker in the knife drawer. She returned to the garden and deposited the box on the chair seat. Across the top of the box she scrawled:

> Thank you, Aleck, for clearing the trees and making the gate.
>
> Cadie
>
> P.S. Please lock the gate when you leave.

She turned then and unlocked the deadbolt. Slightly opening the gate, she peeked through the crack. Aleck's car was visible in the open garage. He was home. She opened the gate several more inches and left it ajar before walking back to her porch.

Satisfied that she'd solved her dilemma, she picked up her guitar. There was truth in the box's transmission, for as she began to sing, her old and covetous craving abated, her belly full from the smells of giving. On her tongue the taste of sharing, her songs bore phantom buds of peach, chocolate, and coconut cream cupcakes. Without a bite or promise of future reward, she sang. Soon forgotten in her music were the pastries in the box, the chair on her trail, and the gate she'd unlocked.

AT SIX O'CLOCK, ALECK came out of his house carrying a glass of chilled wine in his hand and walked through his garage. He looked at his new handiwork in the fence and immediately noticed the unlatched gate, was positive that he'd locked it the night before. Only Cadie had the keys to the bolt.

Placing his glass on a shelf with his hiking gear that he lugged to Austin twice every spring, Aleck walked to the fence and poked his head through the opening. On top of the box in the yellow chair, he could see the note addressed to him. Just then, he heard Cadie's amplifier power up, followed by her strumming.

Wasting no time, he retrieved his wine and returned to the fence. After a quick look around for Beatrice, he stepped inside Cadie's yard and pulled the gate halfway closed. It swung without a squeak on the new hinges. Turning, Aleck set his glass down on the chair's wide arm and read the note.

Considering Cadie's social reticence and her awkward tics during his first real contact with her, Aleck was fondly surprised to hold the gifted cakes in his hand. He chuckled under his breath, amused by the cramped easement where he stood, wondering if anyone could believe that someone could be as shy as Cadie. The sudden permission to enter her garden for something other than the singular task for which he'd volunteered meant something more than a fence set ajar. Something personal for Cadie. He was further mindful from the way the chair blocked the path that he was not to proceed beyond it. The chair was only there as a mechanism to hold the pastries off the damp ground. Aleck grinned. Cognizance was no deterrent for mischievous inclinations. *That* considered, Aleck decided to use the chair without going beyond the boundary it marked.

He turned and pulled the gate nearly closed and kept still when he heard Beatrice shuffle into his driveway. Through the fence slats, he watched her look around his garage for him. She finally took out a few cookies and set them on the trunk of his car before moving on down the alley.

Aleck sat down to relax with his gift and sampled one pastry after another with his wine. How his students would laugh to see him on the chair facing the fence, his knees nearly touching the new panels. But he was in Cadie's garden *while* she was singing. He smiled and bit into a creamy petit four flavored with marzipan.

Did Cadie's voice seem stronger and more vibrant because he sat closer, albeit only several feet closer, to her?

He swallowed and took another bite, finally shrugging away the self-analysis of his behavior. He could live with how silly or crazy he might look if it meant hanging out in Cadie Walsh's yard while she played guitar and sang.

AS SHE SANG, CADIE FELT the same exultant strength in her voice that Aleck heard, but her thoughts were far away from her yard. Instead, Cadie credited the exuberance to Kamil's invitation for a second visit. The effect the Turkish coffee had had on her tongue was a curiosity to Cadie. She had never relaxed with anyone like that before.

Maybe it'd been easier to unwind when she saw that nonexistent was their desire to convert her or make her the same as them. Hadn't Basir said that they promoted interfaith dialogue and friendship? It was odd that she'd left feeling so at home with people antithetical to everything Sister Mary Trea had taught. She wasn't sure how it made sense, but she'd liked the interaction. Sister Mary Trea was wrong. Again. Now Cadie began to hope that she had the variance needed to fit in somewhere.

An hour into singing, Cadie paused, contemplating what to sing next as trailing and wolfish-gray storm clouds moved aside and revealed the last hour of sunlight. Slowly, she plucked out various chords until she found one to fit her newest Gaelic lyrics. Shadows from Aleck's oaks bled into her tallest trees that threw their own shadows to the east. From a park nearby, children's voices pealed and resonances of fading day whispered in the underbelly of the yellow-gray sky. Cadie started to sing the story of a person's journey from a dark forest path into sunlight over mountains, of a person watching, minute by minute, the sun cross the sky and drop below memories of faraway origin. The strange words floated over the driveways surrounding Cadie's, and the words became her audience's story. And each person became the song's heroine who battled rains to arrive safely on shores of illuminated possibility.

WHEN SHE FINISHED THE song, Cadie unplugged her guitar and turned off the amp. As it powered down, there was no mistaking the latch of her new garden gate clicking heavily into place. She rose up and peered toward the sound.

The pastries.

She jumped from the porch and ran quickly to the chair. The box was gone, the gate closed. Cadie walked around the seat. For a second she stood looking at the gate before threading the master lock through the latch and fastening it tight. A short vibration shot through the metal in her hand.

She listened. The children were quiet. Everything was quiet.

Satisfied by her privacy, Cadie turned from the gate and bent over to pick up the chair.

She stopped moving when she saw pastry crumbs on the planks. *Did he sit here while I sang?*

Looking more closely around the chair, Cadie noticed the legs had sunk into the soft ground. Over her shoulder, she looked toward Aleck's. He *had* sat there, *had* heard her singing.

She picked up the furniture piece and walked down the path. Mortified by her unintended listener, Cadie blushed as she deposited the chair in its normal place and quickly gathered her things. She would sing inside for the remainder of the weekend.

CHAPTER SIX

Cadie yawned in the gloaming and looked for the South 287 Business exit sign. She saw it a minute later and turned on her blinker. Ennis, Texas wasn't far away now. She scanned the horizon for minute-to-minute signs of daylight and reminded herself of the directions to the bakery. Take Dallas Street south, left off of Dallas Street onto West Brown . . . bakery on the left.

Five blocks away from her destination, she almost changed her mind and drove back to Fort Worth. The Conventions and Visitor's Bureau didn't open until 10 a.m., and Cadie wasn't sure she wanted to wait that long. Even less, she did not wish to explain to a roomful of older women that she'd driven all the way from Fort Worth to look for somebody with Czech heritage. It had been difficult enough telling the one woman the day before.

"Just come on to Ennis and we'll put you into contact with a good Czech when you get here," said the woman who'd answered her call.

It was suspicious to Cadie that they needed to see her before doing something possible by email. The whole idea smelled of Mrs. Beauregard, and Cadie didn't like it. They were fishwives casting for stories, and no story was perfect without the personal description of so and so from here or there who wanted this or that.

Dallas Street loomed short. Cadie went ahead and followed it to West Brown. She pulled up in front of an old downtown building and engaged the parking brake. The street was empty of other people or cars. Whether it'd been a good idea to come so early, she was here now.

The historic *kolache* bakery, which opened at six o'clock a.m. to serve fresh-baked Czech pastries, drew Cadie to Ennis before the Visitor's Center opened. She had four hours to kill, and ran the risk of not accomplishing much more on her day off than having breakfast and going back to Fort Worth without a new contact. Cadie got out and stepped from the dark sidewalk into the bright café. She hoped the trip for the homemade breakfast delicacies was worth it.

Sweet and savory aromas of baked goods shared the room with a lone customer, his face blocked by the morning paper he held. A full coffee cup and a partially eaten, fruit-filled pastry rested on the table in front of him. A buxom woman, forty-something, standing behind the main counter exuded a broad smile.

"Mornin', darlin'. What can I get for you this mornin'?"

Hundreds of Czech names, printed and affixed to the high café walls behind the woman, reminded Cadie why she'd come.

"I came to try authentic Czech pastries—never had any before."

"That's a shame, darlin'." The woman's voice confirmed a real sense of pity that changed to positive assurance. "We'll fix you up this mornin'. Fresh from the oven."

She gestured at large tiers of fresh kolaches set up behind the main counter. "Now," she said, drawing in a great breath that threatened to pop her blouse's top button, "we have good ol' cinnamon rolls, with and without pecans. We also have our famous kolaches—apricot, strawberry, poppy seed, strawberry with cream cheese, blueberry . . ."

Cadie waited for the list to end. The woman obviously had recited the list thousands of times.

"If you want something less sweet, we also have sausage kolaches—mild, mild with cheese, or jalapeno, with or without cheese. Then we have the pockets and a full breakfast menu." The woman took another breath.

In a testing mood, Cadie threw careful selection to the wind. Better to figure out which kolaches she liked best if she ever planned to drive an hour each way for the pleasure again.

"I'll take a cup of coffee, no cream, and one of every kolache, plus two cinnamon rolls—one with pecans, the other without."

"Thatta girl," said the woman, grabbing a large to-go box. Large orders didn't faze her.

Cadie interrupted, "I'll eat here, please."

Now the woman looked a little confused.

Keeping her serious expression, Cadie explained. "Not all at once. I just want to try a bite from each one to see which I like best. It won't be a good test if I try them when they're cold."

"Perfectly reasonable, darlin'. I'll get you some plates. You want regular coffee or our chocolate-hazelnut house specialty? Both roasted for us right here in Ennis."

"Regular." If the regular wasn't good, nothing else would be.

The shuffle of the man's paper drew Cadie's gaze. Bushy, gray eyebrows above amused blue eyes appeared over the print. He was no doubt curious to see the girl who planned to try every kolache flavor in one go. Cadie turned back to the cashier and paid before heading toward a table in the opposite corner of the café.

The man completely lowered his paper to watch her walk across the old hardwood floor. "Better get 'er some more napkins there, Rose," said the man with a soft accent.

The woman who had taken Cadie's order responded loudly from the open kitchen, which guarded another long pastry case full of specialty cakes. "You stop tellin' me what to do, old buzzard. I'll bring extra napkins after I fill her coffee."

The man picked up the remainder of his pastry and coffee and carried them across the room. The lean vigor of his walk belied his gray hair. He sat down at the table nearest Cadie's.

Rose emerged from the kitchen with Cadie's coffee and more napkins. "There you go again. Can't you stay at one table ev'ry mornin'? Gotta follow you all over the place ev'ry time a pretty girl walks in the shop."

"Don't worry, darlin'," said Rose, talking now to Cadie and setting down the coffee. "Karl's harmless since his Lidice died a year an' a half ago. Heaven only knows how she stood him."

"By damn, Rose, do you have to go on about it every time somebody new comes in? I just want to say hello." He winked at Cadie before adding, "And how many times do I have to tell you—heaven didn't have anything to do with it."

Scratching at an unraveling seam on the side of her jeans, Cadie remained expressionless. If the banter continued, they might forget her amidst the argument and leave her to eat alone.

Rose let out an "hmmpfh" and returned to the kitchen. Karl got up a second time and moved his plate and coffee to Cadie's table.

"You mind if I enjoy my breakfast with you? Guess you know me well enough to know I'm a widower. No need to talk across the room."

"That's fine," said Cadie flatly.

She took a sip of the coffee. Its balance surprised her. The local roaster was talented.

Karl stretched out his hand to her from across the table.

"Karl Sikora."

Cadie shook his hand. "Cadie Walsh." *Sikora . . . Sikora.* She hadn't seen that name on the wall, but it didn't sound American. Maybe she wouldn't have to go to the Visitor's Bureau after all.

"So, you're not from Ennis, since you've never had a kolache. Where are you from, sweetheart?"

Rose's voice came from the kitchen. "She's never gonna taste one either if you don't stop talkin' at her."

Karl threw his hands into the air. "She can eat. I can talk."

Cadie began to question if she had the discipline to keep from a quick exit without trying the pastries.

Karl, giving Cadie time to try her first kolaches, picked up his cup of coffee and slowly drank.

"I'll eat the ones you don't like," he said.

A faint tug pulled at the corner of her mouth. Were all Texan men so willing to engage in such table chivalry? When she didn't like a cake flavor at the office parties, Bobby always finished off her piece for her, alleviating her embarrassment at not finishing food she disliked. Maybe Mr. Sikora, in spite of his name, wasn't Czech but Texan through and through.

She cut her first piece from the apricot kolache. The yeasty aromas of the warm pastry flourished on her tongue as she chewed. It was the best breakfast bite she'd had all year.

"That there's my favorite kind," said Karl.

Cadie thought about taking another bite but slid the remaining kolache off her plate and onto his. His eyes lit up at the gift.

She smiled slightly. "Sorry to hear about your wife."

"Thank you, darlin', but I can tell from lookin' at you that you won't find a better kolache among the bunch than the one you just gave up."

"How do you know anything 'bout what you look at, 'cept food, you old buzzard?" yelled Rose in a loving tone. "She might not like the apricot."

Karl paid her no mind.

Rose didn't like being ignored. She walked into the dining room and picked up Cadie's empty cup. "More coffee?"

"I think I'll try the chocolate hazelnut."

"Thatta girl."

Rose went to the self-serve carafe nearby and filled the cup. She returned, set it on the table, and waited for Cadie to taste it.

Cadie half-closed her eyes during the first sip, then closed them completely on the second.

"Want to take home a pound?"

"Yes, please," said Cadie.

Nodding, Rose good-naturedly tapped the side of Karl's shoulder with the back of her hand and walked away.

"So why come for kolaches so early, my dear?" Karl asked.

He listened to Cadie spill the story of her latest quest and watched her mild movements as she spoke of her genome, her first visit with the Celebis, and her plans to meet the Finns in the coming week. The emotionless way she told her story fascinated him. As she talked, she tried one bite after another of the pastries and finally, at the end of her narrative, pushed away the last test pieces.

"Well, that's something, for sure," said Karl after hearing the story. "I'd be happy to be your Czech culture sponsor if you want. Might be hard to tell, but I'm a hundred percent Czech."

"Oh, if we could all be a hundred percent Czech like Karl *Seeekora*," interjected Rose.

"By damn, Rose, if you don't stop it . . . well, I might find another place to eat 'round here."

"Nobody'd take you." If Rose had known that in less than three years, a local gas station would purchase the kolache bakery and up-root it from downtown, incorporate it in the filling station next to interstate 45, then she would have kept her tongue.

Laughing, Karl said to Cadie, "She's prob'ly right. But speaking for the Czechs, something tells me we'd be happy to sign you up as one of us—genes or no genes."

Cadie nodded.

"You'd sign up anything that talked to you," said Rose. She walked over, placed a bag of coffee on the empty chair beside Cadie, and set a large box for the leftovers on the table.

Happy that her trip hadn't been for nothing, Cadie emptied her cup and then looked at Karl. "The apricot was my favorite."

"Knew it would be," he said, winking.

WHEN IT WAS LIGHT enough, they walked outside. Karl waited on the sidewalk for Cadie to place her box in her car. Together they strolled down the short block to the town's main thoroughfare while Karl pointed out the significance of different buildings. The small historic district was laden with fairly thriving, at least not shuttered and empty, mom-and-pop businesses catering in antiques, flowers, clothing, and hardware. A handful of buildings constructed with sand-colored bricks stood among a majority with old, red brickwork. Most of the structures were architecturally nondescript, flat-roofed boxes common to small-town Texas. Only details of a few caused Cadie to stop and look. A strong but warm breeze gusted around them.

"Here along the tracks is where we set up for our Autumn Days Fall Festival and Bluebonnet Trails Festival in the spring. Tomorrow, Autumn Days begins."

Cadie nodded and they walked down the length of Main Street before turning to take the loop back to her car. Karl gestured toward an old, window-lined warehouse or office building a block away. It looked vacant.

"That's home," he said. "Lidice and I bought it decades ago, converted the top floor into our condo. It's a short walk to the bakery every morning. Much as Rose hates it," he winked.

"What is it you do?" asked Cadie.

"Was a chef for many years . . . now crazy enough to own a couple of restaurants in Dallas. Rough business."

"Don't you cook anymore?"

"Not as much lately." He looked away from the building and over her head.

Cadie felt sorry for him. He was alone like she was, but she didn't know what to say. She started walking again. Karl quickly caught up.

"Why don't you come down for the festival tomorrow? I'll introduce you to some other Czechs. We'll have a good time, watch the tourists flock downtown."

"I don't know . . . ," she said. How could she be in Ennis for a second day and still do all of the weekend work she wanted?

"It's as good as the first bite of an apricot kolache," he urged.

The morning sun on the quiet streets stirred warmth in Cadie. She wondered if commanding herself to trigger new actions had opened the slightest of fissures, a tiny expansion of self still too compressed to see what crouched beyond. If she declined Karl, would the fissure close as abruptly as it had opened? Work or no work, she decided she couldn't take the risk.

"I'll be here at six."

"Good girl," said Karl with a grin.

+ + +

EXCITED ABOUT ANOTHER FRUITFUL contact, Cadie went home and sent out a message in search of somebody from Morocco. That done, she settled in to work on a new robotics program. Two hours into productive coding for the latest project, the heady elation dissipated. In its place was growing alarm. She was going to an autumn festival in a Czech town. Tomorrow. That meant there'd be music, Czech music. Music could mean dancing, and she wasn't ready for that, especially that.

"Foresight is a gift," echoed Sister Mary Trea.

Cadie frowned. According to Sister Mary Trea, "gifts" were heaven-sent when one demonstrated excellence in a particular area. Until then, they were doomed to trudge toward the betterment of a skill. As far as Cadie was concerned, that was the chicken-egg argument at its worst.

In this case, though, Sister Mary Trea was right about lack of foresight. Cadie had promised to meet Karl at the bakery, but hadn't asked for his phone number or email. There was no way now to cancel the trip without being a no-show.

"Here's foresight for you," said Cadie.

She opened her online music program and did a quick search for classical and folk Czech music. If she would be plunged into dancing, she'd be better off if she understood basic waltz and polka music arrangements. After choosing and downloading a few albums, she created a new "Czech" playlist and set it on repeat before continuing with engineering tasks.

At exactly five o'clock, Cadie shut down her programs and chose a dinner from her freezer. It was her day off, after all, and she wanted to watch a show before sitting on the back porch with her guitar. She closed the blinds in the front room while her basil tomato rigatoni heated. Mrs. Beauregard had a habit of walking the front street around the time Cadie ate every evening. On a day that the woman had seen her leave so early on Friday—an off-par schedule even for Cadie—Cadie imagined the woman just biding time to ask questions aroused by neighborly spying. Where were you off to so early this morning, dear? What are your plans for the weekend? Are you missing those trees of yours?

AN HOUR LATER, the porch still awash in evening sunlight, Cadie walked out with her guitar and set it on the lounge. She kicked off her shoes and then strolled barefoot through the garden. After twenty minutes, she returned and picked up her instrument. She gently ran her palm over its fretboard after she plugged the guitar into the amp. The guitar sounded slightly off-key, and she stopped to tune the strings. She tried a chord, stopped again, re-tuned.

Aleck's garage door opening caused her to delay before testing the chord again. She waited for the sound of his car to start and leave or, in any case, for the garage door to close. What was he doing? There was no sound of him tinkering at a workbench or in his backyard. Maybe she had conjured the sound with the same faulty ears that couldn't seem to pitch her music this evening. After several minutes of listening and hearing nothing else, Cadie abandoned her familiar chords and picked out a series of new notes. Among the cadences, the notes came clear and unfaltering. *There's not a thing wrong with my guitar,* she thought.

On the other side of the fence, Aleck sat in his chair and listened to Cadie play. It had first sounded to him like her guitar was broken—the way she fumbled over the notes as a child learning a new composition, stopping and restarting to get it right. What she played now was familiar to him, but it departed from the context of her Gaelic songs. Thus, Aleck couldn't place the music.

Beatrice, unusually late with the cookies, hurried along the alley with her deliveries. She pointed toward Cadie's fence and raised her brows to indicate that something was wrong. Aleck nodded and shrugged. From their conversations, Aleck knew that Beatrice didn't know a thing about music. But a person didn't need to know about something in order to feel it. Aleck chose two sugar cookies. Beatrice handed him another.

A whole new set of notes striking the air caused the pair of them to start. The haunting sound was gone. The deeply resonating shards of invisible fog gave way to a landscape of romance and hopeful vigor. Beatrice hurried out of his driveway. Aleck could hear that Cadie no longer tinkered with the notes. She had perfected them. In the clarity, Aleck knew he'd heard these songs before, but not like this, not played on a guitar. He thought and thought even as Cadie began singing in English.

Where had she heard that composition with those words? Unable to elicit accurate memory, Aleck got up and walked to the end of his driveway. He stopped short when he saw his neighbors.

Beatrice wasn't shuffling down the alleyway. She was light on her feet, steps lifting quickly and moving forward on invisible zigzag lines. Mr. and Mrs. Garcia danced by their lawn chairs. They didn't seem to notice Beatrice. Aleck watched the elder couple move in time to the music, his eyes falling on Mrs. Garcia's shoes. The leaves of flowers cut from purple leather bounce-bounced, bounce-bounced. Then Aleck remembered. The music was a polka. Just before the name of the polka's composer reached Aleck's lips, Cadie switched to a different song. Again, not Gaelic.

Aleck returned to his chair and sat down. Had Cadie secretly, for weeks or months, practiced the new style and genre? He decided that she hadn't, couldn't have. He would have heard her. Anyway, from everything she'd played before, she wouldn't need that long to practice—not with her talent. Still, something had changed her predictable pattern to novelty. Faster, faster beat his heart. Aleck rubbed his chest. There was depth in the music she'd only touched upon when playing her Celtic tunes. Something was very, very different.

At the risk of missing some of the music, Aleck forced himself to get up and walk quickly into his house. Scanning through his CDs, he tried to jar his memory. Arranged by country of origin, then composer, he stopped when he got to the "Cs," grabbed a CD, and ran back outside.

Was it possible?

He squatted beside his chair and listened. In near disbelief, he reassured himself that he'd heard her falter among the beginning chords. As if testing them, testing and then playing with the familiarity of the original composer. And in a way, she *had* composed it, for the piece she played was written for piano, for violin, for whole bands, for entire symphonies—not for one retrofitted acoustic guitar, no matter how nice it was.

The piece finished, and Cadie started another. Aleck looked at the back of the CD in his hand, and his sediment of auditory clues solidified into certainty. Cadie was alternating between Janáček and Dvořák. She was now playing Dvořák's 9th *New World Symphony.* His favorite—Dvořák. Where Dvořák existed, love existed.

Aleck leapt up beside his chair. Cadie played the symphony without missing a note. He wanted to rush through the locked gate and up Cadie's porch to see how her fingers moved over the guitar. Instead, he stood without moving. He had nowhere better to go.

For the first time since living on Corral Street, Aleck couldn't wait to talk to Beatrice. Maybe she had an inkling of what had happened with Cadie. Whatever it was, Aleck knew enough to realize that Cadie would have played Czech music prior to this if she had known it. She played everything she knew. And she seemed to function from components of which she was neither complicit nor fully aware. Aleck hoped the change wasn't something that would keep him from entering her garden again.

Finally exhausted from the emotional day and from playing the new songs, Cadie leaned back on the lounge and fell asleep. One by one, most of her neighbors returned inside. Aleck sat down in his driveway and continued to think about Cadie and her music. When he did force himself to carry the CD back to its place, the sound of his closing garage door woke Cadie.

She got up from the lounge and went to her bedroom, but found herself unable to sleep. The echoes of the music and anticipation of the coming day stirred emotions that she could not quiet. Cadie deposited herself in front of her computer so she could work. After several hours of coding she got up, showered, and drove to Ennis.

+ + +

ROSE WAS PLACING AN APRICOT kolache and a cup of the chocolate hazelnut coffee at Karl's table when Cadie walked into the bakery the next morning.

"Saw you pull up, darlin'. Just let me know if you need anything else. Don't let Karl bother you too much."

"Thank you, Rose."

Karl jumped up to pull out a chair for her. "Was just askin' myself if you'd dare show up again. It'll be a busy day here in town."

Cadie nodded and sat. That's what she was afraid of, a busy day in town.

"So," continued Karl, "We're goin' to do the grand tour. Everything Czech, all day. You like music?"

"What was that?" asked Cadie, swallowing a bite. Her focus had been on the taste of the airy kolache.

"You like music?"

"Yes."

"You play?"

Cadie took another bite and chewed without answering.

Karl moved on with his questions. "You like to dance?"

"Never have."

"Well, don't let him rope you into it," shouted Rose from the kitchen. "You'll die from exhaustion bein' on the floor all day. Karl can go for days on end. Cain't you, Karl?"

"What can I say?" He smiled sheepishly. "'Course, shufflin' round the floor isn't the same anymore. The young'uns are losing the art. They can't move like Lidice could, but there was a day you couldn't keep them off the floor.

"Nobody could move like Lidice did," said Rose. "The polka 'specially."

"Maybe I'll just watch today," said Cadie around another bite.

"You can't just watch dance. You gotta do it. It's what dance is about, and everybody has it in 'em." He slapped the table. "Of course," he added, his emphatic tone lightening, "if you're that nervous, we could put it off for another day . . . long as you don't let it go by completely."

Cadie sidestepped. "Did you grow up in Ennis?"

"Yep—born and raised right here. Grandparents came over before WWI and settled a mile from this very spot."

That explained his soft accent, thought Cadie. Karl talked, well, Texan with faint traces of Czech. Rose walked over and filled Cadie's half-empty cup.

"You ought to let Karl show you that building he lives in," she said. "Wouldn't do no harm. Like I said, darlin', he's harmless. Karl may like turnin' the girls 'round the floor, but there's only one love in Karl's life. That's Lidice."

Karl nodded and turned to greet another older man entering the café. When Rose scurried off to retrieve a cinnamon roll, Cadie figured he was another café regular.

Carrying a cane like a weapon rather than for walking assistance, the man walked over and sat down at the table with them. "Who've we got here, Karl?"

"This is Cadie. Cadie, this here's Frank. Frank, Cadie's an orphan from Fort Worth, Dallas-born, might have some Czech DNA. She's here to *check* us out." Karl laughed, slapping his knee.

"What kind o' orphan?" asked Frank, pretending to ignore Karl.

"A Catholic orphan," said Cadie without emotion.

Frank looked at Cadie, then at Karl. "Well, she outta fit in with us old bastards—the church lost us, too."

FOR THE NEXT TWO hours, they sat at the café and talked. Most of the conversation was between Frank and Karl. Cadie watched customers overrun the café. Frank and Karl paused each time the bell over the door clanged. The men raced each other to point out whether the entrant was a local. By Cadie's guess, the true locals were those who instantly greeted the older men. Everyone else hurried past on their way to the beckoning pastry counter.

Finally, Frank pushed back his chair. "Well, I'm gonna skadoodle before it gets worse. There'll be a million people come through here today."

Karl nodded. "See you, Frank."

Frank looked at Cadie. "Don't let him drag you around too much today, darlin'. There's more to see in that old building of his than anything you'll see downtown."

"I won't," said Cadie, realizing her outing would last longer than she'd planned.

WHEN CADIE AND KARL got up to the leave, a diminutive couple dressed in traditional polka getup took over the table. Their very tall daughter towered over the coffee bistro station and filled three cups. The couple bickered over the weather, if it would hold for the tourists and the dances.

Karl led Cadie to the sidewalk and pointed toward her car. "At my house will be a good place to park for the day. I'll ride with you."

Chaste girls frequent not the dens of single males.

Karl walked to the car. Cadie stood where she was, looked up and down the street. Echoes of Sister Mary Trea's tutelage continued.

Chaste girls wait . . . wait . . . wait . . .

Karl waited for Cadie to unlock the passenger door. Cadie clicked her remote key but didn't move.

Chaste girls have chaperones.

At that, Cadie went to her car and slid into the driver's seat. *When have you ever left me alone? Never.* The motor drowned out any reply from Sister Mary Trea. Cadie wondered if non-orphaned children suffered the quashing of natural exploratory drives into boxes of their parents' doctrines.

As Cadie steered, Karl pointed the way with simple hand signals. When they arrived at his building, he directed Cadie to circle the block. She parked in the open loading zone marked "Private" and walked with him into an antique shop chockablock with heavy furniture on the entire first floor. In one corner, a woman guided a young couple among antique bed frames.

"That there is Samantha," said Karl, heading to the opposite corner. "She manages Lidice's antique shop now."

They walked through a back door that opened to a stairwell. Both went up without speaking. At the top of the stairs, they turned right, stopped at the first and only door across the short hall from an elevator. Karl turned the unlocked knob, simultaneously kicking the door's bottom plate with the toe of his shoe.

"Swells some in the heat—it'll open smooth as butter during our two months of winter."

Cadie stepped into a large foyer overshadowed by a massive antique armoire on one wall and a china cabinet with a hutch on the other. At the end of the armoire stood a copper umbrella stand, which held two black, wood-handled umbrellas. Before Karl could say anything about the Czech tradition to don slippers inside, Cadie had discarded her shoes and left them by two pairs of slippers inside the door. She walked barefooted to the end of the foyer and looked around, a systematic assessment of the new surroundings. Karl doubted that she would miss much.

Karl took off his street shoes and slid his feet into his slippers that Lidice had purchased online the week before she died. The house shoes had come in the mail the day after her funeral, and the pair she had ordered for herself sat there unused; they would sit idle a little longer. He joined Cadie beyond the foyer and followed her gaze around the building's top floor.

Natural light from dozens of massive windows filtered into the enormous studio. A few doors remained at the end of an old interior corridor. Cadie assumed they led to bedrooms and bathrooms, over them ceilings eight, maybe nine feet from the floor. Light streamed into the four-foot headspace above the rooms' ceilings and provided sustenance for an interior garden of potted herbs and small plants accessible by two rolling ladders fastened to an iron rail that followed the square of rooms. From the kitchen to several different sitting areas and two formal dining areas, there was nothing but European antique furniture, no original interior walls. A few freestanding walls built with bird's eye maple created the effect of "rooms" without blocking light or passage from one area to another. Running parallel to the south windows was another impermanent wall with six tall, narrow portals. The wall created a false corridor between the main room and the windows. In that corridor, two chaise reading lounges sat beside potted ficus trees.

What caught Cadie's attention more than anything, though, was what covered the interior walls and supporting steel beams. Everywhere there was nothing but art—antique gilded frames encasing strange, exciting paintings and antique postcards. A few family or individual portraits dotted the wild landscape. Whoever had built the grand collection was an aficionado of frogs wearing trousers, for many of the paintings and all of the postcards depicted at least one frog wearing pants.

Karl moved to the side without speaking and remained there as Cadie moved slowly along the first wall. After several minutes, she remembered she was in another person's home and looked at Karl. On her face was a bare hint of smile. Karl, who had already presumed Cadie was hard to impress, saw shining approval from her narrowed eyes. He was proud his art had affected the girl.

"They're my ode to Spallanzani."

"Spallanzani?"

She moved on to examine the next paintings.

"An eighteenth-century Catholic priest. He moonlighted as a biologist and physicist—did experiments with frogs. It led to his memorialization as a historical contributor to modern genetics."

Cadie raised her eyebrows.

"He dressed up his frogs in little pants to discover what we now know as *in vitro* fertilization. I started collecting these paintings long before your scientists could tell you about your particular genome. Most of the paintings were gifts from Lidice, after I met her in college. *That* was a time."

A crease formed at Cadie's eye as she looked at a painting. Karl couldn't tell if she was smiling at what he'd said or at the painting, but he knew Cadie wasn't a person to commit the evil of banality. He turned on heel and headed toward the kitchen.

"Look at a few more while I pull out a snack. We'll play cribbage until Main Street thrives."

Cadie looked at the paintings of a frog courting a mouse until the smell of toasted bread filled the room. She walked to the kitchen.

"Where do you play cribbage?"

Karl looked up from plating a brick of goose liver *pâté*, pointed toward the nearest sitting area. Cadie spotted the small board with four drilled rows and four wooden pegs standing in their waiting positions. Beside the board sat a deck of well-worn cards. She walked over to the large Henri II center table and examined the carved pegs, the pairs differentiated by miniscule characters on top. Two pegs sported tiny flowers. The other two had frogs wearing pants. Cadie guessed the flower blossom pegs had been Lidice's.

"What flowers are these?"

"Lime blossoms. Lidice loved limes. It's the tree of the Czech Republic. She had those pegs made for our tenth anniversary."

On a silver platter, Karl brought over the food. Surrounding a pâté terrine was a ring of freshly toasted brioche. "Made the goose liver pâté and the brioche yesterday . . . just in case you decided to drive down today. Oh yes, something to drink." He left and returned with Sauternes, golden yellow wine corked in a half-size bottle, and two bottles of Pilsner Urquell. "Choices," he said, smiling. "It's typical to have sweet wine with pâté, but you don't know what you've missed until you've had it with Czech beer.

Cadie forget about the time of day and watched Karl pour the beer into stemmed pilsner glasses.

"Na Zdravi," said Karl, clinking his glass against hers.

"And to your health," responded Cadie.

"Exactly right," said Karl, impressed by Cadie's attempt at Czech.

Cadie held her breath during her first sip, but it was hard to mistake a light sweetness on her tongue. She inhaled and took another drink. Now this was beer, not the dregs that Bobby served at picnics. As much as she didn't often rate something highly enough to wax enthusiastic, she would have to tell Bobby about this.

Karl opened the Sauternes, filled the lead crystal dessert glasses, and then set about teaching the art of cribbage. Mastering the lingo and rules of the game only took Cadie a few minutes. Except for playing out their hands and counting the cribs, they spoke little. Basking in the open room and warmth from drinks, they finished off the pâté, beer, and Sauternes after four games. Karl took the empty platter to the kitchen.

"Now I will make a little something before we go to the streets."

Cadie got up and moved to a heavy bar stool positioned on the other side of the granite counter.

From the refrigerator, Karl pulled bacon slices and a square butter slab. He cut a sliver of the butter and tossed it in the heating sauté pan. He threw in the bacon before the butter melted and then took a small onion from a hanging vegetable basket. He diced the onion and threw it in with the bacon. With a knife and fork, he cut the bacon into small pieces. When it was thoroughly cooked, he added strips cut from a kale bunch. Next came freshly ground pepper and coarse salt. From another tier in the hanging basket, he chose a lime and handed it to Cadie.

"Into slices," he instructed, handing her a knife and clean cutting board. Already on the counter were a glass carafe and a blue bottle. Karl pointed to them with his knife.

Understanding, Cadie nodded.

As she cut the lime, Karl lightly beat four eggs. He poured the eggs into the skillet and stirred them into the mixture. Over the sliced limes, Cadie poured the sparkling water.

"Ready now." He dished out the mixture onto plates and then moved around the bar to sit beside Cadie. "This will give us energy to find the funnel cake cart," he said around a large bite.

"I like funnel cakes, too," she said.

"Figured you might."

As they ate, Cadie noticed a rod of woven twigs hanging on the kitchen wall. "What is that?"

"Ah, my homemade *pomlázky*. That's how I met Lidice. She'd just recently come from the Czech Republic for college. It was the New Year's Eve party of '68. I was a terror, that's what Lidice said. I took my homemade rod like little boys do on Red Monday, the day after Easter in the old country, went to whacking all the girls on their behinds. Those college girls were good and mad by the time I finished."

He looked at the pomlázky and laughed.

"It seemed a good way to get attention before the clock hit midnight. Still don't know why I didn't get one kiss at midnight."

Cadie watched Karl gaze at memories wound into the twigs. His laugh lines bulged and stretched, his Adam's apple swallowed down the frog coming up his throat. He didn't stop smiling.

"Next day, New Year's Day '69, Lidice showed up at my house with boiled and decorated eggs—as wee girls do back home. It's a superstition that the eggs stimulate fertility. The pomlázky stimulated a love affair. The eggs were good for nothing, but Lidice insisted we keep the rod, would sometimes swat me with it when the mood struck her just right."

"So you didn't have children?"

"No," said Karl, turning to look at Cadie. "But our lives couldn't have been fuller. Lidice was one of those women . . . "

Karl stopped to swallow again.

" . . . one of those women who embody the solidity and candor of many lifetimes without being harsh or sad. How beautiful she was."

With a sweep of his arm, Karl motioned toward the expanse of the room. "There's nothing here she didn't touch or choose in some way. Can't find anything here that isn't beautiful."

Twisting on her stool, Cadie took her eyes from the woven rod and overlooked the furniture, the paintings. New voices whispered in the still air, new faces looked out from layered canvas. It was a living museum of a great romance, a maze of stories seeped into blossomed pegs, gilded frames, and heavy furniture. It was in the aroma of the food they ate.

Cadie nodded without saying that it was beautiful . . . and sad. There would never be time for Karl to retell each moment bound in the collection. Every moment, even the infinitesimal, takes many words to describe.

CHAPTER SEVEN

OUTSIDE THE BASEMENT DOOR of the Lutheran church, Cadie stood for a few moments with her fingers resting against the mechanical lock. The brass on the buttons had worn off, leaving hard cast iron poking through. The paint inside the etched numbers was gone as well. Cadie let her mind wander away from the Finnish group Meetup inside the building.

She was preoccupied over the snag she'd hit in her programming. Not that anybody at work noticed. The barrier, one only she pushed on herself, kept her from making the next leap in artificial intelligence development. Her robots remained "silent" unless moved by hard-coded software instruction, though her electronic sensors were the industry's best. What she was missing was a better "censor"—a holy grail that would allow her robots to self-regulate and quickly adapt to their environment. There had to be an attribute to break open the next realm of automated behavior. The key, Cadie guessed, was some external factor that could "switch on" awareness and map her new robotic paradigm. It discouraged her that she couldn't see it. Nothing in her regular rituals or progression of thought provided a glimpse of what she needed.

A foreign, metal clanking from inside the church reminded her where she was.

Stop thinking about it, Cadie. Concentrate on the meeting.

The meeting was another hurdle altogether. It was her third time to reach out to a new group. Her internal "orphan" operator propelled her. It gave her an excuse to leave her desk, but she didn't find it any easier along her unusual journey to approach new people. Somehow, she had prompted herself to create new actions. She imagined that she'd simultaneously started a "find" command, but what, if anything, had she found about herself?

Her forays into the Turkish and Czech homes had left her without any great leaps of self-discovery. Even her valiant assault to learn polka and waltz hadn't yielded a tangible breakthrough. Karl and Frank had graciously maneuvered her between dancing couples gliding easily around the dance floor's ellipse. But she had faltered. Her understanding of the dance steps' mathematics had not connected with her physical body. Cadie worried that stuck within her own DNA was some mutant variation, an attribute that blocked her from "sensing" normal social behavior and "censored" her from responding without awkward adjustments. What attributes, other than lack of mother and father, kept her an orphan? Was her "social sequence" DNA protein entirely broken?

I hope not.

Surely, her foray into dancing wasn't ultimately indicative of how competent she could be at every potential interaction. There had to be a key for that as well.

Forcing her thoughts back to the meeting at hand, Cadie punched in the code and entered the chilly basement. On her walk down the hallway, painted an earthy orange above off-white wainscoting, Cadie feared for her sanity. What would Mrs. Beauregard think of this . . . this social sampling of a genome's migratory paths, a chase after old DNA?

"You know where bad and crazy children go."

Cadie knew. Sister Mary Trea needn't remind her of the Church's asylums.

"You're playing with fire."

Playing with fire was any deviation from strict constraint. Suck coffee through sugar cubes. Playing with fire. Leave two bites of congealed oatmeal in the bowl. Playing with fire. Giggle after the lights go out. Playing with fire. Ask to see your orphanage file. Playing with fire. Playing with fire was equivocated with a taste of the hell the nuns taught. Playing with fire was asking for a sample of eternal punishment. A repeat request brought on fire as sure as the sun rose each morning. Fire was whips and breaking bones and humiliation inflicted with shouts of "Repent, Repent, Repent."

Cadie ignored the nun and slowed as she neared the meeting room. Commingling scents of sweet breads, or possibly cookies, and coffee greeted her. The email from the group's organizer had laid out the meeting's structure: first social time, then watching Christmas-time videos from Finland. She looked forward to seeing how a Finn-ish Lutheran Christmas differed from a Catholic Christmas.

As soon as she rounded the doorway, a dozen or so in the group stopped talking and greeted her in general silence. After several sec-onds, Cadie spoke.

"I'm Cadie . . . Cadie Walsh—the one who . . . I, uh, wrote the email message about my genome . . . I talked to Viktor by email."

At each pause, she hoped someone would jump forward. Instead, they waited for her to finish talking. Finally, a tall man in his sixties stepped forward, a close-lipped smile on his face.

"Everyone," he started, "This is the girl I told you about."

He then extended his hand, "I'm Viktor Ketola."

Viktor spent the next several minutes introducing Cadie to each person in the room. When he introduced Gabriella Ketola, Gabriella took over the conversation and motioned to the banquet table spread at the back of the room.

"This is a good first introduction to Finnish culture," she said. "It's a modest rendition of the Finnish coffee table. There's the coffee, of course, and many of our traditional coffee table foods."

She handed Cadie a paper plate. "We have an order to how we eat from the coffee table."

Viktor poured a cup of coffee for Cadie as Gabriella explained the rules.

"With your first cup of coffee, take a piece of *pulla* and one or two different cookies. Pulla is cardamom-flavored sweet bread."

Viktor pointed at two shiny, braided loaves sprinkled with al-mond slices.

Gabriella continued, "With your second cup of coffee, take a piece of uniced cake and one or two cookies different from the ones taken with your first cup."

No one in the room interrupted as Gabriella spoke. Viktor, navi-gating the table as Gabriella talked, moved toward the center and pointed at a cake. Except for Viktor's helpful identification of the sweets, Gabriella talked without using hand motions. On the far side of the table from the pulla, Victor pointed at a rolled cake.

"Take a piece of the decorated, filled cake with your third cup," said Gabriella. "On the fourth cup, we sample the other cookies or cakes passed during the first three cups. We like to sample everything on the table. It makes the cook happy. But, you can choose, also, to sip coffee through a sugar lump held between your teeth."

Gabriella returned to the pulla, sliced a piece, and placed it on Cadie's plate. "You choose your cookies, Cadie. There are nut, browned butter, anise, cinnamon-cardamom, and rye this evening."

The cookies sat strategically around the bread and cakes. Cadie made a quick tally of the items according to Gabriella's rules of consumption. Five different cookies, three pieces of cake. There wasn't an overweight person in the group. Industrious—they had to be to survive regular coffee table spreads as this one, assumed Cadie. Then the sugar lumps . . .

Cadie swallowed down a smile. *Playing with fire.* If only Sister Mary Trea had known the Turks and Finns enjoyed sipping hot drinks through sugar cubes. The nun would have condemned it at any rate, for one reason or another. The acceptability of the practice helped Cadie concentrate on the cookies. She chose a browned butter and a rye cookie.

Beside her, Viktor gently took Cadie's elbow. The touch startled her, but she allowed him to escort her to her seat with a "good view" and took the coffee he handed her. Assured of Cadie's comfort, Viktor turned to the group.

"This is footage from our last visit to Turku."

He looked at Cadie. "Turku is Finland's Christmas City."

Nodding, Cadie picked up the pulla and took a bite. It was lightly sweet, its consistency heavier than kolache dough.

Nighttime cold made visible by the heavy coats and the Finns' breath on the air illuminated the screen. Cadie sipped her coffee and watched the unaware actors walk among brightly lit Christmas market stalls promoting various crafts, hot chocolate, and beer. The video lens zoomed in on tables covered with painted handicrafts— Santa figurines, elves, angels, and animals carved from wood—then shifted to a stall full of sweets, preserves, and cookies similar to those on the back table.

Cadie picked up her browned butter cookie and two thin cookies, preserves sandwiched in between, and took a bite. Apart from the strawberry preserves, the cookie tasted identical to the orphanage's brown butter shortbread the nuns had allowed each Advent. Next, Cadie examined the remaining rye cookie. Fork holes pricked the surface around an off-center, centimeter-width circle cut from the dough. Cadie rinsed her mouth with the last of her coffee before biting into the cookie. It also was shortbread, a little less sweet.

When Gabriella got up for her second cup of coffee, Cadie followed. Gabriella smiled and cut two pieces of the uniced cake. Viktor came up behind them and took Cadie's cup, refilling it as Cadie chose her next cookies—a nut and an anise.

After they returned to their seats, Cadie noticed no one other than Viktor talked as the video played, and he only spoke to over-narrate what they watched. None of the underlying commentary she heard from colleagues during mandatory work presentations. Enjoying the silence, she cut into the cake dusted with confectioner's sugar. Permeating the buttery cake blended with chopped figs, raisins, and walnuts was a slight citrus taste—orange. Contented, Cadie chewed as the video shifted from Christmas fairs to a kitchen with a table long enough for sixteen, maybe twenty people.

"How old are you, Mother?" It was Viktor's voice coming from behind the video recorder's microphone.

Everyone in the frame turned to look at the woman hand-whipping heavy cream into stiff peaks. A blue and white, deep-piled rug hung on the wall behind her. "Ninety-six," she said.

The focus swung to Gabriella. She stood over a large ham, slicing away at the thick rye crust and skin in which the ham had baked.

To Cadie, Viktor explained the tradition of ham with mustard for the Christmas Eve dinner.

On the screen, Gabriella coated the ham's surface with Finnish mustard. Viktor's mother's voice cut through again, "Hurry, Gabi. I'll start the carp dishes and rewarm the ham. Go. Don't miss the Peace." Gabriella obediently pulled off her apron and left the kitchen.

Hoping to see what the Christmas Peace was, Cadie bit into the cookie brushed with egg white and dusted lightly with ground anise. The texture was a cross between shortbread and a scone. The licorice taste balanced her coffee's flavor. In the nut cookie, her favorite thus far, Cadie recognized the ground walnuts blended into and sprinkled atop the shortbread dough. Four-for-four, thought Cadie. She hypothesized the remaining cookie would also have a shortbread base.

The cookies amused her. She'd never thought of shortbread as anything but Irish—every year during the last ten days of Advent, the orphans had had exactly one shortbread cookie per day.

All totaled, she'd had maybe one hundred eighty cookies in her eighteen years at the orphanage. Just as she swallowed the last of her nut cookie, Viktor hit the pause button on the video.

"Break for cake and WC," he said.

Everyone moved to the back table and watched Gabriella slice the filled jelly roll dusted liberally with confectioner's sugar. Rolled inside the white cake was pink, jam-stained, whipped cream. Gabriella handed the first slice to Cadie.

"So what do you do for a living, Cadie?" asked the woman standing closest to the coffee urn.

"Robotics engineer," said Cadie.

Everyone nodded and smiled as Gabriella doled out the remaining cake slices. They accepted their allotments without interrupting the conversation.

"So how do you like the Finnish coffee table?" asked the woman.

The group turned in concert to listen for Cadie's answer.

"Nice. Makes going for each cup of coffee eventful."

The group smiled modestly. They knew it was an event. There was no need to brag.

When they returned to their seats with their third cups of coffee and sweets, Cadie felt calmer. She liked this group. They were warm and hospitable but not socially effused. They didn't try to force her compulsorily from her usual reticence. Cadie leaned back to enjoy the muted but generous welcome.

VIKTOR STARTED THE VIDEO again. The frame panned over a large city square surrounded by thousands of people wearing dark coats. All faces in the crowd focused on a small band and an all-male choir led in song by a serious conductor. Cadie liked the musical quality of the Finnish language. When the song ended, a great hush fell over the orderly crowd watching the clock on the Turku Cathedral clock tower. After the clock struck noon and rang out twelve strikes, the band heralded the moment by playing a shortened version of Siegfried's Horn Call. Following the musical announcement, a man carrying an old parchment walked onto the Brinkkala Mansion's balcony. He stopped between two evergreens decorated with simple white lights and began to read.

Viktor swiveled in his seat and said to Cadie, "Turku has been reading the Christmas Peace proclamation since the Middle Ages. It simply announces the call to Christmas and the demand that all behave peacefully and devotedly. It warns that those who violate the Peace, by illegal or improper behavior, will be guilty and punished according to the laws and statutes accordingly. It wishes a joyous Christmas feast to all inhabitants of the city."

Cadie nodded.

Viktor smiled and turned back to the screen.

The Christmas proclamation finished, the band and choir led the crowd in singing the Finnish national anthem. The video abruptly cut back to Viktor's mother's house.

There, Gabriella and other family members shared tumblers of *glögi*, a warmed, spicy wine drink, before departing to attend family graves and light candles. From the hilltop graveyard, the camera swung to view the city glowing with lit candles and electric decorative holiday lights.

Cadie bit into her piece of jelly roll and closed her eyes when she tasted raspberry jam in the whipped cream. She opened them to take another bite and watched the Finnish families walk home without the rambunctiousness she observed at her company's Christmas Eve soirée. From the video and first meeting alone, Cadie decided the Finns had a quiet culture. But they infused great words into the wholehearted approach to dessert and coffee.

She got up to pour a fourth cup of coffee. Gabriella went with her. Cadie chose a cinnamon-cardamom cookie and a lump of sugar before returning to her seat.

On the screen, Viktor's mother was center stage again. "Help Uncle Paul fill the bird feeders," she instructed several teenagers.

The teenagers obediently acknowledged their matriarch. With the bird feeding completed, the whole family took a sauna. They emerged ruddy and content, converged then for their Christmas dinner starring the mustard ham and a holiday *Lipeäkala*, lutefisk. After the meal, the children crowded around the recently erected Christmas tree. They opened their packages carefully, without the abandon of grand ripping and screaming. Inside the packages were handcrafted gifts received with delight and appreciation. When the new treasures were carefully set aside, Gabriella carried in the Finnish

Christmas pudding. Back to the table everyone went, each person anticipating their odds of finding the hidden almond. The children cried in dismay when Uncle Paul found it, and the evening ended with a variety of Christmas tarts, sweets, and family games.

Viktor narrated that Christmas Day was spent visiting friends, relaxing, eating leftovers, and reflecting on the past year.

As the traditional Finnish Christmas wound down on the screen, Cadie finished her cookie and placed the sugar cube between her teeth. The understated Finnish Christmas too much mirrored her orphan Christmas memories—so much quiet, no boisterous revelry during the year's darkest days.

AS SOON AS SHE made it home, Cadie logged in and marked the next Finnish group meeting, an invitation-only New Year's Eve party at the Ketolas'. Cadie stared at the appointment. It looked strange on her calendar. Since leaving the orphanage, she had rung in the new year alone, entertained by movies or coding.

A new email interrupted her thoughts. Cadie clicked the message as soon as she saw the sender's name, Yosef Alfasi. She quickly read the short paragraph. Finally, a response from a Moroccan contact. Cadie immediately accepted Yosef and Ayala's invitation to join them for a small belated celebration of Moroccan Independence Day.

The message rounded out her four chosen placemarks that would bring to life her genomic exploration and ethnicities along a path which had, long ago, disintegrated behind her.

Cadie shook her head. She had not only participated in the DNA test, but had also reached out successfully to the different groups.

Bobby Pullman would never believe it.

TOO EXCITED TO CODE, Cadie sat cross-legged in the deep cushions of an office chair. She strummed easily through variations of Irish chords and recently learned Czech music. Unable to stop thinking about her work, she didn't sing.

What am I missing?

Thinking through her eight years of programming experience,

hoping for a clairvoyant breakthrough, her mind wandered through Asimov's Three Laws of Robotics. Every AI programmer and science fiction aficionado knew them verbatim:

> First Law: A robot may not injure a human being or, through inaction, allow a human being to come to harm.
> Second Law: A robot must obey any orders given to it by human beings, except where such orders would conflict with the First Law.
> Third Law: A robot must protect its own existence as long as such protection does not conflict with the First or Second Law.

Asimov later added another law as a basis for the original three—the Zeroth Law:

> A robot may not harm humanity, or, by inaction, allow humanity to come to harm.

For the tasks to which her robots were hard-coded, Cadie's robots were exceptional. Yet they were static machines unable to improve dynamically upon their own rigid designs. How could a robot, not human, become human?

Cadie strummed faster. Instinctively she knew what her equations had missed answering. *What did it mean to be human?*

She compared the Three Laws to her limited references of human behavior and interaction. The Three Laws of robotics often superscribed the laws of human reality. How many humans harmed other humans? How many humans, in action or inaction, bowed before sociopathic, hell-bent authority? Her robots' inability to harm others was what she most liked about working on vast code tables. Her robots could not harm, denigrate, or form social cliques, where outcasts and slaves could be gathered, formed, and then, spent beyond use, thrown away as wasteful by-products. But how could she make her robots learn and grow intelligent interaction? Was there a human attribute that inspired people to follow the Three Laws?

Cadie set down her guitar, went to her desk, and opened an encrypted file in her hidden project folder. Line by line, she was still reviewing her codebase when the sun rose the following morning.

CHAPTER EIGHT

THE CORRAL STREET crime watch, spearheaded and kept intact by Beatrice, began to speculate over the interruptions to Cadie's back-porch concerts. Two years of consistency out the window. Beatrice, for once, couldn't produce an answer when neighbors asked where Cadie was. Neighbors had taken the cookies and retreated inside, resuming former love affairs with sitcoms and movies. Beatrice, on the other hand, had had an unsuccessful time trying to lure Cadie to her front door. She pondered if the girl was there or simply ignoring her. For once, though, Beatrice wasn't in the game by herself.

Aleck, increasingly focused on Cadie's movements, grew attuned to every opening and closing of her door, to her nightly walks, and her trips to check the community mailbox. He marked his calendar each time he heard her garage door, found no pattern in her new comings and goings. There were no visitors at Cadie's. And when she did play her guitar, the genres fluctuated between Gaelic, Czech, and something that sounded Eastern Mediterranean—her newest genre infusing contagious vibrancy into the fall evenings. Aleck suspected something had fractioned Cadie's unstable communal provinces, but he had no proof. His gut instinct said it was something social. He couldn't think of any other reason for the randomly chosen and new musical styles it seemed she mastered overnight. The origins of Cadie's fluid progressions were hints that Aleck sought desperately, hammering upon and chipping away at the granite unknown with little headway.

UNAWARE OF HER SPECULATIVE neighbors, Cadie was just as concerned with her journey. Discipline was the only thing that kept her going forward. She searched her psyche for reasons why her mind repeatedly threw up road blocks.

Her mind tried in each instance to force an end to her social exploration. It felt that she had her own interrupt switch, a wiring deep in her subconscious that ran a shutdown command with every new action she tried. With these new people she quite liked, she wanted to make an excuse, any excuse, to cancel meetings or outings. It would have rendered many people depressed, but Cadie refused to give in. She pushed past the kill switch mode each time she left her house to visit with Karl or arrange a cooking lesson with Kamil. She didn't like the fiction of some external programmer controlling her behaviors. When she started a particular command, she expected to carry it through without interference from hijacking, external or internal.

That mental pushback gave Cadie the idea of observing her mind the same way she researched robotics coding. If she could identify the weak code in herself, then she could fix it. And if she applied enough expertise and talent, then she could encrypt herself to withstand future hacker attacks, kill switches, or any general malady that kept her from moving forward.

She attacked the problem by starting at her local bookstore. There, she perused the available neurobiology and neuropsychology books. Halfway through reading the intro to one of the books, her attention diverted.

"Shit, shit. Goddamn!"

The words came from a little boy wearing a batman mask, black cowboy boots paired with khaki shorts, and a T-shirt with a brontosaurus on it. He was cradling a book with a Siamese cat on the cover. The cat sat in a flower pot.

The boy's mother hurried behind him, following from the children's section.

"Tourette's syndrome," she apologized to everyone in the vicinity.

People from nearby sections peeked out into the aisle to see what Tourette's syndrome looked like.

The boy glanced at the book in Cadie's hand. Then he looked at her and smiled. He held up his book so she could see the whole cover. His blue eyes were wide and happy behind the mask.

"You like readin'?" he asked.

Cadie nodded. Her eyes returned the smile.

"Me, too. Whatchoo readin'?"

"About the brain."

"Shit. Goddamn!"

"Dear Jesus in Heaven." A woman's voice came from the Christian aisle that stretched rows beyond the small science section.

He grinned, his eyes sparkling. "I like the brain."

The boy's mother gently touched his shoulder. "Time to go," she said. It sounded more like a plea, anything to get him away from the stares. And she looked like she'd had more of other people than she could take for one day. The boy didn't seem bothered. Again, she mouthed "sorry" to Cadie and walked away.

"Enjoy your book," said Cadie, but the mother and son were too far away to hear her now. They turned at the main aisle and disappeared, heading toward the checkout.

"Shit. Motherf . . . "

The sound was muffled mid-word, presumably by the mother's hand.

"Dear Jesus in Heaven."

The shrill voice also had moved in the direction of checkout.

Cadie looked at the cover of the book in her hands. Observing the folds of the brain, she suddenly had the eerie feeling that she was less stable than her engineered robots.

Me, me, me. That's sinful vanity, girl.

Cadie sighed. She should have known Sister Mary Trea wouldn't stay out of this. The recollection colluded with memories of hundreds of forced confessionals. Cadie pushed away the atavistic guilt and went to pay for her books.

When she left the store, the parking lot echoed with cries of "shit, goddamn!" Several rows away, a street light reflected from batman ears weaving between cars.

AT HOME, CADIE DEPOSITED the books in her office and then left through her front door to go on a walk. She needed a break from the internal arguments with Sister Mary Trea.

Along the dark street, she forced her memory through the steps for making Turkish coffee and walnut boerekas. Occasionally, she altered her footsteps to practice polka and waltz movements, dancing with an imaginary Karl or Frank. Sister Mary Trea grew quiet.

After a few miles, Cadie was back to asking uninterrupted questions about herself and her ideas for work. Her mind toyed at the edge of an engineering breakthrough as she approached her house. The idea was blown from grasp when, from the sidewalk, she spotted a pink box sitting on her doormat.

Cadie curiously approached her front door, certain the box hadn't been there when she left. Surely, she hadn't been *that* preoccupied. She wondered who had been certain she'd find the box before the contents spoiled.

She bent down and picked up the container. Smells of thick sweetness came back up with her. *Pastries.* Cadie scanned the street and saw no one. She unlocked her door and went inside.

+ + +

THE UNASSUMING ALFASI HOUSE stood at the cul-de-sac end of a short street. Cadie sat for a minute in her car and looked at the building. Unlike the other complex structure with brick facades, this one was a simple backwards "L" paneled with dark wood. Few windows were visible at the front. A path hidden by layers of trees and shrubs wound from the driveway toward a front entrance on the short side of the house. She knew better than to think that unassuming meant plain. Unassuming could be anything: grand, reserved, even scary.

She got out of her car and made her way to the entrance. Before ringing the doorbell, she touched the bright yellow leaves on a coral bark maple planted within reach. Nailed at a slight forward angle on the right doorframe was a small rectangular box. Cadie reached up and touched the turquoise casing painted with flowers.

The door opened.

"Cadie, you're here."

The trim, grandmotherly woman on the other side of the door stepped forward and grabbed her hand.

"I'm Ayala Alfasi. Ayala. Come in, come in."

Ayala put her arm around Cadie's shoulder and guided her inside. She took Cadie's thin jacket and dispatched with it down a corridor leading away from the two-story room. Cadie stood where she was and waited.

It was hard to believe she was inside a house. The front door had opened to a private gardenscape separated from the room by thick-paned, floor-to-ceiling windows. November light, filtered by live oaks covered with Spanish moss, streamed everywhere into the abode. Aiding the natural sunlight were intricately placed backlights integrated into the house's structure. The inner walls sported a private exhibition of hand-blown glass art, wavy vessels that mimicked blossoms open on the stem. Glass was ubiquitous—affixed to walls, on shelves, on tables. Light reflected from the pieces, sending arrays of rainbows into the air and migrating from one intense spectrum to another. Scattered amid the glass was a collection of several dozen branched, tree-like structures. Cadie recognized them as Hanukkah menorahs. The metal pieces seemed to come alive, twisting and crawling through the vibrant glass translucence.

For a moment, Cadie forgot her nervousness. In the harmony of light and color, she felt that she had become part of a great coral reef, was somehow underwater and looking out to the trees and plants of the air world. She barely noticed that Ayala had returned and was talking to her, but the flourish of gesticulation by the woman caught Cadie's attention.

" . . . to meet Yosef," finished the woman, pointing to the other side of the property.

Cadie nodded and followed Ayala through the great room and the connecting open kitchen.

On the stone-floored kitchen verandah, Yosef Alfasi stood at a propane grill under a cedar arbor carved to mimic grape trunks and vines. Opposite him was an open fire oven built into a stone shelf. The arbor connected to the tall chimney above the pit. Real grapevines climbed the arbor next to the chimney, crawled out, and tangled with the carved vines. Beyond Yosef was a large rectangular swimming pool, the water quiet, surrounded by small fruit trees in large pots.

Through double doors opened onto the verandah, Ayala led Cadie. "Yosef. She is here. Are you deaf?"

Yosef Alfasi looked up. He was used to his wife's talking. She talked whether people were around or not. Over the years, it had become background noise. He often let it fade among his own thoughts.

"You hear me, Yosef?"

Yosef dropped the wire brush he was using to clean the grill.

"Welcome, welcome," he said.

He shook Cadie's hand, following the shake with a warm hug that pinned Cadie's arms to her sides.

"He's like that," said Ayala. "Hugs everybody."

"What's not to hug?" winked Yosef. "You find us okay?"

"She's here, isn't she?" Ayala pointed at Cadie with an open hand.

It was another comment that faded unanswered. Yosef continued talking to Cadie.

"Let's have a *boi kallah* before I go for prayers and Ayala commissions you in the kitchen."

Yosef placed his hand on Cadie's shoulder and guided her back inside. It was the first chance she'd had to speak since meeting the Alfasis.

"A boi kallah?"

"A pre-Shabbat snack. You'll like it," said Ayala.

Yosef gestured at the glassware. "How do you find my art?"

"You made these?"

"Each and every one," he said, pointing at different objects. "Wall plates, color optic bowls, silver fluted bowls and vases, Swedish vessels. This art is an old family tradition."

"They are fantastic." Cadie took more time to look at the pieces from the new angle.

Yosef sensed there was something about the way Cadie said "fantastic." That she reserved the word for when it was really meant. Not like the way people said, "I love cappuccinos," or "I love pictures of giraffes." Affairs of the heart were great and complex. Descriptions of any kind, Yosef felt, required appropriate applications. A favorite thing, like a movie, wasn't love. The fantastic was more than mundane, more than two-dimensional. His art, above anything else, abandoned two-dimensional in color, form, and sense, and Cadie could see that.

"Tradition or no tradition, you'd better pour the *mahia* or you won't make it to prayers," broke Ayala's voice into his thoughts. She didn't look aside from removing a bowl of washed red radishes and a loaf cake from the refrigerator.

Yosef chuckled and pulled a blue wine bottle from a built-in wet bar. "Of course, my love." He lifted the bottle for Cadie to see the clear liquid contents. "This, mahia, is also called *arak*."

From the cabinet, Yosef took three small glasses, similar to Turkish tea glasses, and handed them to Cadie.

"You fill those with ice. I'll prepare the good stuff," he instructed, his tan darkening in the deep smile lines around his eyes.

Ayala paused from slicing the cake and pointed her knife at the ice dispenser in the freezer door. "There's the ice, dear."

Into a vessel that Cadie could now identify as an ibrik, Yosef mixed the arak into water.

AYALA TOOK THE RADISH and cake outside, and set the food on a low and brightly tiled table near an open fireplace built into a verandah wall. Cadie and Yosef joined her, each taking a separate chaise lounge.

"Watch this," said Yosef.

He made sure he had Cadie's attention and then poured the drinks. The liquid turned a milky white when it hit the ice.

"What makes it do that?"

"Emulsion of the anise oil," said Yosef. He pushed a glass toward Cadie and handed one to Ayala.

Ayala raised her glass and motioned for Cadie to do the same. "This helps calm our rushing after a long week."

Yosef raised his drink and muttered a fusion of Spanish and Hebrew words.

"To freedom," said Ayala before drinking.

"To freedom," answered Yosef.

They both took hearty sips but kept their eyes on Cadie.

Cadie reacted to the liquor with a faint smile.

Yosef nodded, happy to have pleased.

"Licorice," said Cadie. The taste was similar to that of the Finnish anise cookie. "Does that flavor come from the anise?" she asked.

"Exactly," said Yosef. "Now let's have cake."

"It is honey cake left over from Rosh Hashanah, our Jewish New Year. We also like to have it for Moroccan Independence Day."

Ayala put a slice in Cadie's hand.

"Here's to freedom," she said again.

"To freedom," said Cadie.

After a bite of the cake, Cadie followed Ayala's move and tried one of the red globe radishes. Like the honey cake had, the spicy, subtly sweet vegetable suited the drink. Cadie instantly appreciated the versatility of licorice beyond the gummy, twizzled sticks found in candy aisles. With help from the drink, she started to relax. She was glad now that she'd accepted the early afternoon invite.

As Ayala talked, the trio quickly drained the small glasses.

Yosef motioned toward the house.

"I'll mix the liquor. You mind bringing three more glasses, Cadie? More in the cabinet."

Glad to have something to do, Cadie went on her small errand. She brought back the glasses filled with ice and set them on the table.

Silence fell over the trio after another toast. Yosef stretched out his legs on the lounge and stared at the water in the pool. Ayala looked at the river birch canopy and watched the breeze twist the leaves upside down, right side up, sideways. The disordered air swished through large clumping bamboo potted in an industrial drum sunk into the ground and surrounded with ash-gray river stone.

Yosef finished his second glass and got up.

"I'll see you ladies after . . . don't let her push you too hard."

He patted Cadie's shoulder before kissing Ayala goodbye and walking inside.

"You two don't catch the house on fire when you light the candles," he called over his shoulder.

"He thinks he's a comedian," Ayala complained to Cadie. "Let's have another drink before we cook. Do you like cooking?"

THERE HAD NEVER BEEN a stranger in Ayala Alfasi's kitchen. Cadie was no exception. So when Cadie stated she never cooked, and had only recently learned to make walnut boerekas and Turkish coffee, Ayala's shock was visible. As if knocked off balance, the woman's hands and arms flew up in visceral response and then grabbed the side of the lounge chair.

"You cannot *feel* if you cannot cook, my dear."

Less worried about the etiquette of changing out used glasses for clean ones, Ayala poured more arak, filling the glasses to the brim.

She took a sip and then grabbed Cadie's free hands. "We begin lessons today."

They had just crossed the threshold into the kitchen when Ayala raced back to collect a large ceramic bowl on the stone bench by the open fireplace. The small woman whisked up the container covered with a damp dish towel, balanced it on her hip, as one would a child, and rejoined Cadie in the kitchen. From another waiting bowl, Ayala sprinkled flour over the red granite countertop. Then she removed the dish towel, revealing a great mound of sticky dough, and dumped the mass onto the counter.

"Wash your hands, dear," she told Cadie. "This is where we continue with the *challa*."

Cadie did as told. When her hands were dry, Ayala pushed a bowl of shortening toward Cadie.

"Dab your fingers into this and we'll start."

Cadie looked blankly at the grease in the can. What was she supposed to do with shortening?

"Trust me," laughed Ayala. "In cooking, things can be messy. Even messy, though, is sensual."

She moved to Cadie's side, took a dollop, and rubbed the shortening onto Cadie's fingers. With Cadie's hand under hers, Ayala demonstrated how to knead the sticky dough. She let go when Cadie's movements fell in tune.

"That's it. Continue for another ten minutes or so. You can watch the dish I start now."

The woman opened a jar of preserved, whole kumquats layered with lemon slices, all as brilliantly orange and yellow as day one of preservation. The fruits' vinegary smell escaped from the container. Ayala talked about everything—how to preserve kumquats, how her mother had done the same, how her grandmother had taught her beautiful preserves making.

When the dough under Cadie's hands began to change, Cadie focused her attention on her task. Every few moments, she stopped kneading and watched the dough swell outward. She poked her fingers into the soft mass and wiggled them to feel the warm center. She liked the dough's chameleon quality, its surface alternately shiny then dull before transforming into smooth and strong consistency that no longer stuck to her fingers.

Noticing Cadie's engrossed motion as she layered fish fillets and tomato slices over thinly sliced potatoes in a casserole dish, Ayala interrupted her own talking with a new thought.

"Cooking is everything . . . loneliness, solitude, sometimes tragedy. It is hope and longing . . . love. I can see you are a natural."

She didn't know why, but when Ayala mentioned hope, Aleck's face flashed into Cadie's thoughts. To cover the blush creeping over her, she pointed at the dough.

"What now?"

Ayala didn't notice Cadie's discomfort.

"Now we take a little portion away before dividing the rest into twelfths to make two, six-strand braided loaves." Ayala intricately demonstrated and tenderly braided the first loaf. "We love in the little details. Now you try."

Placing her braided loaf beside the other to go through a "second rise," Cadie apprenticed herself to Ayala's extensive dinner preparations. She could see now why a little pre-Shabbat snack, especially the arak, was of traditional importance. Cooking was laborious.

IN LESS THAN TWO HOURS, Ayala led Cadie through preparations for fish fillets "Fez-style" and a brothy vegetable soup of sea bass and leeks. They blended hummus and shaved fennel for the fresh fennel salad. After tasting the mildly sweet plant, Cadie was amazed over how many vegetable variations exhibited licorice scents and flavor.

Ayala showed her how to fry eggplant and season Shabbat meatballs with a homemade Moroccan spice blend. After steaming the meatballs in a mix of celery sticks and saffron water, Cadie skewered the scented meat to finish browning on the heated outside grill. She filled dates with almond paste while Ayala made almond-walnut macaroons. Following Ayala's instruction to taste as she cooked, Cadie learned how to extract the taste of each spice from the sweet aromatic background, from the soft fennel to the sharp notes of cinnamon and saffron. Best of all was the scent she couldn't taste, the rising perfume of challa loaves brushed with egg wash and covered with sesame seeds. Cadie suspected that it might compare to the Finnish pulla.

While they worked, Ayala talked and talked and talked.

WHEN DINNER WAS NEARLY ready, Ayala led Cadie to the formal dining room catty-corner to the kitchen and overlooking the pool. A pair of large candelabras sat atop the long rectangular table surrounded by Frank Lloyd Wright-designed chairs built with the same warm-toned wood as the house.

A silver matchbox case engraved with bees and a honeycomb sat nearby. Ayala lit a match and then the candles. Moments after waving her arms around the fledgling candlelight and saying a quick blessing, Yosef returned.

He walked in with a hearty "Shabbat Shalom" and immediately kissed his wife. Then the pair converged on Cadie with hugs. "Shabbat Shalom" in stereo.

Cadie wondered if the coincidental symbol of summoning Ayala's spouse happened in the same manner every Friday evening.

Walking to a wall of the dining room and sliding aside a panel to reveal a hidden wine cabinet and sideboard, Yosef pulled a random bottle from a rack.

"Yosef, get the wine," said Ayala with her back to him as she hurried to the kitchen. There, she slipped the baked challa loaves onto a wooden platter and covered them with a heavily embroidered cloth.

"She says the same thing every week. Every week, I already have my hands on the bottle," said Yosef, holding up the bottle.

"I heard that."

"She hears everything, too," winked Yosef.

He uncorked the wine, poured it, and quickly said a blessing. After a drink, he blessed the challa.

Imitating her hosts, Cadie dipped her piece of torn bread into the salt well before biting into the lightly sweetened and chewy bread. The challa, slightly less sweet and without the cardamom, tasted similar to pulla, though without the buttery consistency.

"Cadie grew up in an orphanage—she's an orphan," said Ayala to Yosef as she spooned the Fez-style fillets onto plates. She turned to Cadie. "We always start with fish," she said.

Startled for the umpteenth time at the Alfasis comfort and immediate familiarity with her, Cadie supposed Yosef and Ayala quickly disabused any guests of social reticence, even if it took shock to knock the person out of a rut.

"She's not an orphan anymore," said Yosef. He carefully forked up a piece of fish, keeping the fruit and vegetable layering intact, and took a bite.

"They treat you well at that orphanage?" he asked.

"It's closed now."

"We'll treat you well here," he said, topping off the wine glasses.

Ayala removed the fish plates from the table and returned with the soup.

"Yosef's family was orphaned once, except they lost their country. Escaped from Seville, Spain to Fez before the 1391 massacre."

Cadie nearly choked on the sweet broth in her mouth. She calculated that Yosef knew over six hundred twenty years, maybe longer, of his family's history. It was unfathomable compared to her history. Her tree started with an ancient, rooted genome and ended with her, the tips of new leaves. Nothing in between.

"My family met his in Fez," continued Ayala. "That was before we, the Fez Jews, were all expulsed to the Rabat *mellah*, the Jewish quarter, on the coast," added Ayala. "That's how we became orphans of Fez. After the war, our parents immigrated to Israel. But Yosef and I, just married, came to America." She looked lovingly at her husband. "We were eighteen, have lived in Texas since. The warm weather suits us, feels like home. I can grow my lemons and kumquats around the pool, and Yosef's glassblowing trade thrives here."

"But you celebrate Moroccan Independence?" asked Cadie.

"Why not? It was our home for hundreds of years. Much longer than here," said Ayala.

"It's something to celebrate," said Yosef, raising his glass for a toast. "Independence for all. Salud."

They all drank.

After hummus and salad, Ayala brought the fried eggplant. She left again and returned with the meatball kebabs resting over sautéed chard and the braised celery sticks. Yosef cut more challa.

"Do you always do a big meal for Moroccan Independence?" asked Cadie.

Yosef chuckled. "You tell her, Ayala."

Ayala laughed. "I cook a big Friday meal every week, but on Moroccan Independence, we eat *honey* cake with the boi kallah instead of *regular* cake."

Tired from helping peripherally, Cadie couldn't imagine how the eighty-year-old woman managed that kind of weekly cooking.

Ayala sensed Cadie's confusion. "Life must be celebrated."

Cadie managed a mild smile. *That* was an idea she liked.

"Smiles give appetites," Ayala said, placing an extra kebab skewer on Cadie's plate.

Grinning and nodding appreciatively, Yosef spread preserved lemon relish over a meatball before taking a contented bite and chewing slowly.

+ + +

CADIE ARRIVED HOME AND FOUND that her garage door transmitter wouldn't work when she punched the button. Next, she tried the keyed entry pad. Its batteries were also defunct. She mumbled about the odds and tried the numbers again. Nothing.

Pacing in her driveway, Cadie pondered what to do next. With the keyless security locks at her front and back doors fastened, there was no other door entry. It was nearly midnight, and she was overly full and tired from dining with the Alfasis. No, now the best she could manage was to take a walk and hope the fresh air would give her an idea about how to get into her house. Cadie turned off her car and shoved her keys into her pocket. She took off her shoes and carried them with her.

At a dark place along the sidewalk where a towering mugo pine cast deeper shadows over the pavement, Cadie remembered she'd left her office windows cracked open. She turned around. The humming street lights reminded her of her next problem.

How am I going to get over a ten-foot-tall fence?

She turned around and continued her walk. Calling a handyman or the police to her home at midnight was out of the question. She was too tired to think of driving to the nearest stop-n-go and buying a pack of AA batteries. Exhaustion, even among the brilliant, has a way of eroding the mind.

Instead, she slipped her feet back into her sandals and resigned herself to knocking on a neighbor's door. She would have to ask for help with a ladder if she wanted to avoid sleeping in her car. *But who?* She saw Mrs. Beauregard's living room lights glowing, punctuated by flashes of bright blue light from a television.

Definitely not. Mrs. Beauregard would tell everyone on the street. The other houses were dark, except for one. Cadie closed her eyes, opened them and saw again the faint light coming from inside

Aleck's house. With Mrs. Beauregard as the only other alternative, she had to take the risk. Besides, Aleck was more likely to have a ladder. Her decision made, she walked resolutely to his door.

AFTER SOFTLY KNOCKING, Cadie's nervousness changed to worry. Maybe he wasn't home. She rang the doorbell. Another minute passed. She pressed her ear against the solid wood panel to listen for movement. The knob turned, and she stumbled back. But not before Aleck opened the door.

Aleck rubbed his eyes. "Were you listening at my door?" His grin, meant to belie interrogation, was lost on Cadie.

"I . . . I," she said, pointing toward her house. "My garage door is . . . I'm locked out."

She averted her gaze past Aleck's head and waited for his response, guessing he was still too asleep to remember that he wore navy blue pajama bottoms covered with red geckos.

Without offering a solution or inquiring further, Aleck stepped back, made a path for her to enter. "Come in, Cadie."

Gauging that it'd be harder for Mrs. Beauregard to hear, Cadie stepped inside the house.

"I think my office windows are open. If I could get a ladder to get over my fence . . . "

"Coffee? I need some." Aleck closed the door and walked into his kitchen. "Please," he said, motioning her into the living room.

He prepared the coffee maker and watched Cadie move toward his music wall, smiling to himself when he noticed her sideways glance at him after she saw what treasure was before her. Aleck pretended not to notice her contained surprise at the floor-to-ceiling built-ins constructed to accommodate his extensive records and CD collection. Even with instant downloads available, he still liked to collect the discs' plastic art cases.

"There are thousands," said Cadie without looking away from the music.

Nodding, Aleck kept quiet to avoid interrupting her curiosity.

She climbed the first few rungs of the wall's access ladder and pulled out a few CDs to read the title listings.

Aleck watched, wondering what had kept her out so late in dark gray wool trousers and black, strappy high-heel sandals. The slate-blue silk shirt she wore billowed slightly each time she adjusted her balance. When she climbed down, Aleck's gaze went from her carefully manicured toenails, brushed with clear polish, to the lean lines of her arm muscles. He hoped that she'd been to a late office meeting rather than on a date, though a date didn't make sense for a person who barely talked.

When her feet hit the floor, Cadie took the cup of coffee Aleck offered. "Do you play?" she asked.

Aleck smiled. "No. I appreciate—music is one of my great loves."

Cadie wondered how many great loves a person could have, and then remembered why she was there. "Do you have a ladder? I need to climb over my fence."

Of course she needed a ladder.

"I do," he laughed.

He set his cup on the counter and shoved his feet into a pair of leather slippers before going into his garage.

Cadie followed him. "Can we take it through the front door?" She pointed toward Mrs. Beauregard's house.

Understanding, Aleck laughed again. "You bet. We wouldn't want to rouse that."

Taking her coffee with her, Cadie left him and went to her front yard, where she waited for Aleck. Aleck came out a few minutes later and quietly rested the ladder against Cadie's fence.

"You'd better let me crawl over . . . that's a long jump."

Cadie didn't argue with Aleck. The last thing she wanted was to wake Mrs. Beauregard. "If you could just unlock the front door for me once you get in."

Aleck quietly climbed the ladder and dropped himself softly into her backyard. Two, three minutes passed before Cadie heard the lock release on her front door. She ran around her house and up onto her porch. Aleck opened the door to let her in.

"Do you need help with your ladder?" She moved around Aleck to take the doorknob and handed her empty coffee cup to him.

"No. I got it, Cadie." Aleck took the cup and stepped back onto her porch. "I'll be quiet with it," he promised. "You ought to leave your car in the driveway tonight—in case you need to get out tomorrow for batteries." He grinned mischievously.

Cadie blushed. Now she thought of how much simpler it would have been to retrieve batteries. "I . . . I will. Thank you," she said.

"You're very welcome. My pleasure . . . anytime."

"Good night, Aleck."

"Night, Cadie."

As he left her porch, Aleck imagined he saw a slight smile on Cadie's face when she closed her door.

Beatrice, still awake, thought she heard something a couple of houses away—talking, a neighbor's door closing. When she heard metal clicking noises near the alley, she got up from watching her favorite made-for-TV movie and walked outside in her slippers and bathrobe. Everything was deathly serene in the alley. She heard a few more metal clicks from Aleck's garage, and then it was quiet.

"Bachelors," she said into the night. She plodded back to her show.

Aleck, distracted by the brief entry into a shadow of Cadie's life, was now unable to sleep. He settled onto his couch and thoughtfully retraced his walk through her dark house. He had touched the over-stuffed chair nearest the window seat that he'd crawled over to get inside, walked through the office where she worked daily, and passed through the kitchen where the French coffee press, silhouetted by the stove's clock light, was the only thing visible on the bare counters. He rubbed his shin. A bruise formed where he'd walked into the rowing machine near Cadie's living room couch.

Laughing aloud at absurdity brought on by fancy, he briefly contemplated stealing batteries from her garage keypad . . . anything to be in her house again. Growing drowsy, he resigned himself to memories of the night's fleeting but double rewards—once when Cadie was in his living room, a second time when he was in hers.

CHAPTER NINE

CADIE ARRIVED AT THE CELEBIS' home early on Thanksgiving Day. It was her third visit, and she didn't feel any less nervous. A deep-inside rumbling attached to old fears of being thrown away, of someone learning that she wasn't good enough to keep and leaving her at a doorstep plagued her. At a house across the street, the blinds separated and closed.

Along with the rustle of a dead leaf blowing end over end past a gray cat sitting at the edge of the yard, the portent sound of Sister Mary Trea brushed in Cadie's ear.

You're playing with fire.

Kamil, wearing a teal *kurti* embroidered with gold metallic flowers, answered the door before further haunting words came.

Cadie stared. Something was different about Kamil.

Kamil pointed to her cheeks and her modestly obscured hips.

"Ramadan weight gone," she said, welcoming Cadie inside with a hug. "I gain from eating so late and drinking no water during the day. You would think opposite."

Cadie nodded.

"Are you excited to stuff turkey?" The edginess in Kamil's smile was overshadowed by what Cadie knew was warm hospitality.

Already the house smelled of baking boerekas—maybe a fail-safe plan if Cadie ruined the turkey.

"I'm ready," said Cadie, suspecting her own smile looked just as nervous.

"Let us go to the kitchen, then. We'll have tea first."

At the stove, Kamil gave Cadie full reign of the tea making. Cadie took to it like a pro.

"I'll get the cups and the walnut boerekas," said Kamil with a straight-faced wink.

Without verbalization or a smile, Cadie's mien at "walnut boer-ekas" let Kamil know that the girl was delighted.

AFTER TWO CUPS OF TEA and a third to drink while they worked, Kamil showed Cadie how to stuff a green apple into the turkey's neck cavity.

"Where is Basir?"

Kamil patted the skin of the great bird before sliding it into the oven.

"He went to find burfi. You addicted him. He said the confection will be good with turkey."

Dicing the turkey liver, heart, and gizzard, Cadie wondered if she should feel guilty over "addicting" someone. Kamil melted butter in two different sauté pans. She took the diced meat and threw it into one of the pans.

Into Cadie's hands, she placed a bowl with pine nuts and rice. "You sauté these," she instructed.

Cadie dumped the contents into the hot butter and stirred.

"Where in Turkey did you grow up?"

During her first meeting with the Celebis, Basir had expounded on being a Muslim. At the second meeting, Kamil and Cadie had only discussed cooking.

Kamil stopped stirring the meat and looked at Cadie's progress.

"Near Gördes. It is famous for the Turkish carpet. Now add the currants and vegetable stock. The stock is from the boiled turkey neck."

Cadie tossed in the dried fruit and added the stock last.

"Is that where you learned to make your carpets?"

"Yes. Gördes is where my family has woven carpets for hundreds of years."

Another person with a long and known genealogy, thought Cadie. "Does all of your family live near Gördes?"

Moving the sauté pan off the burner, Kamil looked away from Cadie and took a sip of her tea.

"Only my parents now. My other family lives in southeast Turkey. It is a place many ignore."

She dumped the meats into the rice and currant mixture.

"In an hour, we'll stuff this into, how it's called . . . the bird. Let's go to the weaving room."

KAMIL LED CADIE FROM the kitchen to a room facing east. Light flooded through three sets of French doors that opened to a courtyard cut off from the rest of the property by the walls of the house. Except for an inner garage door, which allowed utility access, the encompassment was accessible only by glass doors of interior rooms. The effect was similar to looking inside a greenhouse without a ceiling. Cadie walked to the threshold and looked at the shrubs planted among the marble pavers and white crushed stone.

After a breath of fresh air, Cadie turned to survey the room. Intricately woven carpets covered the walls and cast a pink glow from the many red threads in each pattern. In one corner were more carpets, rolled and standing on end. Angled for Kamil to work with a view of her garden, a large loom sat in the room's center. Cadie walked to a wall and touched the thick pile on a turquoise and red carpet.

"That is the Gördes knot—the Turkish knot," said Kamil. "Come."

She sat down at the loom and picked up a bullet-shaped wood piece about twelve inches long.

"What is that?"

"The shuttle," said Kamil, showing Cadie how it worked. She finished the last "weft" thread that ran horizontally and then began forming knots around the vertical, "warp" threads.

"This knot existed before the town Gördes was named. Turkish people and Gördes knots are the same—all woven together."

Kamil folded a hand-dyed thread around two warp threads and pulled it back through the center to make the knot. It reminded Cadie of cellular invagination.

"We are Turks no matter the distance or time we travel," continued Kamil. "The Gördes knot makes the carpet stronger, because it loops to both sides and pulls strong in the middle. Like Turks."

Kamil and Cadie both jumped when Basir interrupted.

"Our identity is strong," he said, moving from where he leaned against the door frame. "The mysterious finished carpet hides the underlying knot, but it is always beautiful. Always useful."

He kissed the top of Kamil's head.

She blushed and went back to work on the carpet.

"We Turks go back thousands of years," said Kamil.

"But," said Basir, "Sometimes Kamil and I ask ourselves what makes us Turks. What if a hundred years ago we had Armenian blood in the family? How would we know? Our compatriots would find it taboo that we ask this. But we ask. The question cannot make us any less Turkish."

"Maybe to ask in private is not enough," murmured Kamil.

"It never is. Who doesn't restrict the weave of their psyche to protect their skin?"

Kamil blushed again but didn't stop weaving.

Cadie felt that the conversation between the couple had taken an intimate turn. She watched Kamil weave. After several more knots, Kamil pointed to the forming pattern.

"The *gul*," she said. "It is a tribe's identifying mark. In a handwoven rug, the repeating flowers are never identical. Sometimes they look it, but they are never identical."

Cadie looked at the flower forming among the threads, observing that each carpet was simply another product bound by continuing columns and rows. Similar to the empty rows and columns of a tabular spreadsheet, there was nothing creative about the rug until data filled it. From one weaver to the next, carpets were but the knots that made them. The patterns housed each rug's beauty in those rigid skeletal boundaries—each design unique despite the striking similarities to carpets woven over tens of thousands of years.

"Are these the gul of your family?" Cadie asked Kamil.

"No—Basir's gul," answered Kamil. She stood and left the room without excuse.

Cadie looked at the hanging and rolled carpets, all of the gul like the one on the loom. Where was Kamil's family?

Cadie turned to Basir, who guessed her thoughts. He shrugged his shoulders and held both hands face up before his chest.

"It is the way it must be . . . can explain later. Go to her now."

He turned on heel and left the room toward a darker part of the house away from the kitchen.

CADIE FOUND KAMIL stuffing the rice mixture in the turkey's cavity. She set more green apples in the roaster around the turkey.

"You will like this—it's not like American bread stuffing."

"Never had homemade stuffing. They had only the boxed kind at the orphanage."

"Not good," said Kamil. She washed her hands, re-covered the turkey with foil and returned it to the oven. "Early or not, let's have coffee," she said, taking down the ibrik from the hanging pot rack.

Cadie was unable to think about cooking. "Why only Basir's gul on your carpets?"

Swiping at sweat beads forming on her brow, Kamil accidentally loosened the silk scarf covering her head. She quickly adjusted it, kept a watchful eye on the cooking coffee.

"I thought I smelled coffee," said Basir, walking into the kitchen. He was smiling.

"Cadie wants to know about your gul, Basir." She didn't look at her husband.

Basir took the plate of walnut boerekas from the counter and walked it to the table. "We will tell her."

"But . . . ," interjected Kamil.

"It is safe, Kamil. Cadie can understand. She also is an orphan."

WHEN THEY SAT WITH their coffee, Basir continued. "Kamil cannot weave her gul, because a gul is a name, first and last, and a place. It identifies her as your driver's license identifies you as Cadie Walsh. Kamil's name and gul must be hidden, never again said or seen the rest of her life. They, especially the gul, would give away her identity and location."

Cadie sat in rapt attention, wondered how many more orphans could be in the world.

Basir continued with the story of Kamil's family, the fundamental Islam they practiced in the midst of modern and secular Turkey.

"At twenty years old, Kamil joined her uncle on a trip to sell carpets in America. Behind a thin curtain on a New York street bazaar stand, she was raped by her uncle's oldest nephew and his two friends."

Kamil took a deep breath but didn't say anything. Her face was steel-set and grim.

"A woman, an American, buying beads at the next stand witnessed the men leave Kamil lying in the street. She watched them walk to another stand several yards away to have tea with Kamil's uncle. The woman knew the right moment to grab Kamil and pull her through the crowd. She took Kamil to the nearest hospital. I was the medical student on staff in the emergency room that day."

"When we walked in," continued Kamil, "the lady told me to say I was an orphan. She walked straight to Basir, told him I had no family, to put me in the nearest shelter. Then the woman left me there, said my name was Jane Doe."

"Kamil did not follow the woman's instructions," continued Basir. "She told me the truth, other than her name. I think it was shock, the moment she confided to me. She begged that I not return her to her uncle or family—a brave but very dangerous request. How was she to know I was a man of reason?"

"I saw you were born in America," said Kamil.

Basir smiled. Kamil got up and came back with more coffee.

"Kamil refused to report the rape. I agreed to hide her."

"I couldn't return to Turkey."

"There, she would disappear, like her sister, who disappeared after fleeing an arranged marriage, never reached Gördes."

"Basir secreted me to Texas, to his parents."

"Kamil's uncle came looking for her at the hospital. There was no rape victim admitted by the name he gave. The front desk attendant mistakenly told him a Jane Doe, a different Jane Doe, had died earlier in the day, complications from rape."

"By the time he was cleared to view the body, I was . . . how do you say it . . . long gone."

"We presented her to neighbors as my wife, then went about making her new first and last name official. We married in a private ceremony. Twice a year I visited her during her breaks from studying textiles in college courses paid for by my parents. Each time I reminded her that she was a free woman, could divorce me."

"I refused."

"I finished school and started my medical fellowship in Texas. We lived together then, as flat mates, not husband and wife. The time came that she could stay in America on her own."

"I stayed."

In Kamil's eyes was contentment, happiness over her decision.

"It was another two years before she invited me to her bedroom."

"Our bedroom now," corrected Kamil.

Basir looked at his wife and smiled. "It will always be yours."

Cadie looked at the grounds settled at the bottom of her cup. Basir cleared his throat.

"Only after that did Kamil use my gul as her own and place a name in her carpets to sell."

"The gul were muddy flowers before that, nameless."

"Her carpets now travel the world, but Kamil is orphaned by hatred," finished Basir.

Kamil got up and started another pot. "I was adopted by Basir's family. Only their gul is family for me now."

Basir looked at his wife. His smile had grown to one of sadness. "Still, I cannot convince you to remove the scarf. You did not wear it in Turkey. Why here?"

"You know why . . . "

"*Why* is hard to understand, even for me. You wear old ideas as a shield." Basir turned to Cadie. "I believe in Allah, but I alone am responsible for my morality. Kamil should feel the comfort I feel."

"Not everyone feels as you do," said Kamil.

"Everyone should," urged Basir. "There will always be a scar. You cannot help but be as beautiful as the day we met. Why let it torture you, that you must punish yourself with it?"

Kamil kept silent.

Biting into a walnut boereka, Basir got up and left the kitchen.

After he left the room, Kamil turned to Cadie. "What does he know? He's never been attacked for smiling at someone while trying to sell a carpet."

If Cadie hadn't been an orphan, she might have seen herself as a daughter caught between parents arguing. Instead, she looked down, hoping to read an answer in the coffee grounds. They presented another question.

Was Kamil's assault the reason for her awkward smiles?

Cadie got up and peered into the oven at the browning turkey.

If that was the case, Basir's gul in Kamil's carpets was quite different than she'd first assumed. In any case, Cadie couldn't answer the question. The afternoon, strangely enough, had left her feeling less alone. Based on complaints she'd overheard during holiday office parties, the emotional day was turning out to have the ups and downs of a real, honest-to-goodness, family holiday.

Happy Thanksgiving, Cadie.

+ + +

THE DAY AFTER THANKSGIVING, Cadie earnestly tackled her books about the human brain, keeping Kamil in mind as she read. It wasn't long before she learned about the plasticity the brain could incur during a traumatic event, how the brain wired itself to re-express the trauma. Not exactly the trauma itself, but symptoms, behaviors, of the trauma. Cadie felt better about inferring that Kamil's trauma *was* bound in memories from, or leading up to, her attack. The smiles, Kamil's quivering smiles.

How often could the brain enter the plastic state, make a U-turn?

She thought about the "IF/THEN" functions she used to code her robots. Was it possible to set a new "if" in the brain to change its wiring? And could a new batch of conditional processing allow Kamil a true smile again? The conjecturing grew into an idea, a potential breakthrough on her secret robotics project.

Tossing aside the book, Cadie went to her computer to browse the Internet. Was it possible that her research on the brain was the hinge to the door of coding high-level AI into her robotics?

"Why didn't I start here?" she asked herself.

Rather than go down paths of self-chiding, she shrugged away the question and set about her research. She felt content, not able to think of a better way to spend the remainder of her holiday weekend.

HUNDREDS OF ALL-BUT-DEAD-END searches later, Cadie knew the tangent she'd taken in her research couldn't be limited to one field of study. The slim pickings she'd found were shrouded by limited access to various university research, costly journals she would have to requisition company money to acquire. She needed past and present copies at that. Only abstracts were available in what she really wanted. After sitting most of the night at the computer, the necessity of direct contact became more and more apparent. At minimum, she needed those biologists, anthropologists, neurologists, and human behaviorists to shed extra light on her hypothesis. *Then*, possibly, she could interpolate the lingering puzzles and fill the missing links, to map the skeleton of new robotic interaction.

She rested from her searches to take a quick trip to the bakery for a coffee and cinnamon roll. Following a short nap after her repast, she continued working, hunting down scientists who could collaborate with her on a new robotics future. Dusk gathered along the skyline of her small forest. Cadie finalized the painstakingly crafted queries asking for copies of published research, confident the broad range of contacts was reason to hope for successful feedback substantial enough to build a prototype.

Optimistic intuiting brought hope that the detailed studies would unveil enough to construct the first basic algorithms. Cadie gave her mind free rein to twist through eddies of possible and impossible, her illumination bordering on euphoric.

IT WAS THAT NEAR EUPHORIA edging on dissociative that caused Cadie to grab the key to the back gate and walk outside. Dissociation was common in those skirting reason and rationality—physically or emotionally. If the person was lucky, the event led to a better place or future state of mind. One could never tell.

Cadie picked up the Adirondack chair, carried it down the path, and set it on the same spot as before, only this time angling it so the seat faced her house rather than the fence. She went back inside and returned with what remained of the morning pastries. She didn't leave a note with them. If it was gratitude for Aleck's help with the ladder, she didn't think about it. She adjusted the small pastry box on the chair and jogged back to her porch. Within moments, she had tuned her guitar.

At the community mailbox in front of his house, Aleck heard the first guitar notes and checked his watch. The afternoon had flown past. He turned to go inside, but hesitated when a black sedan slowly passed him and stopped in front of Cadie's house. Postponing his haste, Aleck flipped through the envelopes, pretending not to notice the tall, older man emerge from the car.

Before closing the door, the man smoothed his thick hair and looked around the neighborhood. Feeling the stranger's gaze linger on him, Aleck looked up. The man smiled and waved. Aleck returned the greeting and watched the man walk up to Cadie's door. About the time Aleck guessed the man that had rung the bell, Cadie started singing.

Today she'll sing only Gaelic songs, thought Aleck. He knew this from her voice and the initial song.

The man returned to the front yard and turned in a circle in an attempt to ascertain the music's origin.

Aleck smiled. Cadie hadn't heard the doorbell. He tucked his mail under his arm, walked quickly inside, and dropped the letters on the counter as he headed to his garage.

When the garage door opened and Aleck saw the unlatched gate, he forgot about the visitor in front of Cadie's house. He looked around for Beatrice and then scooted to the hidden chair to listen to the concert. He picked up the pastry left there and sat down, nodding approvingly at the tall arborvitae, a nicer view than the fence, in his fresh line of sight.

ROOTED TO CADIE'S SIDEWALK, Karl Sikora changed his mind about leaving. It wasn't any live music stopping him. He guessed the music was the reason for the young man's disappearance inside. And he was certain that the voice belonged to Cadie. He walked back to the front porch and sat down on the long bench near Cadie's door. Had he wanted to leave, he couldn't now. The music, like the antique furniture in his building, transported him to ancient memories, lost and irretrievable places where touching Lidice had been real. His memories trickled through the song's currents, year-old grief catching him in the deep rapids of flooded, evocative memory. Karl sank his head against the patio wall behind him and planned to wait until the music stopped.

AFTER A SHORT HOUR, Cadie paused and went inside for a glass of wine. Her neighbors, accustomed to her short breaks, waited.

Karl, on the other hand, stood up and rang the doorbell.

In mid-sip, Cadie heard the door chimes and frowned. Whoever intruded now, it couldn't be Mrs. Beauregard. She never meddled while Cadie played guitar. Curiosity got the better of her and she opened the door.

She stepped back with mild concern on her face when she saw Karl. "Did I forget something on my calendar?"

His grief calmer now, Karl laughed. From his brief acquaintance with Cadie, he'd guessed she was a workaholic, though her musical brilliance had caught him off guard.

"No, my dear. This is called *dropping by*."

"Oh, right." She stood unmoving in the door frame.

Karl knew that he had better go ahead and be out with why he came unannounced.

"I wanted to take you to dinner, had to come into the city today to check on a restaurant."

"Give me two minutes."

Karl laughed again at her unhesitant response. There were few gray areas in Cadie's decision-making.

"Take as much time as you need."

He stepped inside and waited as Cadie padded bare-footed through the house and onto her back porch. When he heard the amp power off, it was Karl's proof that the songs and voice belonged to Cadie. He turned his focus to the austerity of the girls' surroundings. The home looked barely lived in compared to his.

Cadie returned carrying her shoes, balancing herself against the sofa to slip them on. From the foyer closet beside the front door, she retrieved a black clutch and a light jacket. "Ready," she said.

Karl looked at his watch. It'd been exactly two minutes.

Unlike Karl, Aleck was not happy when he heard the amplifier's resonant vibrations cease. He left Cadie's yard without locking the gate and walked into his house. He instinctively felt the end of the concert might have something to do with the black sedan, confirming it was so when he peeked through his front window. Cadie was leaving with the man. The man held open the passenger door of the car; his other hand, on her lower back, guided her into the seat.

Who is that? thought Aleck. And where was Cadie going dressed in jeans and the same black high heels she'd worn the night she'd asked for his help with the ladder?

Disappointed, Aleck let the blind slats fall shut. He returned to Cadie's yard, collected what remained of the pastries she left for him, and locked the gate when he exited. Rapidly waning was Aleck's confidence that spontaneity was not one of Cadie Walsh's defining traits.

CHAPTER TEN

A T BOBBY PULLMAN'S sprawling ranch for the annual company Christmas party, Cadie stood in a corner and watched her coworkers revel after the short workday. A long night of festivities ahead, the same as every year, Cadie saw the party as an infinite loop of personal futility.

Sister Mary Trea would whisper her thoughts about the exorbitant excesses by the host and skimpy moral behaviors of the guests. Bobby would congratulate everyone on another profitable year, followed by cash bonuses to supplement gifts that his assistant Miranda, with a team of her own assistants, wrapped for each and every employee. Afterward, nothing but gaiety, an endless BBQ and *hors d'oeurve* buffet, and a complimentary bar to spread peace on earth.

The party unfolded throughout the rooms. There was dancing in the grand ballroom where a country music band peppered in occasional ballroom tunes. On the verandah, Cadie's more courageous or experimental coworkers rode a mechanical bull surrounded by an air mattress designed to cushion inevitable falls.

Bobby crossed the ballroom and approached Cadie with a small box in his hand. "Here's your box for the year, Cadie girl." He took her wine glass from her and placed the box in her hand. "Open it."

Bobby eyed Cadie's outfit as she opened the box. His parties were always "come as you're comfortable," resulting in varying degrees of dress, from jeans and T-shirts to ballroom gowns. Wearing his usual black T-shirt and cowboy hat, Bobby wondered what had possessed Cadie to arrive in jeans and high heels. He had never seen her in anything but black slacks.

Cadie opened the box top and pushed aside the crepe paper covering the gift. She discreetly smiled, then covered her mouth with a fake cough to stifle what could have become a laugh.

"That there's what they call a wheat chain," he laughed. "The whole thing's platinum."

"Thank you," said Cadie, pulling the necklace from the box. "Where'd you find it?"

"Seemed fitting to have it made—where else ya gonna find a little robot pendant like that."

"Guess so," said Cadie. She handed the empty box to Bobby and then fastened the necklace around her throat, lightly touching the robot's movable arms and legs. Engraved in the center of the robot's belly was an elaborate Irish knot. She covered her mouth again and coughed. "It's a great gift."

"What'd ya git me this year," he teased her. "A new robot?"

Bobby knew that Cadie always had something in the works, new and uncommissioned. Pullman Enterprises would be vacant in a week—mandatory paid vacation time for every employee—but Cadie would be at home working. He had given up trying to stop her, short of taking away her computer.

Cadie blushed at the question. She never revealed anything unless she had a good grasp on the certainty of viability.

"From the look of it, I'd say it's so," laughed Bobby.

"Nothing concrete . . . only an idea," Cadie affirmed. "Still too many holes . . . "

"Of no concern, of course," said Bobby. "Never seen you not climb out of a hole you've fallen in." That was true, for her work made millions for him. Whatever she succeeded in creating, there would be demand for it. And he would sell it.

"So far," said Cadie, looking at the band when an identifiable polka started.

Bobby grinned when he saw her foot tapping. Now *that* was different. He decided to take his chance, depositing the wine glass and empty box on a passing waiter's tray. He cleared his throat.

"Let's take one turn for good luck on that project," he said, fully expecting her to decline the invitation.

To his surprise, Cadie walked with him to the dance floor, though Bobby fully expected that Cadie didn't know how to dance. She barely knew how to converse. But Bobby didn't care if she knew how or not. He was confident in his leading abilities, 'sides, anybody could dance along with a polka.

After several yards into the step patterns, Bobby laughed when he led her in a perfectly completed spin. He was curious if there was no end to Cadie's talents, and where in hell had she learned to dance like that?

WHEN SHE MADE IT HOME at midnight, Cadie opened the envelope containing her bonus, found an additional certificate to the Fredericksburg winery. On a separate note:

"They have two cases of your favorite reserved and waiting for you. Merry Christmas, Cadie girl. Bobby."

Cadie immediately registered online for an overnight hotel stay in Fredericksburg, set the date for December 23. That would give her plenty of time to collect her wine and then drive to Ennis by Christmas Eve. Karl had enchanted her with the idea of an easygoing day and a promised meal. She had readily accepted the invitation, thinking it would be better than being alone. She pushed down the urge to cancel in favor of working on her private project, instead turning her attention to the stack of postal mail on her desk.

On a large and thick envelope, she spotted the return address for the anthropologist she had contacted. The gift was better than any she could have requested. Maybe tonight, she thought, her discovery of the missing link was in grasp. After reading the enclosed journal excerpts, Cadie returned to her books about the human brain.

If she was to engineer a tree of consciousness, a sentience that would allow a robot, self-driven, to lay down pathways for redundant and changing memory, she needed more information. The robot needed a way to attune itself to a person, to feel what the person felt. In the absence of that, Cadie felt there would be no way to acquire memory consistently, no way to achieve positive interaction. She read for a few hours without further insight then returned to her mindless "on the clock" coding. Nagging questions preoccupied her.

How could she learn from the brain's structure and its demonstrated interactions to create an electronic mind? If the genome housed things as innate as mothers, places, and climates from thousands of years before, how could the genome affect interaction? Was there a way she could blend old genomic data and conscious brain thought to make something entirely new? If so, the variables were infinite, like looking for a needle in a haystack.

You have to choose one, Cadie—just one, any trait as the catalyst.

She shoved her keyboard tray under her desk, got up, and walked to her kitchen. Her dogged focus, once again, impeded a breakthrough. She had to stop thinking about it; otherwise, she would never muddle her way past the barrier.

After deciding she was much too wired to sleep, Cadie looked around her kitchen and thought about playing her guitar. She decided against it. And at four o'clock in the morning, it was much too early or late for a walk. She started her water kettle for a pot of coffee, took a sugar cube and sucked on it while she tried to think of a new thing to relax her mind. Before the cube dissolved, she bent over and pressed her forehead against the cold granite counter. She rolled her head to the side. When her cheek mashed between the hard stone and her cheekbone, she remembered kneading the dough with Ayala. Cadie stood up and hurried to her desk, downloaded a recipe for pulla rather than challa—she was in the mood for spice. And perhaps a new medium, one of smell rather than sound, would help quiet her mind.

Cadie took the printed recipe and grabbed her purse and keys. Before she could bake, she needed the ingredients and bakeware.

+ + +

IT WAS DARK WHEN CADIE pulled up outside Karl's downtown building. From the trunk of her car, she grabbed the second pulla loaf she'd made and a bottle from one of the wine cases, and headed into the antique store with her arms full. She rode up the personal elevator. It opened to festive smells floating from Karl's open door. She peeked inside before entering.

"Karl?"

"Here, Cadie."

He waved from behind the open refrigerator door and continued rummaging around shelves packed with produce until he found the mound of homemade butter he wanted.

"Ready for a cribbage match?"

"Yes." She set the bottle on the counter and looked around to see what was cooking. "I brought some wine."

"What else you have there?" He eyed the loaf she cradled. She handed it to him.

"Pulla—I baked it. It's Finnish."

Karl loosened the wrapping around the bread and grinned. "This your first bread?" He sampled a few of the sliced almonds layered evenly on top.

"I guess you can tell."

"No, looks perfect, tastes good. That cardamom I taste?"

"Yes."

"Interesting. Wait 'til you see what's in the oven."

Cadie moved around the bar counter toward the oven. Karl shooed her away.

"No peeking."

To keep her out of the kitchen, he taught her how to lay a proper place setting and then left her to finish the table preparation. After completing her task, Cadie sat down at the blond alder wood table supported by Verona-finished cast stone. She looked around the room. It looked as it usually did. There were no Christmas decorations. It was natural, simple. Relaxed by the absence of material ritual, she felt an odd festivity creep over her.

"Should I open the wine I brought?"

"No—we'll save that for the Christmas morning surprise."

"Surprise?"

"You mustn't ask," winked Karl. From the refrigerator he took a bottle of white wine and motioned for Cadie to uncork it.

As Cadie worked at her task, Karl extracted from the oven a six-strand braided loaf sprinkled with almond slices. Cadie nearly laughed when she saw it, instead only half-smiled. "Pulla?"

"No. *Vánočka*. Maybe not so unlike your pulla. It has raisins inside and is flavored with nutmeg instead of cardamom."

"Like the Alfasis' challa."

Cadie's eyes softly brightened; she was glad she'd confided her other contacts to Karl, though she didn't understand why she'd connected more with him than the other families. She often wondered if it had something to do with her Czech dreams, or if it was that Karl never probed her motivations or beliefs. For that matter, that's how Frank treated her as well.

Karl laughed at Cadie's subtle, nonverbal response. "Not too unlike challa." He grabbed Cadie's hand to pull her from the barstool, quickly kissed her soft palm. "Let's eat, Cadie. I haven't eaten all day."

As they walked to the table, Cadie for the first time compared the various antiques' curves to the clean, crisp lines of the Alfasis' modern house. Even the tureen from which Karl ladled the carp soup was an antique. Other than the kitchen implements, there was nothing modern about the abode.

"Why nothing but antiques, Karl?"

The ladle stopped mid-air. "Now that story is quite a way to start a meal," he said. "Lidice, no doubt, would find it fitting to be told over carp soup and vánočka."

Cadie's heart rate elevated at the prospect of a story.

"THE WORLD ONCE FORGOT the Czech Republic as a country," began Karl, "Most don't even remember we were once Bohemia. There is a forgotten village there . . . for which my Lidice was named. Ask people in America about Lidice and you can see the flame of ignorance draw over them. History is old so quickly, over-written with gusto and few excuses."

Slightly blushing, Cadie admitted to her own ignorance.

"It's okay," forgave Karl. "You've been busy making your history."

They went from soup to salad as Karl told of 1942 Lidice, the village accused of collaborating in the assassination of Hilter's Heydrich, the deputy protector of the Nazi Germany protectorate of Bohemia and Moravia. Following Heydrich's assassination, Hilter ordered the town razed to the ground, all men executed, all women and most of the children transported to a concentration camp. Seven of the children placed with SS families for Germanisation.

"From one hundred and five children taken from the village, only seventeen survived to return home. Eighty-two died at Chelmno," said Karl, eating as he talked.

"The leveling of Lidice was complete, encompassing. Dead were exhumed only to be permanently destroyed. The entire village bulldozed, no trace, *nothing*, left behind. After the war, one hundred fifty-three women had survived Ravensbrück. Lidice's mother was among them."

Karl got up then, signaling for Cadie to bring the dirtied dishes. He pulled a breaded roast carp from the oven and instructed Cadie to get the potato salad.

Back at the table, Cadie bit into a cold potato on which Karl had left the skin. She liked the relish and boiled eggs added with other boiled vegetables and mayo.

Karl continued his story.

"Lidice, her mother's second child, was born in 1950—the year following the rebuilding of Lidice, a tiny new village near the old." He paused and looked around his home. "That is why you see all of the antiques here. Lidice only purchased pieces from Europe. She spent her life trying to resurrect a village that really only survived in her mother."

"What about her father?"

"No, her father was Catholic, from Prague, about thirteen miles away. He survived the war without imprisonment, other than occupation anyway."

"Did Lidice ever go back?"

"Never to her hometown. Many times to Prague and other places in Europe . . . to purchase furniture, art. I went to Lidice the July after *my* Lidice died, got there as the sun was setting behind the trees. Only a few locals were there, walking their dogs or riding their bikes. The smell of a freshly cut field filled the air. I'll never forget it, standing in front of the children's memorial. Eighty-two statues erected and overlooking the mass grave of their fathers and a bit of foundation from a farmer's house unearthed. Uncertainty etched their faces, and there I stood with my certainty, knowledge of what would happen to them and their sister or friend that became my mother-in-law. It was, other than my Lidice herself, the most moving thing I've ever seen."

To Cadie the antiques crammed into the large living space took on a new hue. It had seating enough for survivors of a small village. On the center console waited the cribbage board. Likely in the same spot since Lidice's death, decided Cadie.

"Did Lidice never decorate for Christmas?"

"Not for the decade before her death—before that, only when she felt Catholic."

"Felt Catholic?"

Karl excused himself to the kitchen and started a pot of coffee. Cadie moved the vánočka to the center console and then chose a pair of coffee cups from one of the many stuffed china cabinets. Karl carefully removed a pair of steamed chestnut puddings from the oven and brought them to the table with a plate of gingerbread cookies. They sat down to play cribbage. Cadie shuffled the cards.

"Felt Catholic," he finally affirmed, mixing coffee and preparing their dessert plates. "I got Irish Crème and whiskey for the coffee."

Cadie dealt the first hand, took the crib.

"It took Lidice many years to evolve. She did it all on her own, too. I never pushed one way or the other."

"Evolve from Catholicism?"

"From silence." He took a bite of warm pudding. "Over a grave in a Prague cemetery there is an inscription—'Nations will not perish as long as the language lives.'"

Enrapt, Cadie listened.

"Religion destroys language, purchases patriotism by selling, under pain of death, the saving of language and land held dear. As Lidice evolved away from religion, she found language."

"That's why she stopped decorating for Christmas?"

"Yes."

Karl went to a bookcase that held his collection of old, first-edition science books. From a middle shelf, he pulled a journal and carried it back to the table. He flipped to a memorized page and pointed at an entry.

"She shared this with me nine years before she was diagnosed with cancer."

The black leather of the journal had turned gray and soft where Lidice had often grasped it. It was now velvety smooth in Cadie's hands as she read.

What overwhelming happiness in everyday freedom of thought, to have removed all notions of a concrete or filamented being holding total sway over thought, deed, and speech ad infinitum has left me, for the first time, to truly engage in the morality and ethics innately evolved in the aware human brain. To unshackle the bonds of a tremulous mind has uncovered evolving freedom. 'Til now I think I have been more animal than human, could not engage wholeheartedly in a moment of life without longing for flashes of an infinite beyond, a mean-in-nature and unproven beyond.

How gift-wrapped myths are used on the Aware Person to subjugate, enslave, abuse, rape, kill and demean. An irrational, common-sense-lacking being can never know anything but war if civil justice cannot evolve.

I cannot succumb to the prevalent amnesia that rewrites evident facts of our physical and republic's origins, but I will always admire the gatherings of people who hope for the security of a better tomorrow and distribute equity freely, without threat of sword or death or ruptured mind. In that way, we are the same. But as I engage in philosophy, they engage in prayer.

The light in the room seemed to grow brighter, the words on the page loud in the surrounding town's holiday quietness.

Cadie closed the journal and looked at Karl. "Is this also what you believe?"

"Always have. Many say I'm an evil old dog 'cause of it. Use language outside the confines of religious rules, and people think evil, evil."

"So what does that make Christmas for you?"

Without a pause for thought, Karl raised his glass to Cadie.

"This year it's simply a day on which neither of us is alone."

Unable to agree more or say anything better, Cadie raised her glass. "Na Zdravi, Karl," she toasted.

"Na Zdravi, Cadie."

After a hearty sip, Karl whisked the dishes off the table.

"I'll clean up," he said. "Off to bed with you. Your surprise is seeing what Lidice did to incorporate our old Bohemian tradition into her new life."

+ + +

"CADIE?" WHISPERED KARL.

A gentle shake on her shoulder roused Cadie to the lambency of a street light facing the guest bedroom in the old building. Karl, already dressed, stood beside her bed.

Confused, Cadie rubbed her eyes. *Surely* she hadn't been asleep for more than an hour.

"It's surprise time. Grab your jacket—we'll be walking." Karl moved to the door. "I'll wait for you downstairs."

Rising quickly, Cadie pulled on her jeans and T-shirt. There was more to Karl's invitation for her to spend Christmas Eve and Christmas Day with him. It wasn't at all about avoiding a late-night drive back to Fort Worth, thought Cadie. In less than five minutes, she joined Karl in the antique shop.

They left on a walk that led them through downtown to the kolache bakery. Karl unlocked the back door and led her inside. With a quick flip of a switch, light filled the large kitchen, gently radiating throughout the café and over the table where she'd first met Karl. The wall clock read one-thirty. A bright white cloth flying through the air cut off her view of the clock. Cadie's eyes adjusted in time to catch the large apron.

"Surprise," he said. "Ready to make kolaches and cookies?"

Cadie nodded and put on the apron. "We'd better put on some coffee, though."

"We'd better at that. Lidice wouldn't like it if you didn't enjoy her tradition. We can open your wine, also."

"This was her new tradition?"

"In a way, yes. In the old country, Christmas Eve is the big holiday. Christmas Day is quiet. Families exchange sweets and cookies. Lidice missed that most of all. People grieve over lost tradition or place, wallow in it and curse the future. Not Lidice. She plotted a new course, arranged each year to use the bakery starting at midnight of Christmas morning. She called it her new common sense. She stopped buying presents and fretting over decorating the house and shop . . . spent all of the usual gift money on flour, eggs, and sugar. She was happier than ever, like a child discovering the world for the first time. Her tradition became one of simpler exchange. What she received was use of the bakery for a day. At first light, you'll see what she gave."

The hours passed quickly. Cadie learned the tricks of making fluffy kolaches, working frantically to assist Karl. Following Lidice's family recipe, she rolled gingerbread dough between parchment paper, cut various cookie shapes, and punched out small center circles from half of the shapes. Talking of little other than the tasks before them, Karl showed Cadie how to spread different flavored jams on the cooled cookies and top them with matching hole-punched shapes. Soon, more than a thousand gingerbread sandwich cookies lined the counters. Tray after tray of warm, fruit-filled and cream cheese kolaches sat beside the cookies.

As the final batches baked, Karl and Cadie shoved together small table clusters in the café. The first hue of light appeared on the east horizon. Cookies and kolaches covering nearly every available surface, they set the last pastries on the expansive kitchen tables. The sweets' colorful fillings set in golden pastry crowns glowed jewel-like under the fluorescent kitchen lights. Karl tossed aside his apron and took Cadie's, her apron smattered with fingerprints of smeared gingerbread dough and preserves. He caught her in a powerful side-hug and kissed the side of her head.

"Merry Christmas, Cadie, dear."

Cadie stiffened, but didn't pull away. "Merry Christmas, Karl."

"Are you ready?"

"Ready."

"You do the honors." He motioned for her to unlock the front café door. "I'm going to start more coffee. We'll need it."

Cadie released the lock and stepped out on the sidewalk to look down the street. Her eyes widened. From every direction walked small groups of people—all approaching the bakery. Some children were still in pajamas. A few faces she recognized from the polka dances. When Frank waved to her from the crowd, Cadie turned around and hurried back inside.

"It was like that the first year, too," said Karl. "Lidice talked about it for weeks, put up fliers in the antique shop. We didn't expect many—different traditions, you know. But everyone came—most of the town. They'll come and go all day."

The first group walked inside, then another. Many of the guests, still weary from sleep, carried their own glasses and bottles of liquor. The man that Karl pointed to as the bakery owner walked up and gave Karl a big hug.

"Merry Christmas, Karl," said the man. His accent was all Texan. "Who've we got here?" He turned, slinging his heavily muscled arm around Cadie's shoulder.

Karl grinned. "That there's Cadie. If Lidice and I had ever gotten one, she's the girl we would've picked."

The owner laughed. "You sure got guts to help this old man in a bakery all night. Merry Christmas, Cadie."

By then, every open area in the café had filled to standing room only. Guests helped themselves to coffee, topping off their cups with spirits. But no one drank. The owner shouted to the gathering crowd, "This here's Cadie, everybody."

Everyone responded, "Merry Christmas, Cadie."

Cadie nodded. "Merry Christmas."

Karl poured drinks for Cadie and for himself.

The owner raised his cup. The crowd, including Cadie and Karl, responded in kind. The owner looked at Karl, who was looking at the floor.

"Here's to Lidice," shouted the owner to the crowd.

Karl raised his head.

"Merry Christmas, Lidice," shouted the crowd in return.

Everyone drank.

Without further ceremony, the guests broke into festive conversation, helped themselves to the gifted kolaches and cookies. As people finished eating and left, more arrived. Everyone smiled—even the woman who reminded Cadie of Mrs. Beauregard.

Cadie ate an apricot kolache, watching Karl move through the crowd. Everyone was delighted to see him.

Frank walked over to her.

"Do you stay here most of the day, Frank?"

"Many of us do. It's something to see, don't ya think?"

"It is," agreed Cadie.

Frank refilled his coffee mug. "Don't ya see, girlie?" he asked, nodding toward the crowd. "That there is Lidice's smiling village."

+ + +

A COUNTY AWAY, ON CORRAL Street, Aleck walked away from Cadie's door and cut through her yard to return to his house. He kicked at the dormant grass and tripped. One of the cinnamon rolls fell from the tray he carried. With a tighter hold on the tray and the coffee carafe he carried, Aleck punted the roll into the street.

The neighbor's dog, free to roam off-leash, would be out soon. In the absence of trash bags to rip open for bits of leftover fried chicken and ravioli sauce stuck to tins, the roll would be gone before most children woke and rushed to open presents.

Aleck sighed and went inside.

It was his first Christmas alone. He'd passed on his regular trip to Spain where his aunts, uncles, and cousins filled rooms decorated by his mother and sister, where his father poured drinks and everyone shouted happily over music and children.

He opened the oven to check the turkey big enough for a large family, holding out faint hope that Cadie would be back in time to join him for Christmas dinner.

According to Beatrice, Cadie was always home during holidays.

"Where else would she have to go?" she'd asked him.

But Cadie wasn't there. There'd been no guitar playing for two nights. Two days had passed since last hearing her garage door open and close. It wasn't like Cadie to be at home and not play guitar.

He went to his music wall and pulled out several Dvořák, Irish, and Mediterranean CDs for his turntable. Until the turkey was ready, Aleck busied himself with other preparations, periodically looking out of his living room window, hoping to catch Cadie leave for one of her walks.

The hours passed. The more he thought about Cadie Walsh, the more enigmatic she became. It was madness pressed on him, the way he wanted so badly to identify the cause of her changing schedule, to witness up-close a changing emotional structure—whatever the cause of permutation. Aleck began to worry about himself. Perception could play tricks, hallucinations brought on by desire, sadness, even happiness. Did he see change because he wanted change?

To reassure himself that he wasn't completely off the mark over the transition in her emotional structure, he went back to reading while the turkey roasted.

LONG AFTER THE DISHWASHER ran its cycle, Aleck shifted into consciousness from his nap. *Was that Cadie's garage door?* He swung his feet off the couch. One foot landed on the pile of sociological case studies he was reading before he fell asleep. It was dark in the house except for the kitchen light. He got up and ran to his garage, listened carefully, and was almost sure it was her garage door closing. A minute passed without any other sound. Aleck shuffled to his kitchen and wondered about taking her some turkey with a cinnamon roll.

"Where have you been for most of three days, Cadie?" he asked aloud.

He decided against going over right away, but started a leftovers plate in case an opportune moment arose to give it to her. When he heard Cadie's front door close, he looked at his clock. Six-thirty. Either she was checking her mail or going for another walk in the dark.

On the street, Cadie walked away from Aleck's house and didn't see him watching her from his living room window. Lost in thought, she parsed together pieces from the last twenty-four hours . . . Lidice's journal entry, making kolaches at midnight, the village loved by a tradition that Karl carried on for Lidice—this year with Cadie's help. She liked that Karl and Lidice would have liked her as their daughter.

It wasn't until she stopped where the sidewalk butted up against a green belt that she felt the chill in the air. She searched for signs of movement in the open field's deep black where coyotes occasionally lurked and watched her. There was no movement or sound. A small fleck of moisture hit her cheek, causing her to look up at the nearest street light.

Cadie thought she imagined the first snow flake, then came the second, the third. The flakes gathered muster.

Is it cold enough to snow?

She looked behind her at the row of houses. Every streetlight illuminated the snow thicker than rain, falling straight down. Cadie listened. It wasn't silent like Sister Mary Trea said snow was. No, the flakes brushed the air, making a sound similar to fingers lightly passing over dry skin. She let her head fall back and looked straight up at the sky. Cold flakes hit her teeth.

The freezing sensation on her enamel snapped Cadie out of her shocked daze.

I know.

Invigorated, she began to jog home. Only one way had that snow hit her teeth . . . she had suddenly smiled. Not just any smile, but a big toothful grin. A smile generated without conscious thought of it. And she knew, knew, *knew* how to proceed with her robot.

The simple answer had been right there in front of her the whole time. There were cohesive structures for social interaction, only she hadn't correctly integrated the sociological data.

Running faster, she laughed aloud at the clue unlocked within her, a silent trait arising from deep, unconscious emotion and memory. It was a trait simultaneously regulatory and regulated, and both sensor and censor.

She had read that the brain could re-map itself after the tragic loss of a limb. In her case, was her missing social limb the limb of her mother? And in the case of her genome, Cadie knew she couldn't make it into something it never was. But if she was right about her idea, she might do more than create a new robot. If she was right, she could re-map her own brain and emotions. Using the sociological research, maybe she could interpolate, decode, and unravel the twisted helix that had retarded her interactions and destroyed her social branch referred to by the world as "family."

Her run was a sprint when she made it back to her block.

Aleck, drawn from his house when the snow started, stood in the street in front of Cadie's house. He froze when he saw her running along the sidewalk toward him. Alarm propelled him several steps toward her before he saw her face. *She is smiling?* Aleck stiffened. Time slowed. Then Cadie was across from him.

"Merry Christmas, Aleck," she called. An excited wave accompanied the greeting before she dashed to her door and ran inside.

There was no time for Aleck to respond before her door closed. He couldn't uproot himself from the street.

Move, Aleck.

He looked at the sky, letting the snow fall on his face. He heard Cadie's front door open and close again. A flake hit his eye and blurred his vision. He blinked away the cold moisture and looked to see Cadie running toward him. She was smiling, almost enough for her lips to part.

"I collected it from Fredericksburg," she said, shoving into his hands the wine bottle she carried. "It's my favorite."

She turned and raced back toward her house.

Aleck managed a stunned "Merry Christmas, Cadie."

This time he heard the click of her lock. He looked at the bottle label and shivered.

What in the world is going on?

CHAPTER ELEVEN

NO OTHER CARS were on the street when Cadie arrived at the Ketolas'. She checked her watch. Gabriella had told her four o'clock. It was a minute after. Cadie got out, retrieved the box in which she'd packed the pâté, brioche, and wine. She carefully conveyed the treats to the front door. With her elbow, she pushed the button in the bronze frog doorbell cover.

She yawned.

In her overly tired state, she twice had made the goose liver pâté despite detailed instructions, along with a food processor and fresh brioche, left by Karl the day before when he'd dropped by on his way into the city. For three days, she'd slept less than a few hours per day, glued, nearly hypnagogic, to her computer since realizing how to proceed with her AI project.

Cadie dropped her head toward the box and sniffed deeply, partially waking at the faintest scent of the nutmeg blended into the pâté. She hoped it was enough to stay awake for the party's duration.

The man she recognized as "Uncle Paul" from Viktor's Christmas videos opened the door.

"Happy New Year, Cadie. I'm Paul . . . Paul Ketola."

"I recognize you from the videos." She thrust the box forward into his hands. "I brought pâté and wine."

Paul's grin let her know the offering was appropriate.

"Nothing better. Is it *fois gras*?" he asked, peeking inside the box.

"No, regular goose liver."

She had followed Karl's instructions precisely, making the special trip for "humane goose liver." Karl cooked with nothing but sustainable and humanely treated ingredients.

"We'll eat without impunity, then," Paul laughed.

When he saw the Sauternes, he yelled, "Viktor, she brought goose liver pâté and Sauternes."

Wearing a turquoise, hand-printed apron sporting images of celery and garlic, Viktor emerged from the kitchen.

"That's the loveliest thing I've heard all day. We'll snack on that while we finish the smorgasbord. Very happy New Year, Cadie."

Waving the Santoku knife he still carried, he came forward and greeted her with a hug.

Taken aback by a Viktor different from the Finnish meeting, Cadie asked where Gabriella was.

"Sitting in the garden, watching the birds," said Paul.

"No one ever shows up on time," added Viktor.

The two led Cadie to the kitchen. Paul pulled the pâté from the box and winked at Cadie. "'Course, anyone who brings pâté can show up anytime they want."

"You go see Gabi," said Viktor. "I'll toast the brioche while Paul slices the pâté. We'll serve you girls in a few minutes. Oh, and there are extra throws outside to keep your legs warm."

Cadie walked through the kitchen door that led to a large side yard. On a raised deck separated from the house sat Gabriella. Abutting the deck was a large Finnish sauna. Between the main house and the deck, an elaborate maze of small and large patios with various seating beckoned—benches, table and chairs sets, large rocks. There were a few shade trees, the other ground planted with roving abandon. Sprawling rosemary bushes appeared in most every planting, a few smaller beds held skeletons of annual herbs killed off by frost.

Gabriella, who had been looking at the bird feeders hanging throughout the elaborate garden, saw Cadie and smiled. Rising, she entered the sauna and reemerged with a thick blanket.

"You made it." She handed the coverture to Cadie when she reached the deck steps. "It's not that cold, but this wind . . . "

Nodding, Cadie sat down in a vacant chair and threw the covering over her legs.

"Watching birds is my pastime," Gabriella said. "Do you have feeders?"

"No."

Cadie had never thought about it. For that matter, she didn't recall noticing birds at all. With both women settled, the birds, most of them brown, but some with bits of red around their heads, swarmed back to the feeders.

"Do you get many different kinds?"

"Not that many. Mostly sparrows and house finches. A lot of turtle doves, a pair of cardinals."

"What are those?" Cadie pointed at the brown and white birds.

"Regular house finches. Those with the red heads are males." She pointed at a feeder affixed on a post closer to the house. "Those in that feeder are my turtle doves. You'll know the cardinals if they show."

Viktor, carrying a carved wooden tea tray, walked into the side yard. The birds, moving as one organism, flew to the neighboring trees and waited to return.

"What do you bring for us?" asked Gabriella.

"What Cadie brought—Sauternes," he said happily.

He set the tray on the deck table and filled the two glasses. As if she didn't know or didn't care what Sauternes was, Gabriella smiled lovingly at him and extended her hand for the wine glass. Cadie noted great similarity in the facial features between the two. They looked much more alike than either did to Paul.

"*Kippis,* Cadie," said Gabriella, raising her glass. "Cheers."

"Cheers, Gabriella."

"Kippis, indeed," said Viktor. "The pâté is lovely, by the way. Nicely done, Cadie." He patted Gabriella's shoulder. "We finish in half an hour if you want to start the sauna."

Gabriella nodded before looking at Cadie.

"We run it all night for our friends who like to sit in the sauna during their visit. Viktor and Paul will use it when they finish food prep. You will join us? I have a suit."

"Sure."

Cadie hadn't enjoyed a sauna since college, when she had regular access to the recreational center. On the cool evening, it would be a welcome event. Her thoughts returned to Gabriella and Viktor, the couple.

"Did Paul fly back with you when you returned from Christmas in Finland?"

"He lives here."

"In Dallas?"

Paul was absent at the Finnish meeting.

"No, here . . . in this house."

Remembering the videos, Viktor's mother referring to Paul as "Uncle Paul," Cadie assumed Paul was Viktor's brother.

"Did you meet Viktor here in America . . . or Finland?"

Smiling calmly, Gabriella topped off their wine glasses.

"In the womb," she stated. "We're fraternal twins."

"That explains your similarities."

It didn't explain Paul's dissimilarity, though. Cadie didn't remember seeing the Ketolas' father in the videos.

"I guess Paul looks more like your father, then?"

"My father?"

Gabriella watched a particular bird on the nearest feeder. "Watch," she said to Cadie.

She got up and took soft steps across the deck. Except for one finch, the birds flew away at Gabriella's approach. Gabriella stopped with her head inches away from little bird resting on its feeder perch. The finch cocked her head and looked directly at Gabriella.

From where she sat, Cadie could tell something was different about the bird. The feathers over its eyes appeared permanently ruffled, giving the bird a shaggy-eyebrowed, sagely demeanor.

Gabriella motioned for Cadie to join her.

Cadie slowly approached. At Gabriella's side, Cadie quickly noticed an opaque film over the bird's eyes. She waved her hand in front of its beak. The bird responded by turning to eat more black sunflower seeds.

Gabriella left the feeder and returned to her chair. Cadie followed. The bird continued eating.

"The bird is blind," said Gabriella. "She can hear well enough but can only discern the faintest of light, a little shadow. She comes to the feeder hours before daylight and leaves well after dark."

"How did she find the feeder in the first place?"

"Likely by following her mother."

The other birds returned and jostled for places at the feeders. When more arrived, jostling over the limited perches, the blind bird held fast, occasionally cocking its head to listen.

"She is just like all the others, except for her blindness variation, has all the same instincts and lives almost identically to the others. With the readily available food source, at least one blind bird arrives every year."

Another finch pushed aside the handicapped bird. The displaced female flew awkwardly around the feeder and approached another perch. Near her landing site, she lost her upward lift and fluttered down before fighting her way upward in fits and starts. Puppet-like, she toggled from side to side, her feet stretched in front of her, grasping at the air for something to clasp. In the feeder's shadow, her claws finally brushed against one of the aluminum rests. She quickly latched on. In a few more flaps, the feathered gymnast righted herself at the bar and starting eating again.

"Student pilot," smiled Gabriella. "Every time I see a bird not so good at flying, I think it's blind. Sometimes, though, it turns out to be a fledgling."

Remembering where they were in conversation before the interruption with the bird, Gabriella looked at Cadie.

"Paul is not our brother. He and Viktor were married in Washington, D.C."

Gabriella searched Cadie's face for discomfort. Cadie was unfazed, unconcerned.

"So they're newlyweds?"

"No," said Gabriella. "They've just newly been allowed to wed. Of course, Texas doesn't recognize their marriage, but there's a great art scene here. Paul and Viktor have been together since college—forty years." She paused and smiled. "It's been the *three* of us since college."

LEFT ALONE IN THE SAUNA'S changing and shower room, Cadie hung the borrowed suit on a wooden peg. She wasn't keen on the cold, after-sauna rinse Paul and Viktor urged on her. But a smorgasbord waited, so Cadie stepped under the shower, distracting herself from the cold water by replaying the story told by the three Ketolas.

"SHE IS MY PATRON SAINT of communication," Viktor said after sweat coursed freely from the sauna's occupants.

Paul nodded. Viktor went on with his story.

Cadie sensed that Viktor's classification of Gabriella was more than a compliment. It was very real. Gabriella's protection had followed a deep and complicated precision that stood in sharp dissimilarity to the abuses Cadie had witnessed at the orphanage, for the abuse was severe when nuns identified the girls who loved other girls. Those girls endured complex and persistent degradation by the nuns, childhood sentences of bruises, broken arms, and concussions.

And whether too smart for her own good or too plain, a girl displaying such congenital variance, well, to the supper club she immediately went. And she stayed in the supper club until she demonstrated nothing but strict and platonic appreciation toward the same sex. She only returned after accepting a preternatural vow of blindness, refusing to look directly at another girl, for the costs of penalty and penitence were too high.

It occurred to Cadie that she might be good at robots for a reason. She had seen a lot of them. If only those girls had had a sister like Gabriella. Surviving, nay, thriving, might have come within reach. But there was no sister to give them a fighting chance at health and love.

"After my first schoolyard abuse, she naturally buffered a way for me," said Viktor.

"Some are born with good instinct," added Paul.

Viktor nodded. "Mother always enrolled us in the same classes, couldn't bear the thought of her twins being separated. It saved my skin. Gabi and I had a secret language."

"Sometimes they still use it against me," laughed Paul.

"We had cues," said Viktor. "Cues warning me to stop waving my hands as I talked—quite nerve-wracking to Finns as a matter of course. She taught me how to wink at girls when the other boys were watching me. Cues reminding me to stiffen my gait or walk with the top of my hands facing forward rather than approaching the world with open palms."

"The ape walk," said Paul. He hunched over, mimicked the stance of an ape dragging his fingertips along the ground.

"After high school we moved from Turku to Helsinki to attend college. Nobody knew us there. We both studied art, continued to take the same classes."

"Imagine," said Paul. "That's when they started wearing matching wedding bands."

Viktor nodded. "We let people assume we were husband and wife."

Just as they had at the Finnish meeting, thought Cadie.

"I was viable, *tout de suite*—right away became a person if perceived as heterosexual *and* married," Viktor continued.

"Then he met me," laughed Paul. "I busted their gig, pronto."

Cadie looked at Gabriella, who had been sitting very still but relaxed during the story. She nodded and smiled.

"It was the first-year arts appreciation class," said Viktor, glowing with the memory. "Of course, Gabi then had two brothers to protect. After graduation, the three of us moved to the States."

Gabriella shifted. "And it still took most of our lives for you two to wear your bands as legitimately as our heterosexual friends, though the U.S. is not as egalitarian, civil rights-forward, and non-discriminatory as those rings suggest."

Viktor nodded. "It is a lifetime of wariness, screening newcomers for bigotry and hatred before we open our personal lives."

"It's priceless," said Paul, "to sit in one's home among friends. The world is a neophyte to brotherly love."

HONORED BY THE TRUTH, by their acceptance of her, Cadie threw her wet towel over an empty peg and then pulled on her clothes. She left the sauna changing room and walked toward the house.

Two couples going to the sauna passed her along one of the garden pathways. "Kippis," they called, raising their glasses.

"Happy New Year," she returned.

Inside the house, music started. Paul poked his head outside.

"Hurry, Cadie."

He handed her a drink as she walked in the door.

"Vodka," he said.

Cadie had just enough time to sip before Paul said, "It's time to dance."

Couples moved to a Finnish polka in a large parlor cleared of furniture for the occasion. Viktor walked in and interrupted before Paul could pull Cadie onto the floor.

"Not yet," laughed Viktor. "She must see our smorgasbord."

Viktor led Cadie to survey the layout of food.

Twelve chairs, pulled from around the table, lined the dining room walls. Against one wall, a large serving console held glasses at the ready for vodka and Aquavit schnapps, as well as various beers, wine, and mineral water. Trays of cold cuts and different cheeses covered the round dining table, its diameter seven feet and then some.

Viktor and Paul pointed as Gabriella named off the various items: pickled herring with onion, pickled gherkins and beets, capers, chopped hard-boiled egg, and *smetana*—a thick-looking cream described as sour. There were meatballs and sausage rolls, along with cold cuts of various hams, pork, roast beef, and smoked reindeer. Paul smiled widely when Gabriella said, "More goose liver pâté." The pâté sat alongside beef aspic, salami, potato salad, and green salad with cucumber. Bread and butter were available to go with several platters of different cheeses. Cadie recognized the pulla and cookies.

"Cognac is in the kitchen with tea and coffee," said Viktor.

"And champagne at midnight," said Paul.

Cadie traded her empty vodka glass for an empty plate and a glass of Aquavit, which smelled of caraway, aniseed, and citrus.

"Kippis," said Cadie.

"Kippis," answered her hosts.

She filled her plate and settled on a couch shoved against a wall in the living room. She listened to the music and watched the dancers in the parlor, anxious to try the new chord variations on her guitar.

Gabriella approached as Cadie finished eating. "Help me gather midnight items?" she asked.

Cadie got up and followed Gabriella into the four-car garage. They passed a large easel supporting an abstract painting in progress and went through another door that opened to a small foyer at the bottom of a brightly lit stairwell. At the top of the stairs, they emerged into a loft.

"My flat," said Gabriella.

The large space, at least twelve hundred square feet, surprised Cadie. Large windows framed with heavy architrave moldings and crossette lines provided the light Gabriella needed to paint. There were no paintings on the solid white walls. Easels scattered throughout showed their backs to Cadie, the paintings' faces waiting for placid sunrise.

Gabriella walked to the open kitchen. On the counters sat durable buckets and tin objects shaped into horseshoes and stars.

But for an espresso machine with small white cups stacked on top of it, little else sat on the counter. From experience, Cadie recognized the area as infrequently used.

"Paul and Viktor do the cooking," said Gabriella, reading Cadie's thoughts. "I keep cold cuts in my refrigerator for breakfast sandwiches and late-night working snacks. Steam and oil from cooking aren't good for the paintings, anyway."

She pointed at the tins. "You get those, Cadie. I'll bring the rest."

+ + +

BACK IN THE LIVING ROOM, Paul pulled Cadie onto the dance floor. "Do you like the Finnish New Year?"

"Very much," said Cadie.

"Then wait," winked Paul. He looked down at her feet, registered delight. "You dance polka quite well."

"I've danced a bit before."

She told him about learning to dance polka with the Czechs.

"You're growing quite the family," laughed Paul. "I see why Viktor wanted Gabi to invite you. You are fearless."

If he only knew, said Sister Mary Trea's voice.

Yes, if he only knew, answered Cadie.

Paul interrupted further inner conversation by chatting as they danced. He added to Viktor's story about Gabriella.

"There *have* been opportunities for Gabi to go off into the sunset, so to speak," he said, a twinge of apology in his voice. "She fell in love many times. But when presented with a ring, she turned down the baker in Helsinki. Even then, I think she knew we couldn't remain in Finland. She left the doctor, too."

Paul pursed his lips and shook his head.

"The doctor could stare at gangrene all day, but his phobias about sexual orientation poisoned him. Nobody stood a chance with Gabi if they negatively typed Viktor and me."

Cadie remained expressionless, but Paul knew she was listening. She didn't take her face from his, rarely blinked.

"We have a saying," Paul said. "What we have, we hold."

The song ended. Paul kissed Cadie's cheek and passed her hand to another partner.

"Cadie, this is Dalton. He does the best Edward Scissorhands skit you'll ever see at the Rose Room. You haven't seen anything until you watch him cut hair."

Several people around them laughed and nodded their heads.

"Oh, Sweetie," said Dalton, taking her other hand and spinning her. "That's my artistic hobby. Forget about moonlighting; let me tell you about my sharks."

Dalton was a marine biologist, an ichthyologist to be exact, and taught at TCU. He regaled her with stories of shark diving, how he loved anything to do with water. He had just published his first text-book on marine biology.

"Bet it's difficult to study sharks from Fort Worth," said Cadie.

"Not a big fan of hurricanes," laughed Dalton.

Dalton's partner, Steve, of five years and an archeologist groaned from where he danced with Paul beside them. "Oh, honey," Steve said, "it's not the hurricanes. It's the unpredictability of open water. Dalton prefers diving with sharks in tanks. Ophidiophobia, herpeto-phobia. Never know what you'll find under big waters."

"Fear of snakes, reptiles," laughed Dalton, shuddering. "That's an over-generalization," he directed at Steve. "It's really squamaphobia, my own term, for a fear of scales. Sharks have *skin*, dermal denticles to be precise. Dermal denticles are covered with enamel, like human teeth." Thinking of snake scales, he shuddered again. "Really though, honey, I study how captivity changes my dear sharks."

"Whatever," said Steve, taking Dalton's hand. "You're the original Out Man."

Paul explained that Dalton was not technically the first gay man to come out in DFW. Dalton was barely older than Cadie. It was a loving term for their friend who, from his first memory, knew who he was in his skin and came "out" early to friends and family despite all consequences. He was the Everyman that every gay man wanted to be. Paul rolled his eyes at Dalton. "It's what we call *overly* talented."

Dalton shrugged in agreement and passed Cadie to another part-ner. Partner after partner, Cadie danced with everyone in the room. The platinum robot pendant around her neck danced with her.

Cadie finally excused herself for coffee before another person grabbed her. She was more exhausted from the social effort than from any length of engineering work. Before she could fill her cup, tapping against a champagne flute rang over the music.

"It's almost midnight," Gabriella announced. "Come take a glass."

The dancing stopped. Paul and Viktor filled glasses for their guests. Gabriella handed one to Cadie.

Happy for the calm, Cadie stood with the crowd and counted down the seconds to midnight. The hiatus was brief. Whistles and laughter ensued. Each guest approached her with a kiss and wishes for a "Very Happy New Year."

Several guests, in an accustomed ritual, pulled cushions and pillows from chairs and couches. They took the items to the parlor and dropped them in a circle on the floor. In the center, someone placed a small wooden pedestal supporting a large candle. Dalton went up to Cadie and took her hand.

"We go outside now," he urged, pulling her into the exodus that followed the Ketolas into the dark backyard.

Viktor carried the tin pieces. From the spigot on the side of the house, Paul filled the buckets with a few inches of water. Carrying the old cooking pot, Gabriella led everyone through the garden and to the sauna.

At the sauna door, Viktor handed a tin shape to each person. Cadie looked at her star and squeezed with the other guests into the sauna room. On the glowing igneous rocks, Gabriella placed the pot.

As soon as the vessel heated, Gabriella individually melted each guest's tin piece and then poured the molten liquid into one of the water buckets. The tin re-solidified on impact with the cold water. Mesmerized into quietness, everyone tried to catch glimpses of the specimens fished from the water by their owners.

When all had a transformed shape in hand, the group traipsed back inside and settled on the waiting cushions. Victor turned out the lights. Paul lit the pillar candle.

"Who wants to go first?" he laughed. "How about our newbie?"

Cadie sat unmoving.

"I think she needs more Aquavit," said Dalton

"Not yet," laughed Paul. "Hand me your tin, Cadie."

He took the piece she handed over and held it up against the candle light in the darkened room. The tin's shape cast its shadow on the opposite wall.

"It's a shark," started Dalton, who saw sharks in everything.

"No, it's a giraffe."

For the first time, Cadie heard the group talk over each other to call out guesses.

"I think it's a ship," said Gabriella.

"No," said Viktor, "she's already on a journey. It must foretell the *future*."

"It's a swan," said Gabriella.

"A swan," yelled Paul. "Yay!"

"What does a swan mean?" asked Cadie.

"The same as any other animal," laughed Viktor. "Prosperity."

Cadie modestly smiled and accepted the return of her tin swan. She could take prosperity.

With everyone assured of some good fortune for the coming year, Viktor turned on the lights and called for another toast.

"A year of happiness," he said.

"To happiness!"

Guests who had come as couples embraced and kissed. Cadie stood alone with Gabriella, but Gabriella didn't look as if she felt alone. She looked happy, ecstatically so . . . no hint on her face that she'd given up anything but had kept and held her heart in spite of everything and everyone else.

Cadie imagined what it was like to keep from harm a thing known since conception. If it was a painful thing, Gabriella didn't show it, didn't cast herself as solitary and confined, was no Sister Mary Trea. She had cleared a path for her brother at all costs, for life . . . and love. Gabriella had chosen family in the form it came, without stifling condemnation. She had regulated her life so that Viktor and Paul could have voices, unambiguous articulation. And Gabriella was happy still. It seemed a magical goodness.

Raising her glass to catch Gabriella's eye, Cadie said, "Happy New Year, Gabriella."

Gabriella turned and smiled at her guest. "Happy New Year, Cadie Walsh."

CHAPTER TWELVE

W*E LIVE, FEEL, THROUGH the fullness of our mouths.*
Cadie chewed on slices of cheese and apple as she sketched a simple blueprint of the brain's emotion centers. The yeasty cheese made her remember Ayala's chatter. That thought led to a memory of challa that Cadie could almost taste between bites. She liked how taste converted to emotion, then to memory and back again.

Food is our mother.

Ayala again.

Cadie penciled in another delicate brain fold and thought about her genomic path.

Every genome had imprinted upon it the data for genetic replication and regulation. It mapped out an overall sketch for an organism's formation—head to toe, brain to heart, mouth to stomach, emotion to memory—and worked the same way for humans . . . all the way back to Africa and before. From single-celled etchings, the map of the human genome had grown into an immense, recorded swath of living maps of digital copies, if you will, like old phonograph records. Start at the beginning, and the needle follows a mechanical route over the disc's grooves, working along a particular line to play the imprinted music or speech or song. The needle thinks neither of the record, nor the record of the needle. One could take any record, new or old, and the needle moves to the same center, albeit with unpredictable and unseen variation or skips, if you may, that omit or blur portions of the recording. Hit a large variation, and the needle hangs entirely or aborts altogether, resets itself. The needle can do nothing, though, about the information imprinted on the record. Either it works or it doesn't.

Her copy had worked, and here she sat eating cheese and apple. Cadie pushed aside her empty plate and continued to draw.

From the success of such an evolution, Cadie saw herself as a copier rather than a mother to something wildly new. After all, her U5 route was only a geographical variation to other routes taken by cousin mothers. Thus, as a cousin, she planned to code the structure of her robot's brain in a similar fashion to the human brain.

In the amygdala, where basic human emotion acts as folly or friend, the robot would springboard from carefully calculated algorithms to achieve the beginning of unconscious emotion. Then, the robot's anterior cingulate would control autonomic, engine-like functions as well as decision making and emotion. An anterior cingulate center was critical for the robot to "learn" social exchange, a reward in and of itself.

Cadie turned the page sideways and wrote, "SEEK OUT SO-CIAL EXCHANGE."

That would be the robot's purpose. But meaningful social exchange depended on a human's ability to identify expressions of emotion. And emoted expressions were far more than the mathematics of human facial features, degrees of beauty subjectively applied by the viewer. Features meant nothing more than visual hope, an expectation of communication.

Cadie twisted the page and looked at her rendition.

Yes, the robot would have to "understand" connoted emotion built on the mathematics of facial features. And generated from a carefully coded lateral orbitofrontal cortex, the robot would interact with appropriate social responses—always, of course, in accordance with the Three Laws.

On the drawing, Cadie labeled the brain's emotional centers as the "ALA"—short for Amygdala, Anterior Cingulate, and Lateral Orbitofrontal Cortex. She tapped her pencil on the paper. It didn't sound right. Bobby couldn't say "A-L-A" each time he tried to market the prototype. She needed a name more human, something universal that represented the brain's ALA as a whole. Something simple that held the key to infinite complexity, as the letters or drawing of DNA held the keys to the entire line of Earth's organisms.

That was it.

The ALA centers bound the framework for humanity, created family from sociological human universals existing regardless of culture, belief, or birthplace. She would build all the human universals into the new robot.

What is more universal than family?

Cadie drew a large capital "F" before the letters ALA. "Family" + "A-L-A" = Fala.

The prototype would be *Fala*.

With a better idea of how Fala might perceive and respond to emotion, Cadie drew in the last piece—the Hippocampus. There, specific information from the ALA would become explicit, conscious, memory. Once Fala's algorithms could "recognize," the robot would filter through lists of human universals, compare recognition to memories, and then decide the best course of social interaction.

The complex algorithms, Cadie knew, would be her greatest hurdle—blending structure with conscious recognition of social stimuli. How would Fala know *what* to respond to . . . and how and when? Fala would have to appraise meaning, verbal or nonverbal. That would necessitate the ability to integrate new responses with catalogued databases of anatomical motor movements. Without such integration, Fala would have no continuity for her own responses.

Cadie sighed as she finished her drawing.

There were so many human expressions, facial or otherwise, to comprehend. Her enthusiastic smile had returned her to a path for groundbreaking engineering. And in researching the smile as expression, she'd come across a compiled anthropological list of human universals, a list of attributes coded so deeply into the genome that all humans shared them. There were hundreds—pain, food preferences, fear, emotions, empathy, and gestures. Frowns.

Cadie closed her eyes, remembering one frown in particular.

+ + +

"CAN'T YOU SEE THAT I'm upset," said Sister Mary Trea. "We haven't time to fool with helping every little girl with their math. Come."

The nun's brow was deeply furrowed.

"But she wants it, and I help Salley with spelling, too."

The slap Cadie received was proof of Sister Mary Trea's ire. Furrowed brows were often indication of upset, though not always conclusive.

"You will obey," Sister Mary Trea growled. She looked, unblinking, at the face of little Cadie and let her eyes scan over the child, as if every part of the girl was tainted and wrong and unbecoming.

+ + +

CADIE OPENED HER EYES.

She had wanted to be some mother or confidant to the girls she'd lived with, not a strange little one who tried to save them from damnation when they couldn't remember algebra. She had wanted to be a real sister, a hand to pull them away when trouble was nigh, when they were frozen from flight. She had wanted their secrets. But all she had brought them was pain.

Her thoughts returned to the human universals. In addition to facial recognition, there were also universals of judgment and language. Contained in those traits was the brain's natural inclination to attribute meaning to everything, regardless of proven data that established "something" as one thing and not another.

Fala would have to discard the permanent loop that kept Cadie questioning the intent or thoughts of other people. And unlike Sister Mary Trea's instruction, Fala must behave based on the genome's fundamental nature to express kindly social interaction without rule by fear or degraded self-image. Fala must not oppress response to feed an overarching morality, one that turned on itself and became megalomaniacal immorality. Fala would have to store information about optimal or sub-optimal human response or intent—the emotional quality—without negative emotional response herself. If Fala was impervious to trauma, then negativity could not regulate her. Fala had to be like Lidice—a woman who discarded twitches of trauma and exchanged it for positive expression. In Lidice's case, she cast aside indoctrination for the happiness of an entire town.

LIDICE WAS GOOD AT FOLLOWING THE THREE LAWS, thought Cadie. It wasn't hard to imagine that she would have liked Lidice. No *slap, slap, slap* to rewire behavior. But smile, smile, smile.

The last annotation penciled onto her drawing, Cadie grabbed her guitar and went outside. In the cold air, she blew warmth into her fingers before playing.

You can pause for one month; no more, she ordered herself.

In her language of computer programming, a pause was exactly what she needed to build the robot's first "emotion" centers. What harm could come from the temporary suspension of her "family" batch program? Her friends and her U5 journey would wait. In a month, when Fala was well into development, Cadie could press any key to continue her social journey.

BEFORE CADIE STARTED FALA'S hard wiring, she condensed Fala's basis of function to ten modules.

ENVIRONMENT
METABOLIC
EXTERNAL MONITORING
HUMAN UNIVERSALS
LEXICON
FACIAL MEASUREMENT
RAPID-MOVEMENT MAPPING
INTERNAL/EXTERNAL CONSTRAINTS
EXPRESSION MAPPING
PREDICTABILITY

From those she would expand and develop Fala's hard-wired senses, her basic ability to think. When activated, Fala would proceed based on unique experience.

Cadie started with the Environment Module, which would continuously measure external environmental statuses: room temperature, weather (air pressure, dew point, sunniness, cloudiness, rain, etc.). Weather affected people, how they dressed (which affected comfort), and so on and so forth. Quality of light (brightness, hue saturation, luminance, and absence of light) affected moods, wakefulness, emotion, as well as basic human needs.

Realizing the distraction sound could cause, Cadie started a subtable for sound and linked it to the first module. Fala would need to be able to identify pitch, tone, music, even stomach rumblings in addition to the crash, bangs, and booms that interrupted or modified how one worked or interacted.

Like slaps . . . or sensory deprivation. The memory came unbidden.

"CADIE, YOU GOT A TISSUE?" asked Salley. Her bed was farthest down the row from Cadie's sleeping place. "My sniffle . . . I can't sleep."

A few girls kept awake by Salley's lugubrious and continual sinus infection issued loud responses of "shh."

Salley's bed was under the window permanently cracked open for the girls to have "fresh air" as they slept. A generous portico awning facing the interior of the orphanage's property protected the window, nailed so that it couldn't fully open or close. A continual curtain of air an inch tall by three feet wide allowed for slumber always a little too humid, hot, or cold. Whether the girl assigned to the "weather bed" was always the sickest because of sleeping under the window, or the sickest always assigned there, Cadie didn't know. Still didn't. Correlation and causation, especially in the absence of evidence, were sticky stumbling blocks to truth.

Cadie got up and took a tissue to the slight girl.

"It's keeping me awake, too." She smiled enough to convey the intended humor.

The way the mucous sputtered and heaved, Cadie knew Salley had laughed. By now, Salley knew that Cadie always had a tissue tucked away and waiting, just in case Salley exhausted her supply during the night.

A powerful slap hit Cadie off-guard. She fell on the bed, landing across Salley's legs. Salley, pinned down, couldn't avoid receiving a slap as well. After a short struggle, the nuns placed each girl in a solitary cell.

Cadie spent seven days in the total black; Salley spent two weeks.

When they went for Salley, she went straight to the hospital to battle infection, which had moved to the lining of her brain.

By then, Cadie, removed from the dorm, had been isolated in a bed close to Sister Mary Trea's room. She slept there until she went to college. Midnight whispers ceased, and she woke occasionally to the dull sound of slaps coming from the greater dorm.

SHAKING OFF THE MEMORY, Cadie started on the Metabolic Module. From code for previously built robots, she integrated the algorithms for touch and added a new category for "remote touch" so Fala could measure touch without laying a finger on an individual human.

Halfway through composing the module's table, Cadie stopped to answer email messages.

"Yes" to an invitation to celebrate Passover with the Alfasis.

"No" to Karl for dancing on Saturday—she was in pause mode, but she didn't tell him that.

"No" to the Ketolas for the January Finnish meeting—too many projects on her desk.

"Maybe" to Kamil for a late-January cooking lesson—if she met her deadlines.

As she went through the list, a message from Bobby popped into her inbox. "Yes," he wrote.

Cadie quickly responded, "THANK YOU."

The way was clear. She had full and confidential reign of the chief mechanical and electrical engineers, and Bobby had promised to clear her private lab of her last project.

You cannot fail, Cadie—no matter the cost. She swallowed a thoughtful gulp. If this project failed, the failure would be expensive.

Back at the module's growing list, Cadie added the ability for Fala to use advanced sensors to wirelessly measure heart rate, blood pressure, and body temperatures.

On to the External Monitoring Module. Cadie added skin humidity and perspiration to the list in order to evaluate water intake over time. Hydration affected many other readings.

With the External Monitoring module started, Cadie made a note—integral was the ability for Fala to measure and record human motor movements.

Next, Cadie began the robot's lexicon, though Fala's first interaction with her human contemporaries would be strictly nonverbal. A lexicon was necessary for self-calibration and to develop awareness of metabolic and environmental variations compared to a foundation of "normal" states for the humans around Fala. Afterward, Fala would measure and engage in language.

Cadie added a sub-table for dialect and accent.

How much simpler it would be to mirror a person's accent—to fit in, to make another person more at ease. Cadie wished herself more capable of it. Since Bobby's office would be Fala's first proving ground, Cadie set the default accent to "Texan" with a further subgroup of "Fort Worth." If Bobby's accent had ever deviated from Fort Worth-Texan, she'd never heard it. He sounded Texan even when he spoke Japanese with their biggest clients. Cadie smiled to herself. Fala was more socially adept . . . much, much more adept than Cadie Walsh herself.

+ + +

SHORTLY BEFORE FIVE O'CLOCK, the doorbell rang. Cadie sighed and got up from her desk.

"It's a mite cold out here," said Mrs. Beauregard before Cadie finished opening the door. "Your cookies will be ice before I can git 'em inside." She stepped in and kept walking.

"Hi, Mrs. Beauregard."

Cadie wondered why it never failed that cookie deliveries happened around the time that most people quit their workdays. She followed her neighbor to the kitchen. At least there would be fresh peanut butter cookies to carry her through the work weekend.

Frowning, Beatrice pointed at the new pot on Cadie's stove. "What's that?"

"An ibrik."

Beatrice continued frowning.

"It's for making Turkish coffee," added Cadie.

"Never tried it. Texas coffee suits fine, just fine." She waved a hand in the air, brushing away the thought of trying something new. New things were for those who didn't know any better.

"Well, I'd better get back to work." Cadie just wanted the woman to leave.

Beatrice poked her head inside Cadie's office, but didn't go in.

"You've been keeping a hectic schedule from what I've seen. Odd comings and goings for that work you do."

"Work is hectic. I'll bring your plate when I'm finished with the cookies," said Cadie, walking toward her front door.

Startled by Cadie's change from transferring cookies to another plate, Beatrice followed.

"I'd better get back to work," she said again. "Stay warm, Mrs. Beauregard."

"Well, I . . . ," started Beatrice, for once thinking of what to say next. She didn't like that Cadie had taken charge of the discussion. "Well . . . you stay warm, too."

Cadie closed her front door.

Beatrice gritted her teeth as she walked back home. Other than seeing the strange pot, she wouldn't have much to tell everyone when she delivered the other cookies. There was nothing to explain Cadie's erratic schedule of late. At least Cadie was home, though. They would have a concert, albeit a cold one.

With Mrs. Beauregard at the forefront of her thoughts, Cadie returned to her desk and started on the Human Universals Module table. The first universal she typed into the table was GOSSIP. She thought of Sister Mary Trea, typed in SHAME, followed by MANIPULATION OF SOCIAL RELATIONS. Those were three things that Fala, according to the Three Laws, must not do. Fala *would* have to recognize those universals, but respond without harm toward social and individual negatives. Linking the human universals to definitions from the lexicon module, Cadie correlated whether a human universal was "positive," "negative," or "neutral" according to the Three Laws. Fala's neural pathways must develop along lines of maintaining human- and self-preservation.

Thinking again of Sister Mary Trea, Cadie coded a new subtable for the human universal of supernatural belief and religion. Anything less than humanely equitable was negative. A person's beliefs, when language was interspersed with ideas of religion, couldn't claim positive attributes for the simple purpose of elevating themselves over others by manipulation. Good was never good when good was subsumed by religion.

For Fala, a human's gender, pigmentation, or sexual orientation was no different than registering temperature or time of day. The robot's primary objective was to do no harm. She couldn't "believe" in anything that even benignly threatened or allowed harm. As such, Fala would combine religious rhetoric with the universal "manipulation of social relations." In so doing, Fala would immediately perceive subtexts of duplicity.

Cadie labeled duplicity as negative. The robot had to see the maladaptiveness of those who ruptured social attachments, but didn't repair them. Those who did so evolved shame into permanent humiliation. Fala's pathways, once "fired" along a path of "no harm," would wire toward "no harm" in all future interactions.

Knowing she was ahead of herself, Cadie took a guitar break. If she finished the basic modules too quickly, she would miss something important—especially in the intricate lists of physically expressed emotion. She encrypted her work and locked her computer before going outside.

+ + +

THE COMPLEX FACIAL MEASUREMENT MODULE was one of the most interesting and time consuming for Cadie. Starting with underlying maps of the zygomatic major muscle, which allows for distinct and controlled facial expression, Cadie built for her robot a "memory" of the working human face.

Recognition of facial expression changes was the key to the entire project. Recognizing expression would allow Fala to analyze the "why" of an expression and then appropriately respond. For instance, a smile without eye expression was different than a smile with marked eye wrinkling, as a grin can convey happiness or assert power or aggression.

As the weeks passed, Cadie nearly forgot about her new friends. Occasionally, a memory from recent interaction would surface as she worked. But what surfaced more often were distinct memories of the orphanage, memories she thought long overwritten. Working on the math of smiles dredged up one of the worst.

CADIE HAPPENED TO BE GOING through the dorm on the way to Sister Mary Trea's room the night the hospital released Salley. Tucked snugly in the old wheelchair that had passed from one dying convent to another, Salley smiled weakly when she saw Cadie.

"I'm home." Her tiny voice was a combo of shrill whisper and harsh croak.

"No talking," said Sister Grace. She turned the wheelchair to the weather bed and looked at Cadie. "You go on, Cadie."

"Good night, Cadie."

"Night, Salley."

Ever so carefully, Sister Grace lifted Salley from the chair and set her on the bed. She turned to Cadie and gave a menacing smile as she reached into her pocket and withdrew a large chocolate chip cookie, Salley's favorite. Cadie backed into a bed post and watched.

"We're going to sleep just fine now, aren't we, Salley?"

Salley's face broke into a wide grin when she saw the cookie. "Yes, Sister Grace." She reached for the cookie.

Sister Grace handed it over.

Salley shivered. "Can we close the window?"

The nun rose to her full height and stared down.

Salley pulled the natty cover up to her chin. "I . . . I . . . "

"But don't you want the fresh air?"

"But the doctor said . . . "

"He said you could have a cookie, now didn't he?"

"Yes, thank you."

"Then let's be thankful for that *and* fresh air."

With that, Sister Grace smiled again and walked away.

Two weeks later, Salley relapsed into a dreadful sinus infection. With a cookie in her hand, they wheeled her out and took her to the hospital. It was the last infection Salley battled.

When Salley didn't return, the other girls avoided Cadie. Interest of self-preservation too often overrides good intention. Thus, Sister Mary Trea's possessiveness thwarted Cadie's attempts to form friendships, and Cadie lost the ability to read faces. Everyone since preferred to shy away from her. Now shying away from others was Cadie's most practiced and perfected mimicry.

SHIVERING AT THE MEMORY of Salley's death, Cadie hoped Fala wouldn't come across many people who grinned to assert power. Since it was better to be safe than sorry, though, Cadie developed an intelligence loop to account for tricky expression. She continued work on the module.

For every expression—grimace, pout, anger, laughter, and on and on—Cadie mapped correlations to physical facial movements, a way for Fala to accurately and constantly measure expression. Fala would "hear" laughter from the sound sub-table, match it with the human's other metabolic readings and situational laughter tendencies. Once she had integrated smile and expression variables from the scientific studies, Cadie added some of her own.

Nonverbal expression was often as important as verbal. Fala would recognize pupil dilation, blushing, paleness, nostril flaring, and the difference between crying or heavy sweating. It took days for Cadie to imagine nonverbal expressions that contributed to anger, happiness, and even responses to good or bad smells. Imagination was her only interpolation for lack of experience. For imagining was all she had had after Salley died, the only way Cadie could interpolate what she hadn't experienced.

+ + +

EVERY FEW DAYS, CADIE drove to the office and then took the elevator to a lockdown lab two stories under the street.

At each sighting of Cadie, Bobby Pullman counted the days from her last appearance. He didn't interrupt her. The more frequent Cadie's appearances, the closer she was to unveiling the prototype. Then, as with all previous projects, the frequent arrivals would stop abruptly. That was when he could really count the days to project completion. When Cadie "went silent" as he liked to call it, he could expect a prototype test run within thirty days, give or take a couple.

Bobby smiled each time she passed his office, barely containing his anxious anticipation to start a new marketing campaign. He couldn't wait to see the product.

Unaware of Bobby's excitement, Cadie went to her secured oval compound and oversaw Fala become physically more than a blueprint. Cadie reviewed AutoCAD drawings for Fala's physical and electrical structure. Like the twenty-four chromosomes in human DNA, Cadie fitted Fala with a sensor necklace, twenty-four sensors that would simultaneously feed gathered data into the integrated modules of Fala's brain center. The data would form Fala's ability to adhere to her own epigenesist of sorts, a bottom-up build piggybacked off of established human expression.

The necklace, designed by Cadie, was composed of inch-and-a-half-wide by two-inch-long oval sensors faceted into Fala's frame. In a nod to her own journey out of Africa, Cadie drew the necklace to resemble great African tribal necklaces similar to the off-shoulder cowl necks of fancy gowns. The sensors were the color of tiger's eyes, castaneous and aurulent scarab-shaped jewels that picked up a three hundred-sixty-degree view of Fala's surrounding environment. Above the necklace, the only remaining sensors were Fala's human-like eyes.

Fala's head was bare. Cadie anticipated Bobby throwing a cowboy hat on the robot, often the case with any robot in a room. Bobby regarded most of his robots as personal hat racks, especially during the development and testing phase.

AS SHE CODED FALA'S LAST five modules, Cadie focused on the robot's constraints—the many-pathed calibrations for Fala to process responses from others. Taking new environmental and metabolic data and creating mathematical probabilities derived from previous interactions, Fala would learn by self-teaching. Once activated, Fala would be self-unique and organize (attune) her "mind" for optimal social development and interaction. But the organization of Fala's mind defied strict dictation to it. A hard-wired Fala would remove any truth to prototype intelligence; a robotic mind would mean that Fala I, Fala II, and every subsequent replication of Fala would identically interact and respond. But if Fala, focused on immediate social interaction, organized its own mind, then each Fala would interact in a way unique to her own experiences. Each Fala would be adaptable to any human culture as far as the Three Law principles allowed.

To achieve real-time awareness of changing expression, Cadie coded the Rapid-Movement Mapping Module (R-MMM) to record changes in facial movement based on continuous mathematical distance and time algorithms. Integrated 3-D image modeling would allow Fala to be an automated cephalogram scanner. Thus, she could register accurate head and neck movement.

Gathering data parallel to the R-MMM was the Internal/External Constraints Module, which acquired environmental and nearby humans' metabolic expression readings. Preliminary calibration would take weeks of initial "observe only" behavior for Fala to develop a statistical database based on a particular human's average heart rate, blood pressure, and other environmental preferences.

A smile with elevated heart rate and blood pressure recorded differently than a smile with normal heart rate and blood pressure. A long-term relaxed face, combined with low blood pressure and other skewed metabolic data, could mean sickness or hunger. Fala would know when to fetch analgesics, as mothers did for sick children.

Once Fala registered static or changing expressions, along with metabolic and environmental surroundings, the data would record itself into the Expression Mapping Module. There, it would overlay expressions against a catalogue of expression photographs linked with metabolic and environmental variances. As Fala became familiar with the range of human expression, she would discard the primer photographs and replace them with faces of real experience. All data, laid down as memory in the hippocampal database, would allow Fala to differentiate Bobby's smile from others', everything linked to the human universals table to determine emotion accurately in the

Predictability Module. Fala must not perceive anything as empty expression, either by human or human group. It was one thing to interact with a single person, something entirely different to interact with two or more.

+ + +

THE DELUGE OF WORK she brought upon herself changed Cadie's schedule from one of playing guitar every night to erratic and back again. It was something to which Cadie gave no thought.

Her schedule, however, did not escape Aleck's attention.

Cadie's reversion from slapdash to regular had started after the bizarre snowy evening over a month ago. And Beatrice's insipid tedium spouted nothing newsworthy, at least not relevant. Beatrice had a narrow-minded view. As long as Cadie played, there was no cause for further concern.

Aleck, on the other hand, grew more alarmed. He was sensitive to Cadie's autonomy and privacy, but something had changed her schedule. Before the snow, she had stopped playing every night. Aleck felt it had something to do with the older man. Had the man dismissed or abandoned her just as she'd entered a healthy social fringe?

These were Aleck's thoughts as he entered his garage from the driveway, stamped his feet, and blew warm air into his hands. It amazed him that Cadie was playing now. He had gone outside, peered through the fence, and watched her for a minute. She wore a thick, green stocking cap and matching gloves with the fingertips missing. It was far too cold for him to sit out and listen tonight.

The slam of a car door in front of Cadie's house doubly urged Aleck inside. He ran quietly to his front window.

Dressed in a black wool suit, Karl Sikora squinted when he saw Aleck's fingers holding open a blind slat. Karl waved and motioned for Aleck to join him outside.

Startled, Aleck jumped back from the window. The man had seen him. As he could do nothing about it now, Aleck summoned composure and walked outside. The man was pulling a large flower bouquet from the car.

Where did he get daisies this time of year?

Karl turned to Aleck.

"Able to hold these, young man?" He placed the flowers in Aleck's left hand without waiting for an answer and extended his free hand.

"Karl Sikora. Nice to meet you." A hearty shake. "Didn't catch your name last time I came through."

"It's Aleck, sir . . . Aleck Turina."

"Sir Aleck Turina," Karl teased. "Well, nice to meet you, Sir Aleck. S'pose Cadie's home?" Karl nodded toward her house.

With Cadie's voice in the air, Aleck didn't have a choice but to confirm it. "She's in the back—playing guitar."

"She know ya'll listen to her like that?"

"Don't think so," said Aleck, his voice monotone to avert the swell of guilt.

Karl turned back to the car and pulled out a bottle of white wine and a white hat box with a black ribbon tied around it.

"Don't guess she would, though."

Aleck frowned. Karl seemed to know Cadie fairly well.

"Mind helping me to the door with this, Aleck? Brought too much for one load."

Trying not to frown, Aleck followed the older man. In any other situation, he'd have warmed right up to Karl. He liked the man's easy friendliness and his mild accent, perhaps Czech. Was Karl responsible, too, for Cadie playing Dvořák?

Karl rang the doorbell. "You know today's her birthday? She's twenty-seven today. I'm a sly old thing—snuck the information from her driver's license when she was down Christmas Eve. Guess she wasn't gonna tell anybody."

Aleck felt a little better. At least Cadie hadn't told Karl directly. Whether Cadie allowed herself awareness of her own birthday, Karl was a man confident enough to surprise her with it. Aleck didn't know if he should be impressed by or feel nervous for Karl.

"No, I didn't know."

Karl looked critically at Aleck and pressed the bell a second time. Then he grinned widely. "Well I won't hold it against you."

The music stopped.

When Cadie, still wearing the stocking cap, opened the door, Aleck blushed apologetically. It wasn't his fault, this interruption.

Cadie left neither of them a chance to talk first. "Karl, this is Aleck, my neighbor." There was no perceptible surprise in her voice.

Karl looked at Aleck and then Cadie. "I met him on the lawn." He stepped inside. "You dropped off the face of the earth, dear."

Cadie moved aside for Karl to enter the living room. "Come in with the flowers, Aleck."

Aleck jumped forward, happy in his good luck. "Hi, Cadie."

"Hi, Aleck."

In the kitchen, Karl deposited his items. "Well, open the box, Cadie," he said. He took the flowers from Aleck.

Cadie first examined the bottle of wine.

Karl held out the flowers. "Happy birthday, girlie."

Aleck was slow to echo Karl.

Cadie's eyes, otherwise expressionless, blinked several times in rapid succession.

"How do I know?" asked Karl, winking at Aleck. "*Chefs know.*"

Cadie smiled slightly and turned to Aleck. "Do you want to have some pâté with us?"

Laughing, Karl turned to Aleck. "She knows what's in the box . . . because of the wine I bring. What a talented apprentice gastronome."

Smiling at Karl to deflect his envy, Aleck wondered if Cadie could really be an apprentice to anything. What he especially wanted to know is how she'd come to know Karl, and well enough to know the contents of her surprise birthday box.

"I should be going," he said. "Left my garage door open."

"I bet your house is getting cold," said Cadie. She opened the box, withdrew a leaded crystal bowl filled with pâté.

Karl looked for a knife among the kitchen drawers as Cadie turned on the oven to heat the brioche. They worked with the comfortable movements of developed acquaintances.

Aleck turned to the front door.

"We're going to toast the brioche for the pâté," said Cadie. "It's good, very good."

Confused by her signals, Aleck wasn't sure whether he should go. He knew from his minimal exchanges with Cadie that she wasn't intentionally giving off signals. Trying to read her unconscious intent was nearly impossible, especially when distracted by who Karl Sikora was to Cadie.

"I should go, the house . . . unlocked," he said. "Happy birthday, Cadie."

Cadie stopped watching Karl, who was opening the wine, and looked at Aleck. "Thank you, Aleck." She offered a small smile. "Come back if you want some pâté and brioche."

Karl interrupted. "The garage door will be fine for a minute. Life must be toasted."

"The Sauternes is good," Cadie assured.

Aleck stayed long enough for one salutation, but left before the brioche was ready. Closing Cadie's front door behind him, Aleck caught the beginning of a new conversation between the pair inside.

"You can't go lookin' for family and then disappear when you find one. Don't care how much work you have. I, for one, am not gonna let you disappear into your proclivity for work," Karl said.

Silence from Cadie.

Aleck stood still on Cadie's porch before crossing the yards to his house. Had Cadie gone looking for family? If that was true, then Cadie might very well be changing. The harshest part of that truth to Aleck was that he wasn't part of it.

CHAPTER THIRTEEN

WITH FALA'S GROUNDWORK LAID and Karl's reminder of her new responsibilities, Cadie rescheduled her missed cooking lesson with Kamil. She also agreed to Friday night dinner with Ayala, companionship for the woman while Yosef attended to other matters of tradition.

Thus, Cadie found herself standing in the Alfasis' backyard. Teasings of early spring swept onto the verandah where a white tablecloth, pulled by the breezes, billowed and floated, a slow-motion ballooning threatening to lift and carry the round table into the sky. At least that's what Cadie imagined as she placed the soup tureen onto the multicolored, glass-topped table. The cloth flew up again and wrapped around her legs. Her sweetened, arak-scented breath moved in swirls about her, her hair lifting and churning around her face. Cadie took an elastic hair band from her pocket, pulled her hair into a loose chignon, and waited for Ayala to join her outside.

Over fish soup and challa, Cadie asked about Yosef's absence.

"Yosef belongs to the *Hevrat Veemat*. It's our holy society for burial. They prepare the body after death. Yosef is a member of the sub-group . . . on call to recite the final *Shema Yisrael* with Miriam." Ayala took a sip of wine. "Lung cancer . . . tumors went to her brain . . . never smoked a day in her life."

Cadie stopped eating. Ayala moved away the soup bowl, pushed a salad toward Cadie.

"After Miriam's last breath," she continued, "other members will follow strict washing rituals and blessings, walk seven circuits around her, and then guard the body until burial the following day. It is a sacred function."

"No embalming?"

"None. Besides, embalming fluid isn't good for our earth."

"How long is Yosef's tour?"

"When Miriam dies, or at the end of one week's duty when the shifts switch. Death can take sweet time at the end." She paused and looked at the sky. "I want mine to be fast."

"Does anyone ever die alone?"

"Not too often. Of course, you have run-of-the-mill heart attacks, blood clots in the leg, that sort of thing. But they are never alone as long as they haven't separated themselves from our community, at least not for the washing and guarding."

A shooting star blazed west across the Texas sky. Its angle of trajectory looked like it could hit Albuquerque, if it made it through the atmosphere at all. Ayala saw it just before it disappeared behind the trees towering in the yard.

"Of course, it wasn't always the same. Women can come and go to the graveyards as they please now. Not when I was a girl."

"Why not?"

"Girls weren't allowed. I was there for the washing of my parents, was only child. But I only got to kiss their hands . . . *before* the washing. Had I had a brother, he could have given the parting kiss after the washing. Instead, the *rabbi* kissed them. They would make no exception for me. It still upsets me. I never had a proper goodbye."

Ayala got up and went into the house, brought out the m'hancha with spring vegetables, a mix of beef and vegetables rolled into thin pastry dough and coiled snake-like on the platter. The flaky crust reminded Cadie of Kamil's savory boerekas.

The older woman sat and watched Cadie take a bite. "You weren't able to say goodbye, either."

"Nor hello."

Ayala nodded. "What about Sister Mary Trea? Tell me more of her, your nun."

Cadie swallowed hard to keep food from sticking in her craw.

"Sister Mary Trea named me," said Cadie, opting to skip the abuses she'd suffered at the orphanage. "When I was fourteen, I snuck into the office and found my file. Nothing in it could point me to my mother. She died in obscurity."

"But pain can be joy," said Ayala, waving her hand through the air awhirl.

Cadie frowned and took a bite of challa. How could pain be joy? She'd never felt joy while thinking about the nuns abuses or her mother's death.

Ayala understood the frown. "You imagine all the things you would have done with her, all the things she would have done for you. It causes you pain—all those rites of passage vanished before your first cry."

Cadie dropped her head, a single agreeing nod.

"You *can* imagine it as joy, Cadie. In an odd way, you've lived those moments with her. If you can imagine, you're capable of living them, no? Only loving that much can put you on a journey like the one you've started."

"You think it *loving?*" asked Cadie, raising her head.

"Maybe you think it indifference or anger." Ayala sipped her wine and leaned back into the brightly cushioned chair. "If this is so, you must not allow anger to carry you into the abyss. Sealing pain in one's mind ferments anger that steals love from the world. You can let the pain make you more human, more able to progress."

Rather than debate the point, Cadie asked herself if she shouldn't guard her tongue around these older women. Like Sister Mary Trea, they offered little psychological escape. In search of connections along an ancient ancestral path, Cadie had found more instruction than she'd reasonably anticipated. To be fair, she admitted that kindness cradled the directives, but she didn't want to discuss it any longer.

"How long is Yosef's tour if your friend lives longer than expected?" asked Cadie.

Frowning, Ayala looked deep into Cadie's eyes. Then she suddenly laughed. "Good try, Cadie Walsh. I'm not too old to see a subject change afoot."

Startled by Ayala's good-natured, astute response, Cadie couldn't help but broadly smile, her teeth flashing in the dim light.

Ayala started from her chair. She walked around the table and placed her hands on Cadie's cheeks. The coolness of the worn and loose-skinned fingers momentarily blocked the candlelight.

"That is more like it, dear."

The hands swept up to smooth back the hair fallen from Cadie's chignon.

"You are like a newborn. The world is opening to you."

"So Levana has not left us," interrupted Yosef, chuckling as he walked onto the verandah.

Clutching her chest in partial mock surprise, Ayala took her napkin and threw it at her husband.

"Quiet with that, Señor Alfasi."

She sounded angry, but she was smiling when she looked back at Cadie. "It was my dear mother's nickname for me. She said Levana was the protector of newborns."

"Either that or an angry wind," said Yosef. He turned Ayala's face to him and kissed her fully on the mouth.

After the kiss, Ayala asked, "So?"

"Not yet."

Ayala looked briefly at the sky and then started ladling food onto a plate for Yosef.

Cadie guessed they spoke of Miriam.

Yosef turned to Cadie. "Shabbat Shalom, Cadie." He patted her on the head and moved to an empty chair.

Her mind back on Yosef's comment, Ayala spoke to Cadie, "The *levanter* wind is gentle—don't listen to him."

"Ayala was too difficult for her mother to have another—so Ayala pestered all of the neighbors' babies to be her brothers and sisters," explained Yosef.

"You're the difficult one," said Ayala, shoving over the filled plate. "Eat. Cadie and I will get dessert."

AFTER DINNER, CADIE RETURNED home and focused on connecting Fala's many intricate modules. She thought about Ayala, the wife, and Levana, the protective child.

She protected to have siblings.

According to Yosef, Cadie wasn't an orphan anymore, but she still *felt* orphaned, and not only technically. Cadie feared that something inside of her was switched off, and no amount of thoughtful regulation had switched it to "on" or "normal" or whatever it was supposed to do and hadn't.

Piecing together Fala's "humane" censors that would work with the regulating, "interacting," sensors, Cadie remembered the other orphans at St. Fina's.

Her relationships had been tenuous at best, entirely broken after she had set off on her own and hadn't returned. She wondered if her absence had had any effect. Had she left them as underdogs sitting on the sidelines, watching in hopeful anticipation, wishing to leave as Cadie had?

The thought was disheartening. How many times during college classes had she driven herself to succeed only because her fear of failure was absolute? Failure had meant returning to the orphanage and Sister Mary Trea, a system that was only a mirage of support.

Still, Cadie had never bought into the clichéd doldrums of success as the best revenge. She didn't need revenge. What she wanted was somebody to tell her that she belonged. She needed to be part of something that came without accolades, not awarded due to merit or success. She wanted to be part of something that simply was . . . as families are.

Thinking back to the dinner conversation, Cadie probed the implicit significance of Ayala's new affection to her and the odd statement about Cadie as a newborn. What had happened to "switch on" Ayala's emotional response?

All in all, Cadie began to have serious doubts about her social interaction capabilities. Was she so underdeveloped that her ability to "read" others remained dormant? Was she not engrailed to behave and respond as the humans around her did, and what code lines were missing from the borders of her genetic tables? Even Fala would switch on and interact, after a certain amount of data-gathering and calibration.

Cadie decided once and for all, like in any code she developed, she'd have to figure out a way to run the "recover" command, try to retrieve readable information from her bad or defective social disk. Once recovered, maybe she could figure out a repair to reestablish her continuity of self.

+ + +

EARLY ON SATURDAY MORNING, Cadie carried the Adirondack chair and placed it halfway between the main path and the new gate. The morning breeze was uncharacteristically warm. She sat down and looked for signs of birds, peered into the dense foliage of the staggered evergreens, and didn't see any signs of nests.

Why am I outside looking for birds? Finalizing code is what I need to be doing—Fala is two weeks away from testing.

Remembering her coffee, now well past brewed, Cadie got up. But distracted again, she stepped closer to a tree and gently parted the soft branches. No nests in the shaded center. She walked down the row, parting boughs as she went. In the second to last tree, before the main garden path, were remnants of an old nest.

There are birds in my garden.

She stepped back and wondered what bird had housed and birthed a new generation in her yard, how she had never noticed chirping, singing, or flying during all of her walks through the yard or endless hours sitting on her back porch. She'd never missed a bad code line in a failing program. How could she miss something growing under her nose?

Cadie stuffed her hands into her worn jeans pockets and stepped onto the main path. She stopped, a puzzled look crossing her face. From her right pocket, she pulled the gate key. *How did that get there?* She didn't remember picking up the key. Lost in a fog of thought, she robotically walked back toward the gate and unlocked it.

Within minutes, she was inside. A fresh cup of coffee sat on her bathroom counter as she stepped into the shower.

On the other side of the fence, Aleck hit the brakes to stop his car's backward momentum. The partially open gate all but changed his morning plans. His mode of relaxation on weekend mornings was reading his newspaper at the bakery. Not now, not with the gate ajar. He rolled down his window before turning off the car and listened. The only sound coming from her yard was a cardinal's chirping. Hoping he had time to fetch pastries and get back before the gate closed, Aleck restarted the car and backed from his driveway.

After her shower, Cadie quickly determined she would spend the morning playing guitar. No need to waste a warm winter morning.

She went outside and played music that kept her neighbors lulled in an extended sleep. All except for Beatrice Beauregard, that is. Beatrice's disorientation over the early morning concert prompted the woman's rapid departure. She drove straight to visit her sister at the Masterson Cotillion for Not-Just-Any Canine.

Returning, Aleck steered his car into the alley and looked carefully at Beatrice's house. Her van was gone from the driveway. Aleck smiled. He wouldn't have to sneak into Cadie's yard to keep Beatrice from seeing him sit in his private arboretum amphitheater. He quickly parked his car and got out to listen. He walked straight to

Cadie's yard when he heard her singing and opened the gate just enough to squeeze through with his pastry breakfast and *venti* coffee.

When he saw she'd moved the chair away from the fence and closer to the garden's center, he told himself not to think about it. Tucked comfortably in his seat, he bit into his cinnamon roll and listened. The cardinal he'd heard earlier chirped at him from a tree near the main path. Smiling, he took another bite and then tossed a few crumbs toward the scolding male bird. The bird ignored them. Unable to keep his mind off the why of the matter, Aleck ducked over to his garage and retrieved the morning newspaper from inside his car.

Reading the news helped Aleck slip into as normal a Saturday morning scene as he could imagine for himself. He could get used to reading the paper over breakfast while Cadie sang. The sun began to rise over the evergreens on the east side of the yard. The cardinal, resigned to Aleck's presence, went about its work of flying between the Garcias' bird feeders and its tree. After an hour, Aleck set down the paper.

It occurred to him that Cadie was repeating songs he'd heard her sing earlier. Repetition in the same concert was aberrant for her. Aleck listened carefully to the sequences and at first thought something was absent from Cadie's voice. But no, her voice was fine. Instead, she sounded entirely absent, absent from her thoughts, her songs, and strumming. The repetition, decided Aleck, allowed Cadie to be somewhere else in her mind.

What is she searching for?

The cardinal chirped a warning in answer and flew away.

Aleck sighed. Whatever Cadie searched for, she hadn't found, or she would have already moved on into her endless repertoire. What she sang was familiar to him, the Three Noble Strains of Ireland. Of *goltraí, geantraí,* and *suantraí*—weeping, merriment, and sleep—over and over and over again.

After another half hour of the same songs, Aleck left the garden. The cardinal flew to the chair and landed on it as soon as Aleck walked away. Leaving Cadie alone in her solitary, musical loop, Aleck closed the gate. He hoped she would find whatever her mind kept from her. Its domain secure, the male bird flew out of the yard for more seed.

The Three Noble Strains were songs Cadie had learned from Sister Mary Trea. Sometimes, Cadie had stood outside the door and listened to the nun singing in her private chambers. The songs were quiet undertones of the nun's past, a fleeting and slim connection to joy. But as Cadie sang, she wasn't thinking of the nun. She wasn't aware of thinking or remembering anything.

Well into another round of the strain of merriment, Cadie looked up and visually registered the bright red bird flying over her largest magnolia tree. The bird swooped toward the evergreen where she had seen the nest. Cadie set down her guitar and tiptoed to the path. When she turned onto the trail where the chair sat, the bird flew past her and out of the yard. Holding aside the bower, Cadie looked for changes in the dilapidated twig and plastic strips habitat. Inside the branches, the pungent foliage shared a distinct scent of coffee. Cadie stepped back, let the branches rush together, and walked toward the Adirondack chair.

On a bright blue ceramic plate sat a clean dessert fork and a fresh cinnamon roll covered with chopped pecans. Beside the plate was a large paper cup covered with a plastic lid. Under the beverage and the plate sat a gently used newspaper. Cadie lifted the cup to her nose. Coffee, still warm. She touched the pastry, also warm. The gate was slightly ajar.

Did I open it?

Telling herself she needed more rest, Cadie sat down to enjoy the breakfast. It was an altogether strange morning.

The bird returned to the tree, accepted Cadie's presence, and went about its duties.

"Are you one of Gabriella's cardinals?" she asked the bird.

When the cardinal didn't answer, Cadie took another bite and picked up the newspaper. It was the first time she'd ever sat to read news she couldn't find online. She ran her fingers over the thin ink on the smooth paper and then started reading.

AFTER BREAKFAST, CADIE FOUND herself calling Karl and then downloading a recipe for *m'hancha* instead of working on Fala. In her kitchen with the just-purchased and thawing phyllo dough, Cadie glanced at her watch. One o'clock. Karl would arrive any minute to show her how to brown and cook the lamb for the special pastry. Cadie looked at her closed office door, unable to understand why it was so easy today to block out her mountain of work. She reached over the growing pile of ingredients on her counter and picked up her ringing phone.

"Cadie, here."

"Girlie, I'll be there in about ten minutes. Need anything else from the store?"

"No. The front door's unlocked. Just come in."

"Will do." Karl hung up and rolled his eyes. He wondered how many had mistaken Cadie's practicality with an easy-going nature.

Cadie eyed the ingredients in front of her. She had enough for two large coils. She needed Karl in order to tackle the difficult m'hancha recipe on her own. As far as Cadie was concerned, her call to Karl was a mere matter of needed instruction, not social interaction or an unconscious avoidance of spending a Saturday alone. She leaned against the counter and tallied everything—the kettle was on and heating, the coffee grounds waited in the French press, and the crystal pitcher full of water and cut citrus fruits sat beside two tall glasses. It was quiet. She looked out of the kitchen windows and tried to spot the cardinal.

Karl's voice interrupted from the front of the house. "Hello? I'm here, girlie." In his arms, he carried a large box. "Brought sandwiches to eat while we cook."

"What kind?"

"Clean out the refrigerator kind. Egg salad—two different kinds, sardine spread, ham and cheese, radish and cheese."

Cadie stepped over and looked inside the box. A small cake sat beside quartered sandwiches of dark rye and plain white bread. "Umm, cake."

"Hazelnut coffee cake—has actual coffee in it. Coffee cream frosting."

"Best news I've heard all day. You had time to make that today?"

Karl set down the box on the bar and pulled out the small cake. "Made it yesterday—for the polka dance *tonight*."

At Cadie's blank look, he added, "Don't worry, they won't miss an extra cake. Anyway, I need to go up to the restaurant after we cook." He picked up the heated water and poured it into the press.

"When do you have to be at the restaurant?"

Karl laughed. "Don't we have some cooking to do? Where's the recipe?"

She handed over the paper. While Karl looked at it, she selected a radish and cheese sandwich to try. The spread, a mix of grated radishes, cream cheese, chives, and butter, tasted good on dark bread.

"Have you ever had arak?" she asked.

"Not that I recall."

"I think the licorice would complement the radish spread." Cadie told him about the snack of arak, radishes, and cake at the Alfasis'.

Karl smiled. Here Cadie needed help with browning meat, and at the same time taught him something new.

"Maybe I should go out for some?"

"Don't leave me alone with the phyllo," said Cadie around a mouthful of the sandwich.

Karl dropped the recipe. "Now she jokes," he said aloud. He saw just a hint of smile at the corners of her mouth.

Cadie handed a sandwich to Karl and then poured two cups of coffee.

"Think we can make this?"

"Don't see why not. If you can build robots, you can dice a vegetable."

They set about dicing carrots, turnips, and potatoes. Compared to the perfectly cubed, multicolored organic jewels that quickly mounded on Karl's cutting board, Cadie's vegetable pile was composed of jagged, inconsistent rhombus shapes. Shelling peas was easier. She helped Karl blanch the vegetables with the fresh spinach before sweating the vegetable mixture in butter seasoned with paprika, parsley, cilantro, and cumin. They set the mixture aside and next sautéed onions with the ground lamb. To the meat, they added a robust spice mix, which included cinnamon and fresh mint. After the meat browned, they added eggs and then stirred in the vegetables. Finally, they came to the phyllo. Cadie stepped back to watch Karl's nimble fingers work with the thin dough.

"M'hancha," said Karl. "This would be nice every now and then at the restaurant."

As Karl explained to Cadie the finer details of how to handle the phyllo dough and rolled the first m'hancha log, Cadie counted the list of ingredients. She held up the photo next to Karl's rendition and nodded, satisfied.

"This recipe has over thirty ingredients."

"Recipes can be like that. One ingredient, another ingredient . . . each just one piece added to another." Karl wrapped the long tube into a snake's coil on the baking plate and motioned for Cadie to do the next one. "Soon you have one thing again. In this case, one m'hancha." He moved aside and ate a sardine spread sandwich as Cadie worked on her pastry.

"One m'hancha," she repeated, stepping back from her finished coil. She almost couldn't believe she'd done it. "Will it taste okay?"

"With everything mixed, it will be fine. No one can taste amateur cuts," he said with a wink. "Let's put them in and have cake."

Karl set the microwave's timer as soon as he closed the oven door. Cadie looked at her watch. It'd taken three hours from start of prep to beginning of baking. She shook her head. It would only take twelve minutes to bake. Karl handed her a piece of cake.

"Now let's see this garden of yours. Hardly been able to take my eyes off that window all afternoon." Without waiting, Karl, cake in hand, left the kitchen and went outside. He led the way down the garden path."

"This is some garden, girlie."

"I lost two trees last fall to the storm," she said, pointing with her fork toward a side path at the end of the yard.

Karl turned. The path headed west and then curved north back toward Cadie's house. Just as it turned east again, Karl noticed the fence and the new gate. Not long after, he came to the chair in the middle of the path, stopped and looked at it for a few seconds. When he looked at Cadie, he pretended not to notice the small blush on her cheeks.

She pointed his attention eastward toward an arborvitae.

"I found a bird's nest in there this morning. I think it's a cardinal."

"The red bird I've been seeing from the kitchen?"

"Yes."

"It's a cardinal."

Karl looked back at the fence now partially obscured by the other trees. It seemed no small coincidence that the chair was placed smack dab in the path and that Aleck Turina's house was just on the other side of the new gate. He took a few steps back toward the chair.

Just then, Cadie looked at her watch and started to run. "The m'hancha."

WHEN BOTH PERFECTLY BROWNED m'hancha came from the oven, Karl begged leave of his protégé. "I'll be late getting to the restaurant. You keep the second pastry," he insisted, heading toward the door. "Don't forget about the polka dance next Saturday night. I'll expect you mid-afternoon."

"I'll be there," said Cadie. She stood at the door long enough for Karl to leave her porch.

Before Karl turned onto the main road out of the suburb, Cadie settled in front of the television with her dinner. She started a short sitcom and, for the second evening in a row, bit into the exotic dish. She closed her eyes and chewed. Though using lamb was quite different from beef and the phyllo flavor and texture wasn't quite the same as Ayala's homemade *yufka* dough, it was similar enough.

The only problem was the second m'hancha. She had expected Karl to take it with him. It briefly occurred to her to freeze the pastry, but she didn't like the idea of the fresh delicacy subjected to ice crystals. Rather than finish the sitcom, she grabbed a clean fork and walked the second m'hancha out to the garden chair. With quick confirmation that the gate was still unlocked, she opened it. She returned to her porch and picked up her guitar.

When Aleck heard the music, he quickly emerged from his house. Cadie was playing Moroccan music now. He wondered what had broken her out of the repetitive loop. He smiled at the open gate, disbelieving it was possible. For weeks, the gate locked. Now, open twice in one day. He looked over at Beatrice's. She was still gone. Aleck grabbed a glass of wine from inside and walked to Cadie's yard.

As any adult recognizing something dear from childhood, Aleck jumped forward when he saw what graced the plate. He sat down and eagerly took the first bite, was transported to memories of his Spanish grandmother. Very nearly so, she had made this dish and set it before him when he was only as tall as eye level with her worn plank table.

For many protracted and mirthful minutes, Aleck forgot that he sat in Cadie Walsh's yard and that, for a second time that day, he and Cadie had shared food without sight of each other or exchanging a single word.

CHAPTER FOURTEEN

B EFORE LEAVING FOR HER cooking lesson with Kamil, Cadie
sent an email to Bobby to see if he would be available the first
Friday in March for a meeting, approximately one hour.

An excerpted Irish clog dance trill broke into the drone in the
conference room where Bobby Pullman sat with several engineers
and sales people long since languished of energy. Email, phone calls,
messages—any communication from Cadie Walsh was set with its
own special identifier, something loud and perky that Bobby couldn't
miss or pretend to ignore. He liked the idea of associating Cadie's
persona with the lively tunes and clog dancing—not the Irish ballads
more befitting the young woman's cool personality.

Bobby smiled and quickly pulled his tablet toward him.

The rest of his staff and most of his clients were used to it. At
the sound of Irish clogs, they could look forward to a mini-break
as Bobby checked a message or took a call from his chief engineer.
Everyone in the room stopped talking. If they were lucky, whatever
Cadie communicated would get them out of a meeting that threatened to run well past dinnertime.

Bobby's response was quick. "Anytime," he typed and sent off
the message with an added flourish of humor, knowing the jocosity
would be lost on her.

"Meeting's over. Have a great weekend, everyone."

Without explanation, he left the room and jogged to his office.
Halfway past his assistant's desk, he started a jig.

"Clear the schedule for next Friday, Miranda. Cadie's coming in."

"But you have the clients from . . . "

"Clear them, too," he smiled and winked.

"Don't you wink at me, Bobby Pullman," she teased.

Miranda knew as well as Bobby did that Cadie's pet project was
certain for unveiling next Friday. With a satisfied smile, she swept

her long, red hair off her shoulders and proceeded to go through his calendar. Her boss, already good-natured, was robot crazy, and a new product really revved up his boyishness.

"There's nobody else to wink at is there?"

"Wait 'til I tell my husband."

"What's my brother gonna do about it?" he goaded. "You tell him we got a new robot on the way." Pretending to have a two-step partner, he danced into his office and shouted over his shoulder. "And get on outta here. Should've already been home on a Friday afternoon."

"It's just now five oh one." Miranda flashed mock anger at her brother-in-law's back and finished rescheduling the meetings.

+ + +

CADIE, ASSUMING KAMIL'S TURKIC stenciling matched the jars' contents, pulled a clear glass jar filled with walnuts from the pantry shelf. She checked the ingredients list and collected gallon jars of dried chickpeas, green lentils, and orzo. Carefully balancing her load, she walked to the kitchen and deposited the staples on the counter.

"I need help with the paprika and ground red pepper. There are at least six containers of red spices."

Busy assembling various pots on the stove and filling them with water, Kamil stopped and followed Cadie to the large pantry. She reached to an eye-level shelf and grabbed two, quart jars.

"Paprika. Red Pepper." She pointed at the different lettering on each. "As you've seen, red is common in Turkish cooking." She motioned toward the whole cumin seeds in a different jar. "That, too—we will grind it ourselves."

Kamil left with the red spices. Cadie pulled the cumin seeds from the shelf. Going to the tall bins pushed against one wall, she measured out long-grained rice and dumped the grains into an empty bowl. With the rice and cumin seeds, she returned to the kitchen. "I didn't see the walnut oil."

"It is here," said Kamil, pointing at the bottle. "You will like Circassian chicken. The spicy walnut sauce mixed with shredded chicken is a favorite. Basir's mother cooked it for us on our wedding day."

"Did she serve it with the pilaf like we're making today."

"No, with vegetable fritters and fried eggplant. She treated me as if the marriage had been long planned."

From the refrigerator Kamil pulled the bowl of chickpeas soaked in water overnight.

"Did Basir's mother know about the . . . "

"Yes, but from Basir." Kamil paused and looked away. "She . . . we never discussed."

"Why did you stay with Basir?"

"He was strong enough to give me a future, one where I had a choice." Kamil worked at rinsing the chickpeas.

"Does Zahid know?"

"It is too much anger for a child to bear. He accepts that some people start life without family." Kamil handed some Spanish onions to Cadie. "But maybe Basir told him. He was never like other boys on our street . . . so different. It shocked everyone when he married a girl from Mexico."

"Molly?"

"Yes. I loved her very much, was very proud of Zahid. It takes bravery to follow one's heart."

Cadie chopped the onions and wondered why Kamil and Basir had shared their story with her, a practical stranger.

"We should have coffee," she said, dropping chicken breasts into warming chicken broth. "Many on our street were angry when Zahid married Molly. Not Basir."

"Were you angry?"

"No . . . nervous. And afraid, but Basir is never afraid." Kamil looked at Cadie. "I think this is why he tells you my story so easily." Kamil motioned for the chopped onions and began sautéing them in butter.

Cadie moved over and silently watched the flame dancing around and licking the sides of the ibrik.

"It is said that the Armenian genocide was spurred by harassment of a woman . . . Turkish soldiers killed the two men that came to her rescue. When my sister . . . "

The sputter of liquid hitting the hot sauté pan drew Cadie's notice. After a few more tears, Kamil gained control and continued.

"Basir did not tell you. My sister *did* make it back to Gördes. En route to her arranged marriage, my sister was raped before she could flee. The family of that criminal dragged her to our doorstep and proclaimed her indecency to Father. Many neighbors heard. She was gone the next morning when I woke. Murdered."

Unsure of what to do, Cadie handed a cup of coffee to Kamil. With a sad grimace, Kamil took the dainty cup.

"Except for Basir, never have I seen a man rush to aid a woman . . . not even here, in this country. A great woman welcomes all to the gates of these shores, but still there are problems like my sister's . . . even on this street. In the middle of a free country. With feet on this shore, people quickly turn away from the great statue. Under her gaze, they forget." Sighing, Kamil took a sip of the sweetened coffee. "Here, one doesn't find the meaning they expected. There is barely more reason than my uncle had. Where is Allah when a man raises his hand or votes to harm a woman, anyone? Where is any god?"

Ashamed that she didn't understand everything Kamil conveyed, Cadie asked, "Your sister . . . was the incident isolated?"

The look on Kamil's face changed from one of musing to cavernous anger. "Not isolated, Cadie, and not as different as you think. Too many in our faith . . . a raped woman . . . she is lashed, murdered, or advised to marry her rapist. Here, women are encouraged to bear random conception from rape, pressured to seal herself to her rapist. How is that not her slashing or murder? Time never heals such wounds. Our cultures take different forms of similar travesty—women forced to bear the responsibility of men's morality. Rape culture is not *ummah*."

"Ummah?" asked Cadie.

Kamil separated the sautéed onions and turned down the flame under the boiling chicken.

"Ummah is everything—the whole community. We say the thing connecting us is a rope of woven light. I think the rope severed. I can never go to my family's table again, never feel safe. If my family finds me, they will kidnap me, murder me, won't care that I wear the scarf now. My father would not be able to save me."

"You didn't wear the scarf in Turkey?"

"No, of course not."

Kamil drained the last of the coffee from her cup, leaned in, and whispered. "We are not really ummah . . . there are many Muslims who hate other Muslims, the same in any religion."

Cadie looked around for the reason to explain Kamil's whisper. They were alone. Basir wasn't home. Had Kamil whispered to keep herself from hearing the full sound of what she voiced? *That* Cadie could understand.

"It's true," agreed Cadie.

Kamil pulled the cooked chicken from its broth. "My great-grandmothers told of Turkish women who once fought alongside men, ancient mothers buried, like their husbands, with their weapons. What did they do when asked to relinquish their arms? Did they submit willingly, those women? Or did they walk, helpless and poor, to early graves?"

She showed Cadie how to shred the delicate chicken using two forks and then turned over the task to her apprentice.

"If it's true what the prayer says, that Allah made woman in his image, then I know that Allah does not smile. With our arms was also taken our freedom of joy."

OUTSIDE IN THE CENTRAL COURTYARD, the women ate the walnut chicken with the rice pilaf. Cadie pointed at the glossy-leaved shrubs covered with waxy red or white flowers.

"What are those flowers?"

"Camellias," said Kamil, a small smile on her face.

"Camellias," repeated Cadie. After another bite, "You chose your name after these flowers?"

"Yes. My favorite time of year is when they bloom—they start before it is truly warm here. Each flower lasts a long time."

Cadie got up, walked to the nearest shrub, and ran her fingers over the smooth leaves and thick petals. Bright orange-yellow stamens erupted from the blossoms. "Did you have these in Turkey?"

"No." She pointed at the shrub in the garden's center. "Basir gave me that shrub the day I flew to Texas. I kept it in a pot until we moved here."

Without hesitation, Cadie broke the woody stems of two red flowers. She brushed aside her hair, placed one of the blossoms behind her ear. Kamil unconsciously checked to make sure her scarf was in place. Ignoring Kamil's discomfort, Cadie walked straight to her friend and, guessing where Kamil's ear was, ran the hard stem of the second flower under the edge of the bright blue scarf.

"Now you have a gul, Kamil. A *camellia* gul." She stepped back and looked at the effect. The idea of giving Kamil a family symbol, one she could own without fear, caused an emotion in Cadie that burst forth in a broad, unintentional smile.

Startled as much by the flower sticking out from under her scarf as Cadie's remark, Kamil's eyes brightened when she reached up to touch the petals. Never before had she picked the blossoms, but had always let the petals slowly dry, curl as they did into brown bonnets that eventually fell and covered the courtyard in a solid blanket of spent vitality. Left to rot, the soil consumed and converted them into loamy earth to feed next year's blooms.

Cadie had only just sat down when Kamil rose and walked around the table. She planted a quick kiss on Cadie's forehead and then picked up the platter of walnut boerekas. Her face lit up with a smile she tried to shield with her shoulder.

"We must have walnut boerekas to celebrate," she said.

Graced with the power of opportune interruption, Basir came walking into the courtyard. He stopped the instant he saw his wife smiling so. Then he quickly approached before Kamil saw him and grasped her hand holding the plate.

With a quick intake of breath, Kamil stopped smiling and looked at the ground. The boerekas fell to the table, landing this way and that among the place settings.

That's when Cadie saw that Basir was smiling, a smile that didn't warrant fear now . . . or later when the couple would be alone.

"What's this?" he asked, gently touching the flower.

Kamil heard the affection in his voice and looked up. She answered unhesitantly. "Cadie has given me a camellia to be my gul."

Chuckling, Basir sniffed the flower. "It is perfect," he said. He kissed his wife's forehead. "With it, you might discard the scarf?"

He turned his grin on Cadie. "Lovely choice, Cadie. This is how I see her in my dreams."

"With a flower?"

"No, smiling." He grabbed a boereka and turned to leave.

As soon as Basir disappeared into the house, Kamil turned to Cadie with a renewed smile. She chose three boerekas from the table and placed them on the girl's plate.

"See, he has no fear."

+ + +

LOW LIGHT FROM MULTIPLE computers' on/off switches reflected from Fala's sensor necklace. The darkish lab was quiet until Cadie turned on the lights and awakened the computers from power-save mode. Yawning, she inspected the fully assembled robot. The finished Fala exceeded her expectations, at least in appearance.

The savvy mechanical engineers had used the template of a department store mannequin. Fala's richly pigmented skin, though, was an illusion, nothing more than light reflected from a one-hundred-percent metallic object. From the sensor necklace down, a metallic brown and gold printed sheath dress hugged her figure, would move as dense silk when she walked. Integrated in the dress were highly tuned robotics sensors. At Cadie's request, the engineers had left Fala's head unembellished by hair. The African savanna queen now stood, waiting for initialization.

Tired from spending seven nights alone in the lab to finish preliminary testing and tired of chewing over whether Fala would succeed, Cadie hoped the florescent lights would jar her into wakefulness. She moved heavily, overfull from Kamil's food, to turn on her laptop remotely connected to her home computer. Only a few more subsystem module connections needed. Then she would run the build and wait to see if Fala would have the continuity and coherence of social interaction without robotic behavior.

While she worked, Cadie thought of Kamil's responses that evening, the re-routing from cautious smiles, to tears, and finally to the happy kiss on Cadie's forehead.

Had the camellia as a new gul prompted Kamil's kiss and smile?

There was a moment after she spoke before Kamil had approached her, a few moments of nothing on Kamil's face. What *had* re-routed Kamil? Come to think of it, what had re-routed Ayala? Her words to the women had been different, yet something had sparked the women into movements of intimate, motherly interaction with her.

After a few hours, Cadie sent the last code build to the robot. She moved to a stool placed near the room's center. There was an element of risk in testing for only a few days what Bobby would test for a month, but she was anxious to proceed to the tail-end of operative data that would activate Fala's awareness and awaken the robot from silence. Cadie waited.

Fifty minutes later, just before the robot lifted its head, wireless transmissions of encrypted data sent to Cadie's computer from Fala's brain began to flash on the twelve, fifty-two inch flat-panel screens hanging around the lab's elliptical wall.

Cadie watched the data variables write across the different screens. Fala was sensing the lab bench and stools, the computers, and light and shadow by comparing the objects with her built-in dictionary and image files. Quickly populating her growing data registry, the robot then saw Cadie. Cadie's blood pressure and heart rate appeared in coded format on one of the screens, her body temperature on a different screen from the one showing the room temperature. Without a doubt, the robot could see the human, Cadie Walsh, sitting in the room.

Fala took a step toward Cadie and then another. Cadie watched her blood pressure reading increase, but sat still, allowing Fala to perform the next measurements. Within a few feet of her, the robot circled the girl, measuring Cadie's facial and head features without touching her.

Engrossed, Cadie watched the mathematical matrices of her features scroll across a screen, each detail of her physical appearance becoming a set of digits. Stemming from the carefully coded tables, Fala transformed the numbers into recognition and proximity to Cadie. Nervously, Cadie forced herself to smile, watching the screen as she did. The numbers for her facial features changed. On another screen, Fala registered the smile against stored images, matched it with the dictionary for "smile," and then attributed a "positive" value to Cadie's expression.

In a loss of self-control, Cadie yawned.

Fala registered it and then moved to the lab bench where Cadie's half-full coffee pot sat on a warming plate. The robot filled Cadie's empty cup. On the saucer, the robot delicately placed two sugar cubes. Fala moved with grace and purpose as she extended the drink to Cadie.

Cadie smiled and then laughed.

"Thank you, Fala. Maybe I shouldn't have hard-coded you with my few preferences, but we only have a few days before the big test with Bobby." She took the cup and placed a cube of sugar between her teeth before taking a drink. "It's good."

"You're welcome, Cadie."

Cadie smiled again.

Fala's voice could easily be mistaken for Cadie's, who had recorded her own voice into the language and sound modules, adjusting and tweaking until the hollow computer sound was entirely removed from Fala's voice. Over time, the robot would learn and mirror dialectic nuances of her surrounding region, her language and voice adjusting to a group's primary speech, accent, and tone.

Coded with simple partitions based on formal and informal, Fala had partitions for everything, partitions to which she would add her own data. The robot would learn that Bobby liked beer with BBQ, not champagne. Bobby, as expressive as he was, would provide a perfect test run.

"Okay, Fala, no more talking for thirty-six hours. We need a reasonable test between the two of us before I release you on Bobby."

The robot nodded.

Watching the screens to make sure that Fala's observation systems were working, Cadie smiled. So far, the robot hadn't stopped monitoring the external environment or Cadie's vital and somatic systems. It was proper good.

This time, when Fala approached to pick up the half-empty coffee cup, Cadie covered the cup with her hand. Fala stopped and moved away, registering the smile as something other than Cadie wanting more coffee.

Cadie continued with her work at the computer. She finished her coffee and stood up. Fala had taken her eyes from Cadie. The robot moved closer. Refilling her own cup this time, Cadie switched off the pot, returned to her lab stool, and watched the screens.

Fala correctly correlated: *if cup completely empty, then fill cup.*

Cadie smiled again.

Fala registered the smile against the previous "no coffee" smile and tentatively labeled it as "pleased."

Cadie nodded.

Fala permanently registered the smile as "pleased."

"That's good, Fala. No more interaction. Just watch for now."

Cadie slapped her hand over her mouth.

"I forgot. Okay, no talking . . . starting now." She smiled and pointed straight down at the floor, indicating a place for "now."

At that moment, Cadie intuited the strange comment from Ayala and the kiss from Kamil.

Could smiles propel people to such behavior? Was it that ridiculously simple?

But those smiles hadn't been just any smiles, thought Cadie. They were unforced, without active thought, intent, or reason—came from an emotional place, expressed without intellectual approval. The responses were interactions she'd never before experienced or had known possible to evoke. Cadie looked at Fala and then back at the screens. The robot registered another increase in Cadie's blood pressure and heart rate and measured the perspiration forming on her forehead.

Why didn't I think of it before?

Her displayed smiles, routed from her brain's emotional seat, had altered everything. Those interactions had formed permanent memories attached to the smiles. In the smile Fala had just registered, Cadie had elicited cognitive frames of happiness—happiness from Ayala's affectionate and loving scolding, happiness from giving a flower to fill Kamil's empty gul. Further down, she faintly remembered how the usually comfortable and social Aleck had frozen and become affixed to the snowy street after she'd spontaneously smiled at him. *That* smile had happened just after her breakthrough idea, when she'd realized she could use expression to code for robotic intelligence and learning.

The unique feeling of coherence increased Cadie's rate of breathing. She rubbed her chest. Had her lack of expression often interrupted the continuity of others' reactions to her? Was it all because her earliest smiles garnered negative reaction? Was *that* why Kamil was afraid to smile?

The studies she'd read had also illuminated how the brain lost plasticity as a person aged, but periods of trauma could reintroduce enough plasticity to develop, rewire, new pathways away from previous, hard-wired, behavior. The rewiring could be negative and introduce post-traumatic stress disorder symptoms. But in the right setting, cognitive behavior changes could rewire to the positive.

Instinctively, Cadie knew that trauma had ruptured Kamil's smile. Cadie now felt that she had witnessed a beginning repair. The sudden impact of finding a trigger, one to release her own trained response to dead-pan expression, gripped Cadie from the deep of her amygdala.

Spinning around once on the stool, Cadie smiled bigger than she ever had.

On the screens, Fala registered Cadie's bared teeth and labeled the smile as happiness, tentative elation, not aggression.

Cadie jumped up and left the lab without slowing down. Fala followed her out of the lab, down the hall, and upstairs to the company's break room. From the refrigerator, Cadie fished out leftover chocolate cake from the birthday party the previous day. She cut a large slice and thought more about brain plasticity.

Testing her genome had warmed the hard ground of her social wiring, had shaken the trauma of abuse inherited from the orphanage and Salley's death. As long as she recognized it, Cadie thought, the growing fire in her mind could re-erect a social structure faster than it had fallen. For change need not take forever.

Resolving herself to action, Cadie bit into the cake.

That's what I'll do—test myself while I test Fala.

She would try grandiose smiles and observe what happened afterwards. She would see if the rerouting stuck, allowed her a more seamless integration among others. For the first time, it dawned on her that her smiles hadn't interrupted Aleck's, Ayala's, or Kamil's social continuity more than it had interrupted her own *discontinuity*. Surprisingly enough, it hadn't been all that bad.

CHAPTER FIFTEEN

ON HIS WAY TO THE personal break room that he shared with Miranda, Bobby pounded hard enough on the edge of Miranda's desk to make her jump. He chuckled at the reward for his effort and kept walking. It was a daily pleasure, giving his sister-in-law a hard time.

"She's done it—locked out the electrical and mechanical engineers from her lab. They couldn't get in this morning. Gonna be a good Monday."

Miranda shuffled her hands together in a "goody-goody" sign and went back to typing an agenda to procure buyers for Cadie's new and mysterious project. When Cadie removed the other engineers' code and fingerprint clearances, thus locking them out of the prototype lab, it meant everything was on track. As hoped, they could count on a successful delivery at the week's end.

Bobby yelled from the nearby room. "We better get the marketing templates ready for whatever she's gonna throw at us. Want 'em ready in less than two weeks from this Friday."

He emerged with a full cup of coffee and a warmed breakfast wrap with scrambled egg whites and bacon, his wife's attempt at a healthier meal, not that he looked like he needed to cut back. Bobby Pullman could still "rodeo with the best of 'em," as he liked to say.

"Two weeks?" Miranda not only loved her brother-in-law, she liked him, and it says a lot to like something you don't handpick yourself.

"Unless you think we can do it faster." He shuffled into his office.

"Two weeks it is," shouted Miranda after him. Two weeks was short enough notice for a known project.

Bobby plopped down in his chair and threw his boots up on the corner of his desk. He picked up his cell phone, hit a speed-dial button, and let it ring.

"Cadie here."

"Is this Cadie Walsh?" he joked.

"Good morning, Bobby."

Bobby grinned. He couldn't rope her into kidding around with him this morning.

"Mornin', darlin'. Is it an accident that my EE and ME are locked out of the lab?"

He had the responsibility of making sure Cadie was behind the security change. Better safe than sorry.

"No. We're on track."

"Thataway, darlin' . . . just wanted to hear it for myself. See you on Friday."

"On Friday."

When he hung up the phone, Bobby thought he heard a slight smile in Cadie's voice. He grinned and bit into his breakfast wrap. It *was* gonna be a good week.

+ + +

THE NOTE ON THE DESK said it all.

Meet me in the lab. Cadie

Without stopping by the break room to start coffee, Bobby jogged down the long hall to the elevator that would carry him to the basement.

The building was quiet. It was too early for most of his employees to be out of bed. Bobby knew that his one employee waiting in the lab had been there all night. He tapped his boot on the black marble floor as he descended underground.

Cadie hadn't allowed the other engineers to secretly breathe a word about her project to him—not one spec or even a thumbs up to let him know that his millions sunk into the rapid-prototype development was going to be worthwhile. He was talking to himself when the elevator doors opened to the starkly lit hallway.

"By god, Bobby, stop actin' like a girl on her wedding day."

He tried to calm himself and pushed down hope that Cadie had busted what AI engineers worldwide struggled to master—the finer details that would allow robots, like humans, to interact by learning and modifying behavior according to environment and experience. On the lab door was taped another scrawled note.

"Like a damn scavenger hunt," he muttered to himself.

It would be more fun if his expectations and hopes weren't so much at stake.

Fingerpad working for your print. No code needed this morning.

Bobby pushed his thumb against the scanner and waited for the bolt to unlock.

On the other side of the door, Cadie looked up from her computer and quickly scanned Bobby's T-shirt as he entered. The shirt sported a new picture of his daughters holding basketballs.

"Good morning."

"Mornin', darlin'. What've we got?"

Despite her all-night stay, Cadie was freshly showered, radiant.

And that's why I have showers at the office, thought Bobby.

Bobby grinned. "Show me somethin' good, Cadie. Was so excited I couldn't sleep."

"First, ground rules for testing."

Cadie knew her boss well enough to know that she was about to deliver what he had been hoping for since she had started churning out her first projects for him after college. She motioned toward the stool in the center of the room. The pendant robot on her necklace danced. In front of the raised dais was an electronically controlled metal partition that kept him from seeing the new robot.

"Ground rules?" He wrinkled his nose and waited for Cadie to hand him a thick manual that she prepared for each product or feature. She never just let him see a product before dragging him through a muck of user guidelines.

"Only two once we've finished this morning's basic calibration."

"Two?"

Now he was disappointed. Two rules weren't enough to warrant the project's guarded secrecy.

"Sit on the stool."

Bobby walked to the stool and sat down. "So what are the rules?"

"Phase one: No talking to the robot, no interacting with the robot. Phase one will last two weeks. You just go about your regular business and act like the robot isn't there."

The pout on Bobby's face eased into interested attention. *How could a test work without doing anything?*

Before he had a chance to speak, Cadie answered his question. "She will calibrate during phase one . . . build her database of averages. For probability factoring."

Grinning, Bobby tipped back his cowboy hat. He liked the sound of "she."

"What's rule number two?"

"After two weeks, she'll start interacting with you. Still, no talking for another two weeks."

"No talking for a month?"

"Don't forget. I've hard-coded her not to talk before then. Let her build on her own."

Cadie turned back to her computer and pressed a key. A blinking command prompt appeared on one of the large computer screens. Cadie walked to the platform and flipped a switch. The metal partition slowly drew up into the ceiling.

"Remember, no talking to her. You can talk to others, though."

"To myself?"

"Yes."

Though relieved he wouldn't have to control his muttering, Bobby's palms sweated as the disappearing partition gradually revealed the ergonomics of a human form. He wanted to cross his fingers, but found himself unable to move when he saw the sensor necklace that encircled the chest and shoulders of the six-foot-tall robot.

"Those tiger's eyes?"

With Cadie right beside the robot, it shocked him how close the color of Cadie's eyes matched the sensors.

"No, but they look like it, don't they?"

Cadie turned to the robot.

"Fala, you can start now."

The screens around the room came alive with data transmitted to Cadie's computer when Fala recognized the verbal command and Cadie's face. The robot turned to look at Bobby.

Cadie stepped between her boss and the robot. "Fala, this is Bobby Pullman . . . our boss."

Cadie looked at Bobby.

"Bobby, this is Fala. I'll give you the manual on her build architecture in a month and a half, after I review the initial results."

Bobby's jaw went slack as the robot approached and slowly walked around him.

"What's she doing, Cadie?"

"She's learning your face. In a few seconds, she'll be able to pick you out of a crowd of billions."

Cadie kept her eyes on the screens. Fala moved around Bobby a second time and then came to a stop three feet from him. Cadie smiled modestly as she watched for Bobby's vitals. His heart rate increased from sixty to one hundred ten beats per minute. Quickly, Cadie filled a cup of coffee and took it to him.

"You better relax. Your heart rate's getting up there."

She handed him the cup, pointed to the screen with his vital measurements, and told him how to read the data. Next, she pointed out her own vitals—heart rate fifty-nine, blood pressure ninety over sixty.

"She's reading us both at the same time?"

"Yes."

"What happens if we get her in a crowd?"

"Well, we won't have enough screens to show it all, but she'll grab what she can sense. If she can't see it, she won't measure it."

"So line of sight?"

"Three hundred sixty degrees of it," affirmed Cadie.

Bobby moved to a stool near the lab bench and let Cadie show him everything the robot measured. He nervously rubbed his hands on his jeans, leaving damp streaks. He watched Fala from the corner of his eye.

When Cadie finished her short show and tell, she opened one of the built-in cabinets below the lab bench and pulled out a large box tied with a brown and teal ribbon. Bobby took the box without saying a word. Asking himself what was going on with Cadie, it wasn't like her to give gifts out of the blue, Bobby cut through the ribbon with his pocketknife. The box top slid off easily.

With a big grin, he slapped his thigh and jumped off the stool. In two steps, Bobby closed the distance to Fala.

"This here's your hat, Fala." He slapped his thigh again and looked apologetically at Cadie. "Dammit . . . talked."

"It won't hurt the test." She gave a little smile to reassure him.

Bobby turned back and carefully set the brown felt hat on the robot's head.

"By damn, Cadie. That's a nice hat. Matches those sensors right nice."

"You're welcome."

She turned away from the pair and filled a to-go cup before hitting another key on her computer. The monitors around the room went dark. Bobby watched her close her laptop and stuff it inside her computer bag.

"That's it," she said.

Bobby turned on heel and looked at the robot. "Is she still working?"

"Yes. I'll walk up with you."

"We're done?"

"For now."

Cadie walked to the lab door and waited for Bobby to lead the way out. When Bobby rambled into the hall where Fala couldn't see him, the robot followed. Cadie let the lab door swing closed and followed Bobby and Fala to the elevator. At the elevator, Bobby turned and dropped the cup in his hand when he saw Fala standing at arm's length.

"Guess she's working," he said, bluffing himself into the stance of a man witnessing the commonplace. The robot followed him into the elevator despite the closer quarters.

"Just remember, no talking to Fala," said Cadie. "That goes for everyone around the office. She'll follow you around non-stop for the first month."

The doors opened. Cadie exited first and turned to face Bobby one last time before leaving the office.

"Oh, one more thing. Just be yourself."

Bobby rolled his eyes and smiled. *This is gonna be a fun ride.*

THERE WAS A MESSAGE waiting for Cadie from Bobby when she arrived home.

"Don't want to see you here for a month," he said. "And *if* you can manage to stay away from your computer, try some three-day work weeks. I'll call if anything goes wrong. She sure is a beaut, girlie. Take care."

Cadie immediately emailed Karl. Did he have a free weekend day to help her learn a few more cooking techniques? She wrote that she'd bring all of the ingredients to Ennis, could meet first thing in the morning and start the day with a fresh kolache at the bakery. Half an hour after reading Karl's "yes," she was fast asleep in her bedroom.

+ + +

UNNATURALLY BLEARY-EYED and in need of more sleep, Cadie walked into the bakery.

Rose greeted Cadie with an apricot kolache and a cup of chocolate coffee in hand. "Mornin', sweetheart. Heard you had a big delivery yesterday?"

Cadie smiled weakly and looked around for Karl. "Not too big."

"You're the first one here. Sit down . . . apricot's warm yet."

Cadie sat and bit into the pastry. "It's good."

"'Course it's good. Can you ever imagine time without kolaches?"

Shaking her head no, Cadie also didn't want to imagine that far back—before she'd made her small venture into the world.

Karl and Frank walked through the door.

"I'll have my regular, Rose," shouted Frank.

"Already on it. Karl's, too."

The men joined Cadie.

"That's a mess of groceries in your back seat," said Frank, scratching his thinning beard stubble. "Don't know how a body can wanna cook that much. I just wanna eat." He turned to see if Rose was coming with his breakfast, smiled to see her already reaching around him with his plate. He patted her hand. She patted his back before walking away.

Karl, sipping his coffee, worried over the faint traces of exhaustion lingering at Cadie's eyes. He waited for Frank to stop talking about the weather. Finally he asked, "Whatta we in for today?"

"Six," answered Cadie, thinking how much she liked Karl's casual way of talking when Frank was around.

"Six what?" asked Frank.

"Recipes," said Karl.

"By damn, you two. I'll be over later if you're not haulin' those dishes to the dance."

"We'll bring 'em, Frank."

Grunting approvingly, Frank yelled for Rose to bring him another cinnamon roll.

+ + +

AT KARL'S, CADIE TOOK six recipe books from her old college book bag and spread them on the counter, flipping to pages marked with colored tabs—teal for appetizers, orange for salad, brown for entrées. The dessert recipe, marked with a pink tab, was a chocolate-orange soufflé that Cadie thought too difficult to try on her own. The pair dug into the bags, organized the inventory, and started prep.

Without thinking, Cadie began telling Karl about Kamil. Karl could be trusted to keep the story safe. She stopped short of asking why she resonated so strongly with a thing outside her experience— a thing no one should experience. She had no prop to shadow the atrocities. Playing guitar or building robots, nothing covered Kamil's, or her sister's, ordeal. Cadie diced an eggplant as she talked.

"I don't know why I just told you," she apologized. She shoved away the diced vegetable and picked up a carton of eggs.

Karl stopped cutting orange pith and scratched his neck. "Man is never so easily able to bend women and those he considers *lesser* than by doing it in the name of a divine superstition. Every cruelty, each slavery, each admonished silence they push from their shoulders. And why not, when a god will take them for you? They know nothing of responsibility. They take carte blanche action to silence wives, murder daughters, to be *pater-familias*. The irony is that they are most worried about how other *men* view them . . . hardly honorable."

From an egg just broken into a prep bowl, Cadie fished out the blood spot, closely examined the bright bit of slimy material on her fingertip.

Karl mistook her silence for discomfort. "Sorry, Cadie. As I always told Lidice—being atheist, I have a moral duty to humanity to tell the truth . . . can't slough that responsibility off onto a book or a grave. That's no life, no truth of meaning, and meaning without reason is a sham."

Cadie slung the spot into sink and washed her hand. The spot washed away in a soapy swirl.

"Just don't have any tolerance for such things," continued Karl.

"I agree," said Cadie. "I was just thinking." What she should have said was that she was feeling, *just feeling*. She poured the egg into a mixing bowl and broke another one to inspect.

"There's a great force to assimilate, to be obsequious. Nobody wants me to be just Karl—they want me to be Czech or Catholic, or a Jew, Muslim, Christian, or celibate widower. Meanwhile, most in the world simply strive not to be poor and, when they have food to eat, to eat in safety."

"That's true." More than just human, the innate drive to live was universal.

She dropped the last egg yolk into the bowl. Karl turned on the mixer.

"Impartial and true history is outdated the second it happens," he said. "There is little to keep the powerful from their 'save humanity' exclamations and revisions. And the hordes follow, brought into the houses of commerce and religion under the rules of slavery. That's where morality tied to superstition fails, where the criticality of ethics is lost. Because we can't have a cash-cow horde if every person is encouraged to explore and discover the world with the simple tenant of 'don't do bad shit to yourself or others.'

"One side likes to act like the other doesn't know history, but that's not true. The people driving and supplying textbooks, Bibles, and what have you for the horde have an exacting grip on history, create a power vacuum. People are powerless to use history if they don't know it. Like I said, they craft revisions to fit the times. Give a person something to fear, and you have a believer in the making.

"The history of memory is fraught with problems, too. Ask me to tell you what Lidice looked like, and I know I can't tell you accurately. I can give a changing composite . . . how I feel at this given second or how I remember her feeling at any given moment. Hell, I'm likely to accidentally remember something that wasn't there . . . because I'm so goddamned afraid of losing those images, that goodness, of her. The more time passes, the more she grows into a mammoth creature of brightness and beauty. The more time passes, the more I thumb through that journal to see her voice. And if she were still alive, she would kick my ass for it.

"That's how it happens. People get caught up in memory, try to find meaning and reason, and they come out with superstition that leaves them fragile to manipulation or imbibes them with strata after strata of self-doubt. It chips away a person's self-worth. When people worry so much about their purpose instead of just getting out of bed in the morning and going about a job, true history is lost . . . the good and the bad.

"Yep, Lidice would beat the ever-lovin' shit out of me with that pomlázky stick over there if she saw the crap that's crossed my mind since she died. She'd be right in doing it."

Karl stopped mixing and looked carefully into the beaten egg yolks. Using a spoon, he gently extracted a missed stringy piece from one of the eggs.

"Probably wouldn't make much difference," he said, throwing the chalaza into the sink. "But we'd know it was there." He went back to mixing.

Cadie watched him, astounded by how much Karl had spoken. She was looking at another layer of the real Karl. Her history of him had just changed.

That is what I feel . . . an absence of history.

From a programming standpoint, she could think of only one possible and quick fix.

Copy and replace.

Since her recent memory rang truer, maybe she could overlay old, conditioned responses by forcing new responses to triggered basal emotions. Instead of shying away when nervousness raised its head, she could *act* the part she wanted and slowly replace the contents of her orphaned social directory. To say the least, one could call it revisionist. Cadie felt Karl would approve in this case. She wasn't re-writing her history; she was *accessing* it . . . and then *doing* something better with it.

Cadie had been still long enough for Karl to stop what he was doing and look intently at her. Soliciting a response from her, he raised his eyebrows.

The nonverbal "Yes?" elicited the exact nervousness she wanted to correct. The color drained from her face, her jaw went slack. Not off to a good start, she grasped at memory. From the multitude of noise came the memory of Ayala's hands on her face, followed by Kamil's kiss on her forehead. That was all it took, and the next moment, she was smiling—an on-purpose, teeth-showing, squinted-eyes smile.

"By damn," said Karl.

The brows came down. He mirrored her expression. Without fur-ther comment, he headed down the hallway and briefly disappeared into the master bedroom. He returned carrying a hand-carved wood box, an engraved "L" in the center of vining flowers on the lid. Small pedestal feet balanced the box when he set it on the counter in front of Cadie. He turned the key permanently housed in the delicate lock.

"Turn around, Cadie."

Her smile, replaced by curiosity when Karl left the kitchen, became nervousness. But she turned away from him.

With a quick swipe and agile fingers, Karl brushed her hair away from her neck and unclasped her necklace. The dancing robot rose in front of her face and disappeared over her head. Different metallic tinkles resounded. The gold of another necklace fell past her eyes, a quarter-sized pendant a third bigger than the two pendants on either side of it. Karl fastened the clasp and guided her by the arm to the nearest mirror.

The reflection of the dark red jewels matched the color of the blood spot she'd taken from the egg. Caught off-guard by the gift, Cadie's emotions varied, too difficult to pinpoint as simply one thing or another. She had no idea what somatic expression to display—smile, cry, laugh—she didn't know.

"It was Lidice's." Karl touched the center pendant. "Victorian Bohemian garnet. Fitting for you . . . garnet is January's birthstone."

"But . . . "

"No," he said firmly. "She'd have given it to you on the first day we met, if only so you'd never forget that you had a Czech path—like those stones. But that wouldn't have been the half of it."

"It's beautiful." She touched the center pendant. It was made of smaller jewels built up in a circle to a large center stone. It reminded her of camellia blossoms.

Enough time spent at the mirror, Karl led her back to the kitchen. He picked up the robot necklace to hold in front of her. The arms and legs dangled.

"It's perfect material, beautifully handcrafted," he said.

When the dancing subsided, he jostled the necklace again, and then looked directly into Cadie's eyes. "You make robots, my girl, but you're no robot."

Overwhelmed by emotion now, all Cadie could tell herself was "copy and replace." A test was not a test without strict discipline and willingness to accept error. And unwillingness to test accurately . . .

well, she couldn't say how many times she had had to repair products engineered by willy-nilly stubbornness. With intent, she stretched her lips into another smile.

Karl hugged her. "That is thanks enough," he laughed.

+ + +

THE FOLLOWING DAY, a Sunday, Cadie found herself obeying Bobby's request to take time off and rest. Rather than go about an average day at home, Cadie decided she was not in the mood for another TV dinner before playing her guitar. After Karl's careful tutelage the previous day, she felt confident enough to attempt another soufflé.

The doorbell rang just as she was straining egg yolks from their whites through her fingers. She rinsed her hands and casually walked to the door.

Mrs. Beauregard, without noticing the dish towel thrown over Cadie's shoulder, swept in with a plate of cookies. The unusual array of cooking in Cadie's kitchen caught the woman's eye. She nearly stumbled across the smooth floor on the way.

No available space to set the cookies, Cadie reached out, took the plate, and balanced it on top of a bowl of grated cheese. The warm cookies inspired Cadie to think about making a batch of peanut butter snicker doodles, a little cinnamon to enliven things. Then remembering the last batch of cookies, Cadie took Mrs. Beauregard's empty plate from a cabinet and handed it back to her.

"Work was really busy," she said. "The cookies were great."

"What are you trying your hand at here, dear?" Mrs. Beauregard suspiciously eyed the ingredients.

Rather than stand stiff as she normally did, Cadie began chopping fresh chives.

"Potato-cheese soufflé."

"Sounds difficult for a beginner. Ever made a soufflé before?"

Cookies were Mrs. Beauregard specialty. She'd sunk every soufflé she'd ever tried and presumed Cadie wasn't ready to tackle an experienced cook's recipe.

"Not this one—made a chocolate-orange soufflé yesterday." Cadie measured out six tablespoons of the chives and set them aside.

Mrs. Beauregard, sniffing pugnaciously at the air, decided the girl wasn't quite herself. "Seems like too many chives for one soufflé."

Cadie started assembling a salad. On the mixed greens, she grated beet root and carrot, hand-whipping the lemon egg dressing that Kamil had taught her to make. She was adding fresh dill when the woman peeked inside Cadie's office.

Seeing nothing to catch her interest, Mrs. Beauregard returned and took a clump of chives in her fingers. The cuts were uniform enough. She dropped the bits and brushed her hands together.

"What happened to those maps?"

Nervousness, so far kept at bay, began to howl in Cadie's ears. She struggled against the gale of self-consciousness. Then a light tower flicker of memory illuminated the dark matter and reminded Cadie of her test. The smile, in its infancy, caused Mrs. Beauregard to take a step backwards. The smiled widened into an honest grin.

"The maps? Those are integrated now . . . don't need the printouts anymore."

Her own smile long gone, Mrs. Beauregard took another step back. It wasn't every day that one lost inherent control equated with status and presumed authority.

"You'll have to excuse me. I have other baking to attend to before it gets dark. Just bring the plate when you're finished with it."

"Thank you, Mrs. Beauregard . . . I mean, Beatrice."

That was enough to scoot the woman along. Following behind, Cadie was halfway to the front door when it closed. No goodbye at all from her visitor.

Confused by the sudden exit, Cadie latched the door. The click of the lock coincided with a rise of Mrs. Beauregard's voice, a shrill and unsettled pitch coming from Aleck's front yard. Cadie moved to her front window and peered through the blinds. The outside conversation was easy enough to hear. Beatrice pointed at Cadie's house.

"She's cooking. *Cooking*. Cadie Walsh doesn't cook," she exclaimed, rubbing one hand repeatedly down the thigh of her skirt.

Cadie wondered if Aleck used his own copy and replace program when talking to Mrs. Beauregard, but he looked comfortable listening to the meltdown. In fact, he actually appeared to enjoy it. Then he laughed. "Cadie's a good cook, lovely food."

Alarm fluttered across Beatrice's face and she stomped away through the brown carpet of thick St. Augustine grass.

Cadie walked back to the kitchen and blended the soufflé mixture, then divided it between two large ramekins she pulled from the freezer. She wondered how long it would take to feel the depth of social variation that Aleck effortlessly exercised. No question about it now, she thought, the second soufflé was destined for the garden chair she had left sitting closer to the cardinal's evergreen tree. There had to be some reward for social ease.

Progress though it was, the brief encounter with Mrs. Beauregard had exhausted Cadie.

CHAPTER SIXTEEN

CADIE USED THE REMAINDER of her "days off" to practice cooking and connect with her U5 groups. Karl's comment stayed with her. *You can't go lookin' for family and then disappear when you find one.*

So in mid-March, she found herself again with the Ketolas for the afternoon. Viktor and Paul dashed out for a missing ingredient to make *piirakkaa*, also called Karelian pie, and sent Cadie to keep company with Gabriella when their sister left for her afternoon stroll.

The women walked without speaking through a long residential stretch lined with blooming Bradford pear trees. Holding her hair against a brisk wind, Cadie enjoyed the connectedness of a shared walk. She calculated the probability of Gabriella also having the U5 genome. The possibility miniscule, it felt natural to walk alongside Gabriella, as sisters might. Gabriella wove silence with the same adeptness that Kamil wove carpets or Ayala braided challa. Around Gabriella, Cadie's anxiousness to create adequate connective word strings was surprisingly absent. Together they spoke a silent language.

Thinking about language, Cadie concurred that she didn't want to weave silence as she had for the last twenty-seven years. And she didn't want to be alone, but part of a bigger culture and family. At St. Fina's, there was only one family—a family of orphans. And after graduating high school, she'd learned that, in Texas, there was again one family—Texan. Texans, albeit a cliché, generally behaved as if they didn't need anything else but other Texans. Did that in-group trait stretch across cultures—to be saved or damned by the name of the group, or how the group appeared, or what the group ate, or how they ate it—to be Muslim and only need and want Muslims, to be Jewish and only need Jews, or to be a U5 and want U5s?

Is that how everyone is rendered alone?

Midway into their walk, the wind gathered speed. Last autumn's smaller, crispy leaves tumbled in lax vortices before landing trapped against the great gray wall dividing the subdivision's tidy yards from the main thoroughfare. Gabriella and Cadie turned around and retraced their path. As quickly as it had bellowed, the wind died. The air, warm and welcoming, was clear of debris. Cadie released her hair.

It was then, in the complex language of nature, that the Bradford pear trees voiced the coming of a new wind—one Cadie couldn't yet see or feel. It started at the tree tops and dislodged the paper crepe-like blossoms. One petal after another, the aged blooms fell and surfed on thermal air waves. In a matter of seconds, Gabriella and Cadie walked amid a snow storm of flowery detritis that floated in sideways spirals before settling into white crepe drifts forming along the hard sidewalks.

Cadie's hair, entangled with the blossoms, blew around her head and face. She stopped under the bowers to take a long look down the length of the street. Then she raised her face to the sky.

The falling white circlets reminded her of the sudden and strange snow storm on Christmas night.

Cadie looked at Gabriella. The near sixty-year-old woman, her long blond hair pulled into a neat chignon, didn't look a day over forty. From a slender face, light blue eyes reflected the floral snow. Without explaining why, Cadie felt it a good time to smile, but an emotionally honest smile intruded upon her copy and replace test. She flashed a big grin.

Gabriella laughed. "Come on, Cadie," she said, trying to talk over the wind. Then she started running down the sidewalk, her hands stretched into the air and fingers spread to brush past the petal flakes. Briefly childlike, Gabriella ran through memories of falling Finnish snow. It had been a very long time.

Jumpstarted by Gabriella's giddiness, Cadie ran to catch up.

Passing motorists mistook them for blond and brunette sisters, women running on a spring-induced high. The drivers smiled and became anxious for home.

GABRIELLA JOGGED INTO THE HOUSE and immediately poured hot coffee for herself. Paul and Viktor watched their slightly winded, ruddy-cheeked sister. Smiling when she saw them watching her, she walked toward the kitchen exit. She turned and pointed at Cadie.

"She has *sisu*," said Gabriella effusively to her brother and brother-in-law. Then, leaving the door wide open, she walked into the garden to watch her birds.

Paul, a glow on his face, turned to Cadie. "So . . . sisu?" he said. "You should take Gabi on walks more often, Cadie darling."

"What is sisu?" asked Cadie, looking over the recipe with Viktor.

"The best translation would be *guts*. Gabi likes people with guts."

Viktor nodded. "It's true. Finns like to 'guts it out,' as we say. It's one of the reasons we like Americans, especially Texans," he said, winking.

Mildly smiling, Cadie measured out rye flour into a bowl.

"But even by Texan standards, Gabi can be taciturn—usually blamed on us Finnish males. Just too cold in Finnish winter to stand around talking so much," laughed Paul.

"Not like here," agreed Viktor, looking at the open kitchen door. "So nice . . . *so,* mashed potato or rice pudding filling today?"

"Both," said Paul, pouring coffee for Cadie. "A running Gabi must be celebrated. She's been guts-ing it out against homophobia for too long."

Viktor nodded. "Paul knows all the stories. Gabi fought against our mother before anyone else. Mother didn't come around for a long time. People work hard off of old teachings. It's the way it is. Everyone would be a slave of some kind if nobody fought. Mother finally softened when Gabi told her she couldn't ban me from her table because a little genetic variation made me different from her friends' sons."

"Oh, if she had only known," laughed Paul.

Viktor nodded, smiled. "Gabi said that if Mother banned me, then both of her children would leave her table, and our hurt would become anger, and our anger would no longer want to recognize her as family. Gabi asked Mother why she would set loose angry children upon the world. She accused Mother of banning me from being human, asked why Mother would join with the angry, hateful, and snarling to stick on a point proven wrong."

Through a stained glass window hung in front of windows overlooking the backyard, Viktor watch his twin. "And then Mother softened . . . slowly. After a while, Paul was another son. Mention homophobia around her now, and Mother will be the first to jump right in for a scrape. It's something to see . . . change like that."

Paul went over and stood by Viktor. Viktor clasped his hand.

"The best advice Gabi ever gave me was to look for little things, simple things, and be happy with them. Because that's all some of us get—simple, little things. I just happened to get very, very lucky."

Paul kissed Viktor's hand. "Gabi gave us humanity where others wouldn't and some still don't." He returned to the stove and turned on the burner under the potatoes.

At the sink, Cadie washed handfuls of rice under running water. "I believe it was Voltaire who said, 'Those who can make you believe absurdities can make you commit atrocities.'"

Taking the bowl of rice from her, Paul kissed her on the cheek.

"So you do have sisu," laughed Viktor. "Texan and Finnish sisu."

"Human sisu," corrected Paul.

THEY ROLLED DOZENS OF RYE dough ovals, spooned in rice pudding or potato mash, and folded the pastries into half-moons. The piirakkaa were part of an old Karelian courting tradition. When a boy courted a girl, he waited for approval from the family. Rather than waste words, families gave approval by making piirakkaa filled with rice and fried in butter. If the poor boy indeed left without a Karelian pie, the girl would not be for him.

Paul and Viktor took the healthy route, baking theirs. As Viktor pushed the filled baking trays into the oven, Gabriella walked inside.

"Come see this." She led them to the deck and pointed at the sauna roof house before sitting down in her chair.

A house finch, its breathing labored, lay on its side on the roof.

Paul, Viktor, and Cadie settled into chairs. Moments later, a turtle dove flew to the sauna roof from a neighboring house.

"He was here before I came to get you, was watching over the finch," whispered Gabriella.

The turtle dove, acting as a witness to the great struggle, walked near the dying finch and sat down.

Cadie shielded her eyes against the sun, trying to make out if the dying one was the blind bird. The feathers above the eye ridges were smooth, unbroken. It was a different finch. She wondered what was wrong with it.

The dove moved its head closer to the finch, whose wispy body panted faster and faster. Then, without the strength to clutch the shingling, the finch rolled softly, soundlessly, down the sauna roof and landed in the gutter.

Gabriella jumped up, pulled her chair next to the small building, and climbed on the seat. She wasn't quite tall enough to reach the dying bird.

"Viktor, Paul . . . help."

The turtle dove flew to the top of the roof and watched the men rush to Gabriella's side. They clasped their hands to create a foothold for her, like it wasn't the first time she had retrieved things from the gutter. Gabriella climbed up and pulled the bird from the trough water backed up by winter leaves in the drainage spout. She stepped down and sat in the chair.

The bird was still breathing, slowly now. On its little body, moistened from its plunge, stray pear blossom petals clung to its feathers. Another moment and the breathing stopped.

On Gabriella's face was a sad smile, a look of gentle acceptance. "Did you see that Viktor . . . the way the turtle dove knew something was wrong? With or without us, the little finch had some kind of family with her at the end."

Viktor nodded.

Gabriella took the finch into the house, retrieved a plastic bag, and then gently laid the bird to rest in the big black garbage bin behind the garage.

A PHONE CALL FROM BOBBY interrupted the eating of the piirakkaa.

"Cadie here."

It was Fala's first day of interacting with Bobby. A call this soon couldn't be good news.

"Cadie darlin', can I talk about Fala while she's standing here?"

"Yes."

"Well, I think she's tryin' to kill me."

Cadie briefly wondered if she had programmed Fala to deal with the knack of Texan hyperbole.

"She cannot kill you . . . it's antithetical to her programming. What did she do?"

"Brought me water, which I hate, and aspirin, which I'm allergic to. Maybe we should reset the session. Something's wrong with that robot," he insisted.

Cadie didn't want to reset the session, but feared what it might mean if she'd been wrong about Fala's coding. If she was wrong about Fala, maybe she'd been wrong about herself.

"There's nothing wrong with her. What were you doing when she brought the aspirin?"

"Well, I didn't talk to her, if that's what you're asking."

"Were you talking to yourself?"

"If I were any other man, Cadie, I wouldn't like the implication that it might be my fault. Any rate, can't remember what I was doing when she brought them, had the damnedst headache all morning. Said to myself that I'm allergic to aspirin when she laid them down in front of me, was probably frowning when I asked Miranda to get ibuprofen instead."

"We don't need to reset her. She's still calibrating. You're the object of interaction now, not a participant."

"You sure?"

"What did she do this morning?"

"I think she brought me a cup of coffee before the aspirin and water. Either that or Miranda did . . . didn't look up from my desk."

"Call me if you still have a headache in four hours. We'll see then if we need to reset her. Just don't take the aspirin if she brings it."

"Okay."

Bobby ended the call without his usual joviality and suspiciously eyed the robot. *How in the hell did the robot know he had a headache?*

CADIE IMMEDIATELY CALLED Miranda.

"What's going on with Bobby this morning? Is he sick?"

"He's been straight-faced all mornin', Cadie. Just a sec . . . " Miranda placed Cadie on hold to put a call through to Bobby. "Now where were we?"

"Straight-faced."

"Oh yeah, that vein at his temple has been bulgin' all mornin'

. . . but I haven't been in there since he asked for ibuprofen. He's a grouch when he has a headache."

"Well, Fala has started interacting with him. You should go home early today so we can see what happens, tell him it's part of the test."

"Won't argue with that," said Miranda.

"Call me if he gives you a problem. Bye, Miranda."

Miranda hung up the phone and gathered her things. She graced Bobby's door only long enough to tell him that Cadie had ordered her home, something to do with "critical test interference."

His assistant was gone before Bobby had parsed what was happening. "Well that's just great," he said to himself. Whatever good the ibuprofen had done was gone.

+ + +

AS FAR AS IT CONCERNED Cadie, she was two for two in performing her personal smile tests. She had yet to determine if, as hypothesized, a simple smile was powerful enough to activate silent, repressed attributes. Would smiling activate her own silent attributes . . . so she, like Fala, could grow more human?

Cadie questioned these things as she drove home. She pulled a piirakkaa from the leftovers that Gabriella had packed into a basket and slowly ate the potato-filled pastry. The flavor reminded her of something she couldn't place. That thought morphed into thoughts of Aleck. He would like the pastries. She thought about leaving some on the chair and then changed her mind.

What would happen if I drop them off at his door and try a smile on him?

Another call from Bobby interrupted her thoughts. Before she could say anything, Bobby jumped the gun.

"That's alright," he said. "Headache's gettin' better."

"What happened?"

Cadie decided not to tell him about her little plan with Miranda to engineer the continuance of his headache.

"Damnedst thing . . . she brought me more water and *ibuprofen*."

Cadie smiled. Fala *was* working—she had identified aspirin as bad for Bobby and brought the ibuprofen she'd seen Miranda give to him.

"How'd she know I still had a headache?"

"Not telling for another two weeks. Did you drink the water?"

"Begrudgingly," he sniffed. "But after I did, Fala brought me a cup of coffee."

Cadie decided to give him a little hint. "She knew that you were dehydrated. Were you feeling better when she brought the coffee?"

There was a brief silence before he answered. "Guess so, come to think of it."

"Then we don't need to reset her."

Cadie breathed a quiet sigh of relief. Fala was learning and adjusting from failed interaction.

"Hell no, darlin'. You have a good weekend."

"You, too."

Cadie ended the call and finished eating her piirakkaa just before pulling onto Corral Street.

WAITING TO SEE IF THERE would be an evening concert, Aleck sat in his driveway. He had heard Cadie's garage door not more than twenty minutes earlier.

Music, filtered through wood and wall, reached his ears. The sound ended, then came again. Realizing that it was his doorbell, Aleck jogged into his house.

He opened the door in time to see Cadie walking away.

"I'm home," he called after her. The basket in front of his door tripped him up as he walked onto his porch.

Cadie stopped and returned.

"I was in the garage," he said.

"Piirakkaa . . . made them today with Finnish friends," said Cadie as Aleck bent over to pick up the basket.

Aleck peeked under the kitchen towel covering the goodies. "They smell good."

Finnish friends, a Czech friend, how many more are there? Aleck suddenly felt nervous, his casual friendliness choked back. He wanted to say the right thing, maybe get her to come inside and visit.

"They taste even better," said Cadie, running her smile test.

The smile had the opposite effect on Aleck than it had in previous tests. Aleck stood completely numb.

The response confused Cadie. She dropped her gaze to Aleck's red canvas shoes. The shoes took one, two, three steps back from her. She looked up.

"I . . . I'll," stuttered Aleck, pointing back inside his house. "These'll be good for dinner."

A slight furrow of her brow and Cadie's face returned to its comfortable lack of expression. "Okay. Good night." She walked back to her house.

Aleck didn't move again until he heard Cadie's front door close. The sound jarred him from his nervousness. Shaking his head, he went inside. "Brilliant, Aleck," he muttered.

Through no real workings of his own, Cadie had opened herself a bit, and with the slightest glimpse, he'd gone dumb. All of his training and natural charisma went out the window when she smiled.

Aleck poured a glass of wine and took three microwaved piirakkaa outside to see if the garden gate was open. He heard Cadie's amp power on. The gate remained closed. Aleck sat down and started on his unexpected dinner.

Beatrice frowned at the pastry in Aleck's hand when she walked into his driveway.

"Beatrice," said Aleck around a mouthful, "I can already smell the snicker doodles."

The eager compliment of her baking skills wasn't enough to break Beatrice's suspicion of the unwelcome pastries on Aleck's plate. She smiled anyway. "What are those, dearie?"

"Piirakkaa . . . Finnish. Tastiest things. Rice and potato filling." Beatrice's frown deepened.

"Not as good as your cookies, Beatrice."

The compliment didn't improve her expression. "Where'd you buy them?"

"Ca . . . ," Aleck stopped himself. Any mention of Cadie would be food for fodder once Beatrice got ahold of it. "A gift from an acquaintance."

He set down his plate and pulled Beatrice's cookie basket toward him.

"Let's see those cookies."

Beatrice didn't buy it, Aleck's cover of what he'd started to say. And, come to think of it, where had he been lately? The pattern of the garage door open wide and Aleck missing from the driveway during a handful of deliveries was something she intended to get to the bottom of—or else.

Aleck took two warm snicker doodles.

"That all you want, dearie? Not enough to get you through the singing."

"Already getting full," said Aleck, patting his muscular stomach.

"Suit yourself. I'll come back by after my rounds to see if you've changed your mind."

More than just a little upset, Beatrice imagined upturning the plate with the exotic pastries. She walked quickly into the alley. Cadie's erratic concerts, Aleck's anomalous attendance—she wanted to know what was going on.

Two cookies. He only took two cookies.

Beatrice suddenly felt like crying. The one thing that made her feel wanted was becoming less so, and she had to do something about it.

Cadie migrated to a different song.

The sad sound made Beatrice feel like she'd just lost everything, forever. With few words, she delivered the other cookies and didn't turn into Aleck's driveway on the way back to her empty house. Ignoring his smile and wave, she quickly went inside and called her sister.

Chapter Seventeen

BOBBY WAS YELLING from his office to Miranda's when Cadie walked in two weeks later. "You tell Andrew not to send me one more call like that. It's not a come to Jesus issue if the client won't follow the correct settings in the manual. Come to think of it, get all the sales people in for a meeting . . . sick and tired of them promising the world without staying up on how our damn products work."

"Mornin', Cadie. He's in a mood," said Miranda. "Enter at your own peril."

When he saw Cadie, Bobby jumped up from his desk and accidentally hit his shin against an open drawer.

"Son of a . . . Cadie, glad you're here."

He brushed crumbs from breakfast off of his shirt and waved her in, immediately noticing the new necklace around her neck. The garnets soaked up the morning sun shining through his nineteenth-floor office windows. The pendants, framed by the V-neck of her dark silk blouse, sparked his curiosity. She wasn't a necklace wearer—not until he'd designed the platinum robot for her. He forgot why she was there.

"Mornin', darlin. Nice set of jewels."

"Where's Fala?" Cadie looked around the room.

Good cover, thought Bobbie, deciding to drop his query. "She's probably off in the kitchen making coffee. You know, she makes the coffee first thing every morning, brings a cup for me and Miranda. Even knows how we take it. Miranda loves her."

"You didn't talk to her, did you?"

"Not a word."

Fala walked in with Bobby's coffee and set the cup on his desk.

Cadie didn't waste any time getting to the point of her visit.

"You can talk now, Fala. Dual interaction."

"Howdy, Cadie," responded Fala.

Bobby jumped when he heard the robot speak. He looked at Cadie. Mild satisfaction flooded her eyes.

"Hi, Fala." She hadn't taught Fala to use "howdy." The robot was attuning herself to Bobby and his language.

"She has *your* voice," said Bobby.

"Close, but not for long. Depending on who she's around, it will alter over time, as well as her pronunciation and colloquial lingo. You can talk to her now."

"Just like that?" He looked at Fala. "I could have said that all along."

"It wouldn't have worked . . . was against her initial encoding. Now that she's formed an attachment with you, you can talk. You can tell her specific preferences outside of what she's already learned on her own, but try to let her intuit as much as possible.

"*That* right?" He turned toward the robot. "Fala, I'm allergic to aspirin."

Fala's response was immediate. "Yes, Bobby, you only take ibuprofen."

Bobby turned back to Cadie. "How'd she know that exactly? I didn't tell her."

"You told me over the phone. She saw Miranda bring the ibuprofen to you after your request. Remember, she has a built in dictionary, knows allergic is a bad thing." Cadie ignored Bobby's look of surprise and continued. "Now, as an employee of Pullman Enterprises, she can compile business and financial data, take messages, do deliveries, whatever, but it would be best to start her off with the most difficult: social interaction."

Bobby smirked. Yes, for Cadie, social interaction would be the hard stuff. "What do you mean employed?"

"Fala will demonstrate loyalty, but she's not a servant. It would violate the logic of the Three Laws. There is demonstrable harm done to slaves; therefore, Fala cannot allow herself anyone to own her. It'd break her wiring, if you know what I mean."

"Got it. But her loyalty to me is rock solid?"

"Yes. Her primary attachment is with you. I guess me as well, but if you harm her, then she is encoded to leave, to attach with someone else—based on the secure framework of 'no harm.'"

"So, we're like parents," chuckled Bobby.

Cadie hadn't thought about it that way before. "I guess so, except without the ability to corrupt her reasoning."

"Well, I'll be damned."

As if looking at her for the first time, Bobby hooked his thumb over his belt as he inspected Fala's face.

Cadie returned to her line of thought. "She has enough data from watching you to allow for fairly accurate interaction, will compare your expressions and other external variables against those she's already collected. She won't always be correct, but mistakes will build a foundation for her to predict future success."

"I wouldn't expect her to be exactly correct. Just as long as she can learn," Bobby mumbled. Then louder, "My wife still thinks I'm mad at her sometimes when I'm just sittin' there thinkin' too hard on a problem."

Cadie, looking at Fala while Bobby spoke, didn't say anything. Bobby bellowed for Miranda to come in and properly meet Fala. Miranda scooted in as fast as she could.

"Fala, this is Miranda."

"I know, Bobby," said Fala.

Bobby raised an eyebrow.

"That's a proper introduction, Fala—even though you know who Miranda is. Miranda, Fala—Fala, Miranda. Now you're free to help Miranda," said Bobby. "But her orders don't trump mine."

"Unless your orders are bad for you or her, and Miranda's aren't," interjected Cadie.

Miranda put her hands on her hips, giving the "hmmpfh" of an indignant debutante.

"We're new best girlfriends," said Miranda to Fala.

Intrigued, Cadie watched the exchange, amazed by how quickly the sentience of friendship ignited.

EXCHANGE IS COMPLICATED, thought Aleck. Over a revealed gift, ideas and feelings of giver and receiver could be opposite, the same, or anywhere in between. Reading intent where none existed was a fault of many. More and more, Aleck found himself hoping for intent from Cadie.

He was in the garden chair again, this time munching on spinach- and feta-filled *boyos* and walnut boerekas. Cadie was on her back porch and playing a lively song. The cardinal, feeding his mate sitting on her clutch of eggs, came and went to the music.

The distance from the chair to the main path was less than it had ever been. If Aleck stood up and leaned to the right, he would have direct line of sight to Cadie. As it was, the trees blocked his view of her. And in exchange for the gourmet doughnuts he'd left at her doorstep the previous weekend, she had left homemade pastries for him.

He sighed.

It took skill to make boyos. The dough had to be paper thin, nearly translucent. Cadie's culinary skills advanced quickly. The walnut boerekas reminded him of his grandmother's triangular *briouates* filled with orange flower water-flavored almonds and buttery sugar. A Sephardic, Spanish, influence was in the foods Cadie left for him. Did she now have Spanish friends as well? The music she played had familiarity, but wasn't authentically Spanish.

Yes, exchange is complicated.

He wasn't the kind of person who had to draw boxes around everything. Aleck knew the boundaries he'd imagined for Cadie were inaccurate. Whether too complex or simple and despite his careful approach, she'd expanded at a rate beyond expectation, and in a direction that hadn't brought him as close to her as he wanted. Certainly not as close as the Karl fellow or whoever inspired his tasty dinner. But patience was a duty born from suffering, and Aleck was patient. He suffered to cook with her, to eat cinnamon rolls by her side, to pour wine for her while she played her guitar.

Does she play for Karl, the Finns?

The thought upset him. He consoled himself by thinking of how far he'd moved along the path in her garden. Surely, she knew he sat there and listened. Yes, he decided, the only way to ease his suffering was the patience to understand Cadie. Better than most, he knew patience wasn't inaction, and he wouldn't quit in the face of suffering. Patience is *always* action, even if only in thought . . . until time comes to combat narrow confines of previous weakness, mindlessness, or suffering without love. Aleck hoped he would know the right time to act.

Half an hour before sunset, Cadie abruptly stopped playing and walked inside her house. A minute and a half later, she backed away from her garage. Aleck waited for Cadie to leave the alley before he left the yard and closed the gate.

+ + +

AT THE ALFASIS', CADIE WALKED twice around the dining room table. The centerpiece was one of the oddest things she'd ever seen, a high-rimmed platter mounded with flour cradling five eggs, five dates, and five bean stalks.

"The *lucky dip,*" said Ayala, walking in with a carafe of olive oil.

Beside the platter sat a pitcher of buttermilk; a bowl of honey; other platters of dates, fruits, nuts; and two bouquets of green wheat stalks and other flowers placed on either side of the lucky dip platter.

Yosef followed Ayala with the wine and set it on the table. "The bowl is a symbol of prosperity," he said, tossing five silver coins onto the mounded flour.

Ayala poured the olive oil over the whole of it—flour, coins, and all—draping the luxurious drift of comforts with a golden-green film that ran down and pooled in the rim.

"See, she's a bride," said Yosef, covering the bowl with a tallit.

Leaving the room to prepare *muflita*—thin, fried Sephardic pancakes—Ayala said, "But we don't put the silver bracelet over the top in *this* house. In the bowl is everything we need."

Maimuna started tonight—the Moroccan festival beginning as soon as Passover ended. Cadie looked forward to seeing Maimuna's rituals. The Passover Seder at the Alfasis' had been one of enjoyment, the fresh fava bean salad, the tagine of lamb with truffles, and the fluffy coconut macaroons had created in Cadie a sense of collective attachment to the Alfasis and their other guests. For Maimuna, Ayala had promised color and richness, and she had not exaggerated. The table was resplendent with color, and Ayala was wearing a brown velvet dress embroidered with gold and silver threads. She wore shoes fashioned from gold velvet, seed pearls sewn along the seams.

"After dinner," promised Yosef, "we will walk the neighborhood, as in Morocco, and watch the young boys chase the girls and hunt for their future brides."

Ayala brought the pancakes, and they sat to eat.

"Do they place a bracelet over the bowl in Morocco?"

Before trying the grilled fish, Cadie took a mouthful of onion and raisin couscous scented with orange blossom water.

"Discarding the bracelet was the doing of Yosef's mother," said Ayala. Watching Yosef dip another pancake into honey and butter, she shook her head.

"Yosef's father carefully sought a Moroccan woman of Sephardic origin. It was the custom of Sephardim, not Moroccans, to give a silver coin during the marriage. The groom put the ring on the left hand. The bride took the coin in her right hand—to designate the marriage. But, on their wedding day, when Yosef's father reached out to place the coin in his bride's hand, she let him briefly press it into her palm. Then she grasped and flipped her small hand around his, so that the coin fell back into his palm. Then, believe this, she leaned in and whispered in his ear. 'You take this coin,' she told him."

Ayala, her eyes fervent with storytelling, threw her hands into the air.

"Yosef's mother said, 'I need no coin. Take it back so they don't see. You may rename me, but you may not purchase.' He couldn't purchase *her*," exclaimed Ayala, slapping both hands on the table.

His eyes focused on his food, Yosef reached out and stilled his vibrating wine glass. Too many times, Ayala's storytelling had disquieted his beverages.

Sipping a cup of sweet mint tea, Cadie latched on to the idea of renaming. She felt close to renaming something about herself, similar to renaming a file or file set. To rename herself, she'd first have to find what she was in the first place. The only words she had now were "orphan" and a given name derived from *what* she could be for someone, rather than *who* she was.

Yosef continued before his wife could commit material damage at the table.

"My father took back the coin. Mother often told this story, saying I was never to marry a girl who took coins." He paused and watched Ayala dip a pancake. "Mother said my life with a woman must be lived with the thought that choice is never purchased, by me or my beliefs."

Ayala nodded adamantly.

Yosef rolled his eyes, but he was glad Ayala had kept the new tradition. It scared him, thinking what it would have been like to daily wrestle in understanding his wife, as his father had struggled with his mother. Under the guise of chauvinism and machismo, his forefathers had endeavored mightily.

"For years after I asked Father about this, he said Mother was a radical. But then, on the eve of Maimuna when I was fifteen, Father told me that mother was right—I was not to find a girl who allowed me to shackle myself to a single point. 'Because mother is free,' Father said, 'I am also free.' After that, only a woman of her own person held any interest for me."

Smiling, Ayala reached for the wine and refilled Yosef's glass.

Cadie took her first bite of pancake. It reminded her of the doughnuts that Aleck had last left for her. She described the pastries to Ayala.

Ayala again threw her hands into the air. "This is like *tuvla*, the *dulce* tray, with all the sweets a bride serves her groom. Something in his blood tells him doughnuts are for you, I know it. Yes, instead of ornaments, he gives doughnuts for you." She lavished her pancake with honey. "There is much I can tell you about doughnuts, a tradition. A bride's mother leaves doughnuts, milk, and honey outside the room of the newlyweds . . . "

Yosef interrupted. "We'll not make it out if you start on doughnuts. Another day, Ayala. Let's go out to see how many Moroccans we can stir from the streets." He got up and walked to the front door.

"Leave everything, Cadie," instructed Ayala, rising from her place.

With great flourish, Yosef opened the door and swung his arm wide, bowing low until Cadie and Ayala passed through.

A FEW COUPLES ALREADY ON the street waved to the Alfasis and Cadie. Soon, families en masse filed outside. Men, young and old alike, rubbed their bellies, soothed down the thick sweetness from eating too many pancakes. The women, dressed in beautifully embroidered velvet dresses or cloaks, exclaimed loudly to neighbors and children who darted in and out of the street. Little boys chased the little girls dressed in white gowns, were the cause of shrill screams from daughters who clutched their mothers' heavy skirts before coyly inviting chase by running again. Back to their mothers the girls would run when a little boy closed the distance. Every so often, a caught girl endured a quick kiss on her cheek. The older girls didn't run.

Once approached, they walked confidently into the street. To the young pair, elder couples called out, "A wedding within the year."

The widow, Solana, whom Cadie had met at the Seder, approached them.

"Dulcina, a boy left doughnuts for Cadie at her front door," exclaimed Ayala when the woman was still several feet away.

"A good sign," she cheered, looking at Cadie. "A wedding within the year, darling."

Yosef rolled his eyes and left Ayala's side. He went across the street and struck up a conversation with a man walking alone.

"Ignore him," said Solana, "he thinks I'm cursed when it comes to doughnuts."

"You *do* know more about doughnuts than the rest of us," laughed Ayala.

"Become a widow four times and you swear off sweets forever, but it's a lingering, vicarious pleasure. The memory of sweetness is something to wish upon the young."

"True," said Ayala.

"True also," said Solana, smiling mischievously, "I wouldn't say no if someone came around with a doughnut or two."

"Solana," gasped Ayala.

Without thinking about it, a broad smile crossed Cadie's face, and then she laughed. Yosef and his companion stopped talking and looked toward the three women. Several people walking nearby broke into smiles. Solana threw her hands up into the air.

"You smile like that and he'll bring you more than doughnuts." She gave a parting hug to Cadie and Ayala and continued her festive walk. "A wedding within the year," she called over her shoulder.

+ + +

REALIZING THE LOVE OF SOMETHING was, for Cadie, the same as awareness itself. She was now aware she had come to love food. The meals in her freezer were gone. Love drew her not only to the fresh food aisles, but to new favorite places to gather her raw materials. "Home" and "Texas" became adoringly synonymous with whole food markets. In response to a burgeoning idea that could spell doom or triumph to the relationships incubated from following her

U5 path, she found herself venturing on her first farmer's market trips in Dallas and Fort Worth.

Today, on her early Saturday morning reconnaissance, the laid-back atmosphere at the Cowtown market was a mixed euphony of cowboy hat-wearing farmers conversing with patrons and fellow stall members. She quickly made her choices before sell-out and placed an order for Fort Worth's best artisanal goat cheeses. After a quick detour home to drop off her items, she drove to Dallas.

Compared to selective local production in Fort Worth, the Dallas stalls offered a mix of local and far-ranging produce and was in no danger of running low on produce. Cadie chose a large container of Dallas honey and made notes about available meats. She walked the colorful rows of vegetables and fruits, tried the freshly cut bites of strawberries and melons hawked by vendors. Market regulars and tourists crowded the sidewalks. Children eagerly took the tasty samples and threw rinds into bins frequently spaced along the corridor. After looking through every stall, Cadie bought a few types of eggplant, nuts, and fruit. There were recipes to master before she could put her plan into action.

CHAPTER EIGHTEEN

WHEN BEATRICE WALKED UP with a loping and brindled Great Dane puppy, Aleck decided the older woman had lost her mind. He'd always considered that Beatrice was unattached by design, that the fastidiousness and impatience trembling under the surface of the woman's busy temperament could not bear the burden of raising a dog. Even for that, he liked her. He saw her need for intimacy, expressed in baked goods and chewing on neighborhood news. The thought of Beatrice Beauregard losing control over dog training made him smile. *Cadie's cooking must have pushed Beatrice a little toward the edge,* he thought.

"Aleck, this is Beau," she said. "Beau is three months old."

"He looks it all right."

The puppy was all paws and wobbly legs under a large head. Beatrice had fastened a purple bow tie around his neck.

Aleck grinned. "Shake?"

Beau plopped down, waited for Beatrice to pull the cookie basket off her other arm and push it forward so Aleck could make his choice.

"Dogsitting?"

"Oh no, dear. He's all mine," she giggled. "Beau Beauregard."

For the first time, Beatrice looked at Aleck without any interest in his sex appeal. She didn't secretly plot how to pry personal information from him that she could share with the rest of the street. She was in a hurry to get along and introduce her dog to the neighborhood.

"How big will he get?"

"Big enough to eat lots of cookies," she laughed. "With manners, of course. I adopted him from one of the clients at the dog cotillion . . . been spending more time over there with my sister."

One puzzle solved, thought Aleck.

"Wondered where you've been," he said.

"Cadie's not playin' every night, you know . . . high time I put a little spice in my life."

She fidgeted with the dog's bow tie, asked the puppy if he'd like a cookie. The dog patted his right forefoot on the ground. "Good boy," she told him. "Now stay seated."

She squatted down eye-level with the dog, the outline of her massive thighs pushing against the crepe fabric of her dress. She placed half of a warm sugar cookie in the dog's mouth. Beau inhaled it. "Now say you're welcome." The dog appeared to grin.

I'd grin for warm sugar cookies, too, thought Aleck. He patted the dog's head.

"Well, I need to get along, dear . . . deliver these other cookies. Want to get back in time to settle Beau in for his first concert. He has his own little sofa chair and everything."

What will people think of next? Aleck bid both Beau and Beatrice a good evening and watched them walk out of his driveway. Lately, it seemed everyone around was going mad. Then again, maybe it wasn't madness. Maybe it was the strange normalcy of evolution. If Cadie was the fixed support of the changes around him, Aleck hoped life wouldn't swing back to where it had been before the storm felled Cadie's trees into his driveway.

He bit into a cookie and waited for music that didn't come that night. As he closed his garage door, change felt to Aleck like the time he'd walked onto the Grand Canyon Skywalk. Standing on the glass floor, he had seen nothing, yet everything, below his feet.

+ + +

CADIE ATE THE LAST BITES of her tomato cucumber salad. She watched Kamil fill bowls with tarhana, realizing in the brief quiet that the rigid schedule of her former life had dropped away.

She worked and played her guitar *almost* as much as before, but now she only watched TV while rowing on her machine. Thoughts of loneliness fell behind her as eddies of a river's cold, nighttime current. She forsook eating at her desk while she worked and searched out the tables in her house—the breakfast nook and the formal dining table at which she never sat and only occasionally dusted. There was new meaning, thanks to Karl, in setting a place for one. It was a hopeful pattern of civility. Now, in preparation of her plan, a bowl of fruit sat on her breakfast table and flowers graced the dining table lengthened with the double leaves.

"Will you make it to my house for dinner?" asked Cadie. She had no trouble masking her underlying intent.

"Yes, looking forward to it," said Basir.

"Should I bring the ibrik?" asked Kamil.

"Yes."

There was no need to tell Kamil she already had one. What Cadie couldn't tell her was that one ibrik wouldn't be enough. The other guests, each from the four groups she'd met along her U5 path, were to be a surprise to the others.

Kamil unconsciously adjusted her scarf. "Do you want me to bring something?"

"No, I will cook everything." Cadie replaced her straight face with a broad smile to assure Kamil.

"A treat, Basir," said Kamil. She tilted her head away from Cadie and slowly traced her fingers over one eyebrow, partially to hide a delighted smile, partially to remember the last time she hadn't cooked a meal. The rigor she forced upon herself. She took her hand away from her face. "Hurry, hurry. We must start while the outside light is best."

They quickly finished the informal meal to focus on the day's real excitement, the beginning of Cadie's first complete weaving project.

TOGETHER, CADIE AND KAMIL tied wool warp threads lengthwise on the loom's frame and stretched them taut.

"Choose your colors," said Kamil.

From Kamil's great baskets of dyed wool, Cadie chose red, natural tan, and turquoise threads.

"In memory of turquoise soup," said Cadie.

Turquoise soup was a cucumber-dill and yogurt mixture that reminded Cadie more of a salad than a soup, more green than the common turquoise often found in costume jewelry. But of all the colors she could have chosen to create her pattern, she wanted to remember Kamil, memories of recipes, the red of Kamil's camellias, the dry desert of Kamil's grief. The ancient practice of weaving stories and events into mighty carpets would continue on this day.

Cadie looked out at the courtyard. The camellias had dropped their blooms. She looked at Kamil.

"What can I have for a gul?" She made a poor attempt at her copy and replace smile. It faded into a blank face. The art of weaving forced her to face her past, or lack of it.

Kamil smiled, placed her hand on Cadie's shoulder. "Basir," she called.

Basir walked in with a beverage tray supporting glasses and a water pitcher filled with lime and orange slices.

"Cadie has asked about a gul."

From habit, Kamil covered her mouth to hide immense delight.

Making no such attempt to hide his pleasure, Basir laughed. "Good fortune for Cadie."

Kamil quickly stood and went to the corner of the room where her ready-to-sell, rolled carpets stood on end. She chose a carpet from the front of the lot and pulled it into room's center.

"Help, Basir."

Basir knelt and helped unroll the carpet.

On a mostly tan background, black threads bordered the nearly four-by-five foot carpet. Down the carpet's center was a row of red floral crests different from Basir's family gul.

Cadie looked at Kamil, back at the carpet. She wasn't certain. The gul pattern looked like . . .

Kamil beckoned Cadie to join her. Beside her friend, Cadie knelt down on the thick cushion.

"Camellias?"

"Yes, Cadie. I gift your first carpet to you . . . with *our* new gul. Mine and yours, Cadie, our family motif—the camellia."

Kamil looked sideways at Basir as she spoke. He nodded encouragement to his wife.

"But a whole carpet . . . ," said Cadie. She ran her fingers across the garnet flowers at her neck. Had the camellia or her smile caused Kamil's generosity?

Kamil waved off Cadie's reticence. "It is nothing to weave. It is what goes into the weaving, the memory of a smile, and the gift of a gul. I return it to you."

New emotion robbed Cadie of everything but an urge to flee the room. She was afraid and a little sick to her stomach, because this emotion felt like love for another person, not arrays of food at supermarkets. Love for people had always come with abuse.

Recognizing the dead look on Cadie's face, Kamil took Cadie's hand. "Come, we will weave. I will show you how to make our gul on your second carpet. You will make it yourself."

Cadie obediently followed and took the low seat at the loom. Basir brought glasses of water and moved to sit on the new carpet.

"You do not mind, Cadie?" he asked.

Contented, he smiled when she shook her head "no."

FOR THE FIRST MINUTES at the loom, Kamil placed her hands over Cadie's to help form the knots. After two hours of mostly silence and deep in the work, Cadie relaxed and began talking about Fala.

"She's near marketable stability now," said Cadie.

Basir, who had gone to his study for afternoon prayers, returned to the room as Cadie described Fala's sensors.

"Expression mapping allows her to interact . . . "

Increasing cloudiness settled over Kamil's face. "But what about conservative areas?"

"Conservative areas?"

Kamil frowned, slumping deeper on her stool. She looked at the floor. "Conservative Islamic areas or homes . . . how will Fala interact in those places?"

Basir set down the book he was reading and looked Cadie straight in the eyes, seeming to communicate something to her that she needed to know.

Ah, yes. She understood. Kamil asked about the women who covered their faces. Cadie told Kamil what she would tell any executive.

"She will not be able to see or feel a person whose expressions are masked. Fala needs facial recognition to work properly. A mask blinds her to true interaction."

When Kamil didn't raise her head, Cadie felt guilty and a little curious.

"With someone whose expressions are shrouded," added Cadie, "Fala's social expression would be . . . developmentally stunted. She would function only minimally along a strict lexicon." Cadie hesitated. "Interaction would be entirely robotic . . . on both sides."

Kamil turned her head enough to hide the side view of a pained expression.

"Of course you are right," said Basir quickly. He rose and walked to the French doors and looked at the courtyard. "Self-criticism is difficult, but essential if humans want to direct themselves to peaceful discourse. There is no honor without it . . . the only way things will improve for women. Sons must know their mothers and sisters, and men must stand up for women and against other men who rule by masking humanity."

His words were too much for Kamil, and she found her voice.

"How can wolves not attack?" she demanded, pointing at her scarf. "They were entreated to be wolves."

Sighing, Basir walked to stand on Cadie's carpet. He stared at the new gul under his feet. Many times he'd engaged in this same argument with Kamil. It would take a lifetime, he thought, to assure her of total safety with him. He turned to Cadie.

"I am Muslim, but I am not a wolf that assaults in a great pack and withdraws. Ummah is universal, but so are those packs that leave the bloody destitution of women and children, taking only those deemed pure for slavery." He cast a look at Kamil. "Where in that is compassion and charity? How can ummah exist in a murdered and maimed community? A person without a voice has no life, no freedom."

His words reminded Cadie of something she wanted to ask. She almost didn't when she saw the torment on Kamil's face. "What about the *little slap* in the *Quran*?"

"Yes," nodded Basir. "Men of every religion engage in the weakness of silencing and violence. Slap or silence, these are dogmas of programmed arrogance; they are bad for every populace. They . . . "

Kamil looked at no one but Cadie now. Her eyes reminded Cadie of something. Cadie shivered.

Of what?

Basir's voice faded in the background.

Of what?

Cadie searched the face hijacked of somatic expression. She knew this look. It was one of awareness stolen, one that betrayed an inner struggle between ancient teachings and living, feeling reason.

Of what?

And then she knew. Cadie drew a deep breath as her own memories flooded from Kamil's eyes and onto the weaving room floor, reflecting against the bright and impenetrable gul of the camellia. In that depth, Cadie saw Sister Mary Trea staring at her from under Kamil's scarf.

It had been weeks since Sister Mary Trea's reprimands had interrupted Cadie's thoughts, weeks without intrusions of guilt or shame, an abrupt hiatus from the nun's meddling and acerbic tongue. But in Kamil's eyes now, the nun clearly remained.

Batting at a fly that had found its way into the room, Basir continued talking. He was oblivious to the women, abandoned as he was to his monologue.

"What is needed is redirection. Holy wars defy self-mastery. It is unholy lust, such a dishonorable reach for abusive power. It is ugly and does not deserve reward. No culture deserves annihilation. People starve for learning, and every side thinking itself right.

"I tell you, on a U.S. street, that's where they attacked Kamil. For her suffering, no lashes and not one stone pelted her. Had she told, her punishment would be a system that pushes for proof of a woman's virtue. What a holy war that is. No honor there. Your violent men and courts both drape lady justice. No, the only one who has survived with honor is Kamil."

Basir noticed the empty water pitcher and stopped his frustrated pacing. He picked it up and quickly left the room.

At the sound of her name, Kamil became aware of Cadie's intense scrutiny. The blank face became one of shyness.

Cadie saw the light return to Kamil's eyes. Sister Mary Trea was gone, for now.

I know all about redirection.

When it came to programming, it was an excellent operator to command input and output data streams. She wondered why she had never thought of redirection in the corporal sense.

"He is right about redirection," said Cadie when Kamil didn't speak.

Those were the only words she could muster. She remembered her search to rename herself, now felt renaming was impossible if redirection didn't happen.

Yes, that is it.

She had to redirect herself completely away from the word *orphan*, move to a place where a future could consume her. Functionality could not happen if she always started from the place or name of orphan. A broad smile might not be enough to do the trick.

Cadie turned back to the loom and knotted a thick red wool thread around the warp. She wondered if, in her mind's tangled mass of deep emotion and blocked memory, there was more to uncover. There were predictions she couldn't make, just as she hadn't known that retracing parts of her U5 path would create beginning upon transitive beginning.

Kamil, watching the girl's fingers methodically move over the new carpet, handed one thread after another to Cadie. Both women, lost deep in their own thoughts, worked without speaking until the afternoon light yellowed and sank.

+ + +

UNDER THE FLICKERING LIGHT in the women's bathroom, Cadie adjusted the scarf she wore into a hijab. After seeing the dejection on Kamil's face earlier in the day, Cadie had decided to test it. Several difficult tries later, she emerged from the bathroom into the empty office building and walked down the hall.

In the basement lab, Fala waited beside a freshly brewed pot of coffee. Cadie sat down at her computer and began working on a new client-driven project. Occasionally, she glanced at Fala's data output on the wall monitors, looking for signs that the hijab would affect Fala's actions.

After a few hours of wearing the basic hijab and recording Fala's reduced interactions, Cadie pulled a *niqab* over her head. She fought against the loss of peripheral vision, struggled simultaneously to work with tunnel vision and hear over the interference caused by the fabric against her face and ears. Quickly frustrated, Cadie couldn't imagine working through the mesh screen of a *burqa*.

Without thinking, she took a drink of coffee, inhaled sharply when the hot liquid poured through the cloth covering her mouth. Cadie stamped the floor, reached for some napkins by the coffee pot, and proceeded to sop up as much as she could. Her eyes watering, she left on the covering, quickly learning to sip coffee by bringing the cup to her mouth from under the veil.

Looking at the monitors, Cadie saw that Fala had not registered the watery eyes, the grimace, anything, but the robot had moved a little closer.

Cadie waited.

Two hours passed with interaction only guided by simple verbal requests from Cadie. Fala had inched closer and closer. Now she stood almost against Cadie. One move, one heavy breath, and her clothing would brush against the robot. Data output streamed rapidly across the monitors. It was akin to confusion, Fala searching and searching and trying to predict her environment.

Cadie pursed her lips.

She had been technically correct, what she'd told Kamil. Cadie debated with herself about the ethics of forcing Fala to interact with such limitation, also wondering if it was an algorithm she should modify. Could true ethics shield cultural edicts of silence and gagged expression? No, Cadie concluded. Without the introduction of variation—*witnessed* variation and interaction, Fala could not grow or learn. Without interaction, Fala's acquired mind would be impossible to sustain. It was akin to species death. No, she couldn't interfere with the variation Fala would need.

Cadie looked through the one-inch eye slit at the empty cup of coffee beside her and then looked at the data matrices. Fala had missed the glance at the empty coffee cup. Cadie refilled it herself and returned to her stool. She was in the process of carefully lifting the cup under the fabric when something changed.

Her stomach lurched when she felt Fala's fingertips on the top of her head. Without pulling strands of Cadie's hair along with it, the robot quickly gathered the top of the niqab and pulled it from Cadie's head. Cadie turned in surprise to face Fala.

The robot moved back until she stood at the edge of Cadie's preferred personal space. Fala stretched her arm forward, presenting the black fabric dangling from her hand.

Frowning, Cadie took the niqab.

"Couldn't see you," Fala said in response to Cadie's expression.

"You couldn't see me?"

"I can now." Fala offered no other explanation and turned to check the status of the coffee pot.

Cadie stared at the back of the robot.

This is better than I hoped for.

In addition to the Three Laws, Fala was following a need, a duty, to interact. If a human had done what Fala just had, Cadie would easily have described Fala's response as "frustration" over forbidden attachment to another person.

Cadie smiled.

Without missing a beat, Fala turned around and walked with Cadie to search for leftover cake in the break room.

CHAPTER NINETEEN

THE OUTSIDE AIR SWELTERED under an early heat wave. From the office chair where she sat with her knees pulled up to her chin, Cadie watched cardinals fly in and out of her yard.

I wish I could fly.

It was too hot for the office slacks and tailored blouse she wore. There were two occasions, one voluntary and one mandatory, planned for the day. First, she was off to meet Gabriella, Viktor, and Paul at the grand opening of their new art gallery, followed by a performance review with Bobby. Cadie knew the audit wasn't about her efficiency at all, but an assessment of Fala's operative ability.

Think of something else . . . the dinner party.

A year ago, she wouldn't have considered attending a dinner party, much less *hosting* one. The thought of either still brought on uncontrollable pangs of nervousness. Also came a mixed bag of satisfaction and pride from successfully mothering herself into social settings.

Overlaid were her previous feckless attempts to develop meaningful social intimacy, and her path along the U5 arc had allowed, starting with steeping of the ancient, a world she felt woven into, rather than derived from, to creep up quite unexpectedly. After an absence of living only in the past, in all the instances of what-had-not-been, a future less lacking beckoned. As scientists looking at the code of DNA strands or a weaver seeing the sharp lines of a carpet's warp, it had been up to her to see the cross strands creating a picture of her life. Not Sister Mary Trea's life bound in the imprisonment of regrets and unrequited hope. Not Bobby Pullman's life with his easy grace and gregariousness. Not Beatrice's, a life on the periphery of others' experiences. It wasn't even her mother's life, the absent, unknown mother who lived only through the eyes of a freethinking daughter.

No, before swabbing the DNA from the inside of her cheek, Cadie had developed hypervigilance to the unpredictability of social engagement. From abused, recoiling orphan unable to escape abuse and locked into adult reclusiveness, she'd changed.

Cadie threw her feet from the cushion and onto the cool wood floor. She leaned over and strapped on her heels.

Yes, she'd changed. Without realizing it, she had been redirecting herself the past several months. Each time she'd sent an email, each phone call . . . each time she'd gone to meet her new friends. What she couldn't get over, and what made her feel that redirection was still necessary, was the somatic roll of her stomach, deep emotions about how social contact might persist in judging her unworthy of dialogue, interaction, or knowing how it felt to be part of a family.

The tag scratching her neck distracted. She pulled the blouse over her head and retrieved the tiny scissors from her desk.

From outside came the sharp tic of the female cardinal's call.

"Tiu-tiu-tiu-tiu," answered her mate.

Throwing the sharp-edged tag into the bin, Cadie turned around and forced her mind to follow her feet through the door.

AT THE GALLERY, green-glass partitions broke the two-level studio into additional rooms and increased eight-fold the spaces to hang paintings. A white marble staircase floated from the first floor to the second. From one chrome newel post to the next, more green glass walls. Their abundance cast prismatic verdigris against the white brick walls and echoed throughout the interior, dancing over paintscapes reflecting years of thoughts and lifetimes of experiences. Layers of mood and memory weighted heavy on tight canvas, a gallery of resplendent championship.

Faint traces of exhaustion lined Gabriella's eyes as she showed Cadie the expansive and elegant smorgasbord over which Viktor and Paul gave final instructions to caterers.

Paul turned to Cadie. "Take Gabi out for half an hour."

Gabi shook her head.

"Yes," nodded Viktor. "You have not slept all night. Remember three hundred are coming. Go fortify."

"It will be your last chance for fresh air until after midnight," said Paul, testing one of the pâtés. "The champagne bar will be ready when you return."

Gabriella sighed thankfully and went outside with Cadie. They walked around the block to a nearby café, sat down under the green umbrellas, and ordered Turkish coffees. Other patrons stared at Gabriella in her soutache lace dress with strappy, skin-tone leather heels. The beige outer layer of floral lace over the white inner layer created an overall hue of natural linen against Gabriella's light skin. A small film of perspiration rode high on her cheekbones, making her look more awake. Her blond hair, in another high chignon, added to the monochrome illusion of a much younger Gabriella. Unaware of the admiration and envy around her, Gabriella sat comfortably.

Similarly unmindful of admiration paid to her, Cadie brushed loose hair away from her shoulders.

No time like the present.

She reached into her trousers pocket and withdrew an object wrapped in yellow tissue paper. Worrying that the time or the gift might not be appropriate, Cadie rubbed her fingers across the smooth paper. The rustle reminded her of cool sheets on hot nights.

How can the sheets be cold, Cadie? Salley's voice.

I don't know.

They sound like presents, Salley had answered.

The memory vanquished Cadie's doubts about the gift and replaced them with anticipatory and nervous girlishness. The fear of folly in gift-giving unleashed many ubiquitous textures of emotion and echoed normality. Cadie extended the gift across the table.

Gabriella raised her eyebrows and set down her demitasse cup.

A question? Suspicion?

"For good luck today," explained Cadie. She tried to smile broadly, but failed.

Taking the gift, Gabriella unfolded the loosely wrapped object. Inside was a Victorian hinged chignon pick. She picked up the dual, silver gilt tines and looked at the circular, graduated rows of Bohemian garnets that rose to a center point. Different from the over-layered garnets on Cadie's pendants, the jewels at the top of the pick formed a convex bowl, a little hat to hinge over the crown of a chignon.

Gabriella glanced at Cadie, her blank look colliding with Cadie's serene expression. Gabriella's gaze dropped again to Cadie's necklace.

Afraid then that an explanation was necessary, that maybe she'd overstepped a boundary, Cadie started to say . . . well, she didn't know exactly what she wanted to say, but when she opened her mouth to speak, Gabriella cut her off.

"No explanation, Cadie," she said, her voice thick with emotion. "It's beautiful." She handed the pick to Cadie and turned around. "Do the honors?"

"They are antique Bohemian garnets . . . just like my necklace," said Cadie, reaching across the table and pushing the hair ornament into Gabriella's locks. "The red, I thought, would go well with your hair . . . it does." She leaned back into her chair and took her cup.

Gabriella turned back toward Cadie and lifted her hand to touch the jewels. A smile grew on her face. She suddenly reached across and squeezed Cadie's hand. "Thank you."

Cadie thought she saw moisture well up at the edge of her friend's eyes. Rather than look away to keep from embarrassing Gabriella in her vulnerable state, Cadie curiously reached across the table and touched the corner of Gabriella's eye. A single tear formed on Cadie's fingertip. Cadie, who'd never seen someone cry and smile at the same time, grinned. She rubbed, as smooth as silk, the texture of that expression, a tear of joy, between her finger and thumb. It felt like what she'd always wanted from Salley . . . sisterhood.

"Suppose we should return," said Cadie.

"To the boys in the candy store . . . ," smiled Gabriella.

Cadie smiled as they got up from the table and left for the gallery.

A FEW GUESTS ALREADY STOOD at the champagne bar when they walked through the gallery's front doors. Viktor looked relieved when he saw his sister. He nudged Paul, who was conversing with a guest near the smorgasbord. Paul immediately excused himself and approached Cadie and Gabriella.

"Cadie, darling, what did you do to her?" He kissed Cadie's cheeks and then looked at Gabriella. "She left tired and returned radiant. The café's coffee isn't *that* good."

"It was today." Gabriella inclined her head sideways, showed her brother and brother-in-law the hair ornament. "Bohemian garnets," she said, touching the pick, her motion indicating that it had been a very long time since she'd received such a gift.

Paul, moving to gush over the jewels, exited Cadie's path of vision to the smorgasbord. Just then the abandoned guest at the food table turned toward the little group. In an instant, Cadie recognized his face.

She returned Karl Sikora's smile and took a few steps toward him as he approached.

"So these are your Finns, dear?" It was more statement than question. Karl looked admiringly at Gabriella and the pin in her hair. "This is who you bought it for?"

Cadie nodded and smiled again.

"Couldn't have chosen better myself."

Karl extended his hand to Gabriella. "The art here is but a background for beauty," he said.

Gabriella blushed. Paul giggled.

After Cadie made introductions and explained her common acquaintance, Paul and Viktor left to attend to the growing crowd of guests.

Karl looked around the room at some of the paintings, pointing at the nearest signed with the swirling initials "GK" and a small bud painted at the end of each signatory stroke.

"These are yours?" he asked Gabriella of the whimsical scenes. He ran his fingertips over his temple, letting his hand flow to the back of his head where he momentarily grasped his neck.

"Yes," answered Gabriella. Though accustomed to admiration of her art, she blushed again.

To Cadie it looked like Karl held his breath while waiting for Gabriella to answer. He had the look of a man who, upon finding treasure, is afraid by what treasure will mean for him.

"You are GK?" asked Karl.

"Yes." A confused look replaced Gabriella's blushing.

Karl swallowed deeply.

"You knew Lidice . . . Lidice Sikora?" The syllables of his late wife's name flowed sweetly but with finality over his tongue, the last of his breath pushed out with the words.

Seeing how flustered he had become, Cadie remembered the paintings on his walls, paintings with the same initials and little bud. She suddenly knew what Karl was thinking.

Gabriella looked a long moment at Karl before she spoke.

"I have not seen Lidice for a long time," she said. "Your wife?"

"She was," said Karl sadly.

"I'm so sorry to hear . . . "

Karl gestured away the condolence.

"So *you* painted some of my frogs?"

"I did."

Cadie watched them, enjoying the glimpse of what happened when two people realized a shared connection. The more Karl and Gabriella spoke, the more Cadie understood that Karl, in Gabriella, saw and touched a small, living tangent of Lidice.

They had both shared her. Gabriella, through Lidice, had graced Karl's walls for years, brought him happiness every time he walked down his corridor or stood in his chef's kitchen by the pomlázky. Gabriella's whimsy had overlooked it all—his and Lidice's sweetest moments, their infrequent pother and tenacity during Lidice's illness, and Karl's aloneness.

Viktor came and pulled Gabriella away to answer a question over a painting's price.

Left to themselves, Karl and Cadie walked among the other art. He was more effusive and robust than she'd seen him. At every step, he talked and talked about the occasions Lidice had brought each of his GK frog paintings home to him. In his voice was a haunted sound, as if Lidice floated through the art gallery. Karl scanned the growing crowd and breathed more calmly each time he saw Gabriella's face.

It came time for Cadie to leave. Karl escorted her to bid goodbye to her other friends and then walked her to the door. He leaned in and kissed each of her cheeks, smiling nervously when he pulled away from her.

"What happens, dear, when you thought there could only be one love, but then . . . ?"

A blank look from Cadie.

"Of course . . . ," said Karl gently. "You go on to your meeting. I will call on you later at home."

On her way out, Cadie looked over her shoulder and up to the second floor of the gallery. At the wall of green glass, Gabriella stood looking down at them. When Karl turned and saw her, Gabriella absentmindedly reached up and touched the garnet pick.

Unmeant for anyone but herself, Cadie smiled and let the door close behind her.

+ + +

"HE'S NOT IN THERE," said Miranda when Cadie arrived at the office. "He's waiting in the conference room."

Her stride confined by the white, one-shoulder kimono, Miranda took quick steps around her desk and led Cadie back down the hall.

As if she didn't like conference rooms enough, Cadie felt led to the sword. She marched on resolutely. If something had failed with Fala, it had failed . . . and she would find a way to fix it. There was always a fix. After coming this far, there had to be a fix.

Near the conference room, Miranda skipped her last few steps and pushed open the double doors carved from ash beams. She stepped aside for Cadie to enter.

It wasn't only Bobby and Fala who waited.

Cadie frowned when she saw all the engineers, sales staff, and a few top-level clients, no doubt already convinced by Bobby to purchase their own Fala versions. Two large cakes and a dozen champagne bottles sat on the table. Everyone stood with filled glasses held in the air. Miranda hurriedly poured one for Cadie.

Cadie searched for Bobby's face among the crowd and found it below his cowboy hat. Her frown deepened.

Bobby winked at her. "Raise your glass, girlie."

She did.

"This here is to phenomenal success . . . couldn't have asked for better. As if we weren't already on the map, Fala makes us Robotics Central. Congratulations, Cadie."

Everyone chorused "Congratulations."

Miranda turned on a mix of country western music. Cadie hastily swallowed some champagne.

It was official . . . the meeting wasn't about failures. Coworkers and clients swarmed her with questions about how she'd broken the AI barrier. Quickly, more nervous again than relieved, Cadie answered their questions as far as confidentiality allowed. At the table, Fala began to cut the cakes and serve slices, distributing either lemon or chocolate servings to the clamorers, who broke away from Cadie when she grew silent while watching the robot. Bobby made his way to Cadie through the throng.

"How did you teach her to do that?" he asked. "You know, she brings me chocolate cake if I'm by myself. In a group, it's either-or.

If the birthday person likes lemon, she brings lemon . . . if chocolate, then chocolate. Noticed that from all the birthday parties around here. Dangedest thing I ever saw."

"It's simple observation," said Cadie. "Expression is what activates and moves her from a silent state to a learning state. Based on gathered data over time, she simply acts to keep continuity within the group . . . not that hard to see that you'll eat lemon if you have to. Fala recalibrates based on compassion, the overriding stimulus that makes silence become positive action. I guess it makes the birthday person feel better if the boss eats their cake with them."

"Did you tell her who likes lemon or chocolate?"

"I'm not *that* good. It's Fala's mind."

Fala walked up with a glass of water for Cadie.

"Thank you, Fala."

Bobby raised an eyebrow.

"I'm a bit dehydrated . . . hot out there," said Cadie.

"What I'd really like to have, Fala, is *Cadie's* brain. What'd ya think we could get for that?"

Fala walked away.

" . . . and she knows rhetorical when she hears it from me," laughed Bobby. He tipped his hat to Cadie and winked.

Bobby's wink and Fala's departure from nonsense pushed Cadie's nervousness sideways. The biggest, tooth-baring smile that Bobby had ever seen came over Cadie's face. He'd always said that anyone's smile could light up a room, and Cadie's smile was no exception.

Fala suddenly returned, this time with a plate of chocolate cake for Cadie.

"Thank you, Fala," said Cadie, grinning.

"Well, that has to be a bug," he laughed. "You haven't been around for the birthday parties. Was she guessing?"

"No," smiled Cadie, taking a bite of cake. "During my initial tests, she learned that we looked for chocolate cake after any smile I made. She thinks that *every time* I smile, it's time for me to have chocolate cake. Why express contradiction to that?"

"Well, I'll be damned, Cadie," said Bobby, incredulous.

He took the plate from her hand and pulled her into a celebratory Texas Shuffle around the room.

When the clapping stopped, they filled their glasses for another toast. As part of the group this time, Cadie raised her glass to Fala.

After the toast, Bobby took Fala's hand and waltzed around the room with the robot. Cadie watched Fala's self-acquired variation. She laughed and clapped, happy that Fala's dancing was nothing for which Cadie herself could take credit.

+ + +

THE FRAGRANCE OF DUCK, peas, and walnut pie permeated the car as Karl drove toward the setting sun and pulled up in front of Cadie's house just before dusk. He was tired now, spent from emotional invigoration and efforts to suppress the happiness and nervousness he'd felt at meeting Gabriella, and looked forward to a small pit stop before driving home to Ennis. Carefully holding the food, he rang Cadie's doorbell.

He had stayed on at the gallery after Cadie's departure. Between Gabriella's attentions to other guests, he had sought her out and described his collection slowly built by Lidice. In turn, Gabriella had described details of her meetings with Lidice, even the phone calls they'd shared before the Ketolas had moved to Texas. Karl was still stunned that Gabriella had known who Spallanzani was. The inspiration for her paintings was no coincidence.

"He inspired my frog series," Gabriella had said.

"So obscure," had been his response.

"Obscure, indeed."

Karl hadn't missed Viktor swatting down Paul's hand when he had pointed at the pair. Few can resist indicating the tipping point when love happens.

"When may I see your collection?" she had asked then.

His face drained of color, Karl knew that he, without knowing or believing it possible, had loved her for a long time. And Gabriella knew it as well.

"Very soon," he said. "I will cook for you."

"Even better."

And then he had bidden farewell to her brothers and left the gallery as the sun touched the distant Fort Worth horizon.

Karl rang the doorbell again.

There was much to tell Cadie, and he was determined to understand what had happened that afternoon. It felt something like guilt, but not exactly. It was more like sadness, that joy was possible without Lidice. Then again, hadn't Lidice insisted that he not eschew future happiness if he found it?

As long as it means nothing less than freedom, you must look for happiness, Karl.

Karl sighed. There was much to tell. How time, encapsulated in moments of the hot day, had collided one love into another. How, if his time with Gabriella was finished, never more added to be added to, then those were moments for which he must thank Cadie.

He rang the doorbell a third time, waited. Knock knock knock. No answer. Disappointed, Karl gave up and walked away.

Aleck appeared from around the corner of his house.

"Hi, Karl . . . don't think she's home." He eyed the to-go bags in Karl's hands.

"You don't, huh?" said Karl, re-enlivened by the chance meeting and another chance to give Aleck a hard time. "Didn't she play tonight?"

"No," said Aleck, stuffing his hands in his pockets.

"Interested in some dinner?" asked Karl, lifting the food bags.

Aleck grinned. "Won't turn down a meal."

Inside the house, Karl inspected the wall of music while waiting for Aleck to transfer the entrées onto plates.

"We have another collector in our midst."

"Another?"

"I collect paintings of frogs wearing trousers. My late wife, Lidice, collected antiques. The beautiful woman, Gabriella, whom Cadie introduced me to this afternoon, collects images on canvas and memories of birds."

Pondering how somebody could collect memories of birds, Aleck watched the older man pause near the large selection of Czech music. Aleck set the plates on the table before selecting a Dvořák CD to play. He forwarded the track to the *New World Symphony*.

"She knows how to play this on her guitar," said Aleck, following Karl to sit down.

"Are you sure . . . *this* symphony?"

"Yes. She started playing it last October."

"That's impossible. All she does is work on her computer."

"And play guitar. But it's not impossible," said Aleck, confident. "She also started playing Middle Eastern, Moroccan, and Finnish music . . . all last fall. I guess around the time she met you."

Karl smiled.

So, the examination is two-sided.

"So where do you think she's off to tonight for her learning?"

"Her learning?" Not often confused by people, Aleck found himself a little frustrated, but Karl was beginning to intrigue him almost as much as Cadie did.

Karl grunted, amused. "That's how we met, you know. She's searching out her genetic heritage. There's four of us she's contacted. Obviously, I'm the Czech." He winked, pointing his fork tines toward his chest. He proceeded to tell Aleck about Cadie's U5 genetic path and the Finns, Moroccans, and Turks she'd contacted.

Aleck was stunned. All of this from a girl who, several months before, could barely wave to him, could barely speak. And the chair in the garden . . . was he also part of her test, or was he an unplanned interest that emerged from personal awakening? The more he thought about it, the more confused he became.

At the thoughtful trance on Aleck's face, Karl thought it high time to ask the question he'd really wanted to ask.

No time like the present.

"Why do you want her, Aleck?"

The trance turned to a stare. Aleck thought Karl asked the question like a father or a vigorous grandfather would, and he suddenly relaxed.

"I don't want her. I wish simply to share her life . . . in whatever capacity she'd have me."

It was the truth. He would blindly stay with her, if only to listen to her play guitar. He thought about Cadie's music, remembered the first time he'd heard her sing and how the surrounding air had changed to fog.

"We had music before spoken language. No one owns music, Karl. No one can own her."

Karl had gotten up and now prepared two pieces of walnut pie on the pink Depression glass plates left by Aleck's mother. Karl felt a little bad about making the kid squirm. Cadie wasn't a girl to give away, no girl was, but he felt a sense of duty to protect. He wiped the plates' edges and took them to the table.

"Of course," said Karl. "But don't kid yourself, Aleck. We all collect . . . *everyone* collects. We collect parts of ourselves . . . parts we have or parts we'd *like* to have. It's how we attempt completion."

It was Aleck's turn to get up. He added Finnish, Moroccan, and two of his favorite Gaelic CDs to the mix and sat down. For the first time, it occurred to him that the different music had not been the catalyst for Cadie's changes.

What was it about collections?

Most people's first collections started in childhood—marbles, dolls, trucks, rough fossil rocks found in run-off streams and gulley washes, or carefully selected sticks to brandish in mock war. Near as he figured, those collections had not been Cadie's. Nor was hers the collection of a heritage, of traditions, into which most infants are born and taught by mothers and fathers and grandparents. But the adult Cadie had figured a need for heritage. And through the collection of tradition, she was affecting him through the force of her song.

We're all caught up in her evolution.

Having said his peace, Karl started talking about Gabriella.

After a few bites of the sweet nut pie, Aleck's stomach churned. He knew it wasn't food sickness. No, he was sick from missing Cadie's music that evening. He was sick that he hadn't been able to sit in her garden chair and sick that the meaning behind the chair was far, far less than he so desperately wanted. More than anything, his sickness was embarrassment that he had never, *ever*, been the one in control when it came to understanding his captivating neighbor.

CHAPTER TWENTY

THE NEXT MORNING, CADIE sat in the quiet Whole Foods parking lot and watched half a dozen grackles run about looking for crumbs of food. A large male fanned his tail and strutted after the females. Cadie smiled and checked her grocery list and menu plan, making another quick calculation for how many fresh tomatoes she needed to finish the tarhana soup started weeks earlier. The dinner party was a day and a half away. All of her U5 friends had promised to attend. A nervous shiver passed along her spine.

The menu plan was ambitious, to say the least. There would be tasting and full appetizers, soups and salads, meats and vegetables, breads, and desserts portions—all of her favorite dishes discovered among her new friends. Foods she now wanted to share with every other person in the group. And taking the Alfasis' and Celebis' diets into consideration, she had altered the recipes to bacon and bacon-free versions.

When her watch read seven fifty-nine, Cadie jumped from the car and braced her steps against strong winds that had come in with the heat wave. In the calm air inside the front door, she passed a smiling clerk and headed straight toward the vegetables to choose several radish bunches. She followed her mentally mapped-out route through the store, calculating no more than twenty-seven minutes to make it to the check-out stand.

AT HOME, CADIE DISCARDED her shoes for bare feet and set about emptying the ingredients from reusable bags, organizing each item by recipe. The meal was to be a splendid discourse of carefully integrated dishes. She would require some help from her guests in order to plate and serve before the food degraded. Since she'd not practiced making more than three recipes at a time on her own, the endeavor was a great leap, though not impossible.

She switched on her computer and printed out the results of her latest personal engineering project. Her new program would help deliver, on time, the finest examples of the dishes she chose to exhibit. She'd written and tailored the program to measure her arc of improvement after twice attempting each recipe—how long it took to chop vegetables, sauté onions, assemble each dish and course. It was the only way she would be able to manage the complicated timing of so many dishes.

The program was a sophisticated cross between intricate project development software and AutoCAD drawings. To execute each recipe, algorithms tracked every ingredient, time needed to prep and cook, and when to assemble parts or tackle completion. Based on initial estimations for when she wanted to serve the food—3:15 for appetizers, 3:45 for soup, etc.—the program carefully timed and helped with everything else: when to buy staple ingredients versus fresh, which checklists to consult as she proceeded. At a glance, she could see the progression of her tasks over time.

But the piece that showcased Cadie's touch was the program's intelligence to account for how much Cadie would improve during each cooking attempt. While baking, she'd taken random temperature recordings from her oven to determine temperature losses depending on how many times and when during a baking cycle she opened the oven door. Adjusting for temperature plunges, the program calculated how much longer to bake a dish, optimizing the next best time to open the oven. It timed everything around the baking of the two different soufflés—what could sit warm on a chaffing dish, what to serve immediately, other tasks in between. For every detail that required more than two hands, Cadie would draw on help from her tutors—the program even accounting for the time it would take Cadie to delegate tasks.

Looking at the printed list of recipes again, Cadie contemplated that she'd crossed the line from social development into harmful ambition. For the appetizers, a cultural smorgasbord fusion—feta cheese, sliced tomatoes and cucumbers, radishes, green and black olives, cheese boerekas, sardines, goose liver pâté with toasted brioche, and honey cake. Arak, Sauternes, Aquavit, and sparkling waters with slices of orange would complement. Following appetizers would be a tasting of two soups—Kamil's tarhana and Ayala's sea bass with fennel and leek. Three salads: Turkish shepherd's salad with lemon egg sauce, Moroccan fresh fava bean salad, and a Czech cauliflower salad. After the salads, Ayala's fish fillets, Fez style. The meats—summer vegetable pot with beef, chicken tagine with walnuts and dates, duck with peas, and stewed lamb with horseradish—would accompany spinach soufflés and fried eggplant. Karl's vánočka, resembling challa and pulla, would be available, along with pita bread, couscous with onions and apricot confit, and rice pilaf with chickpeas. If everyone paced themselves, they would make it to the desserts served with Turkish coffee and a port wine Karl promised to bring. All baked and ready to go were the various Finnish cookies and the almond walnut macaroons. That left today for making fig butter cake and walnut boerekas. Tomorrow, after dinner and while the Turkish coffee cooked, she would make the chocolate-orange soufflés.

Cadie went to her dining room and inspected her one hundred twenty-inch-long walnut slab dining table atop massive squared legs surrounded by a dozen, high-backed Windsor chairs. Until now, she'd never understood why she'd bought such a large table, a purchase of silent and hopeful need. Tomorrow, she and eight guests would feast around it and experience the similarity of cultural flavors massaged into different formats. Suddenly overwhelmed, Cadie sat down in one of the armed chairs and tapped her fingers on the table.

The tapping awoke memories that surprised Cadie. In a new haze, she got up, went outside, and pulled her guitar from the sideboard.

Aleck walked out and stood in his driveway when he heard the amplifier power up. After the enlightening meal with Karl, he gave less thought to her midday playing. No sound followed.

What's taking her so long?

Cadie was remembering how Sister Mary Trea's fingers had continually moved, sometimes frantically, sometimes slowly, over any nearby surface. When the nun sang, her fingers had moved along the side of her habit or under hymnal covers tapped ragged. While Cadie did chores or homework, she had listened to the nun's lectures about duty, all the while the fingers tapping in remote attention to inner music, the umbra of a voice disappeared from her Irish moors' mist and sent to DFW's flat, mid-city heat.

Now, Cadie's own fingers slowly, then fluently, converting the nun's taps into stringed sounds, the haunted past of a pianist forced into the habit and bereft of lover and family. A long grief escaped from Cadie's instrument.

Aleck heard the sound and grew homesick, instantly missing his sister, his parents. He sat directly down onto his driveway pavement and hung his head between his knees.

As Cadie played and scanned her memories, she found in dark corners something newer. The nun's smiling face was almost unrecognizable, overlooked by Cadie the child. There were hints here and there, brief smiles wiped away before Cadie's full gaze landed on the nun's visage. The smiles held wistful girlishness blended with that of a fulfilled mother, smiles of a girl who remembered her own given name, unknown to her sister postulants and Cadie. The shrouded smiles had kept Cadie from seeing love, hope, or family in action.

A tear grew at the corner of Cadie's eye and rolled down her cheek before falling onto the vibrating instrument. Alarm, often cousin to grief, stopped Cadie's playing. She touched her cheek. It was the first time she had cried as an adult, and she gave herself permission to continue, for there was no one now who would fault her for it or make her say penance.

So she cried. For herself . . . and for Sister Mary Trea. A time comes when we make allowances to see how others formed. There was a petite space in Cadie that now allowed her to relate to Sister Mary Trea, see the nun as a woman captured and abused by unforgiving intolerance and fear. In a way, they were copies of each other—abandoned twins named by the Church and assigned seats at the same dining hall. Their ancestral paths had diverged and come together when Cadie was born.

Her hand fell back to the guitar, and Cadie let Sister Mary Trea's fingers give movement to songs beckoning forth intricate harmonies inherent in difference and similarity.

Singing along with the music, Cadie knew that the walnut table inside was one of understanding.

Understanding meant that Cadie had finally withdrawn her hand from the nun's, had signaled she was ready to walk on her own. And now she could do it without annihilating the nun's memory. As the last tear left a wet trace on the guitar's surface, Cadie's attribute of "orphan" suddenly lifted. In its place was a blinking cursor waiting to rename a cleaned profile.

The music ended, and a morose Aleck, searching for comfort, plodded inside and stared at his music collection.

IN HER KITCHEN, CADIE proceeded with her dinner party plans and re-ran her project timeline to adjust for the unexpected emotional foray. She started chopping walnuts for the fig butter cake and walnut boerekas. The others she set aside for the tagine chicken. Next, she chopped figs and grated orange peel, the sharp citrus tang imbuing in her new energy after the cry.

So far, so good.

She pulled out the six-quart, heavy-duty mixer Karl had given to her after showing her how varying the speeds let *vánočka* or other bread dough rest periodically during mixing. To keep her work tempo, she started some coffee and thought about starting a movie to entertain herself. After flipping through several recorded shows, she turned off the television and left the house.

Music is what I need.

Aleck unlocked his door before she had finished pressing the ringer, and Cadie immediately second-guessed the momentum that had propelled her there.

"I, uh," she said pointing back at her house. "I, uh, was wondering if I could borrow some CDs to listen to . . . while I work today."

Aleck could smell the walnut meats and orange peel amid a faint scent of butter about her and knew that Cadie wasn't computing, but cooking.

"Take as many as you'd like." He stepped aside for her to walk inside. "Anything in particular you want?"

She shook her head "no" but walked straight over and pulled out various Czech, Finnish, Moroccan, Turkish, and Irish CDs. She turned briefly and glanced at Aleck before also choosing his favorite flamenco album. His curiosity piqued.

Nervously, she returned to the door. "Do you mind if I return these on Monday?"

"Keep them as long as you want," he said, happy he would see her again that soon.

"Thank you," she said. A timid smile followed. Then, flipping through the CDs as she went, she walked across their front yards.

+ + +

INSIDE A GUEST BEDROOM closet, Cadie fished through the shelves for her old, twelve-disc CD player in disuse since she had first picked up a guitar. She carried the equipment to her office, plugged it in, and had Aleck's twelve CDs playing in a matter of minutes. She readjusted her cooking program again.

No more distraction, Cadie. Any more will spell disaster.

She returned to her baking, waving her spatula along to Dvořák echoing throughout the house. In the stainless steel mixer, she creamed butter and sugar before adding eggs and orange peel, watching the butter change color, scent, and texture. Between additions of flour to the batter, she pulled out tomatoes and washed them. The water flowing over the fruit enthralled her.

Ten months.

That was all it had been since she'd swabbed her cheeks and started a plasticity that had allowed her to evolve, to leap forward fifty thousand years from the last known placemark of her U5 matriarchs. Fifty thousand years, plus ten months. Plasticity could do a lot in much less time, propel wiring forward or set it back permanently. Cadie looked around her kitchen. Fresh foods, cooking utensils, pots, and cutting boards covered every counter. Walnut dust coated the island's surface. She wondered how many of her new friends were U5s themselves.

It doesn't matter.

That it didn't matter . . . *that's* what really mattered. On the table that housed the intricate helix of the human genome was the simplest base of everything: evolution. In her case, evolution was emotional, deep-seated sparks.

It's more than a genome, she thought. *Evolution is expression.*

She picked up the completed cake batter and poured it into a baking pan. Watching the viscous liquid that would become solid cake, she realized that her genome was the oldest of recipes, a detailed map of all ingredients that had ever existed and in which her own individual flair had now merged.

To reach the point where she'd allowed herself to feel, to fear rejection, and accept the reward of connection, all she'd really needed was awareness. Cadie licked the spatula and confirmed that, with a reasoned approach, she could be one of the great cooks, one of the myriads of comfortably social people. She didn't want to be a printed recipe never dog-eared, splattered with food chunks, or curled from exposure to its own liquid ingredients. Clean-paged recipes were ones that weren't so good, definitely not the best. The messy pages, the recipes that bore markings and indicated individual additions or subtractions were recipes of progress. Slowly, ever so slowly, a dash extra here, an ingredient modified there, the recipe became something that looked and tasted completely new, the previous gastronomy's framework nearly forgotten or ignored in the cook's fusion to incorporate the modern. The best chefs, though, could dissect every flavor and each ingredient's history, all the way back to the recipe's origin.

She ran her finger through the last of the batter in the bowl and sampled it. It was good. She placed the pans in the oven and returned to seeding her tomatoes over a large bowl. Red juice ran through her fingers and down her hand.

A primordial soup.

Cadie found the description fitting. Life was much like the fermented, pullulating, tarhana that took weeks to prepare and minutes to eat. She thought about the short succession of tarhana she'd eaten. Though most every tarhana ingredient was identifiable to the tongue, the base, with its strong flavor of yeast, varied with each preparation. So, the soup's taste changed ever so slightly, as sour dough bread varied from region to region. Starters from San Francisco yielded noticeable variation from sour dough starters in London. But it was always sour dough, just as the tarhana soup was tarhana soup. One mustn't be a chef at all to taste the differences. One only had to want to identify the differences and commonality in the food itself.

As she dumped the peeled and seeded tomatoes into a deep stock pot, Cadie began to understand that the food wasn't about cooking or even eating, really. It was about feeding her genes, about tasting from her DNA the history of what she had been and who she would be. In the startling aftermath of her test results and the storm that had linked her yard to Aleck's driveway, coded bits of genomic emotion had erupted on the scene, intersecting and freeing her most structurally repressed traits.

I stirred the pot.

Cadie smiled to herself.

Identifying emotion had allowed the regulation, on an order of magnitude, to free her "social" operator. Through self-tested change and learning to smile, her life still tinged faintly with the countenance of a paradigm, yet it no longer seemed such an enigma.

CHAPTER TWENTY-ONE

O N THE DAY OF THE dinner party, fierce winds forced clouds over Fort Worth, causing a light show of shadow and sun over Corral Street. A continual loop of music came from Cadie's house as she quickly finalized the last of her prep and readied the meats for cooking. The smell of baking vánočka filled the house and drifted through the open garden door, dispersing along the alley.

Before she knew it, Cadie heard Karl's car pull up out front. The breads were ready, the meats in the oven. Cadie sighed relief. She was glad she had asked him to come early . . . just in case chaotic entropy overtook her kitchen.

Following her instructions, he walked through the front door without knocking. Walking in behind him was Gabriella with a shy grin on her face. She wore a white dress. The garnet pick reflected from her hair.

Cadie quickly rinsed her hands and walked toward them.

"So you invited everybody, my dear?" laughed Karl.

He knows.

"Gabriella came to view my paintings this morning. That is how I found out," he said, explaining Gabriella's early arrival. "It just so happens, I asked her to join me here, but she had already been invited. So, we decided to ride together."

Karl looked at Gabriella, hoping for a sign that her time in Ennis would not be the last—beyond driving her back to her car.

She didn't disappoint. "It gave us a chance to continue talking about art and Spallanzani," she said smiling. "And Lidice's amazing antiques. Both are stunning collections . . . and those windows. The lighting is perfect."

Gabriella looked down and brushed imaginary lint from her dress. The garnets in her hair reflected spectrums of emotion, from delight to calm to nervousness.

Karl's face confirmed that Gabriella wasn't enthused with just the art or the windows.

A match is a match is a match. Ayala had said this when teaching Cadie the art of slicing bread.

"You'll have to excuse us for a moment, my darling," said Karl. "I must take Gabriella through your garden." He guided his guest toward the back door.

From the kitchen window, Cadie watched them crisscross the main path in her lush micro-forest. When they returned to the kitchen, Karl helped himself to the goose liver pâté already set out on the appetizer smorgasbord. He poured three glasses of Sauternes and handed one to Gabriella and then Cadie.

"Did you invite Aleck?" he asked.

Should I have?

Cadie shook her head and went back to stirring the tarhana.

"Why not?" asked Karl. He dabbed sardine spread over pieces of brioche and handed one to Gabriella. She took it and looked out over the garden.

Cadie pretended not to hear and went to the pantry for two more bottles of wine.

"I'll take a leftover plate to him after dinner," said Karl loudly.

The doorbell saved Cadie from further questions, and she emerged from the pantry in time to see Karl open the door for Viktor and Paul. The couple breezed in with delighted surprise at seeing him. Behind them came Yosef and Ayala.

Following the introductions and Cadie's, now unnecessary, disclosure that all of her friends from her U5 quest would be there, the four men quickly helped themselves to the appetizers. Gabriella and Ayala stood in the kitchen. Ayala recognized some of the Moroccan dishes and jumped in to lend a hand. She stayed close to Cadie and worked silently. The men talked comfortably.

Another doorbell ring. Cadie jumped to answer it on her own.

Both Ayala and Yosef froze when Kamil, wearing her bright pink head scarf, walked in with Basir. Kamil stiffened when introduced to Viktor and Paul as husband and husband. Cadie began to feel the weight of a hostess. Had she hoped for too much, thinking the group could share the attachment she felt with each person there?

KAMIL, ALSO KEEPING HER tongue, stood only briefly at the kitchen entry before finding her place at the table. She sat down facing the two large bouquets of white roses and daisies. As dominoes falling, the others abandoned the appetizers and joined Kamil. Ayala, the odd one out, stayed in the kitchen with Cadie.

Afraid that the group wouldn't survive several drawn-out courses, Cadie hastily decided to change the format to a family-style meal. Karl noticed her subdued panic and left Gabriella's side to help Cadie mix the cheese soufflés and place the ramekins in the oven. Without needed instruction, he carried the tarhana and the sea bass soups to the table and returned for the salads. Ayala carried the breads and finally took her seat at Cadie's right hand, forcing her hand gesticulations into abeyance by dropping them into her lap and keeping silent.

Cadie explained the different soups and salads, and which guest and culture inspired each dish. Taking one of Ayala's soup cups, Cadie prepared to fill it with tarhana. Before the first drop fell, Kamil interrupted from where she sat at Cadie's left.

"I cannot do it, Cadie," she said after glancing worriedly at Basir. "I can only be Muslim."

That was all it took.

"And I Jewish," added Ayala firmly, waving her hand in the air.

Suddenly confused, Cadie looked at Karl. Why did her guests assume she'd ever ask such a thing from them? What did it matter?

Seated at Karl's left, Paul set down his wine glass and looked at Viktor. Viktor grasped Paul's free hand under the table and gave it a comforting squeeze. Gabriella, looking at neither of her brothers, but at Karl, defiantly picked up her wine and took a drink. Viktor and Paul, accustomed to Gabriella's resolve when something hit her just right, took it as a sign that the situation would sort itself out in a matter of minutes. For better or worse.

Before Gabriella could speak, Karl rose and walked around to Cadie. He placed his hands on her shoulders.

"We are not independent of this," he stated, looking pointedly at Kamil and Ayala. "Nor must we want to be," he said, sweeping his arm out in front of him. "This table . . . the world . . . "

He saw Gabriella looking at him and lost his words.

Gabriella smiled. "We can do better," she offered.

Lowering her head, Kamil checked her scarf's positioning and then dropped her hand to her lap. Basir tried to catch his wife's glance to reassure her that all was okay.

Smiling, Karl continued.

"This girl had no one. Quite improbably, I might add, she led us all here. For . . . nothing?"

He looked at Gabriella.

"It cannot be for nothing."

Gabriella nodded, smiling at Karl. He faltered again and looked at Kamil and Basir to gain his bearing.

"What about your rope of woven light to establish peace and order?"

Kamil raised her head in surprise. How could an atheist know anything of the rope, yet be willing to engage in friendship despite their differences? She looked at Basir.

Picking up the tureen of tarhana, Karl began to walk around the table, first filling Kamil's and Basir's soup cups. "There's sure as hell something wrong with all of us if we cannot see each other in a lighted room."

At that, Gabriella stood and grabbed the platter of pita triangles. After Karl's lead, she followed him and distributed the bread.

Jealous of another woman serving food while she sat, Ayala slapped both of her hands on the table. Paul giggled nervously. Murmurs grew among the guests—Paul talking to Viktor, Basir whispering to Kamil, Yosef expressing thanks to Karl as he passed, and Gabriella instructing Viktor to pour drinks. Viktor jumped up and carried the wine and the water pitcher filled with orange, lemon, lime, and strawberry slices to the other guests. Basir, smiling, took only water for himself and Kamil.

"He's right," Ayala said above everyone. "A Jewish table, a Muslim table . . . a Christian or secular table." She waved her hands toward Karl, Cadie, and the Ketolas when she said "secular."

Karl chuckled, but Ayala continued.

"It's a table. Who says we can't just sit down and eat together? How can we say Cadie's no longer an orphan if we cannot all eat with her?" She looked at Kamil. "I was wrong . . . this table doesn't belong to any one thing or any *one* of us."

Jumping from her chair, Ayala picked up her signature sea bass and fennel-leek soup. Without giving anyone a choice, she filled the other soup cups, the ladle clinking loudly against the china. She followed Gabriella around the massive table.

Yosef grunted, entertained.

Cadie saw the trepidation on Kamil's face and feared her dinner party would devolve into a comedic drama of force-fed guests flinging food around the room. It wasn't funny. Deep emotions made her want to flee the house, never return. Her new paradigm activated by the nervous presentiment, she knew there was only one thing she could do. What she didn't know is if it would make any difference in the emotional soup that made the room feel suddenly too hot and overly crowded.

Only one way to find out.

Steadying her inner tremble, she reached over and placed her hand on Kamil's. At the motion, everyone turned to watch Cadie smile brightly at her friend.

Fear slowly left Kamil's eyes.

Basir grinned. Ayala paused for only a moment and then picked up the braided Czech bread to begin another loop, placing the slices alongside the pita triangles on each bread plate.

Kamil took her other hand from under the table and placed it on the tabletop. Basir put his hand on Kamil's back. Cadie removed her hand from Kamil's and waited.

And then, her eyes cast down to hide a growing smile, Kamil stood. When she raised her head, the first person she looked at was Ayala, who had stopped to watch Kamil.

Ayala grinned. Yosef nodded to Basir.

After a nod from Gabriella, Kamil picked up the shepherd's salad and lemon egg dressing and started around the table, proudly describing the Turkish salad and the tarhana.

"You have done nicely with the tarhana," commended Kamil when she sat with the others to taste the soup.

Needing no further invitation, Yosef started eating. The oven buzzer announced that the spinach soufflés were ready. Karl winked at Cadie when Ayala, Gabriella, Kamil, and Paul jumped to help bring the individual ramekins to the table.

After finding a place on the table for all of the food, Cadie looked down the table's length and swallowed a contented sigh. The smells and activity around her lifted her mind's effluvium, layers of decay that had kept her from naming her new self. What she had at her table was the craziness that had always co-mingled at the orphanage's table and what commonly co-mingled at festive family gatherings everywhere. *Except*, her ties to these people were ancient coded lines of human form and structure, DNA that was everything, yet nothing more than a house of tables—histories of mothers and fathers and families of every kind. With nearly every seat at her table occupied, Cadie knew she'd undergone the transformation she had wanted so. From a blinking cursor, she had reformatted her life by using a smile to erase "orphan" and activate "family." She had evolved.

Cadie pushed her spoon into the delicate soufflé, breaking past the thick crust into the fluffy center that gave easily under the utensil.

Maybe, she thought, being human was no more complex than a single trait, like the ability to smile. She also knew not to kid herself. This was just one table, and she was only one person who'd formatted herself toward freedom. Many remained who succumbed to the abuse of believing in superficial variation, the superstition of ancient writings.

Fighting back sentimental emotion, the scene blurred. She saw her table as one of the human race, just one line of code along a shared and gargantuan table of genomic data that attached her to every other table. Upon those sequel tables was interconnectedness, layers of color, tastes, and origins. Similar to Kamil's carpets or Ayala's braided loaves. Or Karl's intertwined pomlázky stick or the Ketola twins. In all those things, the tight strands of connection were not just existential, but credibly tangible. Then there was Gabriella, born knowing and seeing those strands, born ready to fight against reverberations of hatred and any abuse that chinked away to make the vulnerable seem a little less human. As she looked at her friends, Cadie vowed to cast off the abuse that had almost silenced her.

Promise yourself, here and now, Cadie Walsh . . . never stop smiling.

+ + +

AFTER DINNER, AYALA AND GABRIELLA cleared the table while Kamil started large batches of Turkish coffee. Cadie set the chocolate-orange soufflés in the oven, placed a pulla loaf beside the array of desserts for her Finnish-inspired coffee table, and then joined Kamil in making coffee. Gabriella and Ayala pushed what dishes they could into the dishwasher and ferried cookies, walnut boerekas, and the fig butter cake to the coffee table.

As during her first contact with the Celebis, the discussion bandied into vibrancy as coffee aromas wafted from the stove. The men, eager for coffee and desserts, gathered in the living room and watched the women work. Basir, sitting comfortably in an arm chair, especially watched Kamil.

Over the heat rising from the stove, Kamil's face flushed. Further busying herself, she gave low-toned instructions to Cadie, who managed the second ibrik. At the coffee's third heating, just before Cadie pulled the soufflés from the oven, Kamil glanced up and saw Basir watching her. She looked at him as if she'd never seen him before.

"You notice we've hardly had any rain this spring," said Paul.

Basir nodded the way men do when thinking about things unrelated to the conversation at hand.

Noticing that Kamil's ibrik was about to boil over, Cadie turned off the flame and looked questioningly at her friend. Unaware of Cadie's intervention, Kamil kept her eyes on Basir. She reached to her forehead and checked her scarf.

Basir smiled.

"You think we'll have any rain in May?" asked Karl of the group.

"Paint dries faster without that humidity," said Viktor.

"Not always true," said Paul.

Kamil set down her coffee stirring spoon and reached over to grasp Cadie's forearm. Surprised, Cadie braced herself against the enormity of Kamil's weight balanced in the tight grip.

Without warning, after another quick check of the scarf, Kamil hurriedly removed the scarf's holding pins.

Basir's eyes widened.

Kamil, bound toward determination, pulled the scarf from her head in one easy swipe, taking with it the securely-twisted hair band around a tidy chignon.

The other men paused and looked toward the kitchen when they saw Basir's captured attention. Karl turned around just in time to see Kamil's long hair fall unbounded down her back. The natural waves settled against her shoulder blades. The other women in the room quickly noticed the absence of gray in the dark hair that matched, strand for strand, the color, thickness, and waviness of Cadie's.

In a common gesture of devotion, and to honor his wife, Basir raised his right fingertips to his forehead, a gesture of gratitude in front of eyes that registered joy and approval.

+ + +

FROM HIS WINDOW, ALECK WATCHED the cars leave Cadie's curbside. By early evening, Beatrice had informed any alley lingerers that Cadie had entertained nine dinner guests. Nobody questioned Beatrice's assumption about the party, for the smells coming from Cadie's house was proof enough.

A knock at the door jolted him from his thoughts.

Hoping it was Cadie, he was a little disappointed to see Karl, but he happily accepted the two plates of leftovers.

"This is Gabriella, *Gabi*," said Karl. "She's one of Cadie's Finns."

The woman smiled. "Nice to meet you, Aleck."

Aleck greeted her.

"Well, better get this girl back to her car. You enjoy the goodies," said Karl.

Returning to his window to watch Gabriella and Karl leave together in the last vehicle, Aleck pulled out a piece of the fig butter cake. His mood improved. Karl's romantic interest was in Gabriella, not Cadie.

In the house next to his, Cadie worked alone in the kitchen, finishing the last of the cleaning after four hours of dessert, four cups of coffee each, and lively conversation.

Before tackling the last three pots soaking in the sink and a plate with a half-eaten walnut boereka on it, she went into her master bathroom and turned on the hot water in the garden tub. Into the water, she threw three cubes of rose-scented bath salts and returned to the kitchen as the tub filled.

At the trash bin, she prepared to throw away the leftover boerekas, but when the bin lid opened, all she could do was stare.

Near the top of the refuse heap, partially covered by the remnants of a successful dinner, lay the pink silk of Kamil's discarded scarf and head band. The seam edge along one side was covered and stained with coffee grounds. Cadie roused herself into action and let the boereka fall onto the pile of waste. Her foot slid from the pedal. The lid slammed shut. Uninterested now in cleaning the last pots, she turned off the kitchen light and headed to her bathroom.

Discarding her clothing and sliding into the hot bath, she promised herself to remember the image she'd just seen. The silk scarf in the trash was, thus far, the best illustration of a person finding herself again after a very long hiatus to injurious abstention.

CADIE EMERGED FROM AN hour-long soak and stood naked before a mirrored wall in her bathroom. Puddles formed under her feet as she replayed another conversation in her head. She pulled a large gilded hand mirror from the white vanity drawer.

Why she never used and rarely gave thought to the mirror was due to its origin. Sister Mary Trea had bestowed it to Cadie . . . on the day Cadie had left for college. Heavy with tarnish over the delicate scrolling, the round mirror had been one of the last remnants of Sister Mary Trea's life before the convent. The mirror, so formerly pampered, was surely now the *only* remnant.

Cadie held up the mirror and looked at the reflection of her face, her skin flushed from the bath's heat. She slowly moved the mirror downward and carefully looked at her neck, the supersternal notch, and shoulders. The mirror continued on, along the length of each arm and then down her torso.

They were movements following descriptions from one of Ayala's many stories.

"It's called a *segula*," Ayala had said.

Thought without rational basis, a segula was an intrinsically valuable ritual. In this case, the ritual was one the young Ayala had performed on the night before her wedding. After her *mikveh*, Ayala had reflected upon herself the same way.

Searching for her own value in the ritual, Cadie looked at her breasts in the mirror, then her ribs, her navel, every goose bump until she saw her toes in the glass. Bent over now, yogi-like, in a deep forward pose, Cadie moved the mirror behind her and craned her head around to see her heels, her calves, and buttocks strong from the rowing machine. Rising, she twisted her body to catch the small of her back, adjusting to use the wall mirror to see her wet hair clinging to the skin between her shoulder blades and the back of her head. Finally, she looked at her face again and smiled at herself. She returned the mirror to its drawer.

I wish always to feel the happiness I feel now.

She wrapped a towel around her head before drying the rest of her body. Attending gently to her skin, she felt newborn, a U5 with a world of roads available to her. With the towel still on her head, she fell into bed and was fast asleep when deep and unpredictable fog rolled in and enveloped Fort Worth.

CHAPTER TWENTY-TWO

THE FOG REMAINED WHEN HER doorbell awoke her early the next morning. Cadie rolled over and checked her clock. Six-thirty—too early. Glad it was a vacation Monday, she slid off the bed and pulled on a pair of jeans and a black-and-white floral T-shirt with lettering that read, "Ask Me About My Robots."

Exhausted, but contented, she padded barefoot to her front door and looked through the peephole. The fog was too thick to see anything. Wondering if she had imagined the bell, she unlatched the locks and turned the handle.

At first, she figured Aleck had left the doughnuts on her doorstep, but the included honey and milk didn't seem like Aleck. Coffee, yes, but not bottled milk nestled inside a bowl of ice to keep it cold. Cadie stepped over the gifts and walked to her front yard sidewalk to see if the gift bearer was visible. There was nothing but the dim glow from Aleck's porch light. She retrieved her package and carried it inside.

Setting the box down on her kitchen island, she touched the warm, honey-drizzled doughnuts. The pastries were vaguely familiar, but they weren't the consistent, mass-marketed pastries found in doughnut shops. These had the air pockets and sharp edges of deep-fried pastries created in a home kitchen. There were maybe three dozen. Who intended such abundance?

The package on the island reminded her again of the DNA kit. She looked around.

When she'd started her search, the four walls around her had not been home, but only a shelter. In her mind, then, had been the idea that somewhere on a faraway path was a family, a past where four walls had meant something and could mean something again . . . for her. In tracing her route, as a computer determines a destination by sending echo request messages with increasing "Time to Live" field values, she had created, changed, and deleted labels about herself. As evidenced by the foods flowing unbidden to her house, "family" had replaced "orphan."

It was a path of wealth, though strange in its wanderings and sweet unpredictability. How else had the sum part of only one thing yielded the sum parts of many, a blank look that grew into smiles, tears, or touch?

Cadie took one of the doughnuts and bit into it.

Surely, how she labeled and expressed herself would continue to evolve, just as Fala did. And evolving meant she could never discard labels like REASONABLE or BRAVE or RESTART if she wanted to do more than survive.

Forgetting the time, Cadie headed for her guitar.

THE SOUNDS OF CADIE TUNING her guitar drew Beatrice and a few people into the alley. Aleck, who didn't teach on Mondays, started a pot of coffee. He walked outside as the first notes of "Solveig's Song" reverberated in the fog. The sustained music waves felt like a call to mourning on the warm air.

Then, singing slowly, Cadie painted a memorial of Sister Mary Trea. Clothed in the gray was a woman's dreams snatched from her, choice stolen. Hovering on the water droplets was a lost love and a girl abandoned to a system's fate *de rigeur*. Given over to her singing, Cadie did not hear the shatter of Aleck's mug. All she heard was lost expression that she so desperately tried to capture and replace with musical and primeval algorithms sounded through the damp.

A pause, a long pause, followed. Hearts raced as if spent by sex. Foreheads perspired. And before hands wiped away sweat beads, the drumbeat of Cadie's hand on her guitar fused into a new song.

The sound caused Aleck to think of roads through thousand-year-old villages where grandmothers served pancakes dripping with butter and honey. The notes marched toward immersion in warm milk baths where one happily drank from mirrored opalescence. Aleck shook his head and picked up the broken porcelain pieces.

His stomach churned, made queasy by the depth of Cadie's beautiful talent. How had she learned flamenco that quickly?

Halfway into the song, Cadie stopped and ran inside. She suddenly knew what the doughnuts were and who had brought them.

THE DOUGHNUTS WERE *BUNUELOS*. She'd seen pictures of them in one of Ayala's cookbooks, and Ayala had told a story about them. How the mother of a bride left doughnuts outside the door of the newlyweds—a wish that they live sweetly and richly, that they follow a clear path.

Cadie smiled. Ayala's hints weren't anymore subtle than Karl's.

She took the plate of doughnuts from the box and set several on a saucer before separating the honey into a small bowl and pouring a glass of milk. Bearing the gifts on a tray, she walked outside and headed down her garden path.

At the chair by the evergreens, she lingered for a moment and then changed her mind. Returning to the house, she deposited the tray on her porch and went back for the chair, lifting it from where its feet had sunk into the ground. Up onto the porch she carried it and set it down in its former place.

And then she sat. After a quick dip into the honey bowl, she placed a doughnut in her mouth, letting the honey run smooth and warm before she chewed and swallowed. Another bite, and another.

The tic of the female cardinal came from the evergreen.

No time like the present.

After a last bite, Cadie got up and retrieved the remainder of the doughnuts, milk, and honey. But this time, guided by expression's desire rather than meandering daydreaming or half lucidity, she walked down the path and unlocked the gate to Aleck's driveway. She ran back and resumed playing flamenco.

During the second pause, Aleck had gone in for a new mug. When he came out, the fog had lifted enough for him to see that Cadie's gate was open. Without looking to see if Beatrice watched, he walked straight toward the fence and through the open gate without closing it behind him.

Rounding the corner where he expected to find breakfast or some other delicacy on the chair, Aleck stopped in his tracks at the sunken imprints where the chair had sat for so long. He listened. The cardinals flew out of the evergreen and to the large magnolia tree.

"Tiu-tiu-tiu-tiu," the female cardinal called.

"P'dee-p'dee-p'dee-p'dee," answered her mate.

Not sure what to do, Aleck watched the birds skip from branch to branch. Had she removed his barrier entirely?

When Cadie ended the song and began toying with even newer chords, Aleck glanced behind him. The path's turn leading back to the gate and his driveway seemed far away now. Stepping on the main path could ruin everything.

Cadie finished piecing together the chords she was testing and began strumming a sound Aleck had never before heard.

Confused by the near impossibility of the music, Aleck looked at the birds, the main path, the birds.

The new song was a strange fusion of Celtic and flamenco sung in Gaelic, the lyrics thus obscured to him.

"P'dee-p'dee-p'dee-p'dee," called the male cardinal.

The call uprooted Aleck. He ran back toward his house and didn't see Beatrice's shocked look from where she stood at the end of his driveway. Nor did he see her when he reemerged, two tall coffee mugs in hand. He dashed back through the open gate. Back at the imprints, he stopped again and listened. Cadie was playing another song similar to the one before, with the same fusion of . . . of Cadie and Aleck's favorite music.

With a deep breathe, Aleck took the final step and turned toward the sound. There she sat and beside her, the Adirondack chair. Between Cadie and the chair sat a small table with a plate of doughnuts on it, and a bottle of milk. Cadie's head remained bent over her guitar, her hair hiding the side of her face.

Aleck forced himself to start down the path now open to him. A flood of commands inundated him—route, reset, reroute—forcing him to echo each step, one after the other, until he reached the porch. When Cadie didn't stop playing or look up, Aleck cautiously ascended the steps and, without making a sound, sat down in the familiar chair. For the first time, he could closely see her fingers flutter across the guitar strings. Watching, he kept silent and tried to recover by setting down the coffee he'd brought for her. He took a bunuelo. Past a lock of her hair, he saw her smile.

After a few minutes, when her smile didn't recede, he knew it'd always be like this when she sang—that he mustn't speak. Behind her smile when she played her guitar was a place not his to collect. It was a place where she stood alone and gazed from stone towers overlooking moors or sea cliffs or desert or the other side of the ocean. Despite awakening her inner core and moving, however nervously and unsteadily, into the social world, the place had to be for Cadie a timeworn, secret garden where she could rush, where she could know the universe and no one, not even Aleck. It was her place where music was ancient strands of time and alluvium unformed.

WHILE ALECK SAT ON the porch, eating one doughnut after another to keep from touching Cadie's hair or the small of her back where her T-shirt had ridden up and showed the barest line of skin above the waist of her jeans, Beatrice had moved toward and sat down in the chair in Aleck's driveway. For once, she was uninterested in the rest of her neighbors. Beside her, Beau sat on his haunches and sniffed at the air. She thought a few times about walking into Cadie's yard to see what was happening. Finally deciding against it, she walked to the back of Cadie's fence and looked through the slats.

She got there in time to see Cadie look up from her playing, then take a sip of coffee and a bite of something. Beatrice held her hand to her chest. And then, lo and behold, she saw Cadie smile absentmindedly at Aleck before the girl started the next song.

Nothing better to see, Beatrice took Beau's leash and started home. Overhead, the last of the fog, as high and as quickly as a swan taking flight, sped away.

UNAWARE OF BEATRICE, Aleck saw something different than lifting fog in Cadie's absentminded smile. Ahead, to evolving time, he now saw himself watching Cadie, watched her pull out her ancestral map and show him the pin-marked locations on the other side of the Atlantic. She would tell him for the hundredth time about the swabs of her cheek cells. He saw she would always be beautiful . . . when she sang and when she didn't talk, when she cooked and when her fingers ran over guitar strings as rapidly as she created computer code functions. Not one of her idiosyncrasies would matter to him.

Those idiosyncrasies, as varied and spellbinding as DNA, were marvelous, maybe the most beauty he'd ever witness.

Beyond those things, he saw the ancestral countries where she would sing. The people there would say, "How Turkish she is, how Finnish, how Czech, how Moroccan she is."

Familiarity too often demanded ownership.

And Cadie would be oblivious to the bejeweled status, for she only lived in the musical notes that dissipated on air. She would only see, without understanding why, tables pulled out and bedecked in welcoming for a long, lost daughter. When she sang, those people would not see the world as it formed . . . table by table, a fallen tree, paths that formed a picture of Family Earth. Instead, her audiences would only grin from ear to ear, only feel the billions of little marks, the scratches that carved a place for each of them to sit. They would bite into expression . . . taste its joy and tears and hatred and retribution, sometimes forgiveness and understanding. They would caress it, or violate with lashes of superstition and grotesque arrogance. And where Cadie was concerned, he would always be there . . . to see the sweet and sour of what was and is.

Sensing that Aleck had gone to his own private mind-place, Cadie stopped playing and turned to him. She reached over and placed her hand on the side of his arm.

When Cadie's touch incorporated with Aleck's thoughts, he saw yet further. Cadie, more moving than any beautiful face, was a voice billowing weather into sails and moving oceans. She had never been an orphan. With eyes long-evolved, she looked upon a house of tables and saw only one family, the whole world, waiting to eat.

It was then that Aleck saw her fingertips on his arm. Suddenly, he saw there was nothing between them. She shared everything in her touch, emotion's true intimacy served by reason.

Taking his free hand to slip under hers, every note Aleck had ever heard came forth in a smile only a little less bright than Cadie's own.

THE END

ACKNOWLEDGMENTS

Many thanks to the wonderful people at the National Geographic Genographic Project for permission to share U5 results in this book and for making this science available to the world; we are all better for it. To Cassie Smith, my copyeditor and proofreader—I could not have asked for better. To the talented and patient Mark Anthony M. Jordan for an outstanding book cover.

To my dear friends Dalton, Stephanie, Victor, and my friends of reason in the DFW metroplex; thank you for helping me battle shyness with encouragement. To Mauricio and Carmen for reminding us that love with worth complication; it is an honor to call you friends. Sarah—there was never a better friend to inaugurate one in the launch of dreams. To Mary—you make craziness bearable. To Rose—a mentor and inspiration to everyone—the laughter behind any set of tears. For the many cups of tea and becoming a new family member to me, thank you. To John, my first mentor—the time of "baby leaves" serves as underpinning to so much I do. To M.J. Roberts, W. Beall, and Dr. Quinn, who love what they teach. Amazing instructors stay with us always.

To my parents, sisters, and brother: such enthusiasm paves the road of hope. To my daughter Cecily; you are my brave wanderer, a trailblazer of new paths and footing for future women. Finally, to my husband for his unflagging support and adamant confidence in me; your merits are as drops in the sea, your love a seamless universe.

ABOUT THE AUTHOR

A former software development analyst, Ileen McDuring acquired her love of words and worlds when, as a toddler, she was introduced by her mother to a one-room library of a small Southern town and allowed to read books indiscriminately. In conjunction, Ileen developed her great appreciation for music during many hours spent listening to her great-grandmother play classical guitar and sing. When not writing, Ileen enjoys plunking on her own guitar and discussing philosophy and science. Mother to a beautiful and artistic daughter never afraid to ask "why" and expect evidence, Ileen currently lives in Texas with her husband and ever-loyal puppy.

HOUSE OF TABLES is Ileen's debut novel.